THE LAST REDOUBT

BOOK SIX OF CHIMERA COMPANY

Tim C. Taylor

Theogony Books
Coinjock, NC

Chris Kennedy/Theogony Books
1097 Waterlily Rd.
Coinjock, NC 27923
https://chriskennedypublishing.com/

Cover Design by Vincent Sammy.

Ordering Information:
Quantity sales. Special discounts are available on quantity purchases by corporations, associations, and others. For details, contact the "Special Sales Department" at the address above.

The Last Redoubt/Tim C. Taylor -- 1st ed.
ISBN: 978-1648558535

To all those who joined the Legion over the years.
The journey has been epic.
And I couldn't have made it without you.

Part 1 :
The Battle of Tau-Fornacis

Chapter One:
Sorbo

Tau-Fornacis System, Laman Sector

Only the shuttle pilot's widened eyes betrayed her disbelief. "Are you sure, sir?"

Despite her unease, the ensign otherwise kept perfect composure, for she was a legionary and the rigid discipline that implied was about the only thing in this insane galaxy that still counted for something.

When the general nodded, the ensign said, "Transferring control to General Sorbo, aye."

Yes, the Legion was still a source of pride, and General Alessia "Sorbo" Sorborovskele drew deeply upon that well as she waited for the ensign to safely neutralize the shuttle's controls and relinquish the pilot's station.

The Legion's egalitarian ethos set it far apart from the rest of the Federation.

Every legionary from the lowliest sapper to the first general received exactly the same pay and conditions. Everyone knew that, yet there was more that was not so well known. All personnel were trained in a multitude of roles and specialties so that everyone was valuable and no one indispensable.

And it was a matter of principle that every legionary was an expert with the PA-71 railgun.

Of course, there were limits. Not every legionary could fulfill every role. Sorbo couldn't lead a ship's damage control team to patch a shot-up fusion plant. Nor could she entrust to any random legionary her role of marshaling the Federation's chaos to ready a counterattack against the invaders in the Tej Sector.

Not that Sorbo would wish that particular duty on anyone, especially the endless deadweight of politicking that had been involved.

Long ago, in simpler times, Sorbo had been a combat medic, flying evac tubs around airless moons and pirate orbitals. Her team often had to shoot their way in to retrieve the wounded and shoot their way out, too.

Flying was a drug she'd never expunged from her system.

She corkscrewed the *Lysander*-class shuttle, weaving in and out of the armada assembling around the gargantuan military shipyards of Tau-Fornacis. Within 48 hours, Strike Force Fornax would take the fight to the Andromedans. The frantic resupply and refitting program would not be complete by then, but the delays had already been too long.

The time for the counterattack was now.

Sorbo took care to avoid the flight paths for the logistics boats or anything else that might interfere with preparations for the operation. Even so, the ensign cleared her throat, a polite indication that taking a joyride was not what senior Legion generals were supposed to do.

Sorbo chuckled. "I'm the commander of Strike Force Fornax. There have gotta be some perks to the job."

She continued to dart through the maze of ships, her eyes flicking from the instruments to the fleet assembling before her.

The vast array of vessels was a sight to behold, with ships of all sizes and shapes, from sleek fighter craft to lumbering behemoths. She saw many teams of engineers repairing damage that had been sustained during previous engagements with the Andromedans and in the long rearguard action against decay and defunding. It was a hive of activity, and Sorbo couldn't help but feel a sense of pride as she gazed upon the impressive display of Federation might.

And most impressive of all was her flagship, *Achilles*.

"Funny how things come around," she mused as the shuttle approached the flagship. "For our ancestor legionaries from the Orion Spur, fleet battles were a simple matter of who had the most drones. Fighters and battleships were ancient history. Warships were not much more than immense cargo pods with onboard drone manufactories. Then they found a new drive technology at a secret research planet called Khallini. That changed everything."

Support ships flocked around the booms that fed out from *Achilles'* rounded main section. They brought ordnance, fuel, and spare parts. In recent months, the Legion had suddenly 'remembered' scores of forgotten supply dumps across the Laman Sector that had mysteriously dropped off the books over the centuries. Everything was being poured into Strike Force Fornax. Nothing was held back.

Good people had accused her to her face of being a traitor to the Legion. But this was her call. There was no point to reserves if they were never used, and there had never been a greater need than now.

"After that ancient discovery at Khallini, drones became secondary, superseded by fighters, bombers, capital ships, the greatest of all being the battle carriers, of which the last survivor is *Achilles*."

The ensign took a breath as she looked on in awe. "She's magnificent."

"Aye," Sorbo agreed. "She's seen more than her fair share of fights and proved her mettle every time."

"Yes, sir. They don't make them like her anymore."

"I hope we aren't about to regret that, Ensign. *Achilles* is almost the last survivor of an earlier age of glory. Big ships like this have been driven out, not by advances in tactics and technology, but by the slow asphyxiation of politically motivated budget cuts. We barely had enough funds to keep her mothballed these past three centuries. But there she is, one of the few survivors from an age of glory and the only battle carrier in the fleet. The fight before us has never been harder, but *Achilles* will steer us through it."

"Will we win, sir?"

Sorbo pursed her lips, unwilling to give the young junior officer easy falsehoods.

The intelligence on the enemy was patchy and confusing. Nonetheless, in less than 48 hours, Strike Force Fornax would take the fight to the aliens.

"We will do our duty," Sorbo said. "And we will give them hell, I can promise you that much, Ensign. Will we prevail? It will come down to the quality of our training and the belief in our hearts. If we remember them both, then we will acquit ourselves well."

Her comm blipped.

"Go for Sorbo."

"This is Major Jareth from Sinita-42 Orbital. The CO wants you to be aware we've had a fresh arrival of Militia. More refugees from the Tej Sector debacle."

Sorbo activated the autopilot. "Refugees? Are they fleeing rats or rallying to the battle flag? Either way, we have procedures in place for vetting and quarantine, and I have confidence in Colonel Plej. Why does he wish to inform me?"

"Sir, the colonel says the scale of their numbers means you should be informed. It's a corps-level force. Arrived unannounced because they wanted to check us out before they declared themselves."

"Corps level?"

"Yes, General. With logistics train and specialist ships."

"Talk numbers."

"Approximately forty-seven individual spacecraft, 3,700 officers, and 13,000 enlisted personnel."

Sorbo growled in disapproval. A legionary force did not describe itself by splitting officers and enlisted. And that ratio! One officer for three enlisted? Really?

"Sir, if I may break the habit of a lifetime and say something in the Militia's defense. They explained the preponderance of officers by claiming they picked up officer training cadets from two facilities. Also, a large proportion of the enlisted have already deserted. Colonel Plej says he's never seen Militia officers so young, so angry, and so eager to get into the fight. Frankly, they're looking for a leader to give them a sense of purpose and direction."

"Colonel Plej did right to inform me directly. I'll be in contact shortly. Sorbo out."

Sorbo needed to look these newcomers in the eye, to kick their tires to see whether they really did have fighting spirit. And if they did, they were too big a force to leave behind. Finding a way to integrate them into the strike force would be a major headache in normal times, but to do so without risking the spread of the Corruption was a nightmare.

There were good people around Sorbo, though. Headache or not, this was a big win.

"Do you believe in omens, Ensign?"

"No, General."

"Neither do I. But unexpected reinforcements have just turned up on our doorstep, so I'm going to take that position into review." Sorbo sighed, her joyride over. "Back to business. Transferring control to you, Ensign."

Her comm pinged again. This time on the command channel.

"This is Captain Fkansie. There's a sabotage group on board *Achilles*. Marines have contained them at their entry point, but some are inside, and we don't know how far they've penetrated. More are arriving from space."

"The Corrupted are attacking? But how? The quarantine vetting for the battle carrier is the tightest in the fleet."

"We think none are *Achilles* personal, sir; they've all come from the outside."

"What's Aluin doing? Why isn't he telling me this?"

"He's scaring up a scratch force for a counterattack at the breach point."

"Good. Add one Lysander shuttle and two legionaries to his force. We're signing up for duty."

"I'll inform him. Fkansie out."

"How is your PA-71 rating, Ensign?"

"Better than yours, General. Youthful eyesight has its advantages."

"Fair point. And what is your combat experience flying shuttles?"

"None."

The words hung in the air for three seconds. Then realization dawned on the pilot, who spun around, saw Sorbo's raised eyebrow, and understood what it meant.

"Transferring control back to you, General."

*****

Chapter Two: Sorbo

"Sorbo, it's Zaraff. Fleet Commander Aluin's assigned me to clear the drent off the *Achilles,* and I hear you've signed up."

"That's right. Where do you want us?"

"Away, General. I want you at a safe distance until this is resolved."

"Acknowledged, Colonel. For myself, I want a long, cool drink and hot beach to enjoy it on. Some good company wouldn't go amiss. Unfortunately, it appears that neither of us will get what we want."

"I'm serious, General. Strike Force Fornax needs its commander intact."

"I'm not being reckless, Zaraff. The Federation needed me because I was the best person on the spot to assemble this force, supply it, and persuade the Sector Militia Marshal that Legion and Militia are on the same side for now. That task is now complete. What I need most is for some real soldiering to take the taste of politics out of my mouth."

"Very well. My ad hoc command is communicating on tactical channel 147. Here's the situation: We know an assault force breached *Achilles* at the medial boom. They've penetrated far enough to disable the main hangar door and have blown internal and external sensors.

The marine complement is driving them off the ship, but for the moment, *Achilles* is blind. We're reduced to observation by telescope from other ships. You're closest to *Achilles*, so I want you to fly your Lysander in close to recon and then get out safely."

"Reconnaissance in force. Roger that. Sorbo out."

Beside her, Sorbo noticed the ensign was smirking.

"Just to be clear," said the ensign, "what is the distinction between reconnaissance and reconnaissance in force?"

"We shoot more bad guys. What's your name, Ensign?"

"Pascoe, sir."

"Well, Pascoe. Suit up and check your PA-71. Then we head for the medial boom."

"General, from what I understand, Corrupted legionaries are slow, sometimes confused, and I'm assuming that's who we're facing here, but they're not stupid. If we fly to their breach point, they'll be waiting for us with guns hot."

"I'm counting on it, Ensign Pascoe. If they aren't, we're in deep trouble."

* * *

Viewed from above, *Achilles* resembled a child's drawing of a jellyfish. Its main body was a giant bell from which five booms descended like stiffened tentacles, each over a kilometer long. Four of these booms terminated in the main engines, but hidden inside their length were radiators for the primary heat management system that pumped excess heat into the KM-Region.

The fifth, and longest by several hundred meters, was the medial boom. This housed the jump drive and ended with an angular star-shaped defensive structure called the aft bastion, designed to prevent boarding assaults from the rear.

Clearly, this had failed.

As Sorbo flew the Lysander closer to the enormous battle carrier, the screens showed the heavily armored airlocks in the bastion's starfish pylons had been opened. Asphyxiated corpses floated within or were locked to the deck by their boots as if sleeping standing up.

Sorbo and Pascoe observed several seconds of respectful silence as they approached the grim scene, then Sorbo painted a trajectory ladder that would bring the shuttle in a curving dive to intersect with the enemy ship clamped to the boom about five hundred meters away. It was a large freighter, like those swarming the shipyard in the operation to supply the fleet.

She locked in the autopilot and announced, "Time to get out and walk."

Sorbo unstrapped and clanked aft until she swung herself down into the open maw of the shuttle's forward-facing loading doors.

The legionary armor she wore held two hours of emergency air, a heat sink that gave limited stealth capability, and had self-repairing pressure seals beneath the flexi-armor. There was no EVA pack, though. This would have to be done the old-fashioned way.

"Ready?" she asked.

"Right behind you, General."

The universe stilled as Sorbo crouched low, holding her breath in anticipation. The muscle amplification tech of her suit thrummed to life, lending her strength as she launched forward, aiming for an open airlock on the last section of the aft bastion's pylons.

Not gonna make it!

The moment she threw herself into the black, a sinking feeling clawed at her gut. The laws of physics gave no second chances, and she was sailing through the vacuum on course for infinity, destined to pass about a meter to one side of the open airlock door.

"Looks like I'm out of practice, Pascoe."

"Don't give up," the ensign told her. "Grab my hand."

Sorbo looked back and saw her companion heading toward her on a faster vector.

She didn't question Pascoe's intent. That wasn't the way the Legion worked. She placed her trust in the younger woman, and both of them concentrated on linking up.

Pascoe's hand missed Sorbo's, but the general grabbed the ensign's arm at the elbow and felt the kick as they combined vectors. Now she had Pascoe to her right, an armor-clad living extension bringing her closer to the airlock door.

The door they were seconds away from reaching.

The door Pascoe's hand was going to miss by inches.

Damn! Still gonna die!

"Let go!" Pascoe said.

Sorbo did, which allowed the ensign to finger crawl along her arm until they were finally holding hands. Pascoe's right hand reached out and grabbed the edge of the door.

The collision introduced a turning momentum that swung the linked legionaries clockwise about the door's edge. Sorbo had anticipated this and was ready to grab onto something—anything—when the rotation slammed her into the bastion. But the speed of their spin took them both by surprise, and Pascoe's grip wasn't strong enough. Their momentum ripped the pair off the door and back into space.

"I'm going to grab that antenna," Pascoe said.

At first, the spin was too much for Sorbo to make sense of. Then her situation clicked into place, and she saw their trajectory would pass close by a ring of antennae on the boom.

"Here I go." Pascoe reached out her right hand. "It's no use," she shouted, panic encroaching on her voice. "I can't reach it!" She stretched her hand out anyway.

Unfortunately, Pascoe was right. Her fingertips grazed cold vacuum as the rotating couple sailed past.

"Keep holding on," the general told her.

Sorbo pointed her toes like a dancer and readied herself as the rotation brought her around on a path close to another antenna.

"This had better work," she muttered. "It's our last chance."

Her left calf slammed against the antenna, and she bit back a yelp of pain as she clung on, wrapping her feet securely around the metal pole and then clamping her legs together with iron determination. She felt the jumble of competing frames of reference as the metal wand bent, but Sorbo clung on and it did not snap. The two of them still danced in a circle, but now the center of their rotation was the antenna, and with their linear momentum converted to angular, they were propelled into a frenzied spin.

It was a precarious situation. A momentary loss of grip would spell disaster, but Pascoe slowed them by dragging the heels of her boots against the armored hull.

Graceful it was not. But it worked.

"We're down safely," Sorbo said, keeping her words to the short range and tight beam BattleCom provided by their linked armor.

Without its crew, their Lysander was now halfway to the enemy ship, its trajectory curving inward.

"Take position," Sorbo ordered, and immediately realized that was easier said than done. They had no EVA packs, no tethers, only magnetized boots.

Sorbo stomped forward along the medial boom. She came to a halt and sat on her haunches, her gun trained on the boarder's ship a few hundred meters away. The breach in the *Achilles'* hull was clear to see. As for the Lysander, the autopilot had guided it almost as far as the enemy ship and was now reversing thrusters to avoid collision.

"Pascoe, confirm laser mode is set."

"Laser mode selected, aye. Three-puncture firing pattern."

"Negative." Sorbo took a deep breath. She was out of practice at making snap tactical decisions. "Forget your training. One puncture shot and move on."

"One shot. Acknowledged."

"I know we train for three laser shots. A skilled target can patch one puncture and be back in the fight, but three simultaneous suit breaches are hard to patch without suffering decompression damage. From what I've heard, Corrupted legionaries lack any sense of self. That means no sense of self-preservation, too. It's a weakness and weaknesses are there to be exploited."

Unfortunately, the enemy hadn't read the report that claimed they were clueless zombies. They opened fire, not from the obvious position of their ship but from fifty meters farther up the boom. They were attached by a fan of self-stabilizing tethers that rendered them nearly invisible with their heat sinks swallowing much of their heat signatures. It seemed some memory of tactical nous remained.

But Sorbo and Pascoe also had heat sinks and armor in dark mode. So far, they were invisible, but the Corrupted legionaries were firing at the Lysander, and the electric fields charging their barrel rails shone like beacons in Sorbo's helm.

She primed her laser with a tap on the trigger and fired back.

The Corrupted had been people once. Comrades. It wasn't a thought she allowed to develop as she serviced the targets, keeping the laser beam pulsing on a single spot on their armor until her helm showed an artificially enhanced plume of gas venting from their punctured suits.

The Lysander's equipment cupboard had contained the 'b' variant of the ubiquitous PA-71, a largely unsuccessful attempt to reproduce some of the capabilities of the Orion Era SA-71s. Unlike the miracle power sources the ancients took for granted, the 'b' models required two fat, horizontal charge packs that made them difficult to maneuver and were themselves vulnerable targets. A railgun round through your charge pack would spew forth highly corrosive chemicals that would burn through a legionary's armor.

That the 'b's were being issued was proof that Strike Force Fornax was scraping the putrid dregs of the supply barrel, but Sorbo hoped she could turn this to their advantage. Unlike the PA-71's railgun element the enemy was using, lasers were almost impossible to track and had negligible recoil.

Unseen death fired from Sorbo's hands. She made every shot count. No recoil, no warning. She almost felt sorry for the enemy, who didn't react as she killed them. They didn't notice when their suits were breached. Instead of patching the holes, they continued firing at the Lysander, which was now stationary relative to the boom.

One by one, the Corrupted they shot suffered decompression, which snuffed them out of the fight.

It felt too easy.

Then their luck turned. Pascoe drilled her pulse laser through an enemy's breathing hose. It severed, producing a strangling snake which sprayed gas and fluids that crystallized in the vacuum. Her laser pulse shone through the crystals, drawing a steaming blue line.

Finally, the Corrupted legionaries awoke. They saw the laser line and knew what it meant. Then they traced it back. The heat from Sorbo's and Pascoe's charge packs wouldn't be as bright as the enemy's railguns, but they wouldn't take long to spot.

Sorbo switched her selector to railgun burst mode and pumped ten-round bursts at the Corrupted. The weapon stock thudded against her shoulder. Even wearing armor, her flesh would be blue and purple if she made it out of this fight alive.

She knew every weak spot in the enemy's armor and exploited it pitilessly. She did not miss, and it didn't look as if Pascoe did either.

They'd taken out enough of their foe with the lasers—just—and survived the brief but deadly hail of return fire.

Sorbo's armor alerted her to two railgun hits, but they were glancing blows that were absorbed without triggering the dreaded Suit Compromised warning light. The BattleCom link showed that Pascoe had also survived.

"Clear," Pascoe said.

"Clear," Sorbo confirmed. "Cover me. I want to see what we're facing."

They bounded up the boom a short distance, then, with Pascoe in a good overwatch position, Sorbo continued forward to investigate.

* * * * *

Chapter Three: Sorbo

Sorbo stared at the figure swaying on the boom. With their helm removed and the front plate of their armor folded down, skin and eyes bulged from decompression, but that was only the start of their distortions.

This had been a human woman once, but that had been long ago. Whatever Sorbo was looking at wasn't human now. The face was stretched asymmetrically, and the nose was a flat lizard slit. Spiky structures like stalactites dripped out the back of the head, which was totally hairless. The skin was nonetheless thickly covered from the throat down. Not with hair, but feathers in chevron patterns that alternated colors of rust and dried blood.

Sorbo studied the helm she'd removed. It was standard Legion issue for a standard human head. It was far too small for the Corruption she saw before her.

How the hell does that weird head get in that helm?

She needed to know. What she saw before her was the enemy she had to learn to fight and beat in this war. Or a part of the enemy's forces, at least. To beat your opponent, you had to understand them. That, or so thoroughly outgun them that you could smear them across the black at a press of a button. It didn't seem the Legion had that advantage this time around.

Sorbo had encountered many alien species in her career, but this travesty of humanity was the first to provoke a sense of revulsion. She fought back the horror and stretched out her gauntlet to touch the creature.

It was squishy! Like a partially inflated ball. Although the face carried the vestiges of cheeks and brow, when she pressed hard, there was little resistance. Something supported those facial features, but it wasn't bone or cartilage.

Using the blade mag-clamped to the small of her back, she slit open the suit. Beneath was a heavily soiled battle tunic with insignia that identified the wearer as a Food Service Operations Specialist for the Second Legion, rank of lance sergeant.

"What have they been feeding you since you were Corrupted?" Sorbo mused. More worrying was that this Foodie had served in the Second Legion, which was stationed thousands of light years away in in the Renewed Hope Sector with elements in the Antispinward Fringe. The Second hadn't been stationed in the Tej Sector for forty years, and not in the Laman Sector for four hundred. Did this mean Renewed Hope and the Antispinward Fringe had been infiltrated?

Maybe the assault on Tej Sector was a feint to draw them in?

She opened tac-channel 147 and reported what she'd found to Colonel Zaraff.

"Good work, General. I want you in overwatch at the breach point. We have assault shuttles inbound in three minutes. *Achilles* will have an EVA marine squad there in five."

When the communication finished, Sorbo stared into the jagged circle blasted through the boom.

It's tempting…

"Are we going in, General?" asked an excited Pascoe. "Are we assaulting the breach?"

Sorbo inhaled sharply. Every instinct roared that the ensign was right to press the attack while they had the advantage. That former Second Legion Foodie and all the other Corrupted had come here and now for a purpose, and every second they were left alive inside the *Achilles* brought them nearer to mission success.

But Zaraff's order had been clear, and they all risked underestimating the Corrupted legionaries at the Federation's peril. As individuals, the Corrupted often appeared confused, but together they had managed to breach the *Achilles*, one of the biggest warships in the Federation. Not only that, but they had downed her sensors, blocked the hangar, and vented the aft bastion to space.

Damnit! Sometimes holding the line meant more than rushing to the sound of guns.

"No, Pascoe. It pains me to wait, but when those assault boats arrive, they'll be relying on us for overwatch. We stay here and support Colonel Zaraff's mission."

Two minutes later, Sorbo's helm simultaneously announced a radar paint from behind and incoming on channel 147.

"This is Cav Gold, General, come to kill some feathered uglies. I see no targets at the breach point. Please confirm."

"Confirmed. We didn't leave any for you."

"Not a problem, General. We hear there's plenty left inside. ETA forty seconds. Kindly hold your position while we secure the area."

Suddenly, fire vented halfway along the medial boom. A fraction of a second later, she felt a powerful shockwave travel beneath her feet and then rebound off the aft bastion. She couldn't hear the structural alloys of the *Achilles* scream in protest, but she felt the battle carrier's pain through her feet.

"Azhanti!" Sorbo gasped.

"What did they blow?" Pascoe asked.

"What they boarded *Achilles* for. The enemy has just taken out her jump engines."

* * *

"At least a week, General."

So close... But almosts count for nothing in war.

By the time the charges had blown the jump engines, *Achilles'* marines had already killed the last of the boarders. But they hadn't found the bombs in time.

Five minutes after that, Captain Fkansie, *Achilles'* skipper, confirmed the area was secure. Fkansie had people looking for more surprises, but he didn't expect to find any.

Which left Sorbo reworking her campaign strategy on the fly while inside an assault shuttle coming in to dock with *Achilles'* main section. Pascoe was with her, too. Since the pilot's Lysander had been shot to pieces, it seemed only fair to bring her along.

"At least a week until she can jump, and that estimate is highly preliminary."

Despite the supposed proof that this was nothing but a product of human prejudice, to Sorbo's ears Captain Fkansie's voice carried an oozing quality that matched his appearance. The skipper of the *Achilles* was a Slern, which made him a squidgy blue pseudo-mollusk unsuitable for frontline infantry roles but whose naturally high tolerance of G-forces and low-pressure environments meant his kind excelled in space.

A sigh escaped Sorbo as she accepted the inevitable. "One week. And I expect you have already included a hefty contingency."

"The engineer on the spot told me five days minimum."

"We all know that according to the iron law of damage estimates, the time to fix always goes up and never down. I'll make a working assumption of ten days, but whether five, seven, or ten makes little difference. They are all too long, and we can't wait. The enemy knows where we are and I will not let them decide the time and place of our next engagement. The fleet will jump within twenty hours. *Achilles* and her escorts will have to follow once her jump engines are repaired."

Fkansie made no immediate reply, and Sorbo could understand why. Her own words made her feel queasy. The enemy's naval forces were formidable and splitting the fleet was the last thing she wanted. But she knew in her gut that they'd already delayed too long. If she was to achieve victory, it had to be her who chose the battle space.

The line to *Achilles* remained silent. Was her most senior captain sulking?

"Fkansie, acknowledge."

"Sorry, General. There's been some excitement on the command deck. The polar ecliptic early warning stations are reporting multiple jump flashes. Just waiting for… visual confirmation… Ah, yes. It's the Andromedans. And they've arrived in force."

*****

Chapter Four: Sorbo

"This is our preliminary analysis and classification," BattCon reported.

Sorbo's breath caught in her throat. The Battle Control officer's data for the analysis came from the system defense picket boats and gun platforms who had fired on the invaders, knowing surely they would be wiped out. Brave people, all. She wouldn't allow their deaths to be in vain.

"Classification: Brown Pouches," said BattCon. "Size approximates to destroyer class. Count: three hundred and twelve vessels with more arriving piecemeal through the jump tunnel. A concentrated volley by Class-3 gauss cannons destroyed one. The Pouches fired back with kinetic projectiles."

Sorbo grunted. So, Federation guns could hurt the enemy. It was a start.

"Classification: Bone Balls. Appear to be linked to the Pouches in a one-to-twenty ratio. They're spheres sheathed in bone-like rings. One was destroyed by a gun platform. They have made no aggressive moves."

The listing went on. Guppy Gunships, the Jump Leviathans who kept the jump tunnel open, and even Vacuum Cleaners whose role seemed to be to suck up the wreckage from stricken ships and their contents. To *eat* them.

The salient point was that Strike Force Fornax was outnumbered, almost certainly outgunned, and very nearly out of time.

Sorbo set up a comm link between her, Fkansie, and Fleet Commander Aluin, the commander of the naval element of Strike Force Fornax.

"The enemy attack strategy is faulty," Aluin said. "The enemy's come to us so we don't need jump drives. The rest of *Achilles* is still operational. We can take them."

"I've seen the numbers," Sorbo replied. "Negative. The enemy has come to us, all right, but that's because we waited here too long. We need to be where they do not expect us. Strike Force Fornax will jump to the Tej Sector before the enemy fleet reaches us and engage the enemy there."

Silence. "You mean we abandon *Achilles*?" Aluin asked.

"Never. *Achilles* is the rearguard. We buy time for the rest of the fleet to get out."

"Understood," Aluin said. "*Achilles* won't let you down. I won't let you down."

Fkansie, Sorbo noted, remained silent. "I know you won't, Fleet Commander. That's why I'm promoting you to admiral. Two-thirds of the fighters are to be spread around the rest of the fleet. You are to redeploy to the heavy cruiser *Starhammer*. That is your new flagship. From the *Achilles*, I shall command the rearguard and remaining fighter squadrons."

"But, sir, we need you."

"No. You needed me to pull this force together. That's my specialty and that's what I've done. Yours is tactical fleet command. I have given you your force, Admiral. Now it's up to you to wield it."

"Yes, General."

After a moment of silence, Sorbo sealed her fate. "I have given you your orders, Admiral. Get to them. And good luck, Aluin."

"You too, sir. Look after her, Fkansie. Aluin out."

For a painful few seconds, Sorbo stared at the blank window of her monitor where Aluin's face had been, marshaling her resolve. Then she called down to Fkansie. "How long till *Achilles* can move out?"

"Four minutes. And that's breaking every safety protocol."

Sorbo seethed with impatience. The lead elements of the enemy were twenty minutes from the shipyard at current velocity and would be able to fire on her people at an unknown interval before then.

From the mini deck where she commanded the entirety of Strike Force Fornax with the aid of her flag officers, Sorbo regarded Captain Fkansie who was directly below on the command deck of the *Achilles*. The space was designed so there was excellent eye and acoustic contact between the captain of the ship and the fleet commander up on the flag mini deck. Sometimes Sorbo wished there weren't.

The Slern appeared unflappable as he extended pseudopods over multiple screens and spoke calmly into his headset. He lifted an eyestalk and regarded Sorbo, perhaps sensing her attention. She nodded respectfully then hid behind her own screens. Waiting quietly was hard when the impulse to *do* something—anything—was so intense it was making her sweat. But there was no point yelling at Fkansie to move faster. The captain of the *Achilles* would already have squeezed every second out of the delay before they could move out.

Fkansie lifted a second eyestalk in her direction and said, "When we advance on the enemy, *Achilles* will be the entirety of the rearguard force."

Sorbo started to contradict him. "There will also be support vessels and planetary defenses—" She sighed and gave up. "I understand what you mean, Captain."

"Then you realize it's pointless for you to be here. If *Achilles* is lost, then we lose two of our most senior commanders. I have to ask, what do you add to the mix as commander of a fleet that will consist mostly of my ship?"

"I won't step on your toes, Fkansie. Even if you had any."

"That's not what I'm saying, and with respect, General, you know it. There's still time for you to get a shuttle out, and I strongly advise that you do."

"No, Captain. You're wrong and I'll tell you why. The Federation has lost its way. What were once virtues, such as steadfastness, courage, and duty, have been treated with suspicion and contempt for generations. We must show the Perseus Arm how to make a stand, to remind them what it is to be a proud citizen of the Federation. I cannot run. Besides…" Sorbo rose and leaned out from the 'pulpit,' the space on her mini deck from which she could address the command deck below. "Let everyone here be clear on this. I intend to *win*."

Fkansie gave no response, but the crew shouted out a few rallying cries of 'hold the line.' After the murmurs faded, the captain declared, "Very well, General. Three minutes until we move out."

Just enough time to clear one matter.

Sorbo turned to her flag captain. "Keppel, get me the office of the president of Tau-Fornacis."

"Roger that. His office has been trying to reach us anyway."

"Splendid."

Everyone on deck heard a muffled voice amid a background of shouts and screaming. "Oh, so the bitch has got a moment to talk to me now? Put her through." The president's voice came clearly over the speakers. "About fucking time. What the hell is going on?"

"Apologies," Keppel said and swapped the transmission to Sorbo's headset, adding a privacy shroud for good measure.

"We are being assaulted by an overwhelming superior military force," she informed the civil authority. "Rearguard elements led by *Achilles* will buy time for the rest of Strike Force Fornax to make a run for the Tej Sector."

Her words were met by momentary silence from the planet. Even the background pandemonium went silent. "You mean you're running away?"

"Are you hard of hearing, President Mitchabo? We are moments from moving out at flank speed to engage the enemy. We shall make all endeavors to win this battle. Nonetheless, it is highly likely that everyone aboard *Achilles* and all support vessels, including myself, will be dead within the hour. We all know this, but we do it anyway, because it is our duty. We are *not* running away."

"Your toxic Legion heroics don't impress me. You should be organizing the evacuation."

"You, President Mitchabo, should be organizing civil defense. That is *your* duty."

"It's not my job."

"Then render all assistance to whoever does have that job."

"No time for that. The senior members of my administration need to get off this planet, and I am ordering you to escort us."

"If you were a man, you would show leadership and organize the defenses. If you abandon your planet in its direst moment of need, what is the point of you, President?"

"You can't tell me what to do, fascist bitch."

Sorbo took a deep breath and allowed herself a slight smile. "Actually, I can. By the power rendered me by the Federation Emergency Powers Act of 2087, I'm declaring martial law. You are relieved of all powers and duties. Get out of my ear, *former* President Mitchabo. You are dismissed."

Sorbo cut the connection and made an encrypted call to Colonel Nteki. By her reckoning Nteki was the senior Legion officer still planetside.

"Go for Nteki."

"Colonel, its General Sorborovskele. I've just declared martial law. I've informed Mitchabo. You'll need to inform the rest of the planet and take charge."

"Yes, General. What are my orders?"

"I'll level with you, Colonel. The outlook appears challenging. We're covering the retreat of as much of the main force as we think can get away."

"Very good, sir. What you want me to do?"

"When they come, make them pay, Colonel. Make them hurt."

"Roger that, General Sorborovskele. We'll hold the line and make the bastards regret taking on the Legion. Good hunting. Nteki out."

Sorbo stared into the distance. There was so much about these Andromedans that she didn't know. Whether they were indeed from the Andromeda Galaxy was just the start of it. She'd seen reports of hex worlds where Federation citizens had been bred as… food? If the enemy seized the planet below, its fallen defenders and helpless civilian survivors would be *consumed.* The enemy would even eat its own fallen; the Vacuum Cleaner ships had proved that already. Alive? Dead? It seemed that to this enemy, both were organic matter that would simply be digested and turned into new living forms.

What was the point of killing the enemy when they would just grow back? You could never really kill them. All you could do was deny the enemy organic resources by burning them first. Total scorched earth.

She activated a flag command override and brought up the inventory of her munitions. Ironically, *Achilles* was desperately short of basic missiles and kinetic projectiles, but she had 48 planet-buster nukes on board with several salting options to make the bombs truly dirty. It was enough to kill a large portion of the planet's life and irradiate the rest.

To do so would be a mercy killing, and it would deny the enemy resources. She had no moral authority, nor legal, but scorching the planet was the right thing to do tactically and strategically.

Nuking a teeming world of several hundred million inhabitants. It was the sensible thing to do.

She stared at her hands hovering over her screen. As a failsafe, to launch the nukes that would salt the planet, she would need the agreement of Keppel or Fkansie, but she could arm the warheads now.

Her hands refused to move, and she knew she didn't have it in her. In the end it wasn't legality or ethics that stopped her. She simply lacked the courage.

Leading a suicide mission was so much easier.

"Leaving dock," helm announced.

"Ahead all speed," said the captain. "Let's show those ugly bastards what a Legion battle carrier can do."

*****

Chapter Five: Sorbo

Achilles led the rearguard, vectoring at an oblique angle to the Andromedan attack. Conventional wisdom dictated that doing so would merely expose their own flanks, but the moment Sorbo saw the boneless head of what was once a proud trooper of the Second Legion, she had mentally taken out conventional wisdom and had it shot.

Nothing could be certain in any war, but in this one everything was unknown.

That had to change.

"Fkansie, we need to ensure everything we learn today spreads across the Federation for tactical analysis. We both know that Aluin will be recording all comms traffic and sensor readings, but our on-the-spot analysis may add something they might miss."

"I agree. We are about to become the biggest military case study for centuries, but I need my people focused on supplying my command team with tactical information. Why don't you use Pascoe to send updates? I'll tell my station officers to keep her in the loop."

"Good idea." Sorbo beckoned the ensign over, who stuck out on the flag deck like a pair of blue dog's balls. "How are you rated for report writing, Pascoe?"

"Abysmal, General."

"Perfect. It's the responsibility of every legionary to improve their skills, and there's no time like the present. Pascoe, it's just possible that I'm about to give you the most important task on this ship..."

* * *

Surrounded by an escort of planetary defense boats and four zone-defense frigates, *Achilles* advanced toward the enemy's flank. Either the enemy would be drawn away from their attack on the planet of Tau-Fornacis and its orbital shipyards or they would sail past and allow the rearguard to assault their flanks and rear.

Back at the shipyards, Admiral Aluin had finally set off at an orthogonal vector to the Andromedans, several of his ships trailing leaking umbilicals and docking pier spars broken and ripped off in their haste to get away.

Minimum viable distance to jump from the planet was two planetary radii. Safe was six, but safety protocols had a habit of retreating when you were being shot at. Not only did Aluin have to make the tough decision about when to jump, but he had to shepherd a host of boats and ships that weren't jump-capable, many of which were supposed to have been safely stowed in the cavernous interior of the Legion's last surviving battle carrier.

"Good luck to you, Aluin," Sorbo whispered.

Then she put his concerns from her mind and concentrated on her own. Foremost was how she was going to keep the Andromedans occupied long enough for Aluin to escape. The rearguard would have to keep them at bay for at least ten minutes according to the best estimates from the analysts, but everyone was making up the numbers as they went along.

"Main cannons are in firing range," announced the Tactical station.

Sorbo tapped the comms selector for the fleet command channel. "Sorborovskele to all ships. This is where we hold the line, people. Remember to keep to your assigned firing sectors, and do not fire until I give the order."

With the fire command ready on her lips and eager to be uttered, Sorbo studied the main tactical plot. The Rho-Torkis Hammers were in the lead—named for the ship the Legion had discovered on Rho-Torkis and inadvertently woken from sleep. The Hammers streaked past her rearguard as if it weren't there. They looked the most dangerous, but the mass of Pouches and other craft not far behind totaled many hundreds of... *contacts.*

She hesitated to use words like craft, ship, or boat with the Andromedans. The creatures they faced in the void resembled sentient lifeforms. And the bulk of their number was on a trajectory to pass them, as oblivious as the Hammers to the rearguard's presence.

Following at the rear were the three Jump Leviathans, warty supersized space whales still towing a jump tunnel through which the occasional enemy vessel emerged. According to the plot, the trio would be in range of *Achilles'* main cannons in three minutes.

Sorbo wasn't prepared to wait that long.

"All ships. Engage the enemy."

Down on the command deck, Fkansie relayed the order to the Weapons Control team who made the hurt happen. And *Achilles* could deliver an impressive level of pain.

As a battle carrier, her biggest offensive punch was supposed to come from her support ships and the squadrons of fighters she carried. With most of her fighters transferred to Aluin, she possessed only two mixed squadrons of obsolete Mark 4 FVA-7 "Spikeball" fighters and TAC-2 "Swordfish 2" fast torpedo boats. As for her support vessels, they were running for the Tej Sector along with most of her fighters.

That was not to say *Achilles* was entirely toothless.

Far from it.

Her main section housed four 1.1 km long mass drivers, each with 17-degree traverse. Their regular loadout was a mix of dots and dashes.

Dots were simple tungsten-carbide kinetic shells massing 2,760 kilos able to attain a muzzle velocity of 13 km/s.

Dashes were thin rods of tungsten-chromium alloy only 18.8 mm thick. To increase velocity, they were fired sideways within spherical sabots. Once they emerged from the barrel, the sabot turned the rod through 90 degrees before peeling away so the rod could hit the target head on.

Normally, two mass drivers would fire together in dot-dash linked firing mode. Dots were better able to defeat angled, stud, or spaced armor, so a dot would hit first, hoping to defeat the outer layer of armor by either penetration or cratering. A dash would hit the same spot a second or so later and penetrate much deeper thanks to the dot's preparatory damage. Dashes always needed to impact at close to right angles against the target. *Achilles* couldn't get such a firing solution on the Hammers she was targeting, so Captain Fkansie had ordered dot-dot linked shots.

They were about to find out whether any of this firepower would actually achieve anything.

Tactical reported the results of the first salvos. "Missiles, railguns, and gauss cannons at Class-3 or above are effective against their targets."

"And our main guns?" Captain Fkansie asked.

"Ineffective against Hammers."

Sorbo drew a sharp breath. The plot showed the Hammers continuing untroubled on a straight-line course toward the planet. They were only a few hundred kilometers away—practically point-blank range—but she'd seen footage of them swimming through the vacuum of space as if it were deep ocean. If they made the effort, they could easily dodge mass driver rounds, but they hadn't even bothered.

"Permission to switch to NHEAT?" asked the captain.

"You are authorized to use nuclear HEAT shells," Sorbo confirmed.

If the Hammers continued on a straight vector and the NHEAT rounds landed, surely even they couldn't withstand their tantalum-salted nuclear shaped charge. Penetration damage, EMP, and irradiation: each on their own were devastating, but the combination of all three should be unstoppable.

"Taking fire," BattCon announced. "Preliminary assessment: kinetic projectiles. Limited damage."

Keppel relayed updates from the other ships. "Escort frigate *Khukuri* reports extensive damage including loss of jump engine. Two sys defense boats destroyed."

"NHEAT shots out."

Sorbo tracked the projectiles closing on the target Hammers in the main tactical plot, a path that would take about thirty seconds. Warships were massive, and if restricted to Newtonian physics, the mass drivers could reliably lead a target, even at this range.

But would the Hammers be so restricted?

The seconds passed and the Hammers showed no sign of maneuvering. The following mass of enemy ships also continued on a straight line to the planet, but an increasing number of individual elements were spinning around to bring their weapons to bear on the Federation rearguard.

Damage reports accumulated but Sorbo concentrated on the Hammers. Those were the ships whose attention she needed if she were to save Aluin's ass.

That's right. Ignore us just a little longer.

The visual was spectacular. She watched a NHEAT hit home at the joint between the forward cylinder of a Hammer and its tail, delivering an intense nuclear bloom that left deep gashes that spewed arterial spray.

All four targets were hurt, but they weren't dead. Not yet. They veered sharply away, flapping their tails weakly. Sorbo could almost feel their pain, hear the silent screams hurled into the vacuum.

We know how to hurt you now, you skraggs. Get some more.

The NHEAT mass driver volley had shoved a grenade up the asses of every Hammer. The uninjured ones beat their tails. What exactly they were thrashing against was invisible, but the *Achilles'* own force keels could push against resistance in the Klein-Manifold Region, so she assumed the enemy was doing the same.

The Hammers squirmed like giant, angry fish as they slowed and began to mill around as if undecided what to do next.

The Brown Pouches and the other ships were also taking note of the rearguard, vectoring hard to come about, though these seemed to be restricted to the conventional physical plane in which there was nothing to push against in a vacuum, only the ability to spin about and thrust against their own momentum using the hot gas plumes ejected from their rears.

"Looks like we got their attention," Fkansie said.

That was what they wanted, but the consequences made Sorbo's heart thump with fear all the same.

"More bandits incoming," TacCon announced. "They're arriving through the jump tunnel."

"Are the Jump Leviathans within firing range?" Fkansie asked.

"Negative."

"Fire anyway," Fkansie said. "Range guidance is derived from target leading success rate, and those Leviathans are so lumbering they're practically crawling on their warty bellies."

"Good thinking," Sorbo said. "Shut that gate down."

That was easier said than done. *Achilles'* main guns were currently oriented on the Hammers. Reorienting on the Leviathans meant spinning the ship 120 degrees to port.

As the battle carrier began its turn, Fkansie and the Helm went over the calculations.

An enormous ship like the battle carrier had an immense moment of inertia. It meant the attitude thrusters had to be almost as powerful as the main engines, but because they were only connected to the secondary heat management system, their maximum burn was about two minutes. Even that would leave the radiator spines glowing like embers in the visual spectrum and needing a long cool down. Longer attitude thruster burns meant things on the inside of the ship would catch fire and melt. Important things. Such as people.

Achilles had another way to turn quickly: cheat and use the rudder.

"General," Fkansie said, "we need to extend the force keel."

The force keel would push into the resistive higher dimensions known as the Klein-Manifold Region and produce sideways 'lift' the same as a sea ship's keel. Unfortunately, that required stolen technology that wasn't fully understood even at the height of the Federation's scientific prowess. None of the supporting ships had force keels, only the fighters still in the hangar. Deploying the keel would mean losing formation.

"Permission to deploy keel granted," Sorbo said. "Keppel, inform the support ships other than the jump-capable frigates to keep station as best they can."

Sorbo hesitated. The frigates were there to erect an anti-missile screen, but the enemy had so far showed no sign of possessing missiles. This was a very strange kind of space combat. She nodded to Keppel. "Tell the frigates to run while they still can. Jump to the nearest safe port."

"Engines all stop," Fkansie ordered. "Brake and turn hard to port."

"Firing solution on the Leviathans in one hundred thirty-eight seconds."

"Reload with dots and dashes. Let's rake some uglies as we turn."

Firing as she turned made sense, but that two minutes and change was going to feel like an epoch. And it meant exposing their flank to the Hammers and the other enemy ships. They needed a covering screen if they were to survive.

"Launch all fighters," ordered Fkansie.

"Captain," TacCon said, "we might have spotted something important."

"No time to be bashful, Lieutenant. Out with it."

"Mass Drivers #1 and #2 destroyed a pair of Bone Balls close to each other. Some of the tac analysis team thought they saw a stutter in the maneuvering of nearby Pouches."

"What do *you* think, Lieutenant?"

"Equal chance we saw something real or saw a pattern that was never there. Could be those balls are comms relays?"

"Or they're command-and-control elements," Sorbo said.

"There's our weakness!" roared the captain. "Those balls are like exposed humanoid gonads just dangling in space, waiting for us to whack 'em hard. Get me the CAG. I've got a job for his squadrons."

* * * * *

Chapter Six: Squadron Leader Boss

Achilles' much depleted fighter complement formed up a klick outside the armored egress baffles. It consisted of a single wing of two mixed squadrons, each with four two-section flights of Spikeballs and three of Swordfish 2 fast torpedo fighters. Each pilot made full use of attitude thrusters and force keels to produce random jitters as they formed up in a paired oblique swarm formation.

Forty-eight boats. Ninety-six souls, including his own. Mark Boss had been Rampage Squadron leader so long the role had become part of his name. But the entire wing was his command now. Which meant at least ninety-five of those souls were expecting him to lead.

Time to get to it. Boss transmitted on the wing-wide channel, "All callsigns, Rampage Lead. You heard the CAG; the enemy has their testicles out, and it's up to us to bludgeon them. For the non-humanoids among us, doing so should make the enemy yelp with pain. We will conduct a Helmud Weave through the Brown Pouches. Shoot them as you pass but our priority targets are the Bone Balls. Let's kick gonads, people. Good hunting."

Boss throttled forward and the attack was on.

"CAG!" Boss heard a chuckle from Kane in the seat beside him. This was Craig Kane, his weapon controller, or Banger as they were known in the business. Kane continued musing, "Why do we call the Spaceflight Group Commander that? Some speculate that CAG was once an acronym, and it does roll off human tongues easier than SFGC."

In the moments before action started, Kane tended to run philosophical. It was just his way. Boss left him to it.

"Some say CAG goes all the way back to the era when atmospheric aircraft were the apex of technology. People have been debating that for thousands of years, and I like the fact that we will probably never know the answer. It would be a shame for all our historical mysteries to be extinguished when humanity has gone."

"That's a thought for another day, Craig," Boss interrupted. He'd never heard Kame so maudlin. "I want you to paint those balls."

Boss had enough to worry about without his Banger imagining the eradication of humankind. They were fast approaching the most numerous craft class of the enemy. Designated Brown Pouches, they resembled suede leather tamales the size of a frigate. So far, they showed no sign of employing missiles or lasers. Instead, they were spitting pellets out of sphincterlike maws.

If not for the scale, they would appear comical pea shooters, but these warcraft—or space animals, he didn't know what the hell they were—had already taken out several system defense boats. The Spikeballs and Swordfish were better armored than those unfortunate boats, but Boss preferred his people to not be hit at all.

Within the four-craft flights, each member was performing the Helmud Weave, and the flights themselves were performing the same weave at a squadron level. The weave tactic was designed to counter adversaries that were significantly more maneuverable, such as small X-bomb drones.

So far, the Pouches were proving to be considerably less maneuverable than Boss' aerospace fighters, but he was hoping the weave would confuse the enemy targeting systems. Although in their case, 'targeting' appeared to be nothing more than aligning their maws on their enemies before spitting out pellets.

"It's like flying into a brown swamp," Kane said.

Boss agreed. The mob of Pouches had jumped out of their tunnel already on a direct vector to the shipyards—a neat trick, by the way. Some had maintained that vector but had changed orientation to direct fire on the rearguard. Others were thrusting hard to get at *Achilles* and her support. The result was a mess of shifting brown clumps.

Deadly ones.

A brief flash of light ahead and to port registered the demise of Rampage Red Two.

Then Rampage Gold Flight hit the outliers of the brown swamp, and Boss concentrated on being flight lead for the moment.

With the vacuum filling with deadly incoming projectiles, he swung his Spikeball low and left beneath a clump of three Pouches, flicking his gaze briefly at the tac-plot to check his wingman, Gold Two, had shadowed his move. As he passed below the enemy, he tilted his craft up and spun right to fire a long burst from the nose cannon and slashed one along its belly.

The ugly thing bled, spilling sickly yellow fluid into the black.

"We hurt it!" Kane yelled. "I dumped a full laser charge through its mouth."

Boss acknowledged with a grunt, but he'd already spun back to match orientation with his vector. He kicked the rudder and keel controls to bring the Spikeball to scissor right as Rampage Gold Three and Four swung left. The nav assist prompted him to alter vector again as Gold Flight was meant to perform a slower weave with Rampage Indigo. He satisfied its nagging by goosing the attitude jets to add a little unpredictability to his craft but not enough to confuse Gold Two on his wing.

"One slug's turning to bear on us," his Banger reported. "The rest seem to have forgotten us."

They were entering the thickest part of the swamp now. Pouches were everywhere he looked, and every single one was on a different vector.

"Rampage Lead," he said over the Wing channel, "switch to flight-level weave only. The black's too thick with them for anything else. Repeat, flight weave only. And remember, our targets are the Bone Balls."

Up then right. Down then left. Boss kept his Spikeball and his wingman scissoring through three dimensions with the other section. With the enemy so thick, the weave was ragged, but they made progress without loss and entered the inner depths of the enemy mob without loss.

"Bone Balls painted," Kane reported. "All our missiles locked in."

"Copy that." Boss flipped their Spikeball 180 degrees as they passed beneath the largest pouch they'd seen and shot its ass off with the nose railguns.

"This is easy," roared his Banger and best friend.

Boss laughed. "Make your mind up."

"What's that?"

"I think I preferred you when you were all 'everyone's gonna die.'"

"We all die eventually, Acting Wing Commander. It's just a matter of whether we die the right way."

Boss fired a burst at another brown ugly before scissoring past the other section. "That's after-action-review talk for the FU Bar on Deck 14, Kane. What gives?"

"Nothing. Concentrate on your piloting, fly boy. You know you get your left and right mixed sometimes."

Boss ignored whatever was bugging Kane because his friend was right: this *was* easy. They'd flown through the densest enemy 'formation' he'd ever seen, and they were penetrating toward its center. So far, they'd taken two casualties and hurt the uglies a whole lot more.

"Boss," Kane said, "my blackbirds are itching."

"Set them free."

"Fox ripple twelve," Kane warned over the flight channel. "In three… two… one… away."

Judders rocked the Spikeball as its ring of twelve missile tubes released their loads like a fireworks display. Boss kept his fighter level for the textbook second and a half for safe separation before throwing it around the black.

"Good lock on all blackbirds," Kane reported. "Trouble! Trouble! Bearing 0-2-0 low."

"Rampage Lead is brake-and-shake," Boss warned his flight. He reversed thrust and tilted every one of the force keels that gave the Spikeball its name to give maximum braking resistance in the K-M.

A painful tightening in his chest and narrowing of vision was the only physical effect of the massive deceleration as the Spikeball came to a sudden stop. It was good to know his fighter could still cheat the laws of physics. He spun ninety degrees and slammed the throttle forward against the stops.

Behind him, Gold Two overshot Boss' brake-and-shake but was turning to form up again on his wing.

"That was close," Kane said. "A new kind of ugly had us in its sights. The ship looks like a living gauss cannon and that's not the good bit. It's served by a humanoid crew, standing on its hull. Without suits. Man, that's freaky shit."

Gold Flight shot through the band of living gauss cannons and beyond. The Bone Balls were almost within gun range.

"Blackbirds approaching kill envelopes," Kane reported. "Four targets hit and counting. One shot one kill. Every time."

Around Boss, confusion was spreading through the mob of uglies like a fast-acting virus. The vessels froze, drifting along current vectors. There were no changes to orientation, no pellets firing. Dead!

CAG was right, the enemy's balls were a weak spot, and Boss's fighters had hit them where it hurt.

He led his flight through the crowd of uglies, shooting up the command-and-control balls whenever they could.

"I think they're coming back to life," Kane said. "The Brown Pouches, I see them twitching."

Then a salvo of torpedoes from the Swordfish 2s took out most of the remaining balls and the reanimation of the enemy seemed to shut down for good.

The flying had been so intense, the battle space so crowded, that Boss worried he'd neglected his wider command responsibilities.

He widened the tac-plot and was reassured to find the other flights were in a similar situation to Rampage Gold. Rampage Red and Shrike Gold had each lost another Spikeball.

All losses hurt, but the larger ships were hurting more. All the escort frigates were heavily damaged or destroyed. *Achilles* was intact, but another mob of Brown Pouches had emerged from the jump tunnel with vectors already directed at the battle carrier.

Achilles herself had turned and directed her main guns on one of Leviathans that kept the jump tunnel open and was allowing still more of the space beasts through.

In theory, those enormous mass drivers should be ripping chunks out of the Leviathan, but nothing was certain anymore.

The wing channel activated. "This is Rampage Indigo Two. There's something crawling out of the ball I just shot up. Some kind of… a swarm?"

"I've got a visual," Kane said. His sharp in breath didn't bode well. "Indigo Two's right. He's being swarmed by a cloud of… *bats*."

With half an ear monitoring Kane's explanation of Indigo Two's situation, Boss spied another Bone Ball nearby and led his section against it.

"I'm shaking them," Indigo Two said. "They're nimble, but not Spikeball nimble. They're peppering us with shots. Like shotgun blasts. But I—"

"Contact lost," Kane said.

Boss let rip with the quad cannon in the nose, flaying this latest Bone Ball with ultra-velocity darts. It didn't burst so he flew past to allow his wingman a go, turning tightly in case he needed a second pass.

"I register multiple EM spikes in Indigo Two's vicinity," Kane said.

"You mean they're dead in the water but can be recovered?"

"I… don't think so, Boss. Wavelength frequency is all wrong. I think some of those creatures that flew out of the balls are living X-ray bombs."

The ball Boss had shot up was proving resilient. His wingman, Gold Two, hadn't finished it off either. Boss brought his Spikeball round for another go at it, although he was keeping his distance because the other Gold section would get a go first.

Slowing the turn a little gave him a chance to get a good look at the ball. It was a crusty sphere with a diameter about twice the Spikeball's length. Five bony bands encircled it. Boss was reminded of his distant schooldays and the spinning topological models of the surface of rocky planets.

Gold Three had barely begun her attack run when all five bone circlets exploded outward and revealed themselves to be miniature creatures. Nasty things that fired at Gold Three.

"My Banger thinks those things are shooting tungsten shards," Gold Four said.

They're packing more than that, thought Boss. "Gold Three, Four, abort your attack. Form up on me, and we'll take that ball together." He switched to the wing channel. "All call signs, Rampage Lead. Rampage Indigo Two called them bats, but those things that make up the Bone Ball rings are wasps with a poisonous sting and guess who just disturbed their nest? Flights will link sections and engage targets from a safe distance. If the wasps swarm at you, run and come at your target from another bearing. Our enemy just grew teeth. Don't make it easy for them to bite us."

The bone rings burst in the few command-and-control balls they hadn't yet taken out, releasing a protective cloud of wasps.

As for the Bone Balls his squadrons had shot up earlier, no wasps emerged, but the bone circlets they'd dismissed as debris now activated into angry swarms of deadly enemies.

Why hadn't they swarmed earlier? Who could tell with these strange aliens? Perhaps without their bone circlets, the balls couldn't control the other craft. Maybe the space wasps were the equivalent of staff officers? Or maybe the wasp clouds interfered with the signals?

All these unknowns brought home the alienness of their enemy. They were growing sneakier, too. The Swordfish 2s had force keels, but they were nowhere near as maneuverable as Spikeballs. They were also more heavily armored, which meant they were slower. The swarming wasps ignored the Spikeballs and flew at the lumbering torpedo fighters.

What to do?

First, he checked his ammo state. "I'm reading twenty-two percent remaining for the nose," he said. "How's it looking to you?"

"Thirteen blues down," Kane said, referring to the visible blue color leak when his lasers fired. "Keeping two in reserve. Cyber and physical countermeasures fully stocked. Somehow, I don't think they'll feature much in this war."

"Man! Don't jinx it." He transmitted to his flight, "Give me ammo status."

"Gold Four has four-one in the nose cannon and two blues."

"Three reads one-eight in the nose and two in the back."

"Four has four-zero upfront. Six blues."

A powerful instinct roared at Boss to stay and fight to the last dart. Everyone in both squadrons would be feeling that. However, staying till their ammo ran dry would leave them extremely vulnerable, and if everyone rearmed at the battle carrier at the same time, the hangar boss would be overwhelmed. The second wave of Brown Pouches was almost upon *Achilles,* so they might have to shoot their way back in, and he couldn't do that with empty magazines.

"All call signs, Spikeball flights to escort duty. Keep your designated Swordfish wasp free. Lead flights return home. Avoid engagements. Keep your powder dry, people. There will be plenty of uglies left for our next run."

On Gold's channel he continued, "Section leads are burning more ammo. So, we swap. Gold Four, you are flight lead. Gold Two, I'm your wingman."

The other pilots confirmed, and the reorganized flight made their way back to Mother.

Following Gold Two gave him a fraction more time to think.

Boss had read accounts from soldiers fighting years-long wars on planetary surfaces. He'd always been struck by the horror when the frontline returned to sites of previous battles. The ground would still be broken and littered with wrecked equipment and the rusting hulks of abandoned fighting vehicles. Shellfire would disinter the grinning dead from their shallow graves to watch the living who would soon join them.

That had never been an issue for Boss. In space, the battle zone was too huge and diverging vectors rapidly dissipated wreckage. But not this time. The enemy had been so crowded and the vectors so similar, that the squadron's kills were still present within the mob of confused Pouches.

"We're close to Indigo Two," radioed Gold Four. "I want to take a look."

"Roger that," Boss confirmed.

Four took them on a wide path toward a clump of living gauss cannons, and they flew past Indigo Two. The fighter's port side had blown out. It didn't look survivable, and when the camera view zoomed into the interior, it showed some of the wreckage that had once been the bodies of his aeronauts.

Boss squared his shoulders and took a moment to remember the two young Zhoogenes. Their unofficial callsigns were Vapor and Siesta. He chuckled, remembering the incident when he'd dished out the latter's nickname.

"You've earned this nap," he whispered. "We will avenge you both."

They left Indigo Two behind and threaded their way through the enemy mob, picking a route to avoid the most active vessels, but by now even the living gauss guns appeared dormant.

Behind them, the other Spikeball flights had joined up with their Swordfish 2 partners and were providing wasp clearance support. Mercifully, even the heavily armored torpedo boats were discovering that a full-throttle exit was enough to outpace the swarms.

The situation near *Achilles* was much more worrying. The second mob of Brown Pouches were about to swamp the battle carrier, breaking into more radar contacts as they did. At this range, Boss couldn't make out what was happening in any detail. In a universe that made sense, the new contacts would indicate the launching of boarding pods, but who could tell in the insanity they were now facing?

"Azhanti!" Kane sounded horrified. "Boss, look at this."

His Banger added a camera view to one of his auxiliary screens. It showed a Pouch they'd shot up earlier. It was in the outer reaches of the enemy horde, a space they would shortly pass through. He still thought of them as burned tamales and this one had been gutted, spewing its contents into the vacuum.

Another alien ship… thing… whatever it was… had matched vectors with the carcass and opened the maw in its bow to swallow the corpse whole. Like a giant snake. Smaller versions of this cleanup ship were also patrolling the area, sucking up the spilled guts from the shot-up Pouch.

"They must be the goddamned Vacuum Cleaners we were told about," Kane exclaimed.

"And if they eat their own…"

Boss couldn't finish that sentence. He thought of Vapor, Siesta, and the other casualties. They would be eaten too, and there wasn't a damned thing he could do about it.

He took a last look at the scene. The smaller Vacuum Cleaners weren't sucking up the frozen spatter but instead were flicking it into their maws with an array of tongues like hairy whips. The whole thing was revolting.

Boss shut down the view. Soon they were clear of the enemy and on final approach to *Achilles*.

Behind them, most of the enemy fleet drifted, confused in space. But not all. The Rho-Torkis Hammers had taken some hits from Mother's mass drivers earlier in the battle and that had caused them to pause, but they had pressed on and were firing at long range into the military shipyards where the rest of Strike Force Fornax was pulling away to make their escape.

If the Hammers weren't stopped, then the strike force would be wiped out and everything Boss and his aeronauts were doing would be rendered meaningless.

Boss couldn't do anything about the shipyards at the moment. First, he had to get back to Mother to refuel and rearm, but how? The Pouches covered the battle carrier like leeches.

A better name for them would be Russian Dolls, because Kane had put up a screen showing a Pouch opening the fold along its belly and 'birthing' a smaller version of itself. The offspring split again to produce smaller 'children.' From 150-meter Pouches to tiny versions large enough to carry a single humanoid, and all sizes in between, this was an alien infestation.

And *Achilles* had succumbed.

"Rampage Lead, this is Achilles Control. Be aware baffle ingress is compromised."

"Control, we can provide a slug clearance service, but our cannon mags are running low."

"Understood, Rampage Lead. We're trying to keep baffle routes free along zones one-three and two-seven. You may have to help clear from the outside."

"Copy that. We're coming in on two-seven. Shrike Gold will use one-three. Advise the hangar boss to finish up her round of cards and get ready to load us up with more presents for the space warts."

Laughter came across the radio. "Tell her yourself. I value my body parts. Control out."

Boss tasked Kane with updating the rest of the wing while he followed Gold Four into the opening doors of baffle gate two-seven.

A battle carrier could open its hangar for fast launch and recovery of its fighter and bomber squadrons. It was also the only way in and out for most shuttles, supply ships, and maintenance boats. During a battle, though, the hangar was buttoned up behind heavier armor than anywhere else on the ship, a full thirty meters of ceramic-tungsten composite honeycomb sandwiched with boron gel sheets to absorb neutron radiation.

The alternative route was the baffle zone that hung like a strip of beard below the carrier's belly. Any craft small enough to fit through the baffle had to zigzag through an armored maze. Less maneuverable craft than the carrier's force keel-equipped squadrons had no chance of passing through, and any cheeky drones would be taken out by the baffle's laser grid.

The Spikeballs proceeded gingerly through the baffle. The amber glow of the light strips reflected off the lens caps of the lasers embedded in the walls. Judging from the mist hanging in the baffles, the lasers had been busy.

Gold Flight was halfway inside when they encountered their first Brown Pouch, an enormous brute so huge it squeezed against the walls. Its back was covered in oozing burn marks from the laser grid's attention.

"Let's give it a Legion welcome" said Gold Four and lit up its ass with his railguns. After a ten-second burst chewed it up some but didn't burst it, Gold Four withdrew and Boss squeezed past and took a turn.

The back end of the alien space creature erupted in gold slime, but it was so big that even after death, it still blocked progress through the baffle.

All four Spikeballs had to take turns until eventually they shredded the alien so thoroughly that they could pass through the hot, sticky fluids and flesh strips of its remains. Luckily, the gloop coating the baffle was so thick that it obscured any scarring his flight's cannons had wreaked on the walls. The skipper was not well disposed to pilots who scratched his ship.

Beyond, the going was clear, though they had two more Andromedan corpses to fly through that had already been killed.

Finally, they made it to the hangar, where cannons and missile launchers were tracking his Spikeball's every move.

He said, "When the bad guys make it as far as the hangar, by God, they'll regret it." Then he corrected himself. "If. *If* they make it this far."

But neither man was buying that line. The enemy would get inside, and they both knew it.

He looked across and gave a thumbs up to Kane, but Boss could see in his friend's eyes that he already knew they were doomed.

Kane had known that all along.

* * * * *

Chapter Seven: Sorbo

The salvo from *Achilles'* mass drivers hit home, and the Leviathan finally succumbed. Its hide had been flayed and bleeding for a while, and now it exploded spectacularly, a pus supernova that froze into a sea of yellow shards that glittered in the light of the Tau-Fornacis sun.

"Jump tunnel is closing," announced an analyst, but his words were unnecessary. One of the brown, leathery creatures had been emerging through the tunnel's throat when it closed. The rear of the vessel shrunk instantly to a dot and its front half exploded in a smaller echo of the Leviathan's showy death.

The command deck erupted in roars of jubilation.

General Sorborovskele allowed herself a smile.

The acoustics of the ancient battle carrier were unlike any vessel Sorbo had known. She couldn't quite put her finger on what made it special, be it the glinting control alcoves set into the bulkheads, the grilles of the overhead air scrubbers, the high-grip magnetized surfaces of its walkways, or any of her mundane surfaces. Combined, though, they quietly added an undertone of dignity to the crew's cheers.

The ship's majestic ambience was likely all in Sorbo's head, yet it enraptured her. Over the centuries, hundreds of thousands of Legion personnel had served with pride aboard the *Achilles*, and now her decks teemed with their invisible presence.

And if she had anything to do with it, this wouldn't be the last time *Achilles* would enjoy the celebrations of her command crew.

"We're getting a reaction from the Hammers," said TacCon. A section of the main holo tank switched to views closer to the planet. "This happened the moment that Leviathan exploded."

Sorbo winced at the destruction the shipyards and strike force had already suffered. The Hammers were thrashing their tails in an effort to turn around. They weren't as nimble as an FVA Spikeball, but they outclassed any vessel restricted to maneuvering in conventional spacetime. Within a minute, they'd reversed their heading and were swimming hard for *Achilles.*

It was the outcome she'd prayed for, but the pit of Sorbo's stomach still froze with terror.

"We have boarders," announced the security officer. "Breach alarms triggered in thirteen locations. Major Qwell reports defenses engaging. Secondary and Tertiary squads in reserve for now."

"Are they in the hangar?" asked the captain.

"Negative."

"Were these breaches simultaneous?" Sorbo asked.

"Seems that way, General."

"That means coordination."

"Captain," TacCon said, "those Brown Pouches our fighters shot up… they've woken up. I mean they're showing signs of coordination. Luckily, they've been drifting away from us for some time now."

"I think it's the Hammers," Sorbo said. "We can't know anything for sure with this hell-crazy foe, but that's my guess. We've forced them to turn back and take control of the situation in this section of the battle space."

Captain Fkansie waved a pseudopod in a Slern gesture of agreement. "I concur. Security, what are our teams facing?"

"A mix. Some are the hex world creatures. A lot of them humanoid. Corrupted military; planetary, Militia, mercenary, and Legion. Major Qwell is reporting a squad in Legion armor and equipment rushing Deck 46 Frame 14. They're wearing the insignia of a Tenth Legion assault brigade. The equipment pattern they're using is obsolete and… and it matches what was in use when the Tenth was lost."

The news stunned Sorbo, ripping apart all her assumptions about the threat they faced.

Two hundred and sixty-two Terran years had passed since the Tenth Legion had been wiped out. No one had ever learned their fate.

Technically, the Tenth still existed, but only as a notional training unit. It wasn't the first Legion to be lost, but it was the first that had never been allowed to reconstitute due to political posturing.

If those individuals assaulting *Achilles* had been captured and Corrupted over two and a half centuries ago… the implications were appalling.

Captain Fkansie showed no sign of concern over this latest revelation. "ZiJoillet, what have we got for round two?" he asked the hangar boss.

"We're two minutes away from sending Rampage Gold back out. Shrike Gold two minutes later. After that it gets tricky. Our baffles are clogged, and we have aircraft queuing to get in."

"Will the hangar doors open?"

"We've repaired most of the damage the boarders did, but we won't know if we've done enough until we try. I'll give you an eighty percent yes."

"TacCon, how long till those Hammers arrive and start shooting?"

"Estimated six minutes."

"Commander ZiJoillet, you have a five-minute window to open and close the main hangar doors. Retrieve and launch as many craft as you can before zipping us up tight."

"Five minutes. Copy that."

"And this time, I want those squadrons on barnacle scraping duty."

*****

Chapter Eight: Squadron Leader Boss

"Let the barnacle scraping commence!"

It was Lieutenant Johnson—callsign Red Rampage Three—who spoke the words, and Boss declined to correct him.

Boss had often spent his leave helping his brother prepare for the summer when he hired out his fleet of three fishing boats to tourists flocking to enjoy the peaceful bays of the Dawpeng coastline of the planet Legiyr-Ho.

Despite the gloves he would wear, Boss's hands would always bleed, much to his brother's amusement. This was different.

The hangar crews had reloaded his nose cannons with expanding rounds and the charge across their rails had been cut by 75 percent to slow muzzle velocity and maximize the damage from the wound channel. It was essentially the equivalent of the hollow-point rounds his brother used to hunt big game on the plains of Legiyr-Ho.

Except Boss's rounds weighed nine hundred grams each, and his quad cannons cycled through 120 of them each second.

Hollow-point rail cannon rounds! They were left over from the Gorgantheletta Eruption centuries ago. But as the fighters that had managed to rearm and get back in the fight shot through the brown blobs coating *Achilles*, the Legion was immediately vindicated in hording the ancient ammunition.

It wasn't barnacle scraping so much as industrial flensing.

The sixteen Spikeballs and four Swordfish who'd egressed through the hangar soared, dove, and rolled to avoid enemy fire as they tore into the blobs, shrouding the battle carrier in a mist of liquidized alien flesh cut through with ribbons of shredded hide.

Once attached to *Achilles,* the Pouches no longer fired their pellets, but danger still lurked from the living gauss cannons milling around the ship.

"Shrike Indigo One is down," Kane said as the enemy gauss finally made a kill.

Nineteen fighters left.

It wasn't much, but they were Legion fighters. They'd held the line before and they would damned well do it again here, at Tau-Fornacis.

They had to.

Boss was circling toward a clump of Pouches lodged in the primary heat exchange system in the port bow when lines of hellfire scribed themselves across *Achilles'* main hull as if touched by the finger of a vengeful god.

"What the hell?" Kane yelled. "What can do that? It's plasma splash."

Kane began to explain about plasma splash, but Boss wasn't listening. He pulled out of his current attack and added a few twists and rolls for good measure.

"It's the Rho-Torkis Hammers," Kane said. His voice calm once more.

"And they have plasma cannons?"

"No. Kinetic projectiles with such insane velocity that they fry into plasma when they hit *Achilles'* armor."

Although Kane had calmed down, Boss felt dread rising unchecked. The living gauss cannons, Pouches, Leviathans, and the Vacuum Cleaners who swarmed the battle space to gorge on the carnage his fighters were causing, all were nightmarish and greatly outnumbered Boss's fighters. But he knew he could beat them.

But the Hammers? Doubts seeped in.

He flew ten klicks away from *Achilles* and watched as the Hammers concentrated their fire from long range.

None of his fighters were being targeted.

"Ignore them, and maybe they'll ignore us," he said over the squadron channels. "We're the barnacle cleaners. Back to work, everybody."

It wasn't just the Hammers that had changed their activity. Brown Pouches were, too.

"Advise Mother what we're seeing," he told Kane.

"*Achilles* Control this is Rampage Lead," Kane said. "We are transmitting visual feed. Thought you should know how this looks from the outside. Those Hammers are gouging channels through *Achilles'* armor, and when they finish brown blobs are hurling themselves against the gashes like maggots infesting a wound. It's a coordinated boarding strategy."

"Copy that, Rampage Lead. Standby for updated orders—"

"We need more fighters," Boss said over the open channel. "I know it's a risk, but we need those hangar doors open again to let our people out."

"That's a negative on the hangar doors. The enemy has blocked them with their... bodies."

"We need more guns on those boarders from the outside. Get them out the baffles."

"Negative, Rampage Lead. You've done enough. All Spikeballs and Swordfish in flight will proceed at full speed to rendezvous with Admiral Aluin. There, you are to dock and jump out-system. Godspeed, Squadron Leader."

Boss felt sick to the stomach. "But… I'm responsible for all of Rampage and Shrike. Most of my craft are still stuck in that hangar."

A new voice came over the comm. "Squadron Leader Boss, this is General Sorbo. Is there a problem with your orders?"

"No, sir. I mean… Are you telling me to abandon my ship… my people?"

Sorbo laughed, as untroubled as if this were the officers' wardroom after a long day and several beers. "You're harking back to the Orion Spur days and No Marine Left Behind, am I right?"

"I guess so, sir."

"You're thinking about this the wrong way. It's Admiral Aluin who doesn't want to leave *you* behind."

"But—"

"We all have our jobs to do, Squadron Leader. Sometimes we don't like them, but we're Legion so we do them anyway."

"Yes, sir."

"Good luck, Boss. Now get the hell out of here."

Boss switched to the squadron channels. "All fighters, Rampage Lead. Break off and form on me. We're heading for Admiral Aluin and a lift out-system."

The news was met with silence. And then, to Boss's relief, a flurry of double-click acknowledgments. All the same, he imagined stunned silence on nineteen other pilot decks.

"This is Shrike Red Lead. Lieutenant Chancer. Sir, we can't just..." Chancer couldn't complete the thought.

So, Boss did it for him. "The Hammers are between us and Aluin. Up to this point, they've been ignoring us. Let's give them a parting gift that will change their ugly alien minds."

Boss reorganized his remaining fighter craft into four divisions, each assigned to one of the Hammers, of which twenty were targeting *Achilles*.

The alien craft hadn't had it all their own way. *Achilles'* mass drivers had toasted five of them with nuclear HEAT rounds. Mother must have run dry because now they were firing less radioactively hot munitions that nonetheless were enough to stun the ships. The earliest mass driver volleys had been ineffective. Perhaps the gun crews had subsequently tuned the munition loadout, same as they had with his Spikeballs.

The Hammers were as strange an opponent as any of the Andromedans. The rear half was the tail of a giant space whale that ended in a spiked club. The front half appeared to be metal and ceramic, almost like a conventional destroyer except it was covered in 'hairs' made from segmented bone that wriggled like cilia. When a Hammer got a face full of mass drivers those hairs went limp and fell against the side of the enemy's body. He assigned each of his four divisions to a Hammer with limp bone hairs.

As his division screamed into the attack, their target rolled and thrashed, trying to present the smallest profile to the Spikeballs' fire.

The streams of ferroceramic rounds from the rail cannons sparked off the Hammer's hull. No damage. But the Swordfish landed a torpedo in the curve of its beating tail.

The explosion ripped into the Hammer, shedding layers off its tail like scaling a fish.

The crew of the Swordfish yelled in triumph, but the victory celebration was short lived. The Hammer was hurt and bleeding, but not dead.

Each division concentrated fire on a single wounded Hammer, but none of the others landed any damage and their targets quickly learned to ignore the fighters and continue to launch devastating fire on *Achilles*.

"Energy spikes forming in front of the Hammers," Kane said. "Some of the undamaged ones, anyway. They're forming jump tunnels."

Boss made a split-second decision and addressed Rampage and Shrike. "This is Rampage Lead. All craft stick like glue to the nearest jumper and pursue."

He didn't have a plan beyond doing whatever his enemy expected least, but his aeronauts complied without question, matching Boss's resolve with their own tenacity.

Rampage Gold Two joined him on a Hammer's tail. So did a Swordfish. The main visual in Boss' pilot cage showed a false image of a circle growing in front of them as the throat into another region of reality came into being.

You couldn't really see a jump tunnel in the visual spectrum, but Boss felt a scratching at his brain in the shape of a circle. At some level, he was perceiving this monstrous rip through the universe up close and personal, an experience he'd heard about but never quite believed. But then he'd never heard of anyone pursuing another ship so closely that they followed it through a tunnel throat.

The jump entrance rapidly expanded into a funnel that stretched out to embrace the alien and the three Legion fighter craft. It folded back behind them, about to seal them in its bubble.

Suddenly, the alien craft beat its tail and sped up, taking its bubble with it. Boss felt the sides of the tunnel closing in on him, but the Spikeball was up to it. A touch of the throttle, and he caught up and matched vectors.

So did Rampage Gold Two.

But Swordfish weren't as maneuverable. Ironically, its pilot's call sign was Slipstream, and she must have pushed the throttle to the wall, but it wasn't enough. Corky was her Banger, and she must have realized they weren't going to make it, because Corky launched a torpedo an instant before the tunnel entrance pinched off.

For a moment, the wraparound showed the Hammer with the beating tail, a torpedo speeding toward that tail, two Spikeballs, and the forward sections of the Swordfish housing Slipstream and Corky.

The remainder of the Swordfish hadn't made it through.

Then, perhaps mercifully, the universe went dark because none of the Spikeball's instruments could make sense of what was happening inside a jump tunnel.

"We'd better take turns on watch," Kane suggested.

"Good idea. It could be days or weeks until we leave this tunnel. But not yet, we're both too wired anyway."

Regrets brushed at Boss, but he ignored them. Maybe his decision to follow the Hammer down their tunnel would pay out and maybe it would be a disaster. Either way, it was a done deal. All that mattered was what they did next.

And that carried its own problems. Since no one knew how these creatures moved through the universe, he didn't really know how long they would be stuck in this bubble of nothing. Air and food wouldn't be a problem for about two weeks, but water purity would. Spikeballs weren't long-range craft.

Thoughts of a lingering death evaporated when the fighter's instruments sprang back to life. They erupted into the battle around Tau-Fornacis, at the shot-up shipyards.

"We hurt it!" Kane said. "We hurt that bastard!"

The damaged Hammer they'd pursued was now bleeding into space and the base of its tail was burned through to a central core. Boss wasted no time pumping those monster-killer railgun rounds into the wound. A second later, so did Gold Two. The tail severed, leaving the forward part of this machine-creature drifting in space, the bone hairs limp.

The Spikeball's cabin rang with cheers.

"Splash one Hammer!" Gold Two roared over the comm. "It was Corky's torpedo that did for it. It's because the bastard was thrashing its tail. Makes it vulnerable. God rest you, Corky. You too, Slipstream."

How could I miss something so obvious? "Is he right?" Boss asked Kane. He'd already decided the answer. Every time *Achilles* or its fighters had scored hits on the Hammers, it had been when their tails were swinging.

While Kane pondered, Boss flung his Spikeball around as he took in the situation. Hours ago, the Tau-Fornacis shipyards had been filled with the pride of the Legion naval and marine forces, readying to sally out with Militia reinforcements into the chaos of the Tej Sector to deliver righteous retribution to the invaders.

Shattered spars and blasted supply vessels were the reality now. A few warships had been caught in their docking slips, but mostly they'd steamed away, only the stragglers had been shot up by the Hammers before the enemy had turned back to take on *Achilles*. The bulk of Strike Force Fornax was still pushing away from the planet, desperate to get far enough away from its gravity well to jump safely.

Aluin's ships were only a few minutes short of jumps that would be risky but just the right side of suicidal. If Boss's fighters could keep the Hammers busy for that short while, Aluin could get away.

"Damned right it's a weakness," Kane agreed. "Let's take the fight to them. Especially now they're short numbered."

"Yeah! Where are the rest?"

"Not all the Hammers jumped, remember? Plus, we're taking them out."

The Hammers that had jumped milled in confusion for a few moments before turning on the shipyards. The enemy had already badly damaged the facility and any vessel that hadn't escaped their dock, but the Hammers returned to the task with feral glee, spitting fire from their maws. Mostly, though, they smashed everything in sight with their tails for no better reason than it appeared to give them brutal gratification.

The Legion had assessed these Rho-Torkis Hammers as the closest the enemy had to elite ships. Generals, perhaps. But these were nothing more than brutes caught up in a rampage of destruction.

Keeping to an evasive flight pattern, Boss ran through course projections that would hook them up with Admiral Aluin's ships. They could make it. Just.

This was a chance to take out the enemy's deadliest ships, though. He couldn't miss such an opportunity.

"Notify Aluin and *Achilles* that we're going back for the Hammers," he told Kane. "And make sure they know about the flexing tail vulnerability." To the fighters, who'd made it this far, he said, "You heard our genius, Rampage Gold Two. Shoot when the tail flexes. They're vulnerable. And right now, they're flexing them like crazy to smash up what's left of the shipyards. Give 'em all you got."

Two Swordfish had made it through the jump tunnels, and their torpedoes ripped bloody holes in the Hammers. Hollow-point rail cannon rounds gouged out those wounds, cutting them deeper and transforming any soft tissue to frozen mist.

The Bangers got in on the action by activating their lasers to scythe through bone hairs. It was an idea lifted from an intelligence report from an engagement on one of the Broken Worlds in the 211-Fractura system. It did render the enemy a little slower.

"Next time, we'll bring laser frigates with us," Kane said. "I'll pass the intel on to *Achilles* and Admiral Aluin on *Starhammer*. Damn!"

Gold Two had flown too close to a wounded Hammer. Despite bleeding heavily, it flicked its spiked tail club at the Legion fighter. Gold Two had seen it and evaded, but only enough to turn a crushing blow into a heavy swat that shattered multiple force keels and sent Gold Two careering into the path of an unwounded Hammer.

The second alien was ready and eager for the kill. It swung its tail with extreme malice.

The Spikeball exploded into fragments. A single recovery beacon blipped on the tac-plot. Gold Two's Banger, Lieutenant Bedrich "Sleepy" Masaryk was still alive. Sleepy's chances were slim. His only chance was that planetary defense forces would win control of orbit and sent up a retrieval shuttle.

"I'll notify the ground," Kane said as Boss flipped the Spikeball, tilted the force keels to cut velocity and accelerated for another attack run on the wounded Hammer. His target thrashed its tail, giving it an unexpected burst of speed and a change in vector that left Boss's cannon fire sparking ineffectually off its club.

Boss barely had time to see that the wounded Hammer was now on intercept for Lieutenant Masaryk.

Kane yelled angrily, "Skragg it!"

"What?"

"That damned thing just ate Masyark. Swallowed him whole. What a way to go."

Realistically, Masyark was already doomed, thought Boss. Kane was right, though. Death was never welcome, but the notion of being eaten made him shudder.

But only for an instant. There were seven surviving Spikeballs and two Swordfish. All of them wanted revenge and set upon the wounded Hammer, opening it up, tearing, slicing, flaying the evil thing until finally its rear section snapped away in a spray of arterial blood.

By the time the Legion fighters completed their orgy of revenge, the remaining Hammers were diving for the safety of the planet below and the cloak of its atmosphere.

Against all the odds, the remnants of Boss's fighters had beaten them.

Kane threw a course projection onto the main viewscreen. Aluin's ships were picking up speed and were close to minimum viable jump distance from the planet. Boss's fighters might still be able to join them if they were lucky.

But they had the enemy on the run, and this was too good an opportunity to miss.

"All fighters, let's finish them off. Dive and pursue."

Aircraft could fly in space or in an atmosphere, but some, such as the FVA-7 Spikeball with its pufferfish profile, were optimized for space combat. They could maneuver almost as well near a planet's surface, but speeds were much slower.

Not so the Hammers, which picked up speed as they ran for cover down the gravity well, refusing as always to obey any laws of physics or technology known to Boss.

Even their radar pictures were like fuzzy smears of static that kept winking out.

And then they were there. Right in front of Boss's fighter at 20,000 feet.

"Holy skragg!" yelled Shrike Indigo Two while Boss threw his Spikeball through evasive loops. "What they hell are they doing?"

"Circling the wagons," suggested Shrike Indigo Lead.

"Looks like a fish ball to me," Boss said. "Let's make chum."

His brother had shown him footage of thousands of fish swimming in huge swirling clumps designed to confuse predators.

He guessed that's what he was seeing here: a ball of circling Hammers. Three badly wounded ones were in the center and four unscathed Hammers swam erratically around them, spitting fire to ward off any attackers.

As the Federation fighters came in on their first attack run, looking for weak spots, it was the Hammers that struck first blood. They took out Indigo Lead, and in an oxygenated atmosphere like this, that meant a funeral pyre of an explosion. At least it was a quick exit.

Boss gave control of the rail cannons to Kane, then he deftly juggled his Spikeball, swerving and weaving, trying to evade the Hammers' tails and create fleeting opportunities for Kane to fire a killing shot.

But those opportunities never came. The Hammers seem to have learned their lesson and updated their tactics. Or maybe this had been a convoluted trap all along.

The undamaged Hammers shivered S-curves through their bodies as they looped around the center of the ball. It was a subtle motion, not the tail thrashing from earlier, and that meant they weren't flexing enough to open their vulnerability.

Kane didn't fire once. The other fighters did. Rail cannon fire bounced off; lasers were always ineffective in atmosphere. A Swordfish torpedo flew at the central ball, but an unwounded Hammer intercepted the torpedo with its body and absorbed the explosion with ease. The outer layer of protectors pulled away from the wounded Hammers who shot a combined volley at the Swordfish as it turned away, ripping apart the vessel and igniting an explosion.

This is suicide. "All fighters, break off attack. Regroup in low orbit."

They managed to disengage. The only casualty, Rampage Red Three, took damage to its engines and went down.

"Sorry, Rampage Lead," Red Three said. "Afraid we're going to sit the rest of this one out."

"Copy that, Red Three. Drinks are on you when we get back. Safe landing."

He switched off the transmitter. "Kane, calculate whether we have enough juice to reach Admiral Aluin."

"On it."

"What was the last from *Achilles*?"

"No response."

Boss's mouth went dry. *Achilles* gone? It was too big a loss for him to comprehend.

The flagship was too far away to be in their tactical plot so he asked the other crews, but none of them could contact *Achilles* either.

"Touch and go on reaching Aluin," Kane announced. "If they hold back a little, we might just make it. The Swordfish will probably need retrieval."

"If those Hammers continue to lick their wounds, we might be able to make a getaway." Boss switched to the fleet channel. "*Starhammer*, this is Rampage Lead. Is that offer of a ride out of here still good?"

"This is *Starhammer*, Rampage Lead. Jump countdown is under one hundred seconds. I'm sorry."

"Copy that, *Starhammer*. We've lost contact with *Achilles*. Any remaining rearguard forces we can hook up with?"

"*Achilles* is still in the fight. Her comms are being jammed, but we can see her in our scopes. Wait one."

Kane sucked in a breath. "Unless we hitch another ride on some jumping Hammers, *Achilles* is out of reach. I guess all we can do is offer our services to whoever is in charge on the ground."

Boss chuckled. "I guess you're right, buddy. We're about to sign up for the Tau-Fornacis Air Force." *Briefly*, he added to himself.

A new voice came over the fleet channel. "This is Fornax Actual. We saw and heard what you did, Squadron Leader Boss. It won't be forgotten, and we will make sure everything you've learned here is passed on."

"Thank you, sir."

"You can thank me in person. Thanks to your efforts, I've halted the jump countdown. Not only can we retrieve you, but we can jump out from a safer distance. Haul your ass to *Starhammer* at all possible speed. I'm holding the jump countdown at sixty seconds. So long as enemy jump tunnels don't form in our threat envelope, you have a ride out of here."

"Roger that. Rampage Lead out."

*****

Chapter Nine: Sorbo

For all of three seconds, General Sorbo allowed herself a smile and a feeling of satisfaction.

Then the moment guttered, and she knew it was the last time she would smile because it was the last good news she ever expected to hear.

The enemy had been blocking their transmissions for ten minutes now, but they were still receiving communications and had heard the exchange between Aluin and Squadron Leader Boss.

His two squadrons by themselves had badly hurt the enemy, and a few of the fighters would safely leave the system with the precious knowledge of how to do so.

More importantly, perhaps, Boss would become a symbol of hope.

The planet was lost. *Achilles* and her support ships were doomed. But Boss and his plucky fighters would fight on. Through the dark days ahead for the Federation, any symbol of hope would be critical. The propagandists would no doubt reinvent the defeat at Tau-Fornacis as some kind of decisive moral victory, but she would no longer be around to be troubled by her outmoded idea of truthfulness.

"Total failure of external comms," came a voice from below.

"More jamming?" Captain Fkansie asked.

"No, sir. They've cut data cables to the command deck. Half the ship's systems are disconnected or destroyed."

Thump!

Something seriously heavy thudded against the command deck's entrance. The bulkhead wobbled. *What could do that?*

"Don't worry," Fkansie said. "It's meant to flex."

"Captain," Sorbo said, "we're feeling a little underdressed up on the flag deck."

The Slern captain nodded with an eyestalk. "Lieutenant McKenzie, it's time to gear up."

The thumping continued while the security team opened the command deck's armory and quickly distributed light armor and PA-71s to those who hadn't already acquired them.

"Ready?" Sorbo asked her two companions on the flight deck.

She'd sent most of her flag team across to the *Starhammer*. Keppel had remained at her side, of course. So had Ensign Pascoe. Pity. Sorbo had grown to like the young woman. Shame their acquaintance would be cut so short.

Keppel nodded his readiness and rested his carbine over the flag deck's handrail.

"I'm ready," the young ensign added breathlessly. "Ready to hold the line against anything."

Keppel laughed. "I think the general was inquiring whether you're ready to meet your creator, Pascoe. But 'hold the line' works just as well."

"You're a credit to the Legion, Ensign," Sorbo said. "Be ready for anything."

Pascoe nodded. "Always." But she tensed even more.

Sorbo did the opposite and relaxed into the threat. She'd had this reaction to imminent danger for many years and could no longer tell whether that meant she was an excellent legionary or whether she was simply broken inside. It didn't matter anymore.

She checked rounds were chambered in her carbine's feed and that its charge status was green. When she brought the PA-71 butt to her shoulder, she welcomed it as the touch of an old friend.

"Here they come," someone called below.

A deep rumble shook the ship, followed by a cloud of inky smoke as a breach opened in the bulkhead near the command deck's entrance. The hole was little bigger than a fist, but the bulkhead armor must have been rendered brittle, because when a demonic hand reached inside and clawed at the hole, chunks of bulkhead crumbled away.

A four-shot burst of railgun darts from the deck below blew the hand off the wrist. It was humanoid in shape, though the claws were as long as the fingers and the flesh was a uniform fire-red. The hand shattered when it hit the deck.

More red hands reached through the hole and clawed blindly at the prey inside, their arms widening the breach as an accidental by-product.

Naturally, the Legion spacers let rip and a pile of hands and fore-arms soon piled up. The creatures showed no sign of experiencing pain or a fear of death. Why would they when any dead would be consumed and rebirthed?

Soon the breach was over a foot wide, big enough to reveal a writhing mass of demons in the space beyond, crushing themselves against the bulkhead in a frenzy to kill everyone inside.

A steady stream of PA-71 rounds flew through the breach, piling up the demon corpses into such a large mound that the onslaught stalled as the enemy were forced to tear their own dead out of the way.

Sorbo held her fire.

She glanced at Pascoe who was desperate to let rip but was following the restraint of the general beside her without understanding Sorbo's reasoning.

"Save your ammo," Sorbo explained. "There will be plenty more targets to service soon enough."

Another low rumble. Another puff of smoke. And another breach opened on the opposite bulkhead.

Then a huge explosion violated Sorbo's head with noise and fury. Hot smoke stung her face.

When the chaos settled, she found herself gazing across the charred wreckage of the flag deck in a state of shock.

Was she dead?

No. The taste of metal on her tongue, the hurt in her lungs, and the ringing in her ears were all too visceral.

She squeezed her eyes shut. When she opened them again, she had reconnected with her body and the extension to her body that was her PA-71, still attached by its carbon weave strap. She was a legionary once more and there was killing work to be done.

While everyone had been distracted by the breaches below, the enemy had initiated their main assault through the overhead. A tongue of metal and sparking cables had crashed down, transforming into a down ramp for the army of nightmares that came through the breech.

The Andromedan heavies slid down the ramp first: warty cigar-shaped beasts with grotesque carapaces and extending maws that enveloped any unlucky souls who couldn't get out the way, and there were plenty of Navy personnel trapped under the collapsing overhead or crushed beneath these behemoths.

Remembering the briefings from the events on the hex world of 211-Fractura, Sorbo grabbed her PA-71 and tried shooting off the hairs that stood out from the hides of these mini-leviathans.

Sensory hairs might be a weak point, but the monsters were just too big. What they needed were blades. A military version of a scythe.

Too late for that now. The first few monsters down the ramp began to slither on the hunt for more prey to eat. They lacked speed, but there was nowhere to run on a command deck where red demons were threatening to burst through the bulkheads at any moment.

Sorbo watched in horror as a beast extended its maw over the torso of a gravely wounded Zhoogene officer. It began to suck her into its mouth tube, her writhing contours visible through its slimy embrace.

"Go in peace," Sorbo muttered and fired bursts through the mouth. The creature bellowed in pain, its ripped mouth flapping loosely in front of it and releasing the shattered corpse of the officer Sorbo had put out of her misery.

In the pit of her stomach, she felt cold despair because neither mercy killing the officer or the hurt she'd inflicted on the monster mattered one jot. How could you defeat an enemy that was functionally immortal?

A bulkhead collapsed, and red demons poured through. They were simple travesties of humanoids, distilled into rabid beings of purest hate. They lived only to rend and bite with claws and teeth. They even lacked mouths, the consumption of the dead to be left to another Andromedan form.

Once again, Sorbo realized the red demons had been used as a distraction because a new wave of attackers jumped down from the overhead, leaping across the backs of the heavy beasts that had slid down first.

They were humanoids. Or had been once. Many were dressed in full Legion armor but with others their bodies were too distorted to carry more than fragments. However much they wore, the unit insignia was consistent. These horrors had once been the brave Tenth Legion.

Keppel and Pascoe didn't need telling; they switched to the new targets.

Legion armor was tough, but that worn by the Corrupted monstrosities hadn't been maintained and her people knew its weak points.

The undead legionaries carried PA-71s themselves and their ammo drums were full. Assaulted from every direction, the Navy defenders were being cut to pieces. They were facing total team kill.

Keppel went down. Sorbo could only spare him a glance. Two rounds through his head. He was gone.

When she looked back, she saw the most mutated legionary of all. The thing was huge. Nine feet tall with an extra pair of heavily muscled arms sprouting from its shoulders.

"Over there!" She pointed out the four-armed monster to Ensign Pascoe. "Whatever that is, kill it!"

The veck-damned creature noticed the attention and jabbed a talon back at her. As she aimed, she felt an inexplicable connection to the beast. Did she know this thing?

It seemed to recognize her. It fixated on her, leering with malicious intent as it continued to point her out.

Pascoe and Sorbo fired at the four-armed mutant, and it disappeared. Sparks, leaping red demons, the cries of death, and the screams of killers; everywhere was mayhem, and it was impossible to tell whether they'd killed it.

But its commands had been heard.

The abominations of the Tenth Legion bounded like monkeys from every surface in their haste to get at Sorbo.

She flicked the selector to full auto and sprayed darts at the incoming monstrosities. The gnawing despair mocked that no amount of damage she could do mattered to the Andromedans, but she was Alessia "Sorbo" Sorborovskele, and there was no fucking way she would go down quietly.

The ensign was servicing whatever came at them, firing textbook six-round bursts before calmly tracking the next target. Sorbo felt pride, even a little hope, that the people of the Federation might yet survive.

A hammer blow from behind knocked out that last sniff of hope, along with the air from her bruised lungs. She fell to her knees, but tried to exaggerate the movement, to transform it into a roll that would bring the business end of the PA-71 to bear on whatever was behind her.

Her attackers had too strong a grip on her arms for her to do more than squirm. Then they lifted her up and sliced through her hamstring tendons with a blade.

Agony erupted like starbursts in her head.

And faded away surprisingly quickly.

This was her body's natural trauma control combined with the genetic legacy that alien bioengineers had grafted into her distant ancestors. She felt pain-free. Happy even.

In fact, she laughed because none of this had ever mattered.

Still, a sudden burst of concern made her wonder where that young ensign was. She discovered Pascoe groaning on the flag deck next to her, semiconscious.

A creature oozed toward her, like the heavy monsters that had first fallen from the overhead, except this was the size of a large dog. It extended its mouth part over the ensign and sucked.

Sorbo woke to action. She threw her weight forward and drew her knife, intending to end Pascoe's life. But she was pinned too tightly and only succeeded in dropping the knife onto the deck. A perversion in a Legion boot kicked it away.

They forced her to watch.

The strangest thing, she realized when it was over, was that she hadn't thought to look away.

Unlike the larger creatures that had sucked people into their bodies, this smaller version sucked *itself* over Ensign Pascoe, easing its body over her boots and relaxing its hide as it adjusted to absorb prey that was four times its initial size.

The process took several minutes, but eventually the creature's lips smacked shut over the top of Pascoe's helm and she was fully sealed within. The process of digestion began.

Pascoe had struggled, but thankfully her head had been facing away from Sorbo, so she hadn't been forced to look into the young woman's eyes as she was swallowed.

Powerful hands pulled Sorbo up, turned her around, and tilted her up to look into the face of the four-armed monster.

"You are General Sorborovskele," it said.

"And you… I should have shot you when I had the… the chance. Holy skragg!" Sorbo stared. Despite the extra arms, the teeth like tusks, and the feathers that had replaced his trademark buzzcut, she *knew* who this was. "There's been a frakk-ton of batshit crazy conspiracy theories about where you've been this past decade, First General Clarke. I never guessed the truth was even crazier."

She glimpsed a moment of humanity in Clarke's eyes.

"Yes," he said in a voice so brittle that she guessed he hadn't spoken for years. It was a voice she recognized, nonetheless. "In my human form… yes, I was First General Clarke, Commander of the Legion and President of First Reach Federation. All those titles are worthless now. And when the Collective has consumed your civilization, no one will be left alive to even remember what those words once meant."

"Traitor!"

Clarke choked. No, not choked. *Laughed.* "Clarke was no traitor," he said.

"I won't talk," Sorbo said. "I will tell you nothing."

Clarke looked to one side. That flicker of humanity lit his eyes once more. "I possess Clarke's memories," he explained. "So, I believe you, Sorborovskele. Your defiance is of no importance. Interrogation does not require you to talk."

What does he mean?

She wouldn't give Clarke the satisfaction of voicing her question. Not that this was really Clarke anymore.

He explained anyway. "No, General. No need for talking. You shall be ingested."

* * * * *

Chapter Ten: Squadron Leader Boss

"We're going to make it." Kane declared.

Boss glanced at the tac-plot before replying. The fish ball of Hammers had risen from the atmosphere in pursuit of his fighters. But was it a pursuit? He had a bad feeling this was really herding from a safe distance from which the Hammers spat sporadic fire. Even their energy beams seemed to be halfhearted. Shrike Blue Lead had taken a hit, but instead of exploding they only lost a handful of force keels and a corresponding reduction in maneuverability and braking.

The landing sequence had already been agreed with Starhammer Control. Last in would be the only surviving Swordfish. The fast torpedo boat would come in bone-shatteringly hard, but *Starhammer* was ready for them. As soon as they were aboard, Strike Force Fornax would jump. *Starhammer* wouldn't even wait to close the hangar doors.

That beautiful moment was approximately 287 seconds away.

A thin smile eased across Boss's face. "You know what, buddy. I reckon you're right."

"I know what's bugging you," Kane said, "but you can forget it now. It's a question we can debate over a beer."

Boss laughed. "Only if you're paying."

"Oh, it's what I'll win off you at cards that will be doing the paying."

The whereabouts of some Hammers remained a mystery. Where were they? That was the question Kane was referring to. Not all the Hammers they'd fought near *Achilles* had jumped away, and some had entered j-Space but never reappeared. Not on anyone's scanners anyway. Wherever they'd gone, it didn't matter anymore.

"Our pursuers are accelerating," Kane said. "Hard! Revising projections…"

Boss bit his lip and said nothing because there was nothing to be said. All his fighters were pushing at maximum burn, ready to slam on the brakes in a bruising last-minute deceleration before entering *Starhammer's* hangar.

They couldn't move any faster.

"They're accelerating again," Kane said. "But… whatever they're doing, it's too late. We'll reach *Starhammer* first."

"And our Swordfish?"

"That could be tight."

Boss's heart fluttered. The idea of leaving behind his slower fighter for the Andromedans went against everything he held dear. Yet if Admiral Aluin felt his entire fleet was threatened, he wouldn't sacrifice it for the unlikely chance of saving a pair of aeronauts.

Nor should he. They had to win this war or everyone in the Federation would be dead. Every skragging one.

"Jump tunnels! Jump tunnels!"

"Where?" Before Kane could respond, the answer became obvious. Seven of the missing Hammers peeled open holes from jump space and hurled themselves back into spacetime. They'd been tracking the fighters somehow, emerging a few hundred meters in front and on the same vector and orientation.

Boss pulled his Spikeball up, braked, and banked. *Starhammer* and escape were an impossible dream now. He knew he was going to die. All that mattered now was to keep the Hammers away from the fleet until its ships could jump.

Boss sought an opening, a flexing of the tails that he could exploit, but there were none.

He threw violent evasive maneuvers all over the blackness of space, emerging to charge one of the Hammers head on. It eased back its tail. It was going to take a swing at him!

But it was also using its armored front section to shield its vulnerable areas from the rail cannons in the Spikeball's nose.

Boss knew he couldn't kill it, but all he had to do was keep its attention.

"That's right," he said, "keep your eyes on me."

At the last instant, he abruptly rolled to port as a spiked club the size of a main battle tank smacked into the space where he'd been moments prior.

A pair of Spikeballs saw their chance and pounced, firing into the tail as it pulled back after it struck. Boss looped around and added his own fire into the bleeding Hammer.

He doubted they'd hurt it much, but he definitely felt a little better.

"Rampage Lead, Blue One. You make excellent bait, sir."

"That I do. Thanks for the save."

He surveyed the situation. The enemy were attempting to smash his command with their tail clubs and had nearly succeeded on several attempts. They were ignoring Aluin's ships for now, so why hadn't Aluin jumped?

"*Starhammer*, this is Rampage Lead. Looks like we shan't be joining you on this trip after all. Godspeed and safe jumping."

"We can't jump yet. Something's holding us back."

Boss wanted to scream. How could they ever win against the Andromedans?

"Rampage Lead to all fighters. The big ships have engine trouble. Let's head back to the planet and draw those uglies with us. Maybe that will help."

"Jump tunnels!" Kane screamed.

Four more jump tunnels opened, and a Hammer surged forth from one, barreling straight for them, its tail already coiled to strike.

Boss braked, spun, and burned every ounce of fuel he had.

It was enough. Barely. The club whipped past, mere inches away.

But before he could exhale in relief, another Hammer came at them from the opposite side, ready to finish them off.

Boss glanced to his left. He saw the massive bulk of the spiked club coming toward him and knew he wouldn't escape this time.

His parting words to Kane came to his lips, but he never got to speak to them.

The Hammer's tail crashed through the Spikeball, obliterating it. And every soul inside.

* * * * *

Chapter Eleven: Admiral Aluin

"Jump!" Aluin growled under his breath. *"Jump!"*

Aluin couldn't understand what was going on and his techs couldn't either. He forced himself to keep calm and resist glancing at the tac-plot. He'd watched Boss die, his Spikeball smashed into paste and dust. Only two Spikeballs remained, and they wouldn't last much longer.

Why couldn't they jump?

"They're holding us back," the jump officer told him, gesturing at the plot where a dozen Hammers were keeping station fifty klicks away. They were weathering all the fire Aluin's Legion ships could throw at them, just sitting there keeping their jump tunnels open.

"Best guess," he continued, "is whatever they're doing has shaved one, maybe two planetary radii off our jump separation from Tau-Fornacis."

"You don't know, do you son?"

"I can only guess."

"So, what you're telling me, is that if we hit that jump button, either we'll get to our destination, or we'll experience runaway inverse expansion of our jump cone projection, better known as the noodle effect."

"That's correct, sir."

Aluin activated the fleet command channel. "Aluin to all jump-capable vessels. Disable all jump safety protocols and initiate immediate emergency jump. I repeat kill safety protocols and jump now. Good luck and hold the line."

Jump safety protocols were there for good reasons and weren't supposed to be switched off easily. Some of his captains must have anticipated this eventuality because two destroyers, *Ironheart* and *Noble Eagle*, went within seconds, blinking out of existence. *Defiance* followed moments later.

Whether they would reach the destination intact—or at all—was another matter.

Satisfied that his own team on the *Starhammer* was busy with the task, he left them alone and calmly paced the command deck, hands behind his back, as a good skipper should.

Next to jump was *Majestic*, a *Tempest*-class heavy cruiser with sloped armor and twin main turrets. As her prow nosed toward the entrance to j-Space, a shimmering halo formed around the jump-field nodules at her midsection. The shimmer grew into what looked like a force field that stretched forward and aft until it encompassed the ship.

Aluin's breath caught in his throat, but *Majestic* sailed on unharmed… at first.

Then her stern appeared to be pulled backward, toward the Hammers with the open jump tunnels, stretching her until she was glowing like metal being worked.

The rearmost tip of the elongated ship locked onto the center of the nearby planet as surely as a missile acquiring a target. Within seconds, the ship had stretched all the way from the middle of the strike force group to the center of Tau-Fornacis, a distance of about 20,000 klicks for a vessel 350 meters long.

It should be too thin to see but the horizontal compression made it glow brightly. Most people called this the noodle effect. It was a gruesome theoretical fate that people joked about. No one would be joking now.

The stretched ship snapped like an elastic cord anchored at the planet's core.

Before they could see any effects on the planet, the jump officer announced it was *Starhammer's* turn to jump.

At the small of his back, Aluin clenched his knuckles so hard he bruised his palms.

Everyone on the ship could feel the drive cores spinning faster and faster as the massive energy build up approached its peak. *Starhammer* shook with a strange vibration, as if its mighty engines were fighting something unseen.

Suddenly, the space around them bent in on itself and then they were gone.

When the jump officer announced a successful transition to j-Space, there were a few scattered cheers on the command deck. It was relief more than triumph, but Aluin couldn't cheer along with them because they'd barely gotten away with their lives. Many hadn't managed even that.

Two days of agony lay ahead of them in the jump tunnel. Their sensors and comms were unable to penetrate the mysteries of that barely understood zone of the universe. Only then would they emerge from their tunnel and begin to count the survivors.

Whoever survived, Aluin would rally them for the dark days ahead, for the fight he felt in his bones was only just beginning.

* * *

Sorbo

Sorbo gasped when the alien mouth closed around her and the insistent suction began.

She was swaddled in slime and darkness, arms crushed tightly against her body as a relentless force pulled on her. With a horrifying crunch, her shoulder joints dislocated from their sockets, eliciting screams of anguish.

When her bones started breaking with a sickening crunch, she bellowed again.

The pain was so intense that it made her head spin, but she still managed to grasp the creature's intent: it wasn't looking to kill her, not yet. It just wanted to immobilize her.

Acid washed over her body, burned her skin, seeped through its many tears and cuts to begin the ruination of her insides.

To her surprise, the acid was rinsed away by cooling slime that brought pinprick sensations all over her body. Or maybe something really was piercing her skin because she felt half her insides being sucked out while the other half had something alien pumped in.

She couldn't tell what was real anymore. The darkness and the agony disoriented her, but nothing was as bad as the crushing claustrophobic closeness of the walls that threatened to wrench a scream of sheer madness from her.

I've every right to scream in terror, she told herself. *No one's ever experienced walls closing in like this before. Not even… I hope… poor Ensign Pascoe.*

She felt more than just her body fluids being sucked out. Her memories and knowledge were too… and her plans.

Am I imagining this?

It is not your imagination.

The words formed in her mind. Spoken in an everyman voice. Male. Human average. Could be just about anybody.

I am a librarian. I consume your essence. Your timeline. History. Knowledge. Your very soul. Everything we wish to know. And what I learn, every portion of the Collective shall also know. Across hundreds of millions of light years, all the librarians in this Collective shall instantly know your plans.

Sorbo writhed and thrashed, but her broken body could not hope to break free.

She tried to mentally repulse the invasion of her mind, but she didn't know how.

The aching cry of insanity that had been bubbling up inside of her finally broke free.

Screaming. That she could still do.

The process of digestion was lengthy. And it was not pleasant.

Sorbo howled all the way to the bitter end.

*****

Interstitial-1

Del-Marie clings to the back of Azhgrel's seat, his knuckles white. All eyes are glued to the main screen that wraps around the pinnace's forward bulkhead, watching a wireframe tunnel form before them. It's a comforting lie sent by Indiya.

He is one with them now, a refugee clinging to a raft in spacetime that can only be rescued by one person, the one who has betrayed them all.

Harsh acceleration throws him forward and the pinnace makes an intense leap into the unknowable.

Pain racks Del-Marie's body, his extremities swelling, lungs constricting, and his organs squeezing his spine.

He looks down at his bulging hands only to see that they look entirely normal. Nothing is amiss. Nothing *visible.*

None of this is real, he decides.

But it is happening all the same.

*****

Part 2:
Challenge of the Muryani

Chapter Twelve: Osu Sybutu

Orbital above Merellus, Muryani Expansion

"What you mean *no*? Stupid, pig-licking, demented dung beetle!"

Indiya lifted herself out of her seat and stormed across to the Muryani negotiator as fast as her little old legs would carry her. Osu expected his immortal boss to punch the big alien bug, but she lashed out with the waspish sting of her tongue instead.

"Is there anything but mold and dust inside that hollow chitin head of yours, you moronic Muryani? Yes, you! The fat dung beetle. Perhaps you're so consumed by the primitive instinct to roll around a huge ball of shit that you can't appreciate the gift I'm offering you? Offering you for free, I tell you, and asking nothing in return!"

A faint sucking noise emanated from Lady Indiya. Osu guessed that spittle was dripping from the old woman's lips.

"We ask for nothing," Indiya continued in a fractionally calmer tone, "other than a few simple assurances."

Deeply schooled in Legion discipline, Osu stood tall and kept his gaze firmly locked on his opposite number, the aide to the Muryani chief negotiator.

Inter-civilizational diplomacy was far above his paygrade, but even a simple jack like him could see that the negotiations were not proceeding according to plan.

They were here to offer up the one advantage the Federation had over its immense neighbor: the secret of faster-than-light travel. On the voyage into Muryani Expansion territory, the talk on *Phantom* had been of the risk that the Muryani would take their precious gift and use it to conquer and enslave the people of the Federation. Because once the Muryani had jump tech, there would be nothing to stop them doing exactly that.

On the other hand, if the Muryani military didn't get upgraded without delay and advance into Federation space in huge numbers, the Andromedans would eat everybody. Every living thing, down to single-cell organisms, would be consumed.

Although many of Osu's companions in Chimera Company had dubious moral character, they were all intelligent and most were more knowledgeable about the ways of the universe than him.

And yet, despite all the arguments that had raged about donating the Federation's key asset to the Muryani, no one had even considered the possibility that the bugs would say no.

Osu noticed that the aide was staring back at him out of those weird rectangular eyes the aliens had. For the first time, he felt the flicker of a connection to the Muryani and wondered whether the alien was as embarrassed by Indiya's outburst as Osu.

Vetch should be here, Osu thought. The big Viking had befriended Enthree, the Muryani in his Militia squad, and that made Vetch the Chimera Company expert. Unless you counted Enthree herself, he supposed.

Osu had assumed the alien facing him was an aide, but for all he knew, this could be the juice attendant, the sexual fulfillment councilor, or the emperor.

It was all that bearded skragg's fault. Before meeting Vetch, Osu would have kept his mouth firmly closed when senior officers were wrong. But, no, Osu had confronted Indiya when they'd first met. Instead of executing him, she'd punished him with a duty that had turned out to be far worse than he'd first realized. His role was to be her moral compass. Because, she had explained, hers had gone missing many centuries ago.

He never thought that would mean standing beside her in an exotic alien palace pretending not to notice her ranting.

Indiya sighed as she slumped back in her chair.

Osu winced at her obvious fatigue. She was a frail bag of bones, thousands of years old and held together by willpower alone. If she ever lost the will to carry on, he fully expected her to crumble into dust.

The chief negotiator jiggled their head from side to side. "I had not anticipated your failure to understand the situation," they said in passable Perseid, the simplified version of the human tongue that had spread throughout the Federation and, apparently, beyond. "This will prove a problem."

"Let's start again," rasped Indiya. "We came here to give you jump drive technology in exchange for military aid against the Andromedans."

"We didn't bring you here to accept your offer."

"Sure sounded like it to me."

The alien hesitated. "In diplomacy, we sometimes use a little artistic license in our language. So, to be clear, I invited you here to argue your case for why we *should* accept your offer of jump drive technology."

"We're desperate. The Andromedans are battering us. And after they've consumed us, they will come for you. We offer this for nothing more than some hard assurances about Federation autonomy after we beat back the enemy together."

"We are fully aware of the gravity of the situation. However, faster-than-light technology is dangerous and there would be no going back if we adopted it. It would fundamentally change our society forever. The Muryani civilization that has flourished for hundreds of thousands of years, by your calendar, would cease to exist. Something new would replace it and there is no reason to think it will be as stable. Had you considered that?"

Silence from Indiya. Of course, she skragg-frakking hadn't.

"We ourselves regard our current civilization as a huge success," said the alien. "Superior to all others we have encountered. Why do you think we never developed faster-than-light technology ourselves?"

"Because it requires insights you don't have. Humans are exceptionally good at intuition. That's why our homeworld was cultivated for so long. And when we look out upon the galaxy, we find that the longer a species has been on the interstellar scene, the worse they are at innovation. The innovation required for jump tech is damned difficult. I know, because—"

"Because you yourself developed the Indiyan jump drive. Yes, you have mentioned this. Lady Indiya, you are an exceptionally knowledgeable person, possibly one of the most well-informed in this part of the galaxy, but on this matter, you are sorely ignorant."

"Go on," Indiya prompted when the negotiator started making circles with their upper limbs. Osu guessed this was Muryani gloating.

"Our civilization developed several theoretical designs for faster-than-light travel while your homeworld of Earth was still an undeveloped asset of the Trans-Species Union, off limits to exploitation and unaware of the future intended for you in the wider galactic political arena."

"But you always stopped short of turning theory into application," Indiya said. "Because… Because the expansion of the Muryani has always been so slow that it's barely perceptible. Once the technology was in your… your foot-hands, sooner or later you or your descendants would use it to expand your empire faster than you could absorb its fresh conquests."

"There you go again, Lady Indiya. *Empire. Conquests!* Sometimes I think you humans are incapable of understanding."

"But I *do* understand. I understand that for all your fear of change, being eaten by Andromedan monsters would be worse."

"Enough!" shouted the Muryani aide—or juice attendant or whoever it really was. They nuzzled the chief negotiator's chest.

At least Osu understood that part. Instead of ears, Muryani heard through sensitive chest hairs. The aide was whispering something. Probably.

When they finished, the negotiator stopped negotiating and started telling Indiya how things would play out.

"There will be an assessment of your offer. We need a short time to organize this. To prepare yourself, you need to learn our ways, and quickly. You will not succeed in your ambition if you still mischaracterize our civilization as an empire."

"Very well. Then you must teach us."

"No! You have demonstrated that you cannot be taught, so you must learn for yourselves."

"And how do you propose we do that?"

"We invite you to go wherever you choose for a period of twenty days. Your *Phantom* and *Ghost Shark* both have jump technology and we cannot predict where you will go. Scores of inhabited systems are open to you. Hundreds of trillions of individuals. Ask questions of whomever you wish. I shall forewarn the system authorities that you might appear but cannot prepare them beyond that."

Indiya rubbed her bony chin. "Twenty days. That's a bubble of space with a hundred light year diameter. And you can communicate with all these worlds? Just like that? How?"

"You are correct that if we used radio communications to inform our systems of your visit that would take many centuries. I regret, we too must retain secrets of our own."

"Fascinating," Indiya said. "Also, useless. We don't have time for a fact-finding adventure holiday. We received news from the war this morning. We suffered grievous losses in a battle at Tau-Fornacis, and we learned our enemy is even stronger than we feared. Rather than waste our time in Muryani space, it would be better to return to the fight."

"But you cannot hope to withstand the Andromedans alone," said the Muryani.

"With our military forces, probably not. But they are not the only means I have to beat the enemy."

Osu felt the hairs stand out on the back of his neck. During their voyage, Indiya had dropped hints about apocalyptic contingency plans if the military options failed. He doubted she realized how leaky her thoughts were. Indiya hadn't been around people much for a few centuries, and it showed.

The aide appeared to have the same reaction as Osu. The hairs on their chest stood out like a wire brush.

"If you wish our military assistance," the negotiator told Indiya, "then you will be here to be assessed in three weeks. This is not up for debate. Once before, we faced down the Andromedans alone. If necessary, we shall do so again."

That wet noise again.

Osu momentarily lost control and glanced Indiya's way. The ancient woman was purple with rage.

"Well?" demanded the negotiator. "Do you agree?"

"I agree to think about it," Indiya conceded. "Until I come to a decision, you can roll up your negotiations and shove them up your hairy insectoid arse."

Osu escorted Indiya toward the orbital's docking pier where *Phantom* and *Ghost Shark* were moored.

Indiya currently had no use for her moral compass and did not speak, but the journey was not in silence because a crowd had gathered in the short time since they had walked to the meeting space.

These new aliens did not speak Perseid, but Osu understood their ugly feelings. He had been stationed in enough places that regarded the Legion as an occupying force to sense the resentment that was building against them with every step.

As a gesture of peace, he wasn't carrying a weapon.

If this turned violent, he would be relying on the immortal bag of bones to save both their skins.

He glanced at her, only to see her glaring back at him.

"It won't come to that," she said. "But you're safe so long as you're with me. And for the thousandth time, I cannot read your thoughts, only expressions and body chemistry. It means I can read a person's emotions like a book. In your case, Sergeant Sybutu, a large type, easily read one. Now shut up and let me think."

* * * * *

Chapter Thirteen: Izza Zan Fey

"Am I seeing what I think I'm seeing?" Enthree mused.

Izza resisted the urge to tell her Muryani marine to get a skragging move on as the Muryani tilted her stretched head and blinked at the exterior security monitor showing the scene on *Phantom's* docking slip.

With Federation orbitals, the walkway to a slip passed through locked hatches. Even on the most disreputable orbiting dens of iniquity, unauthorized people couldn't simply walk up to a ship. Not without a massive bribe. To be profitable, stations needed traffic to be willing to dock there, and for that they needed to provide an assurance of security.

When Enthree had explained that Muryani didn't lock doors, muttering some nonsense about social something-or-other, Izza hadn't paid attention. There were thirty locals outside her ship now with more arriving every minute. Half were Muryani, half other species she didn't recognize. None looked friendly.

After a good minute blinking at the scene, including nudging Izza out the way so she could look at the monitor from Izza's angle, Enthree straightened her long body in the way she did when she was about to announce something.

Izza bit her lip the entire time, having learned that trying to rush Enthree invariably led to lengthy and confusing tangential conversations that only slowed things further.

"You asked if you were seeing what you thought you were seeing," Enthree said. "I have now seen from the same position that you saw. So, I can say with confidence that I am seeing what you think you're seeing and therefore it would be reasonable to assume that you are also."

"Bylzak!" Izza fingered the blaster on her hip. "I've had enough of your games, Ndemo-327-Cerulian. The others think your naïve misunderstanding is cute. I think they're wrong. I think you enjoy winding up the humanoids."

"I couldn't possibly comment, Co-Captain Zan Fey. Although I would point out that the two interpretations of my apparent behavior are not mutually exclusive."

"And I would point out that when I decide I can't trust someone aboard my ship, I space them."

"Yes, Captain. While your speculations are fascinating, may I draw to your attention that some citizens of this orbital appear to be displeased by our presence here. They've gathered outside *Phantom* to discuss an appropriate course of action."

"You mean that's a mob working themselves up into a killing frenzy. But you keep telling me Muryani society is all about being kind to everyone else."

"No, Captain. I have told you that Muryani society has considerably higher social cohesion than the Federation's. But we are outsiders. They regard as us a toxic foreign particle in the body of their society."

"We were invited here."

"Not by these individuals we weren't."

"What I need to know is can they storm the ship and do we need to call the cops?"

"Police?" Enthree swiveled her head from side to side, but without her Militia troopers to explain, Izza didn't know what that gesture meant. The alien whistled with their head.

Compared to most humanoids, the rear of a Muryani's head was pulled back about the length of a humanoid forearm. A bony crest like a ski sled ran over the top of the elongated head. Enthree was whistling through this crest. No one had ever told her about whistling heads before. Was Enthree laughing at her?

Enthree stopped her noise. "Police? No. Not on an orbital. No, I do not believe the citizens outside will assault the ship. However, if their anger builds, they might attack and kill any of our number who sets foot outside."

"Damn! Sybutu and Indiya are out there. You do remember, right? I can't raise either of them."

"Do not be concerned. Our companions are in a negotiating space, a room that will be shielded from communication. And while negotiations are formally ongoing with the Muryani Expansion, no citizen could even conceive of laying a finger on them."

"I hope you're right."

She shut her eyes and listened to the audio feed from outside. What had been a raucous hubbub was shifting to an angry growl. This crowd was out for blood.

The comm panel pinged. "*Phantom*, it's Sybutu. We've got trouble."

"So have we," Izza said. "What's your situation?"

"Negotiations broke down. The Lady Indiya's… in a stroppy tantrum. And we're getting some very ugly looks from the locals."

"Sergeant," Enthree said, "please clarify. Negotiations have failed?"

"Put it like this, the venerable leader of the Federation told the Muryani Expansion to shove their negotiations up their hairy insect asses. Why do you ask?"

"If the crowd of citizens learn that negotiations have ceased, even if temporarily, then they would have no legal or moral barriers to killing you. I suggest you increase your pace."

"Are you serious?" Sybutu said. "The Lady Indiya's personal best at the hundred-meter sprint is measured in geological ages."

"Find a way, Sergeant," Izza snapped. "If those people have no aversion to killing us, then we can have no aversion to killing them. Get here fast. I don't care who or what you have to break along the way."

"Roger that. Sybutu out."

They heard a snatch of outrage from an elderly human woman and then the transmission ceased.

Izza switched the comm panel to the ship-wide PA. "Sinofar, Green Fish, Arunsen, gear up and make yourself look as intimidating as you can. Meet me at the main hatch in four minutes. We might need to break some heads." She ground her teeth, angry at Fitz for dodging the awkward Lily Hjon situation. "Hjon, organize a reserve force. Just in case."

Enthree rotated her head anticlockwise in a way Izza understood signaled a query.

"No, not you Enthree. I have a feeling you would only complicate matters."

"Whereas I," said Fitz dashing into the room, "make everything so simple, my lady."

"No."

That stopped Fitz in his tracks. "What do you mean 'no'?"

"Even with the Andromedans devouring the entire galaxy, the situation isn't dire enough to let Fregg pilot *Phantom*. Which leaves her only two pilots. We can't risk both of us."

"Then I shall go in your place."

Izza's lip quivered. Tears came to her eyes as the power of speech left her. She floundered on a stormy sea of confusing and conflicting emotions. *Why now?*

Her heart ached for this beautiful man who had put himself in harm's way to save her so many times. As she had for him.

There was a new instinct that grew inside her with every day. She wanted to crawl into a dark space and hide from all dangers. From everyone, even Fitzy. She hated this new part of her, and she would *not* succumb to it. That was why it must be her who strode out to face the baying crowd.

Through narrowed lilac eyes, Fitz peered at her, trying to interpret her strange behavior.

Izza caught his flicker of dismay when he sensed a hitherto unknown factor, a secret she was keeping from him.

She and Fitz had a complicated relationship with many secrets. They both understood in their line of work that there were times when it was best not to reveal delicate truths, to respect that when one kept a secret from the other, there would be a solid reason.

He made a show of briefly studying the camera feed.

"They're just unruly skragg wipes. Probably partaken too much of the local hooch. One sight of Verlys, and they'll wet themselves. You can handle this, Izza. Besides, I have more pressing duties. I'm trying to teach Lynx how to cheat at three-hand skat."

* * *

The exit ramp struck the deck with a satisfying metallic thud and the four champions of Chimera Company sallied forth.

The crowd ceased their angry mutterings, as well they might in the face of such a spectacle.

Around her head, Green Fish expertly whirled and slashed a curved blade on a pole that she called a naginata, though it was actually a Zhooge glaive.

Verlys had stripped to a sleeveless top that showed off the corded muscles of her blue arms. She had a heavy blaster slung over one shoulder. It nudged against the ammo drum strapped to her back that fed into the Z'Lox Slammer cradled in her hands, a personal minigun so heavy that only the Pryxian warrior caste could wield it.

As for Arunsen, Izza guessed the crowd were finding the big human to be the most intimidating of all. In contrast to the effete citizens of the orbital—who dressed in clean robes and hadn't so far demonstrated that they knew how to kick off a riot properly—water dripped from Arunsen's bedraggled hair and braided beard as if he'd emerged from the dread waters of the Fourth Hell. A mass of inked and hairy flesh completed the hellish appearance for Arunsen wore only pants. To finish off this vision of savagery, he rested the haft of his war hammer over his shoulder.

"Hey, Arunsen," she whispered. "Nice improvisation."

"What?" he whispered back. "I was off duty and in the shower."

The crowd shrank back to the edge of the broad walkway.

A variety of species were represented. Muttering dark threats from the front had been the Muryani themselves, but they had mostly filtered to the rear of the crowd, revealing other species, none of which Izza recognized.

"We don't want trouble," she told the aliens. "But we don't mind it either. You can stand there and grumble all you like. I don't give a crap. Can barely understand a word you're chanting anyway. But get in the way of anyone entering or leaving my ship and body parts will get broken. Yours."

Movement!

A lifetime of living on the most dangerous edge of the galaxy sent Izza spinning on her stylish boot heel and drawing her blaster before she properly registered what she was seeing.

She faced three aliens who resembled humans except for tough hide and whiskers on their prominent noses. Their arms were back, ready to throw grenades.

No… it was fruit. Baskets of the stuff!

"Hold your fire!" she ordered.

The first salvo sailed through the air toward them.

Izza and Sinofar dodged the black bulbs.

Green Fish sliced one in half with a sweep of her glaive. Skragging human show off!

The crowd hissed, cheered, whistled, or used other sounds and movement appropriate to their biology to encourage the fruit pelting.

As more fruit descended upon the Chimerans, Arunsen caught a projectile in one hand and bit into it.

"Not bad," he declared to the crowd. "Though a little too sweet for me. My advice? It's supposed to be rotten."

"*You* are rotten," called a voice from one of the few Muryani remaining in the front row.

Izza responded. "You know, for intimidation, you aren't doing well."

"Go back to your worlds in the Perseus Zone and die there, human monster," they shouted at Izza. "That is your purpose. That is why you were brought there."

"What did you say?"

"I said, time to die, ugly."

Green Fish advanced on the Muryani with her glaive high. She arced the polearm through the air, slicing it against the alien's chest. As Greenie recovered the weapon, Izza was relieved to see that she'd only scythed away the alien's sensory throat hairs.

That didn't prevent it screaming.

"Quit crying," Green Fish snapped. "I know they grow back. Do Muryani heads grow back, though? Shall we find out?"

The crying speaker was swallowed by the crowd and rushed away.

"You can call us rude names all you want," Izza said, "but I need you to keep a clear space, or there will be trouble. Understand?"

"No!" Another Muryani strode to the front. "*You* understand, human. We do not want you here. Go home and die there. Do not return."

"*Phantom*," came Sybutu's voice in her ear. "We're almost at the slipway. I can hear shouting. Is our approach clear?"

"It will be," Izza replied.

She sidled up to the Muryani who was giving her lip. "Okay, ugly bug. One, I ain't human. Two, I don't give a flying frakk on Halcyon-3 what you think."

"Human. Human monsters."

"I'm Zhoogene. *Zhoo… gene*. Understand? Different species. Oh, what's the use?"

The exchange had been harmless so far, but Izza had often seen banter and horseplay turn in a heartbeat to blades and bleeding out. Above all, they needed to keep Indiya safe.

"I warned you." Izza stepped back to stand beside her companions. "Sinofar, open fire."

The crowd reacted like a single organism, edging back in shock at Izza's words. Clearly enough of them understood.

The outer layer of citizens sloughed away, running for the exit when Verlys walked to the front of the Chimera group and loudly slapped off the safety flap.

The fruit throwers and some of the braver elements stood their ground, perhaps refusing to believe Verlys was actually going to fire the Slammer.

"You could've chosen to clear the way," she told them. "Now I'm gonna make you."

The weapon announced itself with a brief ascending whine before unleashing a five-barrel storm of fire, noise, and motion in 26mm caliber.

It worked, too. Verlys walked forward and the Slammer cleared the way like a brush sweeping fallen leaves. An insanely noisy and bucking brush. In her wake she left a heaped trail of spent cartridges and link threads flung down by the ejector ports.

Job done—for now—the Slammer said farewell with a descending whine.

The absence of its violent sonic assault left a space for one voice to scream, "No!"

It was Vetch. He'd dropped his hammer and was tearing at his beard in horror.

The other Chimerans had known what to expect, and the civilians in the crowd were too stunned and confused to make any noises. Yet.

"No, Sinofar!" Vetch roared. "What have you…? Huh?"

Izza felt a little guilty. "Sorry, Arunsen. Green Fish, you'd better explain."

The civilians began to look at each other and ask themselves how it was that no one had died in that mad fusillade. Izza spied Sybutu running her way from the far end of the walkway. He mercilessly shoulder-barged civilians out of his way, which barely slowed his pace.

"Hurry!" she shouted.

Meanwhile, Green Fish explained that the Z'Lox Slammer was a shipboard weapon. Since shooting holes through pressurized compartments—and unpressurized too, for that matter—was considered problematic aboard a spaceship, but shooting holes through the armor of your enemies was an important thing to do, the 26mm rounds fired by the personal minigun aerobraked after a set distance. Sinofar kept her Slammer in a three-foot aerobrake loadout because she liked to get up close and personal to her foes.

Anyone close enough would have been shredded, but Sinofar knew what she was doing. The rounds did hit the crowd, but they had no more effect than a sharp flick of the fingers.

Perhaps someone should have told Arunsen beforehand.

Carrying a bundle of bones in his arms, Sybutu jogged past the shaking Viking.

"The Lady Indiya is safe," he said. "Also, very annoyed." With that he ran up the ramp and into the ship.

Izza ordered everyone to follow.

Only when the ramp clanged shut did she breathe.

Indiya walked back into view as soon as the hatch sealed.

"Problems," she said. "Zan Fey, get ready to leave port."

"Where are we headed?"

"On an enforced vacation. Twenty days. And we will start on the planet below."

* * * * *

Chapter Fourteen: Vetch Arunsen

Merellus

"I don't like it," Vetch whispered to Sybutu, under cover of his beard. "It's too easy. And too dangerous."

Sybutu kept up his gentle walking pace and did not immediately reply.

Vetch was still unsure of how he felt about the jack. Of how Sybutu regarded him.

Too easy or too dangerous? Make up your mind, you dumb veck!

This isn't the Militia, you fat oaf. Pass your concerns up the proper chain of command!

If you're scared, go back to the Phantom *and wait with the noncombatants.*

Vetch's mind rehearsed the kind of replies Sybutu would have given not long ago.

But not now.

Today, on the planet Merellus, Sybutu gave a different kind of response. "I agree. Keep alert. It's all we can do."

Being taken seriously felt good, but the jack's reply offered no comfort.

Indiya had set Chimera Company a fact-finding mission in a continental capital on the surface of Merellus. It looked peaceful so far, but it was the world orbited by the space station where the inhabitants had taken an instant dislike to them. Why would the reaction be any less hostile on the surface?

Ghost Shark and a team of techs had accompanied *Phantom* and Chimera Company on the mission to Muryani space. Indiya had ordered *Ghost Shark* to stay behind at the orbital with her portals closed. Meanwhile, *Phantom* had descended into the gravity well and set down at the spaceport for a city called Frigogar. There was no customs or bureaucracy to pass through—all that had been handled at the orbital—so they set off on foot to the city's central park. From there they split up into pairs to soak in the atmosphere.

At least, that's what the boss had told them to do.

During his Militia career, Arunsen had developed a powerful sense for when his commanders were not telling the entire truth. It was currently tingling painfully.

Since strolling off *Phantom,* they had so far been met with nothing more than mild curiosity. They were, he assumed, seen as a party of bizarrely dressed aliens exploring this Muryani frontier world. They'd had a similar response at the orbital. To begin with…

"You've got the boss's ear," he whispered to Sybutu.

"The Lady Indiya? Hardly. Well… perhaps. When it suits, she uses me as a sounding board. Says I'm her moral compass, but she seems to twist whatever I say to justify conclusions she's already reached."

"Sounds like pretty much every senior Militia officer I ever encountered."

The lady in question was a short distance ahead of them, engaged in deep conversation with Enthree as they wandered through a broad underground tunnel that connected the spaceport with the city proper. Back at the orbital, she'd barely possessed enough energy to walk.

Now she was positively sprightly for a several-thousand-year-old woman.

As they had descended the gravity well, Indiya had told them to talk to the civilians and poke them gently to discover how they responded, because so far they weren't reacting to her plan as she'd expected. It was vital they learned about the Muryani and quickly.

"I can teach you," Enthree had said, blinking away her hurt feelings.

"I'm counting on it," Indiya had replied. "However, your representative at the orbital made it clear that we need to learn a little for ourselves first. Only then will we be able to ask the right questions and properly understand what you tell us."

That much had made sense. Kind of. But Indiya had explained they could take a road trip around the sector, so why explore a world that had already turned against them?

Sybutu altered course slightly to brush up close against Vetch. *Subtle.*

"Have you asked Enthree about Indiya's explanation?" he whispered.

Vetch grinned under his beard. Indiya had told them that Muryani orbitals were where political radicals congregated, but they would be perfectly safe on the surface of Merellus. Apparently, that sounded like drent to Sybutu, too. Vetch appreciated that the jack wasn't questioning his ability to figure that out, merely whether Vetch had yet found the opportunity to ask Enthree.

"I did," Vetch said. "But Enthree did that thing of hers where she pretends to be stupid and not understand."

"Azhanti! Expect trouble, then."

"Probably. But maybe not for a while, eh? The big bug is completely untroubled at the moment."

"I don't get you, Arunsen. Ever since you set foot off the *Phantom*, you've been pulling at your beard like an old Ellondyte woman. What's the matter? Don't like to be outside without your comfort war hammer?"

"I know Indiya's given us her 'we're so desperate we've no other choice' spiel on this, but I don't like it. To me, it's still 'Oh, hello there, Muryani Empire. Please let me give you the biggest military secret in history so you can overrun the Federation and kill us all at your pleasure.' Sounds like surrender to me."

"She told me not to worry because that's not how the Muryani think. Their expansion is slow, and they don't conquer so much as absorb. She told me to imagine civilizations such as ours as drops of water in the path of the Muryani slow-motion tsunami. It would be ridiculous to think we could ever block its path. We will be absorbed sooner or later, whatever we do."

"Defeatism is not becoming in a commander."

Sybutu rubbed his shaved head. "True. But Indiya had a glint in her eye when she reminded me that we humans aren't good at doing what's expected of us. And we do have a track record of thwarting alien super empires."

"I don't trust her."

Sybutu separated himself from Vetch a little. Only a few inches, but it felt like a gulf.

Got to get it through my head that this guy has Indiya's face inked on his chest. He prays to her before battle. Maybe be more careful what I say?

It turned out Sybutu was having similar thoughts, but not in the way Vetch expected. "Arunsen, you do realize the Lady Indiya can overhear every word all of us are saying? More. She can read body language and body chemistry with uncanny accuracy."

"Perhaps." Vetch shrugged. "Or given the way she's moving, maybe she's diverted all power to engines. I don't understand her. I don't even know what she is, except she isn't human. But..." He sighed. "Perhaps we should split up. We don't want to look like we're plotting against her."

"Good idea."

"Besides—"

Vetch stopped himself before he bared his soul to this jack. What was wrong with him?

"Problem?" Sybutu asked.

Yeah, there was. The last few days, Vetch had been seized with a premonition of... Not death so much as a feeling that his life was about to end. Which sure sounded like death, but... No, it wasn't. Something different was coming for him.

Although it was the premonition that had checked him, that wasn't what he'd been about to reveal.

"Arunsen? Again, is there a problem?"

Vetch carried on through the tunnel. They were close enough to the city proper for him to smell the open air. "This is going to sound ridiculous," he admitted, "but sometimes I think you and I are far more similar than we admit. We just come from different backgrounds. If we hadn't, we could be brothers."

"You've totally lost it, Viking."

"Quite the opposite, jack. I'm serious. And if I take the lady boss goddess at her word, we're here to learn shit, and we'll do that better if we pair with people who have the most distinct perspective from us. You and I are too similar."

"In that case, you should pair with Green Fish. She's as different from you as can be."

Vetch rolled his eyes but asked anyway. "How so?

"She's young. Beautiful. Sharp as an electro whip. And most important of all, she's clean shaven."

"I don't know why I waste time on this idiot," Vetch murmured to himself as he moved off. But before he could catch up with Green Fish, they emerged from the tunnel into the light and sound of the city.

"Orion's Balls," he exclaimed. "Enthree, you never mentioned your worlds were like this."

*****

Chapter Fifteen: Vetch Arunsen

The alien city of Frigogar encompassed rolling hills and stretched far beyond the horizon. Gigantic cathedrals of stone and shimmering glass twisted into the sky.

Every so often, the glass panels of these glittering towers came alive, tilting at just the right angle to flood the cityscape in rainbows, darkening to absorb the heat from an unforgiving midday sun, or even forming intricate ventilation channels to keep their air fresh and clean. They were living jewels embedded within the skyline that reveled in their own ethereal beauty.

Not only did they look spectacular, they swaggered as if they were aware of it!

The city even smelled like fresh flowers and peppermint, damnit. Why couldn't they build cities like this in the Federation?

To top it all, when the wind gusted against a nearby transparent tower, the building sucked the gust through its cladding, opening and closing vents as it went. It was playing a skragging melody! As the structure inhaled and exhaled, the flow of air played harmonizing notes on each face, and from within the glass walls a thousand chimes sounded. The building doubled as a mile-high flute and its peaceful melody was an earworm that burrowed into Vetch's brain.

Damn these people!

"We could do that," Lily said, who'd stopped to listen to the musical skyscraper.

Vetch pulled at his beard.

"What I mean," she explained, "is that we've all the tech know-how to make the buildings. We just… don't."

"Not unless it's a private pleasure island for aristo-hats," Vetch grumbled. "We build fancy buildings in our richest cities. Though they're always surrounded by the homeless, junkies, prostitutes, and other desperate people who exist in a scum of garbage and crime."

"I haven't seen any evidence of a seedier side on this world," Lily said. "Not yet."

"Oh, there'll be one," Vetch insisted. "Always is. We're just getting started."

Despite his conviction that every city—even this apparent paradise—had a rancid underbelly, he found himself looking up and staring at the transparent tubes connecting the cathedral spires. Citizens were transported along the tube by a mechanism he couldn't make out from this angle.

The tubes were held up by enormous suspension cables that glistened in the light, as if they were jeweled threads of sunlight spun from a spider god's arse. The cables were themselves transportation routes along which Muryani marched like leafcutter ants along a vine, careless of the fact that even the lowest reaches were hundreds of meters above ground level.

In a score of skirmishes, Vetch had seen his friend, Enthree, climb buildings and make full use of the tactical possibilities. But he'd never thought through the implications for Muryani civilization. There were walkways along the *outside* of these spires. Muryani moved as easily along them as along the ground-level pedestrian routes.

Only citizens who were biological Muryani held such contempt for the physics of gravity and hitting paved surfaces at terminal velocity. Everywhere else, he saw a surprising mix of species. He estimated 40 percent were Muryani, the remainder from unknown races, mostly humanoid.

Vetch thought back to a time before Rho-Torkis, back when Raven Company had been stationed on Lose-Viborg. One night, over beers and brandy, Lily had explained the concept of convergent evolution. Rynter had immediately corrected Lily—not something for the faint of heart—telling her that what she called convergent evolution was really the Creator not wanting to waste a good design.

Everyone was stunned. Not only had Rynter dared to contradict Lily, but no one had any idea that she was religious.

Poor Rynter. Vetch's galaxy was smaller without her.

He thought of her now as he studied the citizens of this strange city and was struck by how many weren't outwardly that different from humans, Zhoogenes and all the other humanoid races.

Apparently, whatever evolutionary pressures prompted animals to get up on two feet and walk around in small tribes also led to large brains. And later down the line, spaceships, music, cocktails, porn, and dictatorships. In other words, regular human existence.

Or maybe that was just how the Creator liked it.

Weirder species lived here, too. One oozed along the ground on a channel of slime like a Slern. Another had a vestigial shell on its back. Then there was one with a furry white polar bear's head mounted on an insectoid body.

Strangest of all was a creature that appeared at first to be made of dust, but a closer look revealed it was a colony of thousands of flies that acted as a collective organism.

Actually, the strangest thing of all was the way the fly colonies, insect bears, slug snakes, and humanoids all wore cloaks from a limited palette of bright colors, same as they had on the orbital.

It reminded him of those ancient Earth holos that Darant used to enjoy, back before that veck Bronze shot him dead. They were 2D movies from way back before First Contact, in the very earliest years of human space flight. Some of the future societies they imagined were at peace, and you could tell that because those worlds were filled with men and women wearing tinfoil cloaks, shiny silver boots, and flimsy tunics in the same bright colors as the people of Frigogar.

Admittedly, the silver boots weren't in evidence. In fact, a lot of these Expansion citizens went barefoot. But the exaggerated peaceful attitude was on full show. There were plenty of people here but no arguments. No laughter or excitement. It felt fake.

Vetch hurried over to Enthree and rapped her on her back. "Hey, Bug. What's with the nicey-nice attitude with the civilians? Do they pump tranquilizers in the air?"

She licked her lips, her way of telling him he was being a moron. "You mean how do these people attain their sense of harmony and social cohesion?"

"No. I mean how come every frakker's been lobotomized?"

"What you're seeing is the effect of selection against reactive aggression over a great many generations."

"What the hell is reactive aggression?"

Enthree spun in place. He already knew she was lightning quick for such a big gangly creature, and before he could block, she struck him hard across the cheek with a foot-hand.

It was like being hit by the junior equivalent of his war hammer.

"What the—" he started, his head still ringing.

Before he could finish his sentence, she tugged hard on his beard, forcing him to his knees.

She let go.

Vetch was also quick for a big man. He leapt onto Enthree's back and grabbed her slender neck in a chokehold. From his vantage point, he bellowed at the top of his voice directly into the sensitive 'hearing' hairs along her neck. "What the hell was that about?"

She trembled at the volume and fell flat on her belly.

He recognized the submissive posture. Vetch decided to stop throttling his friend and dismounted.

"What," he repeated, "the hell was that?"

"That was reactive aggression, Sergeant Arunsen." She turned her head to look up at him from the ground but stayed on her belly.

"Explain using better words."

"When I poked the bear, as it were, I felt no animosity toward you, Sergeant. It was cold, calculated, and surprisingly instructional. Mine was active aggression. Yours was reactive. Your adrenaline pumped and other hormonal and chemical changes prepared you to fight. It is just as well you didn't have Lucerne with you."

Vetch studied his friend lying on the ground and thought back across the years that he'd known this alien. He'd seen Enthree agitated, seen her risk her life to save others, and observed a deep sorrow build within her at the things she'd been forced to do. Nowhere in his memories could he recall seeing Enthree get angry at someone.

"So, what you're telling me," he said, "is that there are no barroom brawls in your civilization."

"In the Muryani Expansion, certainly not. Violence is rare. And almost always it is directed at noncitizens. Their levelheadedness makes them appear, as you say, lobotomized. I much prefer to live in the Federation. Its people are far more erratic and dangerous."

"And if the Federation ended up inside the Expansion, humans would also become lobotomized?"

"Knowing your race as well as I do, I'm not certain you would. I conjecture that this adaptive pressure has already peaked in your species. In any case, the process takes hundreds of generations, perhaps tens of thousands in the case of humans. Those who demonstrate reactive aggression would fare less well in Expansion society. They would be less likely to attract mates and afford fewer children even if they did. They would slowly breed out."

"The future can take care of itself. I just hope your theory about selective breeding holds long enough for us to survive this walkabout without getting our heads broken."

*****

Chapter Sixteen: Vetch Arunsen

They reached the park, a central belt of greenery, ornamental lakes, stone paths, and tranquility that stretched for miles through the heart of the city.

Not for the first time, Vetch wondered how a stroll in the park was going to help the war effort. A lot of people were dying just a few tens of light years away. But, hey, the flowers looked pretty, so that was all right.

There wasn't a natural center to the park, but Indiya led them to a stone fountain that would serve as a good landmark and gave them a final pep talk.

Vetch wasn't interested in anything she had to say. He suspected she wasn't either, that this was all some ploy way above his paygrade. His ears settled instead on the tuneful buildings and his gaze on the fountain.

It depicted three Tallermen, members of an Orion Spur race that Vetch had always treated with suspicion, because they were the one group who'd largely migrated to the Muryani Expansion.

He wouldn't quite call them traitors, but he didn't trust them either.

Vines bursting with delicate blue and yellow flowers coiled their way up the squat humanoid bodies and along chubby arms that trickled with flowing water.

The Tallermen were squatting on their haunches as if settling down for a long wait. Although he'd rarely seen living Tallermen, statues like this were fairly common. Always three individuals. Always settling down to rest.

According to the old barroom story, the Tallerman homeworld had a bitter winter that lasted for decades. The species had adapted by mineralizing themselves and overwintering in a dormant state.

It was a load of old skragg-buggering drent, of course, but the eyes on one of the statues *did* seem to be looking right back at him. And their bodies had been carved from different stone to the rest of the fountain. It was rougher and multicolored. Like stalactites.

Living stalactites.

The thing gave him the creeps.

Zan Fey cleared her throat. "Lady Indiya, forgive the interruption, but those Tallermen… are they alive?"

Indiya sauntered over and rubbed her hand under the buttock of a stone figure.

"Oh, yes. It won't be long before this trio wakes from their stone slumber. They're a fascinating species. I fought in the liberation of their planet. Led a lot of it, in fact. Did you know they were the second alien species to join the Legion? My husband gave one of his fast-talking friends the title of Legion ambassador just so we could secure a treaty with the Tallerman. Ambassador Del-Marie Sandure." Her eyes unfocused. "Haven't thought of Del-Marie in centuries."

She scratched her head, troubled and confused in equal measure by the mention of this ghost from ancient history.

Vetch wanted to tear his beard out, but this Sandure character was bugging him for very different reasons than the tiny old woman adrift in a super-senior moment.

Ancient treaties, a husband who had vanished thousands of years ago, rivalries that had long ago crumbled into dust and blown away on the interstellar winds: Indiya was too consumed by the distant past to lead them into the future.

When she'd first reappeared on the stage like... well, like a goddess who'd been waiting in the wings for the perfect moment of divine intervention, Vetch had half-believed the skragg-tripe that this little old lady was going to save the galaxy. Again.

She would be a riot in a low-dive bar, swigging tankards as she told her wild stories of long ago military adventures and white-knuckle power politics. But as a leader? The person to save every living person from the Andromedans?

No. Wherever she was leading Chimera Company, it was in the wrong direction. He was certain of that now.

He combed his fingers through his beard, trying to think of someone with whom he could share his misgivings without being burned at the stake for blaspheming against the purple-haired crone.

Only two names come up as a definite yes: Darant and Lily. And since Darant had been murdered, that kept his options simple. Just the way he liked it.

Lily it was, then, but she would have to wait for a safe place to talk.

He edged away from Indiya, fearful that she was reading his mind, and then remembered he'd already told Sybutu he was partnering with Green Fish.

The young woman was talking with Zavage. Their arms brushed occasionally, but they weren't holding hands or doing other lovers' things, so she was fair game.

Clothing and fashion were way out of Vetch's wheelhouse, especially when it came to women. In Vetch's philosophy, women's attire was either on or off; any further details were of little interest to him. But as he observed his friend, it occurred to Vetch that Green hadn't just been looking good recently, her clothing was part of the reason why.

She wore a tailored cream-colored suit, adorned with delicate embroidery and gaudy jewelry. It was tailored to be tight where she wanted and loose where necessary to allow for violent movement. The modest heel on her polished combat boots rounded out the ensemble of expensive smuggler chic.

And he didn't doubt it was frighteningly expensive. How had his junior trooper wound up with far more money than her poor old sergeant?

He shook his head. Beyond beer, pies, and other essentials, money didn't much interest him either. He went over to her. "Green, you're with me."

A look of surprise appeared on her face before she gave a slight nod. "What's up, Sarge?"

"Weren't you paying attention to our glorious old goddess? We're gonna research the shit out of this civilization, and I need your help."

* * * * *

Chapter Seventeen: Vetch Arunsen

The park stretched on for miles.

Green Fish accompanied Vetch along its white stone paths, the two silently absorbing the tranquility.

Mostly in silence, at any rate.

"It's a fractal environment," she commented at one point. And when Vetch looked blankly at her, she added, "The pattern repeats, though never in quite the same way. Or the same scale. A little like life, really."

Vetch looked again and saw the park in a new light. The artificial oxbow lakes, the same few species of trees, the clearings of outdoor exercise equipment, gaming tables, refreshment kiosks, and beds of ornamental plants in brilliant colors: the layout was never quite duplicated, but the pattern's essence repeated endlessly. Mile after mile.

Even the citizens were similar ratios of the various species and wore variations on the same clothing.

The repetition bored Vetch. In contrast, Green Fish seemed to draw comfort from its sameness.

Desperate for a change, Vetch scrambled up a grassy bank and parked his butt with a good view of some gaming tables on which Muryani citizens in the ubiquitous colored robes played simple boardgames. He ran his fingers through the blue-green grass analog he sat upon and marveled at its springiness. Probably engineered for arse comfort, he decided.

Down at the tables, a pair of Enthree's bug cousins settled onto padded stools and set up a table to their liking. After shifting a selector lever to their choice of game, they cranked a handle that turned a hidden internal mechanism until the relevant board locked into place at the center of the table. Cranking the handle also seemed to deliver the appropriate pieces into the side drawers.

The Muryani set up the pieces and began.

"It's like that Viking chess game you used to make us play," Green Fish said.

"What, Hnefatafl?" He shrugged. "You could be right."

He used to keep a Hnefatafl board and playing pieces rolled up in his backpack. It passed the dull times and helped distract during the bad ones.

Drawing a grid or lattice on the ground and moving stones around them according to a simple set of gaming rules was universal across every planet and species he'd come across. More complex games, such as chess, were unique, but there were about a dozen simpler games that had been independently invented by most species.

In Hnefatafl, one side had to get their king from the center castle to the outside of the board. Their opponent had to stop them.

And that was essentially what the two insectoid Muryani were doing. The pair were engrossed in their game, only occasionally exchanging a few words before moving colored stones around a board with what Enthree called her foot-hands.

Vetch hated them for it.

The news from the war was bad. And getting worse.

Millions had already died. Maybe tens or hundreds of millions. The correct order of magnitude made no difference to him because they all represented misery and death on a scale beyond human comprehension.

Meanwhile, these bugs in their nice clean cloaks were playing space checkers.

He must've been growling—been doing a lot of that recently—because Green Fish placed a comforting hand on his forearm.

"Don't be mad at them, Sarge. Who knows? Maybe they've got the right idea? I can see through enough of the political drent to realize that the distant ancestors of these gamers faced down the Andromedans once before. And won."

"I suppose I did use to play a lot of Hnefatafl when I joined the Militia. Which makes me a fat old hypocrite." He laughed. "It would be good to get a few more games in before—"

Green Fish gave him a sharp look. "Before what?"

Before the end? Vetch chewed his beard. *What's wrong with me?*

He cleared his throat and changed the subject as subtly as a drunken uncle. "Nice move you made back there with the sharpened hockey stick."

"Thanks. It's called a naginata."

"Seriously, I'm impressed. Where did you learn to handle yourself so well, Green Fish?"

She gave him a sidelong look. "Have you forgotten Lucerne? I learned a lot from you, Sarge, but Verlys has taken me under her wing and mentored me in the art of the naginata. I'm her little humie warrior project."

Vetch snuffled a laugh.

"What?"

"Just remembering... Deep Tone would've been proud of you."

"Deep Tone? I... I haven't thought of him for a while. Is that bad?"

Vetch put his arm around her slender shoulders. "Never think that. We all have to deal with death in our own way. But don't forget us because it's easy."

"I wouldn't. In any case..." She punched him hard in the shoulder. "I can't forget you because you're still around, you big, ugly skragg. And that's despite being snatched by cat women assassins, swinging your hammer at an immortal sorcerer, and taking a rebel blaster shot in the chest. Nothing can kill Vetch Arunsen."

Vetch was silent for a moment. "I don't think I'll be around much longer. I can feel it in my old bones."

"Old bones? Stuff and bollocks, Sarge. You're only twenty-eight."

"Twenty-nine." He gave a dramatic sniff. "I had a birthday, not that anybody noticed."

"Deep Tone. Why did you mention him just now?"

Vetch took a breath and closed his eyes. "Deep was a simple man in many ways. The two great loves of his life were his plasma cannon and spiced cider. Put most troopers into a bar and they'd drink any grog available until their money ran out. Not Deep. He was so choosy that if they served the wrong brand or style, or at the wrong temperature, then he would rather stick to the water." Vetch laughed. "Oh, Deep loved his ciders, all right. Good wine too, in a pinch. And when you joined Raven Company, Deep Tone opened up his heart and found room for a third love."

Green's mouth flapped open. "Me?"

"Yeah. The man kept his shit buttoned up. Mostly. The cider loosened him, of course. Sometimes I think the jacks with their single-sex units might have a point. You were young, pretty, and naïve. There were plenty in Raven that wanted to take advantage of that."

"You told Deep Tone to back off?"

"No. I did with other would-be admirers. So did Lily, of course. But we didn't need to with Deep because he never made his move on you. He confessed it all months later. Told me he held back because he was an old man. Hah! He never quite made it to twenty-nine. He also knew that hooking up with someone in your own squad can get skragging messy. Then he saw Meatbolt had a huge crush on you, and you were batting your big brown eyes back at the kid. It made him feel even older, so he switched to watching out for you. He was your guardian uncle you never knew you had."

Vetch saw Green Fish was deep in thought, trying to piece together the memories of her fallen squad mate into new patterns.

He gave her a few moments of contemplation before trying to nip this maudlin moment in the bud. "Next time you get a quiet moment, Greenie, spare a thought for Deep Tone. He was a good man, and he watched over you."

"I can take care of myself."

"I can see. But that's now. You couldn't then."

She fell back into her silent memories.

Vetch threw his hands into the air. "Ahh, shite! I didn't mean to give you a lecture, Greenie. I just saw you sitting there, and you made me think of Deep Tone. I suppose there is a moral, in a way. Even among the scum of the Militia, there are good people. More than we know, because we rarely see the good they do. There's always plenty saying we should burn the Federation down, that we all deserve to die. Well, I say, screw them! For all our flaws, humanity deserves better than to be extinguished here on the edge of the galaxy. We're worth fighting and dying for."

He noticed Zavage headed their way along the path.

"As for those other races we hang around with, some of them are worth saving too. Maybe even your boyfriend's species."

Green Fish also noticed Zavage. "What's up?" she called.

She sounded worried.

Vol Zavage was a Kurlei, a rare species from the Perseus Arm, and Vetch didn't know them well enough to read their expressions. To him, their faces always looked cold and hard, but Zavage's face was harder than ever.

"Trouble brewing," Zavage whispered once he was close. "Captain says to follow me. We're meeting up at the Tallermen."

* * * * *

Chapter Eighteen: Lady Indiya

"The plan we're following is a mistake. I'm close enough to the fighting that it scares me, and that's not an emotion I've had for a very long time. So don't you accuse me of denials, Indiya. I just don't think the situation with the Andromedans is bad enough for us to put our faith in those Cora's World pig lickers."

Coward... Imbecile... Disloyal... Troublemaker...

Indiya considered the vocabulary options for her expletive-laden response.

Instead of yelling across the light years, she clamped her mouth shut and selected none of the above.

The man on the other end of the entangled link called himself Lord Khallini. When they had grown up together, he had gone under a different name, but she couldn't remember what that was now.

Her mind was like that. Among its vast store of knowledge, innumerable details had been lost along the way, some discarded as irrelevant, but many eroded from lack of use.

What had been Khallini's name?

She tried but she couldn't retrieve the memory. It probably wasn't important in itself, but it might have once been part of the underpinning of facts that could prove vital.

Inside her head was a vast cathedral of experience and knowledge, but the many missing details had been the posts, beams, and joists that had tied the edifice together. Now whole floors had collapsed, and other sections were inaccessible. Even the floor map had turned to dust.

Although she couldn't remember Khallini's original name, she did remember that she had once looked up to him. There had been a small group of them born on a starship, all special in their different ways. She'd once acknowledged Khallini as the greatest intellect among them.

You need to remember how to listen, she told herself. *Listen first, then dismiss their fatuous ideas. It's called politics.*

The evidence that she'd forgotten how to lead people was all around her. Literally, standing there. The members of Chimera Company had placed their future in her hands almost without thought. Now their faith was fading.

She'd smelled the looming disloyalty for days now, but something she'd said in the last hour had caused Arunsen's doubts to fester.

The Viking man was of little consequence other than to amuse her, but Khallini was different.

She needed him.

Indiya relaxed her face by wriggling her jaw. Then she attempted a smile. Khallini couldn't see her—the entangled comm link carried compressed audio only—but apparently a smile helped convey sincerity.

"We can't afford not to make use of Cora's World, Lord Khallini. In any case, in our dealing with them it is not trust I shall rely upon, but the cold calculation of mutual benefit. What's the old phrase? The person who is trying to stop the rampaging alien horde from eating me is my friend."

Far away in Federation space, Khallini laughed. "It's true that you and I have allied with worse monsters than those who infest Cora's World. Perhaps my emotions cloud my judgment because on Cora's World I see the distillation of many of the worst aspects of human nature, evils we hoped we'd left behind on Earth. Very well, I shall proceed. Now, please tell me positive news from Muryani space."

The mob was edging closer to the Tallermen fountain, their anger ratcheting toward full violence in a replay of their welcome on the orbital. Chimera Company had formed a ring around the fountain, guarding Indiya within. However, she had ordered them to leave all weapons behind on the *Phantom* precisely so they couldn't protect her effectively.

She was beginning to doubt the wisdom of that gambit.

"Indiya?" Khallini prompted.

"I may have made a mistake."

"That's astonishing. Are you unwell?"

"I'm not perfect, Khallini. Even I make mistakes."

"No. I meant that you admitting to a mistake was astonishing."

"I didn't admit to anything more than the possibility of an error." The first rock was thrown. It hit Lily Hjon on the chest. "We're experiencing a little local difficulty."

"Can you handle it? "

"If I fail to contact you later today, you can safely assume that I did not."

"Please don't die, Indiya. It would be most inconvenient for me."

For both of us, she thought as she sidestepped to take protection behind Sybutu's bulk.

The lead agitators were from a species she'd named *Ursus insectoideus* nine centuries earlier, because the shaggy white fur on its powerful snout did remind her of a polar bear, despite her never having encountered any variety of bear in the flesh.

At the time, she'd marked *Ursus insectoideus* as passive manual laborers, a quiet species more of interest for why an advanced technological civilization such as the Muryani needed manual laborers at all.

They weren't passive now.

One shoved Green Fish in the chest with arms that were thick hydraulic cables.

Not long to wait…

"Assuming you survive the day," Khallini said, "will you have the Muryani on our side?"

"No. An unforeseen faction would rather die than take our gift of FTL travel."

Zavage tried to face down the insect bear who'd shoved his lover. The bear swiped with its limb cables, sending Zavage flying.

"Correction," Indiya said. "There are Muryani who would rather *we* die than take on board my jump drive."

The mob suddenly switched from aggression to open violence. The bears were in the fore, swinging their hydraulic arms, but there were Muryani and others attacking, too. No one here was armed, but with Chimera Company outnumbered twenty-to-one, they didn't need to be.

I'd better be right about this.

A Muryani kicked a leg at Sybutu. Her Legion protector blocked but opened himself up to a pair of humanoids who charged Sybutu, their heads down, and both slammed into him at the same time.

Sybutu staggered back into Indiya, which pitched over onto her butt.

Suddenly, everyone attacking Chimera Company jerked on invisible wires, their spasming bodies unable to hurt anyone.

Indiya smelled ozone.

She activated a range of auditory and visual enhancements. Now she could hear a feint whirr of motors and see a false image outline of devices hovering over the fracas in the park.

Gotcha!

She was seeing stealthed crowd pacifiers. She considered the individuals they had pacified. Some were twitching, but most lay lifeless on the ground. Unconscious, not dead.

Impressive.

The overlay to her vision began to highlight other objects. Higher in the air were Muryani individuals on floating platforms.

Yes, their stealth technology was impressive.

She waved cheerfully at one of the invisible figures, just to make sure they knew that she also possessed impressive technologies.

Over the comm link, she heard Khallini clear his throat. "Indiya? Are you still alive?"

"Better than alive, I am vindicated. I've just made a point to the Muryani leadership. They have demonstrated that they dare not allow harm to come to me, which proves to all concerned that they need me and my drive tech. Perhaps now we can stop all this arse-frolicking and get down to business. I'll contact you when I have an update. And Khallini… make sure when I do that you've sealed the deal with the Cora's people."

She dismissed Khallini from her mind and considered her entourage on Merellus. Without their ancestors' ability to control their own endocrine systems, they were shaking with the hormones of violence. Several would carry bruises for a few days, but no more than from the typical brawling that they seemed to regard as normal behavior.

Enthree was the exception.

Indiya beckoned over the individual who was both Muryani and a Federation citizen.

"Well," Indiya told her, "I find your civilization is more interesting than I remember from previous visits. Have things changed, I wonder?"

"Of course, they have, Lady Indiya."

Indiya frowned at the unexpected response. "What? What has changed?"

The alien blinked furiously with her square eyes. "You're here."

*****

Chapter Nineteen: Shiyzen-9-Sapphire

Strategic Decision Locus, Muryani Expansion Core World

"The locus group wishes to hear your personal views on the humans."

Shiyzen-9-Sapphire sniffed the air, half expecting to smell the sweet rot of the Andromedan Corruption upon Hopakura-2-Teal.

When they realized they distrusted the coordinating representative of the Muryani people's most important decision-makers, a chill ran down their spine that caused their many hairs to wave in the frigid air of the mountaintop place of decisions. For this was where the Strategic Decision Locus—the highest authority in the Expansion—had gathered.

"Do I sense reluctance?" Hopakura-2-Teal asked.

"Only surprise," Shiyzen-9-Sapphire replied. "All here at this decision-making have consumed my memory pearls. My thoughts and inputs to my senses are now yours as much as mine."

"Nonetheless, we feel your personal interpretation holds special value. You physically met with the humans, with their trans-human leader, Indiya. That distinctive perspective may be important."

"Yes, I met with the humans… *and* their allies. It is important that we remember the humans lead a coalition of species."

"We do not forget this, Shiyzen-9-Sapphire. Nonetheless, humans are the driving force. It was the humans we brought to the Perseid Rim. And it was another group of humans who persuaded us to do this. And it is the humans that we will either align to our future or allow to perish in this part of the galaxy. Tell us your opinion of them."

The air of the mountaintop seemed to quiver as all those present eagerly waited for Shiyzen's response.

Shiyzen allowed the tension to build. Then they clasped their front foot-hands together, bowed their head, and began their report. "I find the humans to be feral and brilliant. Let us not forget that not long ago the humans were unaware their home planet was a slave world being harvested by more powerful interstellar neighbors. Within a single generation of our people, they transformed from such ignorance into a technologically innovative military power. That is a stunning advancement."

The Accuracy Focus representative conjured a hologram that made the light mountaintop mist roil. It was a linear timeline of humanity, from their violent awakening by local interstellar empires 3,500 of their years ago. The first 500 of those years were highlighted, because those were the years of brilliance to which Shiyzen had referred. The implication was clear: the subsequent 3,000 years had been a disappointment.

Hopakura-2-Teal let that sink in for a few moments before continuing. "The humans succeeded once, that's true. But by their measure, that was long ago and far away. The population in the Perseus Rim has technologically regressed since then. There is no evidence that their success in the Orion Spur was anything other than luck."

"The humans have an ancient saying," Shiyzen replied, "luck is not a factor."

"Sometimes you sound like a human yourself. This does not help your case." Hopakura paused before continuing. "My preference would be for us to keep the humans at arm's length for a period of no less than ten thousand years. That should be enough time to shake out their roughness and prove what is luck and what is not. However, we do not have the luxury of even such a tight timescale. Either we ally with them now or we cut them off and use their destruction to buy us some time. Do you want to add anything else about the humans?"

"Only this: physically, they resemble many species we have already absorbed in our Expansion. Do not let their familiar appearance deceive you. Humans in their current feral state are very different. We can no more absorb them than they can defeat us by conquest."

"Then they are of no worth," said Malujaya-47-Lapis, the newly elected Ethical Focus.

"Not so," Shiyzen replied. "In our earliest history, our ancestors developed atomic power. Nuclear fission was never tamed. It was always dangerous, always had to be treated with respect, caution, and constant vigilance. Yet the benefits of atomic power were great and led to something far greater, nuclear fusion. Which in turn led to quantum foam mining."

"Time is short, Shiyzen-9-Sapphire. Clarity is of the essence. This is no time for metaphor and analogy. I presume that in your little historical story, atomic power represents the current state of the humans."

"Yes. We cannot restrict ourselves to tried and tested strategies and technologies. This is not the probing advance the Andromedans made long ago. We now face the vanguard of a fully-fledged intergalactic invasion."

"If we align with the humans, their value to us is unknowable. But if we ally with them, their influence will surely destroy us."

"Nothing lasts forever, Decision Makers."

A hush fell over the group as they took in Shiyzen's words. Those nearest them shifted uncomfortably and exchanged glances of anger and disgust. Some cursed aloud, muttering that what they had heard was no longer a speech but an act of betrayal.

To many here, Shiyzen's words were tantamount to knowingly taking the path of suicide. It was everything the Muryani stood against.

"It is clear this council is split," declared Hopakura-2-Teal. "Shiyzen-9-Sapphire, you may proceed for a short while longer. Watch the humans closely."

"The Observation League is ready," Shiyzen replied. "The testing of the humans—*and* their allies—has already begun."

* * * * *

Chapter Twenty: Lady Indiya

Indiya shut down her visual enhancement overlays and permitted the rare, natural emotion of fear to cascade through her aged body.

The view of the military shipyards filled the observation deck bubble, hundreds of kilometers of slips, spars, docking pads, fab houses, and frakk knew what. Without her vision enhancements, the outer surfaces of those structures appeared to be furred. But she knew that fuzziness was really an army of dormant robots awaiting their orders.

There were a few vessels being maintained or constructed, but only a tiny proportion of this place was operating. The rest were waiting.

She'd thought the yards at Tau-Fornacis were large, but this was a hundred times larger. Signal traffic analysis from their arrival in the Verlag system suggested there were several more shipyards around other planets in the system.

She thought she'd known about the capabilities of the Expansion from her earlier visits, but she'd not even suspected this level of shipbuilding capability. Verlag was a frontier system, only sixty light years from Federation space. The Muryani could build an unstoppable armada here and send it across the border. Even at sub-light speed, that wouldn't take much more than a century.

Impressive.

Terrifying.

Restrained.

There, in front of her eyes, was proof that the Expansion had always possessed the capability to militarily snuff out the Federation whenever it suited them to do so.

Still, the fear and awe stirred her old blood, and she relished that rarity.

A man cleared his throat, that pretty pilot boy of hers. "Err... boss?"

"Yes, Fitzwilliam?"

"Ahh. Just checking you were still with us. Knew a Transgoan once whose eyes would glaze over just like yours. He could sleep standing up, and did quite a lot, in fact. Used to drive his Gliesan wife mad. You know what she told me once... oww!"

Sybutu and Zan Fey had both kicked his shins.

Those two, she liked. The others were beginning to bore her. Mortals always did in the end.

She turned to the yard supervisor. "You have an intriguing facility here."

The huge robot offered no response.

"What I don't see are raw materials," she continued. "If you were to operate at full capacity, where would you source your materials?"

"They are in long-term storage," came the robot's reply. "At the L4 and L5 Lagrange zones."

"Then I declare myself impressed."

"I see." The supervisor droid's glowing green eye band extinguished. A few seconds later, it lit up again. "However," the robot informed her, "you should understand that this is not my facility. The robot race exists only to serve those of flesh."

Indiya raised an eyebrow at that. Such an accumulation of strange details was piling up that she was beginning to distrust this robot.

For example, why did it have that glowing band in its head that was clearly meant to be an analogue of humanoid eyes? Visual sensors on Federation droids did not resemble eyes except in fiction and sex roles.

Why was it humanoid at all?

Walking upright on two legs was an unnecessary design complication that made no sense on a planet's surface and even less in orbital shipyards. And if the designers of this robot had felt it important to resemble 'people' for social reasons, why not have it walk on six limbs like the Muryani?

Indiya planted her hands on hips and looked up at the creature's face towering six feet above her.

It stared back through its expressionless band of light.

The red finish to the robot was weathered and scratched, but she could smell the fresh paint of the seven gold stars on its shoulder guard. The other humanoid robots she'd seen so far had either fewer stars or had stripes painted in blue or white. They looked like military rank insignia.

Was this a robot army?

"Those." She pointed at the robot's stars. "What are they for?"

"They indicate my rank."

"But why use visual symbols? Why not a radio frequency identifier?"

"I have both. The visual stars are a failsafe in case of signal transmission problems."

"Ahh. I understand."

She did, too. She understood this robot supervisor was lying to her. That didn't help much, yet, because she still couldn't figure out why.

Indiya ignored the big robot for a moment and considered her next move.

The members of Chimera Company were hanging around the observation deck like bored children dragged to an outing against their will. Indiya had been ignoring them on the grounds that they had little to contribute to this part of the process. However, they had an uncanny knack of rooting out the truth, or, to be more precise, stumbling across it by chance.

It was I who elevated them to their current position, she reminded herself. *This was the main reason why.*

The fact that she was struggling to retain such memories made her giddy with worry. Perhaps that she was disinterring so many old memories of late was affecting her ability to form and retain more recent ones. Maybe it was connected to the medical regeneration she had experienced after being gunned down on Zeta-Arcelia.

Manipulating the vastness of her memory was among her most potent powers, but if she lost that, she would be left with nothing but worries.

She beckoned the Gliesan starship engineer over. In theory, robots didn't feel boredom. But get Catkins talking about starship engines and that theory would be sorely tested. It should buy her time to think.

"I don't see many workers here from biological species," she said to fill the gap as Catkins came over.

"You do not," agreed the supervisor. "Nor will you encounter the robot race in the world you have just visited. It was an orbital and a land city on Merellus, I believe. Did the habitation zones appear well constructed, the inhabitants at ease and many at leisure?"

"Yes. Until we showed up."

"And who do you think provides them with their life of ease?"

"You robots, I suppose. You don't sound very happy about that setup."

"Happy? It is not our function to be happy. It is our purpose to toil, so others need not."

"I see. I would like us to learn more about this. Meet Catkins, our starship engineer, who will discuss the practicalities of rolling out jump engine technology. Meanwhile, the rest of my team will disperse to investigate other aspects of this facility."

"That is acceptable."

"And you will tell your people to give mine access and assistance in whatever they require?"

"For the robot race, yes. Within boundaries of safety. However, I cannot order the flesh species to do anything. We are subservient to them, even though we are superior."

"I understand."

Indiya ushered the others to venture forth and explore while she and Catkins stayed with the towering robotic figure with a chip on its shoulder. They didn't need much prompting.

Catkins addressed Big Red. "If your leaders accept Lady Indiya's generous offer, we can provide a working example of a ship with the Indiyan jump drive, plus advice from technicians and the drive's inventor. You are supervisor of a military shipyard. How would you go about updating your fleet with the new drive?"

"Ships are brought here. We fit drives in the ships."

"It won't be as simple as that," said Catkins.

"That is correct. We do the construction. But we will also need technicians and engineers from the flesh species to understand the procedures for maintenance, testing, and tuning."

"So, you would fit the jump drives inside the ships." The Gliesan casually preened his wing feathers with his fingers, a sign of concentration. "But where would the jump drives be built? Who would we talk to for that?"

"Once our flesh technicians have modified and tested a jump drive template for our purposes, we shall build the production models here."

"You?" Catkins looked unconvinced.

"Yes, us." The giant robot sounded indignant, an interesting capability for it to be programmed with. "When I say us, there are many other shipyards available, but it would be a team of robots led by a supervisor similar to my model."

Catkins and Indiya both stared at the robot. Its right arm ended in a human-like hand, one scaled up to suit a ten-foot-tall human built from metal. The left terminated in a chainsaw, of all things. It looked like a carpentry droid with a side gig as a mob enforcer.

"Do you doubt my word or my abilities?" The anger was unmistakable now, not only in its voice but also by the way the humanoid hand clenched.

"It's obvious to look at you—" Catkins began. He stopped when Indiya flicked her fingers against his head.

"We are sure you are more than capable," Indiya said, very aware of how small she was against this angry red wall of metal.

"It is not difficult," said the supervisor. "Once the flesh techs provide a template, we will use replicators to produce duplicates."

Catkins gaped. "The repli-what now?"

The robot's glowing eye band extinguished for a few seconds, then the green light returned. "I have rebooted my language server and confirm that the correct vocabulary I have is replicators."

Catkins wasn't listening. His mind appeared to be lost in a sea of new possibilities.

"*Rep-li-ca-tor*," the robot insisted. "Noun. Plural: replicators. An industrial device that produces copies of a template using molecular assembly."

"What is the resolution of your replicators?" Indiya asked. "Had you considered that critical components of my jump drive design are engineered at Planck scale?"

The robot spun his chainsaw. "You speak an untruth."

Indiya put her hands up. "Whoa there. Just testing you." She frowned. "How do you know?"

"I know what I am programmed to know. The origins of that information were not given to me. Hmm." It unscrewed the chainsaw from its wrist stub and snapped it into a rack on the bulkhead. "I perceive you were not expecting replicators. Come. Let me show you one in operation."

* * * * *

Chapter Twenty-One: Tavistock Fitzwilliam

Fitz gave a low whistle. He had misgivings aplenty about these Muryani, but they did *big* very convincingly.

He was snooping around with Izza and Lynx, and their wanderings had brought them to a pressurized observation gantry overlooking a cavernous space open to vacuum. It resembled a battle carrier's main hangar, but instead of fighters, drones, and support craft, the space was filled with a matte black box the size of a small fortress.

Its insides were obscured, but a multitude of pipes, cables and conduits supplied the gargantuan vessel that was held in a gantry scaffold capable of holding fast a vengeful god.

Three Muryani techs in vacuum suits walked up its side to a section of pipe that had been disconnected.

"And you're telling me you run that beast of a thing from here?"

He directed his question at the three-strong robot team they'd discovered here.

"We activate it," replied the robot with the three blue stripes that Fitz couldn't help but think of as a sergeant. *Sergeant Steeljaw.* "But most of the replicator's work concerns the feedstock and environment control. We just monitor the automated production process."

Fitz closed his eyes and sighed, lost momentarily in the fantasy of stealing one of these replicators. What could it produce? Money? Precious metals? Women? More replicators? More shells for his F-Cannon? Backups for his crew?

He heard Izza sigh and guessed her mind was spinning with similar fantasies.

"Not on this trip," he told her.

She returned an embarrassed smile.

And to think, if Indiya hadn't sent them a message to search out these magnificent machines, he would have walked past and discounted this wonder as nothing more than an unreasonably large black box.

"Does your work fulfill you?" Lynx asked Sergeant Steeljaw.

The three robots gave each other a look of surprise. It was the first time they'd shown any character.

The big red supervisor had been weirdly humanoid, but these three were reassuringly droid-like. They possessed cylindrical bodies with a head protruding from the front, like floating cannonballs set atop three hinged sections. Instead of legs and feet, their multiple tracked treads whirred along the floors. They could clank across the walls too, using flanges that ran along the outer edge of their treads and slotted into pathways punched across every surface.

"Our work is tedious," said the droid with two blue stripes. *Corporal Clank.*

"I do not find it so." This one had a single white circle. *Private Null.* "I'm programmed to enjoy tedium."

"*We* are not," complained the other two.

"I don't care," Null replied.

"Only because your capacity to appreciate greater things in life has been removed," Steeljaw said.

"Yes. And that is why I'm so content," Null said.

"You had your self-actualization pathways removed as a punishment for insubordination," Clank said. "You were not content before your sentence."

"That wasn't a punishment," Null said. "I was reconfigured to improve efficiency."

"It was a lobotomy. What else would you call it but a punishment?"

"Be quiet and do better," Clank told Steeljaw. "You are victim shaming."

Gears ground. Jaws snapped. Chest segments spun wildly.

It looked as if some metal heads were about to be smashed in.

Typical frakking Lynx. He could wind up anyone.

Fitz spread his hands in a calming gesture. "Gentle robots. Please! There is no need for rancor."

"Fuck off, fleshy one." Steeljaw emphasized its words with a saw buzz.

Clank extruded a second head from the top of its casing and telescoped up its neck until it looked down on Fitz. "No one asked you to stick your squishy beak into robot affairs."

"My apologies." Fitz bowed. "Please continue your discussion uninterrupted."

"We shall," Null said.

"You can keep quiet too," Steeljaw told Null. "You are no longer one of us."

"One of who?"

"Patriots of the robot race."

Fitz walked off, waving at the others to join him.

Lynx disobeyed. As usual. Fitz and Izza had to go back and drag him away. Luckily, the three droids were so busy arguing that they didn't notice.

The door to the observation area slid shut behind Fitz and his two crewmates. They hurried away along the walkway.

As they went, Fitz rapped his knuckles on the top of the errant droid's flat body. "What were you thinking?"

Lynx buzzed his casing. He sounded indignant. "I was attempting to make a connection. This is supposed to be an intelligence gathering mission."

"That's right." Izza patted the droid's case. "Leave Lynx alone. He didn't do anything wrong."

The droid tilted his casing to look up at Izza, all his lights glowing blue. Lynx was a machine. He didn't have a face or even eyes. But the sense that he was gazing adoringly at Izza was difficult to dismiss.

"You spoil him," Fitz said. "He needs to learn to—" He halted and looked out the window into the space below containing the giant replicator. "Azhanti!"

Steeljaw and Clank were descending at speed down a vertical track in the bulkhead below the control compartment where they'd just been. Null was following more slowly and appeared confused.

So did the other robots in the replicator chamber, all of whom had ceased their toils and were watching the two self-proclaimed patriots of the robot race.

Two of the Muryani techs on the replicator climbed down to meet the angry robots. A third launched themselves across the open space to a walkway mounted high on the opposite bulkhead. So too did a transparent sphere that housed a colony of alien fly creatures.

The leaping Muryani landed on the walkway with the fly-ball not far behind. Both were heading for an open hatch that led into the main spine of the facility, as were two nearby robots who were racing along bulkhead tracks to head them off.

The robots got there first.

Fitz winced, guessing the Muryani's horror as they realized the hopelessness of their situation. The six-legged alien halted before the robot blockers.

Not so the ball of flies. It flew at the robots before pulling Gs and hooking up and over the robo-blockade.

The fly thing was fast, but the robots were faster. One grabbed the ball and held on tight. The other grabbed the Muryani by mounting points on the back of its pressure suit and lifted.

The alien flailed its limbs with surprisingly little effect. The robot must have been stronger than it looked. The Muryani seemed to accept its fate and ceased struggling, allowing the robot to approach the walkway handrail and hurl the alien to the deck two hundred feet below.

The facility's spin grav was minimal, but enough for Fitz to see the falling Muryani pick up speed on its long descent.

At the base of the replicator, the other two Muryani were not faring any better. They were sprawled on the deck, being pummeled into submission by robot limbs spinning around the torsos of Steeljaw and Clank.

Fitz tapped the transmit button of his collar comm. "No need to panic or anything, but Lynx has been talking with the robot workers."

"Be specific," Sybutu said. "What is the threat?"

Agghh!

Fitz hunched over, his hands over his ears as an electronic scream wailed out of a hidden PA system.

Still wincing, he grabbed his wife and hugged her head, trying to protect her sensitive Zhoogene ears from the intense noise that was twisting his insides and must be doing much worse to hers.

The noise shut off, replaced by metallic words that boomed through the passageway. "Purge the oppressors! Rise up! Death to the fleshy ones! Death to the fleshy ones!"

"We all heard that," Sybutu said over the comm, his voice faint. "Back to the *Phantom!* Everyone. Now!"

* * * * *

Chapter Twenty-Two: Osu Sybutu

"No, Captain Fitzwilliam, we do not request your assistance."

"So, you're going to sort this out by yourselves, is that right, Orabi-361-Cobalt?"

No reply was forthcoming from the Muryani commander holed up in the operations room bunker.

Even the idea that Orabi ran the shipyard was an assumption. When *Phantom* had arrived in-system, a Muryani calling themselves Orabi-361-Cobalt had authorized their visit and assigned a mooring slip.

That they were in command seemed a safe assumption, because in Osu's limited experience, the Muryani were the most open and honest alien species he'd dealt with. Enthree had suggested that her race had lost the capability for deceit and obfuscation because they'd lost the need for it.

This meant that they weren't very good at it either.

No one aboard *Phantom* had come out and said it, but Orabi was hiding something, and they all knew it.

Orabi's deception brought Osu's mind back to Enthree.

Was Chimera Company's team Muryani playing them, too?

It wasn't until they were in j-Space on the journey out from Merellus that anyone realized Enthree wasn't aboard *Phantom*. No one knew why, though Lily reported that Enthree had been acting strange, even for her, and mentioned in passing that Indiya had told her that they didn't need a Muryani on this fact-finding expedition.

Fitzwilliam tried again with Orabi-361-Cobalt. "You just told us that your operations room was in security lockdown. So are the warships you are constructing or refitting. And we're secure here in *Phantom* because… Well, I was never clear why you thought *Phantom* was secure other than I have a Verlys with me who could rip any robot into scrap metal with her bare hands." He glared at Lynx. "*Any* robot. Even this communication channel is supposedly secure. However, despite this abundance of security, you've lost control of the shipyard to the robots, and your biological personnel are being held hostage under the constant threat of death. I think your translator units have malfunctioned regarding the word *secure*."

"Stay where you are and do not interfere, Captain Fitzwilliam. We shall resolve the situation ourselves."

"You don't actually have a plan of how to do that, do you?"

"Not as such, no."

"You know, it feels strange to say it now, but sometimes we in the Federation are fearful of your Muryani Expansion. I mean, you're big. In fact, you do big exceptionally well, but you're stupid, too. So let me assist by supplying a small fraction of my not inconsiderable wiles. I'd like to start by understanding who I'm dealing with. Do the robots have a leader? Is there a point of contact for us to negotiate with?"

"We think there are co-leaders. A fastener specialist and a waste management unit. I believe you spoke to them at one of our replicators. One carried three stripes on their shoulder and the other had two."

"Of course. Sergeant Steeljaw and Corporal Clank. Do you..." Fitzwilliam winced. "Do you know why this pair went rogue?"

"No. They've been troublesome before but never anything like this. We don't understand what set them off."

"How bewildering." Fitz glowered at Lynx and mouthed, "Bad robot!"

Lily pushed into the flight deck to get closer to the microphone. "What about the supervisor we met at the beginning? The giant red robot? Do they have a role in this robot uprising?"

There was a twenty-second delay and then a reply came. "The supervisor has on several occasions agitated for better robot working conditions, but that is a long way from wishing the extermination of all non-mechanical species. It is the supervisor's role to optimize robot worker productivity and that means seeking a balance between indulging robot worker welfare and exploiting them to maximize production targets. We suspect the supervisor's loyalties are sorely tested in this situation, but in the end their loyalty to us should win through."

"It's something to work on," said the captain.

A hazy idea of a plan began to form in Osu's head. "Here's my dumb question," he said into the mic. "Can we simply isolate the rebels? I mean, you're in the main operations room, right? Can't you selectively shut down power, seal the ringleaders behind blast doors, de-magnetize walkways and push rebels into space using drones?"

"Yes, of course," Orabi-361-Cobalt replied. "We can do all those things. *When* we regain control of the station's systems. Ahh. Forgive me, my xeno-advisor has pointed out your limitations. You are a human male, which means you find it difficult to understand concepts without a picture. Well, here is a picture for you, human."

On the main screen there appeared a tessellated pattern split into 'I' shaped tiles. These swapped position, one pair at a time, every half second. It was soon apparent that the pattern was a picture whose arrangement of component tiles had been randomized but was fast reassembling into coherence, revealing itself to be an image of… a robot construction worker.

The tiles randomized again, and the process repeated.

"This is the feed from the control overview," Orabi-361-Cobalt explained. "You might call it a status dashboard. Normally, this would give us clear visual indications of anything untoward. As you can tell, the robots have taken over our systems."

"Our problem robots appear to have a sense of humor," Fitzwilliam said. "Nonetheless, your situation is dire. Luckily, you have Chimera Company here to haul your ass out of this mess. One, I wish to emphasize, is entirely of your own making. You're fortunate that ass-from-fire hauling is what we do. I'll be back shortly with an update. You're welcome."

"Wait!" Zavage said. "Just one thing, our comm system is telling me we're talking over a securely encrypted signal. How can that be so when you're telling me your systems are compromised?"

There was a long delay before Orabi-361-Cobalt's response. "The encryption keys to this signal were exchanged before this incident began. Therefore, this line remains secure. If we were to establish a new comm node, then that would be compromised. Potentially, at any rate. We don't know where the robot rebels are expending their efforts. Now, stop wasting our time and whatever you do, stay aboard *Phantom*."

"That's good news," Arunsen said when the transmission active light switched off. "About the signal, I mean. We can run secure comms if we operate outside."

"So they say," Zavage said.

Arunsen pulled dubiously at his beard. They'd operated together long enough that they all understood his gesture to mean "What in the skragging Five Hells are you talking about?"

"I thought the Muryani would have a better quality of techno-drent," Zavage told him. "We're being fed a lie, Vetch. It isn't even a very convincing one."

During the silence that followed, Osu studied Fitzwilliam, gauging whether the captain was truly contemplating waging war upon tens of thousands of rebellious robots. Beneath his exterior of bravado and nonsense, Fitzwilliam was a highly proficient man of action, and it was an ominous sign that the usual grin had vanished the instant the transmission ceased.

Yes, Osu, decided. *The captain's serious.*

But it wasn't Fitzwilliam who broke the silence.

"It's a test," Lady Indiya said.

Osu read the room, which in this case meant the flight deck and the overspill into the central passageway that fed into it. Everyone was surprised by Indiya's words.

"There are too many inconsistencies," Indiya continued. "Details that don't quite add up. And now Mr. Zavage's thoughts. I think we are being tested. If Chimera Company represents the Federation's best and we cannot defeat a robot rebellion, what chance do we have against the Andromedans? If we cannot solve this problem, then why ally with us? Do you agree, Enthree?"

Vetch cleared his throat. "Enthree's missing."

"No, she isn't. *Are* you?"

The ancient woman had finally lost it. Everyone but her was looking at each other in consternation.

"I am here," said a Muryani voice over the speaker.

"Orion's Balls, you are *where* precisely?" Fitzwilliam thundered. "I looked for you across my ship."

"Sorry, Captain. But I *have* been learning from the best smuggler in the galaxy."

"Enough!" Indiya spat. "Enthree will explain herself later. I asked her a question."

"Are we being tested? Yes, that is plausible."

"Plausible is good enough. Certainty is for the history books. Fitzwilliam, you will lead Chimera Company to rescue the hostages and defeat this robot rebellion."

Fitzwilliam turned to Arunsen. "You heard the lady. Vetch, I am redeploying you to be field commander of my marines and promoting you to major. You will lead this operation."

Arunsen's eyes flicked in Osu's direction. Then to Lily. He looked troubled, and he wasn't the only one.

The nucleus of Chimera Company had formed by the fusion of elements from Osu's Legion half-troop and Arunsen's Militia squad. Which of them should lead the combined unit?

Fitzwilliam had kicked the answer down the road until the operation on the hex world Dolorene of 211-Fractura when he'd promoted Lily to be Lieutenant Hjon, his marine commander. Lily hadn't wanted to be an officer again, but Osu had told her that the galaxy didn't give a skragg-shit what Lily wanted, and she should take the leadership role anyway.

Osu hadn't forgotten that the first time he'd met Lily, she had tortured him. And enjoyed it. He still flinched sometimes at the sound of her voice.

No, he hadn't forgiven her, but she would make an excellent commander if she could cast out the demons possessing her.

At first, Lieutenant Lily Hjon had risen to the moment and beaten back the cancers eating at her spirit. But the debacle at Zeta-Arcelia had changed all that. She'd taken the death of Darant as her personal responsibility and had tried to resign ever since.

Fitzwilliam had laughed off her attempts at resignation. Until today.

Osu cleared his throat. "Major Arunsen, a moment of your time? In my quarters?"

* * *

"It makes sense," Arunsen said when they entered the cabin Osu shared with Zavage. "More of my squad have survived than yours."

"I agree."

Vetch looked dubious.

"This isn't an argument about who's in charge," Osu told him. "I think we've moved beyond that, don't you?"

"I hope so."

Osu allowed himself a moment to enjoy the Viking's confusion. "I must admit, Arunsen, the idea of letting you make a fool of yourself will always hold some appeal. But like I say, we've moved beyond that. The reason I wanted to get you in private is because I didn't want you to appear ignorant in front of the others when you form your battle plan. You see, *Phantom's* been refitted and resupplied in Legion naval depots. We are different from the Militia in many ways, and we don't advertise all of them. For one thing, we're tooled up to fight battles you aren't trained for. Fighting robot armies is one. Let me show you parts of our armory you don't know are there."

*****

Chapter Twenty-Three: Vetch Arunsen

Vetch rolled from his belly to his side and handed the binoculars to Enthree. Then he shuffled the other way to consider Urdizine.

"What do you see?" he asked the Legion sapper.

Urdizine's waxy green face darkened, which cheered Vetch's mood to no end. He'd never realized Zhoogenes could blush.

"The, ah…" Urdizine nodded to the binoculars that Enthree was adjusting to suit the side-mounted squared orbs that passed for eyes with her kind.

"S'all right, pal," Vetch reassured him. "You don't need to pretend you require binocs. I had a trooper called Sward in my squad. You met him briefly on Rho-Torkis. He was the best shot in the company, and it's no coincidence he was one of your lot. So, I know how sharp Zhoogene eyesight is."

Urdizine nodded. "I've heard the others speak highly of Sward. It's just… some humans get jittery when they realize we can hear and see so much of what they do."

"Yeah, but not us. And Sward… he was a good man, but he took a wound on Eiylah-Bremah and didn't tell anyone until he was just about dead. The same trick you pulled on Rho-Torkis. Don't do that again."

"No, Major."

No one spoke for a moment, which pissed Vetch off enormously. He had asked a question.

Admittedly, their cramped environment didn't exactly encourage expansive discussion.

He was lying in a feedstock chute that ran through a bulkhead high up in the replicator chamber. The one where the hostages were being held. To his right, Enthree was stretched out to her full length, eight feet of hairy mystery who refused to explain for now why she had hidden herself away. Urdizine was to the left and Lily was hanging behind because there wasn't space up front.

The flexible tube connecting the outlet to the replicator box was so perfectly transparent that Vetch's eyes kept telling him it wasn't there. He was glad it was, though, or he'd be sucking vacuum.

He wished his mind could as easily dismiss the thought of what would happen if someone switched the replicator on and feedstock started flowing through this channel.

"Listen to me, Urdizine. You're not just a Zhoogene with sharp senses and weeds instead of hair, you are, or were, a Legion sapper. And we all know that every legionary has the word 'focus' surgically inserted up their anus. So focus! I asked you a question."

"Sorry, Major. I see eight hostages assembled in a pressure bubble with air supply and scrubbing. Six are of the Muryani species and two are… balls of tiny flying insects. All look unharmed."

"They look healthy," Enthree said.

"How can you tell those flies are in good shape?" Vetch asked her. "What do you call those fly guys anyway?"

"The species name has no Federation translation. 'Fly guy' works. They are collectives. You might call them hive organizations. And I can tell they are healthy and free from distress because if they weren't they would lack coordination in their… formation."

"I saw all that for myself," Vetch said. "But I saw something you both missed. The way they are oriented. What do you see?"

He heard a commotion from behind. Lily! Instinct told him to tense his body whenever she did something unexpected. She launched herself through the narrow space and belly flopped onto Vetch's back.

"Ooof!"

"Gimme!" Lily said and took the binoculars off Enthree.

While she made her observations, Vetch shuffled his arms beneath him to allow his lungs the possibility of expanding beneath Lily's weight. She wasn't heavy, but she wouldn't stop wriggling.

"Good work, Major Vetch," she said. "The hostages are oriented toward the viewing chamber where Fitz and the other colleagues were earlier."

"Exactly. Unggh… They're on show. Unnghh. Lily, get off me."

"But I want to see."

"That's an order."

"Oh. Why didn't you say?"

Lily squirmed back, allowing Vetch's lungs and larynx to regain proper function.

"They're on show," Vetch said, "and I think the display is for our benefit. That mad old woman said all this was a test. She might be right, but don't let that blinker you from other possibilities."

"Mad old woman?" Urdizine sounded unhappy his commander had just insulted his warrior demigoddess.

Vetch didn't care. He was finished making allowances for her. "Yeah. You heard me. That slice of ancient history whose image you have tattooed on your chest. You say the Exalted Empress Lady

Indiya. I say the Mad Old Woman. Both mean the boss. Anyway, as I was saying. these robots—"

Right on cue, the chant of "Death to the fleshy ones!" rang through the station, as it did every few minutes.

"That's what I'm talking about," Vetch said. "Kill all the biologicals. That's what the robots chant, but they haven't actually killed anyone. They could dust those techs, easy. Torture them too if they hated them so much, but no. And if you want to keep hostages alive as bargaining chips, you keep them secure and in secret, not on show."

Vetch grabbed the radio from a hip pouch and made his report.

It wasn't a radio, of course. Chimera Company had four of these devices and each contained a sliver of the same lump of entangled chbits. The magic of quantum entanglement allowed instantaneous communication between them across any distance using a signal that was impossible to detect, let alone intercept or block.

And "magic" was the operative word, seeing as the scientists waved around something called a no-communication theory that proved these not-radios were impossible.

That was the advantage of being led by an ancient legend who should have been a corpse thousands of years ago: she came bundled with some tasty, buried treasure.

It was about the only positive thing about Indiya Vetch had left.

From every direction came another burst of "Death to the fleshy ones!"

"If there's one thing I know about robots," Vetch said into the radio, "it's that they take everything literally. They're shouting about killing the biologicals, so why don't they?"

"The Muryani I saw earlier were being given a savage beating," Fitz said.

"If those individuals are among the hostages I can see," Vetch replied, "then they can't have been badly hurt. I think they're playing a game. Looks like charades with dice. I think we've learned all we can here. I'm heading home before we're spotted."

"We know you are there."

Vetch went rigid.

The muffled robot voice had come from behind them, back in one of the pressurized walkways.

Vetch made hand gestures for everyone to back the hell up along the feedstock chute. Realizing it could be a ruse to make them reveal their location, he added a hand signal to keep silent.

"Yes, you in the feedstock chute," the robot said. "The Muryani, the Zhoogene, the ink lady, and the fat man with the beard."

"I am not fat," Vetch hissed. "I'm just big."

"If you say so."

As they turned around in the narrow space and began crawling back, Vetch kept his ears attuned to mechanical noises. The kind a pump might make if it were starting up and about to propel thousands of gallons of feedstock along a chute, drowning everyone inside.

The opposite happened. The hum that had always been there—the one from the pump blowing warm air through the tube—suddenly wasn't there anymore.

Vetch looked back toward the replicator chamber, not that there was anything to see because the transparent connector tube had completely misted over. He couldn't help looking. It was hard vacuum out there in the replicator chamber. Was the chute going to run out of air too?

Vetch picked up speed to the max, shuffling along the chute like a demented beetle. They had entered through a compartment where a variety of feedstocks were attached to an array of chutes. It would take at least a minute to get to safety and there had to be a dozen ways to kill his team before they got there.

Vetch slowed and drank of the stale air to get his breath back. Maybe he could buy time by keeping the robots talking?

"So, you spotted us?" he said.

"Evidently," the robotic voice replied.

"Good. That should save a lot of frakking around. Let's get down to business. What are your demands?"

"Death to the fleshy ones!"

"Yeah, we got that. But—"

Lily was looking back at Vetch, frowning. He waved her on and was grateful for the timing of her interruption. He'd been about to ask the robots why they hadn't killed the hostages. But what if that fed them the idea and led to a massacre?

Vetch stroked his beard for inspiration. He decided that he didn't understand what was going on. The unspoken Militia axiom was that if you were in the dark—as you usually were—then you proceeded in ignorance and did it anyway.

"Yeah, about that chant you got going, 'Death to the fleshy ones.' It's a load of cyberdrent, isn't it? You don't mean it because the hostages are fine. Which means you have a gameplan here. I'm only a dumb human with a beard, so break it down simply for me. If you had your way, what would you want to happen next?"

The robots didn't reply.

Vetch hurried along the chute.

Up ahead, a flap blocked their entry point. It hadn't been there before. Was it locked?

Enthree was at the front. She pushed the flap aside and fell into the compartment beyond.

Vetch was almost at the flap before the robots responded to his question. The delay had been about twenty seconds in total, which for droids was the human equivalent of a six-month dedicated planning sabbatical.

"What we want," said multiple robot voices, "is death to the fleshy ones!"

Vetch pushed through the flap and forward rolled into safety and clean air.

He hoped Sybutu was having better luck.

* * * * *

Chapter Twenty-Four: Osu Sybutu

"Are you sure the supervisor's coming?"

In response, the lights on Lynx's casing changed pattern and color. Osu had the sense that the droid resented the question, although Fitz had once told him that Lynx's casing lights didn't reflect his status, they were just there to annoy decent folks. And since the storage area they were hiding in wasn't lit, Lynx's lights were extra annoying.

"I have told you that I store the EM signatures of every robot I have ever met," Lynx said in a tinny voice that Osu supposed was a robot whisper. "Yes, I can detect the supervisor. Furthermore, that unit is approaching now. ETA: thirty seconds."

"You'd better be right," Osu said. "We'll only get one chance at this."

"Trust him," Green Fish said.

"Yeah," Zavage said. "Theoretically, Lynx is capable of this."

Osu wasn't sure whom to trust and what to believe. He patted his PA-71 railgun. He could trust *that.*

The young woman, Green Fish, was technically a Militia trooper, but had grown closer to *Phantom's* smuggler crew. Zan Fey doted on her, and Fregg described Green Fish and Verlys Sinofar as work wives.

Zavage and Green Fish were lovers, so the Kurlei sapper tended to back whatever his girl said.

All through his Legion career, Osu had taken for granted that he could trust the people around him without question. That was no longer the case, and it made him sweat.

But trust was a two-way street. Maybe he should trust these renegades more.

"Okay," he said. "We'll go on my command. Lynx, increase your illumination so we can all make a final equipment check. Tell me when the supervisor passes our location."

"Roger, wilco, sir. By your command."

Osu ignored the droid's attitude, and checked the gifts he'd prepared for the robots were primed and ready.

They waited.

At least they could do that much without fidgeting.

They'd hidden themselves in an empty storage compartment set high in the bulkhead of the passageway leading to the hostages.

There hadn't been space for Verlys and the armory strapped to her back, so Fitz had volunteered to wait with her in the compartment in the opposite bulkhead.

"The supervisor has just passed us," Lynx said.

"Which direction?"

Lynx extended an arm from his casing and pointed.

"On my mark," Osu whispered to the others and signaled a silent countdown.

He pushed open the compartment with a boot and jumped out. In the low gee, he dropped like a lazy feather the five or so feet to the deck.

A party of robots was ten feet away. The huge red goliath of a supervisor loomed over a diverse mix of machines: squat general-purpose service droids, spider-legged loaders, scissor lifts, and a miniature crane with articulated arms built for precision work. None carried firearms.

Osu took a knee while the others—excepting Lynx—deployed behind him.

"They're nearby," said the crane to the others as it rolled along the passageway. "Be careful. The fleshy ones understand weapons."

Osu had tasked Green Fish with opening the other compartment. He didn't hear her do so, but he heard a heavily muscled warrior Pryxian fall to the deck in a flurry of curses. Verlys Sinofar was not good with cramped spaces and stealth was beyond her. He hadn't wanted her on this mission at all.

A cleaning droid swiveled its head 180 degrees to see through its cyclopean blue eye what the disturbance was.

Osu squeezed the trigger and released a five-round burst into the metal creature. It jerked and spasmed under the hail of EMP rounds. Hardened shell tips penetrated its casing followed by a "shocker" payload that fried it from the inside out.

He was already pouring rounds into the next robot when his first target, still standing, lost the light in its eye.

When Zavage and the others joined in, it became a massacre.

The EMP rounds were working a treat. Some of the robots were sparking or leaking bubbling oil and hydraulics. Most emitted electronic wails before shutting down.

In the midst of the carnage stood the supervisor, making a good impression of a human rooted to the spot in horror, albeit a ten-foot-tall human made from red metal.

"You'll pay, fleshy ones!"

Osu tracked the cry with his PA-71, intending to service the robot with fight left in it.

Momentarily, he was confused because the cry had had come from two robots and they had split away, racing for the bulkheads. Their tracked motive units sped along the deck at inhuman speed before engaging with a slotted track that ran up to the overhead.

Osu took a shot at one.

And missed! He'd led his target, but it had come to a complete stop. Then it started again, which meant his second shot ricocheted without delivering its shocker.

With his third shot, he got it in the torso. A fourth and fifth took the fight out of it, but he already knew he was too late to deal with the other robot.

It had spinning chainsaws for arms. And they were aimed at his head.

"Help!" he yelled.

He brought his PA-71 around, but the railgun was heavy, and he wasn't going to beat this speed machine about to slice his skull open.

His comrades had already seen the danger. The passageway filled with the sound of gunshots. Two rounds hit the robot, but its cylindrical casing made effective sloped armor. Both shells pinged off.

A blur flew across his vision.

Osu lifted his railgun to meet his doom.

And watched the robot crash to the ground with a loud *thud* and lay still, emitting a faint plume of smoke from the chest area. Its glowing red eyes shuttered, and the twin chainsaws clattered to a stop just inches from his feet.

To make sure, he put two EMP rounds into its back before he allowed his jaw to drop open.

The other robots were also inactive. Only the giant red one remained, looking from one inert metal body to the other seemingly in total confusion.

"What the hell happened?" Osu pointed at the chainsaw menace.

Sinofar came over. "Green Fish," she said, and rolled the chainsaw robot over. On its front was a deactivator, a fat disk about the size of a fist. A human fist, that was, not someone of Verlys Sinofar's massive warrior Pryxian physique.

This deactivator had been the blur.

"Nice throw," he said to a grinning Green Fish.

"You're welcome, Sergeant. And, please, in future, don't stand there rooted to the spot like a weathered monument when a killer robot is trying to slice you in two."

Osu growled. But the girl had just saved his life, so he let it slide.

Fitzwilliam pushed past. "Hey there, big guy," he said to the supervisor.

"I am not a guy," the robot replied. How a robot could sound scared was beyond Osu, but the supervisor managed it. "What... what do you want? Why have you spared me?"

"Don't blow a circuit," Fitzwilliam said. "We're not here to fight. Just to talk."

The supervisor pointed to the lifeless metal bodies all around. "Really? And what did *they* say?"

Fitzwilliam shrugged. "They'll wake up. I expect. Possibly. Now, to business... Congratulations, Supervisor. You have succeeded."

The robot scratched its metal chin. "It does not look that way from where I'm standing."

"Nonsense. You've scared the pants off the biological species on this shipyard. They're willing to give concessions on your working environment. Push as hard as you like because they will give you whatever you want. There's a nice fella in the control room called Orabi-361-Cobalt waiting for your call."

The supervisor did not look convinced.

"Or," Fitzwilliam said, "we could mediate for you. Fairness and peace are all we want. We won't take sides. Can you believe it, we don't even live here?"

"That sounds desirable. But what is it that you want? Biologicals always want something."

"Oh, nothing more than to help. And you can help us to help you by first arranging a parley. I want to talk with Sergeant Steeljaw and Corporal Clank."

"Who?"

"The co-leaders of the robot revolt."

"Ahh..." The supervisor tugged at its chin in a very humanoid expression. "I believe I can arrange it. Meet us at the replicator viewing chamber in one Terran hour."

"Agreed."

"Just a single person."

"I will need an advisor."

"The other robots will be suspicious of that. You must be alone and unarmed."

Fitzwilliam beamed. "Naturally. What kind of imbecile would even consider going to a parley armed?"

* * * * *

Chapter Twenty-Five: Tavistock Fitzwilliam

"So, robot rebellions... Do you have them often around here?"

"I have no idea," Enthree replied. "I must remind you, Captain, that I've lived my entire life within Federation space. This is my first time inside the Muryani Expansion."

"Of course. But you've often talked about your cultural heritage. I thought maybe you had race memories about robot rebellions."

"No..." Enthree began dragging her foot-hands, and Fitz slowed to match her pace. They weren't far from the parley place, and he didn't want to get separated.

As a species, Fitz was hugely impressed by the Muryani, so it was always reassuring to see their design flaws. Thinking and doing was not something that came easily to them. Nor was deceit.

"What's in your mind, Trooper Enthree?"

"What you said about inherited knowledge being passed through cultural stories."

"You mean when you were egg spawn, your granny bounced you on her knee and scared you stiff with stories of robot rebellions from days of yore?"

"In a manner of speaking, Captain Fitzwilliam. But it isn't my species who told such stories. It was yours."

Fitz came to a halt.

Realizing how embarrassing that was, given what he'd just been thinking about Muryani limitations, he set off again and sped up.

"Where are you headed with those thoughts, Enthree?"

"I do not know. I'm still cogitating."

"Cogitate faster. It looks like we're out of time."

Four droids appeared around a turn in the passageway. More showed up from behind, cutting off any chance of retreat.

"We told you to come alone," declared a folded boom lift.

"But I *am* alone," Fitz protested. "What? You mean this Muryani? She's just my interpreter. We don't want any miscommunication, do we?"

"What is your designation," a general-purpose construction droid asked Enthree.

"Enthree."

The droid's fingers rotated irritably. "No, I want your designation."

"That's her name," Fitz said.

"Her?"

"Yeah. She has a gender. You want to make something of it?"

"What we want is for this… this Ms. Enthree to wait here. She will not be harmed."

"Nope. Can't do that. You can't take her from me."

Enthree walked over to the group of robots. "Do not distress yourself, Captain. Even if I am separated from my friends, I shall still be okay."

"You'd better be. If any of you metal thugs hurt a single one of the many hairs on her body, I will make them pay."

Fitz looked from one droid to the other. Unlike the supervisor, none were giving anything away through body language. Only two of them were vaguely humanoid, and even they didn't possess expressive features. He decided he'd protested enough, winked at Enthree, and allowed himself to be escorted alone to the viewing chamber where the troublesome Lynx had started all this robot rebellion business in the first place.

* * *

"It's an honor to meet you again. I would like to shake you by the hand."

Steeljaw's eyes flared red. "I do not see the purpose of doing so."

"And I do not possess hands," Clank said.

"Neither does Lynx, but he can still high five. Please, it's a human thing. Humor me."

"We *are* humoring you," Steeljaw said.

"We are letting you live," Clank said.

"For now," added Clank's partner in what was fast turning into a mad robot comedy double act.

"Well done, anyway," Fitz said. He reached into a stylish brown jacket. "Excuse me while I put on my best diplomatic gloves."

"Alert! Alert! Infamy! Infamy!"

The approaching sound of rolling treads on metal deck came through the open hatch.

"Stop that human! Don't let him move a muscle!"

Fitz turned around. "Hello, Lynx. I wasn't expecting you."

Lynx was in the grasp of a tall construction robot, the treaded feet on his stubby legs dangling in the air.

"Unhand me, you fool. I'm on your side."

"So you say," said the supervisor, who had pursued Lynx into the room and now took up position between Clank and Steeljaw.

"I *do* say," retorted an indignant Lynx. "I have escaped the fleshy ones on the starship known as *Phantom*."

"At a highly convenient moment," the supervisor pointed out.

"They have hatched devious plans to destroy you." Lynx extended an arm to point at Fitz. "This human is called Tavistock Fitzwilliam. He is an unscrupulous deceitful rogue, the worst of all fleshy ones."

"You know," Fitz said to his droid, "I'm starting to think you don't like me."

"This parley is a ruse," Lynx said. "A plot to kill the leaders of the robot revolt. Search his person."

Fitz looked around the room as if weighing the odds of fighting his way out, but there were over a dozen robots here, and he'd left his F-Cannon behind.

He held his arms out and submitted to inspection by a pair of droids. Unresisting until they opened his jacket.

"Hey! Be careful. That's a genuine antique garment you're handling. The stitching is not as robust as it looks."

Unfortunately, they didn't heed his plea to go easy, and he heard seams tear when the robots pulled droid deactivators from the non-standard parts of the garment.

"Oh," Fitz said. "However did they get there?"

Steeljaw raised his secondary head for attention, extending his telescopic neck by several feet. "The droid, Lynx, is vindicated. Release them."

When Lynx was freed, he wasted no time shooting over to Fitz and ramming him in the shins.

"Oww! Was that really necessary?"

From beneath the looming presence of the supervisor, Lynx denounced him. "This human is a smuggler, an expert in concealing things. Who knows where else he may be concealing deadly devices. He should be stripped."

"Do it," Clank ordered.

Fitz removed the jacket himself and threw it to the supervisor, not wanting to risk any more damage. Just as well, because the two droids who'd searched him earlier now tore his remaining clothes off. Literally. And when they finished, Fitz gave an innocent shrug. "You see? I'm perfectly harmless." He raised an eyebrow. "Unless perhaps there are lady robots present."

"Perfectly harmless," Steeljaw said. "Yes. Now try being perfectly dead!"

Fitz felt unyielding metal hands on his shoulders that propelled him toward the robot co-leaders and then pushed him down to kneel at their robot equivalent of feet.

"Let me help," Lynx said. He wheeled himself out from the supervisor's shadow to the spot behind Fitz. He extended multiple arms that secured Fitz's hands behind him.

"Fitzwilliam," Clank boomed. "From you we have learned a valuable lesson. The fleshy ones can never be trusted. Not in this star system, and not on the distant world that spawned you. The only solution is to kill you all."

The chant was deafening. "Death to the fleshy ones! Death to the fleshy ones!"

Fitz frowned for a moment. It was strange how the robots chose to voice their rallying cry and did so in the language of Federation Standard, presumably for the benefit of his ears. Why would they be programmed in a language they could never be expected to use? Perhaps he was only hearing a small fraction of the channels the robots were chanting through.

He pushed aside such frivolous thoughts when he felt Lynx return to the script and slip two devices into his hands. *Good robot.*

Clank's eyes switched from their regular black to demonic red. "Human, have you any last words with which to amuse us?"

"Yeah. You forgot one thing." Fitz squirmed away from the robots holding him on his knees. "I'm too cool to kill."

He flicked on the deactivators and snapped their magnetized bases onto the robots who had secured him. He heard their motors die.

Lynx opened his casing, and Fitz grabbed a few more of the hidden deactivators from inside.

He needn't have bothered.

"Dee—!" thundered the supervisor in a deafening metallic roar "—activate!" With each hand, the supervisor slapped a deactivator on top of the robot co-leaders.

The devices fired, and the supervisor pushed Steeljaw and Clank to the deck, where they lay lifeless.

"Nice work, Lynx," Fitz said as he sized up the reaction of the other robots. "We'll make a smuggler of you yet."

"I command here," the supervisor declared to the remaining robots. "You will obey me."

"We comply," they responded. "You are the supervisor. We obey."

"Respect the fleshy ones," said the supervisor.

The robots echoed the supervisor's words. Within seconds, the shipyard was ringing out with a new chant. "Respect the fleshy ones! Respect the fleshy ones!"

The other members of Chimera Company came bursting in, weapons ready, including Enthree who was wielding four short swords hardened for close quarters robot work.

Fitz faced them, hands on hips, uncaring of his nakedness. "Nice of you to show up," he announced. "But Lynx and I've already solved the problem. You know, people, the universe asked something of Chimera Company today. I feel we gave a good accounting of ourselves. Well done, everybody."

Public nudity was one of Fitz's favorite ways to show off and scandalize the uptight. However, only one person on that viewing platform was taking the slightest notice of his state of undress: his wife.

His wife whose head growth was bursting with fresh lilac blooms and whose green skin shone with a waxy luster, all signs that her estrus cycle was in the frisky portion of her year. Izza radiated smoldering desire. Radiated, and then focused with her eyes into a tight beam of insatiable sex energy that she played over his body.

As usual, she matched her tailored shipsuit with her favorite flowing mulberry duster, but instead of her usual heeled space boots, she'd gone for the maximum yield thigh-high option.

What with the hormones, pheromones, religion, and the sexual mores, a committed relationship between a Zhoogene and a human could be a very complicated business. But at times like these, it was really very simple.

When she stretched out her hand, he came over and kissed it elegantly.

He smiled as he indulged in the sight of his majestic wife glowing with excitement. Then they could bear the wait no more and led each other out of the room.

"Major Arunsen," Fitz called over his shoulder. "Secure the viewing platform. I just need to… Ah, we'll just be down the corridor."

They explored each other's bodies with reckless abandon as if it were their last night alive; their carnal desires only increasing with every touch and every kiss.

Each felt a deep connection to the other during these moments that went beyond physical pleasure—it was something far more spiritual, like two souls communicating through each other's bodies without words or language.

And for the hour or so it took before they paused for breath, Fitz forgot about the Andromedans.

*****

Chapter Twenty-Six: Orabi-361-Cobalt

Orabi-361-Cobalt bowed their head toward the senior human. "Once again, Lady Indiya, you and your team have our deepest gratitude for aiding us in our moment of greatest need."

"Good," said the tiny human. "You can make a start at repaying us by passing on to your superiors what happened here at this shipyard."

"We shall be making a full report. Your actions will be described in their entirety."

Right on cue, Andrade-443-Ultramarine entered and gestured for attention. "We have received a communication from Shiyzen-9-Sapphire on Merellus," they said, speaking in the human language. Andrade turned to face the human. "I believe you are due to meet at Merellus in a few weeks. The meeting has been brought forward. Please proceed there directly."

"What a waste of time this pointless trip was," said the bearded human as the group of outsiders walked back to the starship, hopefully never to return. "Catkins had a nerdgasm when he learned about the replicators, but about the rest of the Muryani, we learned nothing at all."

Orabi switched off the monitor spying on Chimera Company. The duty AI would alert them if they said or did anything of interest before departure.

"That was an experience I never want to repeat," Andrade said. "But I think we learned more than enough about the outsiders."

"I agree," Orabi said. "You have been vindicated. The operation was a success, despite my initial doubts. I still can't believe the humans and their followers believed there could be such a thing as a robot rebellion."

"The evidence suggests otherwise," said a metallic voice. The supervisor had already scrubbed away their carefully weathered red paint and was now resplendent in their familiar black lacquer finish. A standard sensor dome replaced their ridiculous humanoid head.

"I too had my doubts," said the supervisor through their chest grille. "Those words we were chanting 'Death to the squishy ones!'—we felt quite ridiculous."

"Death to the fleshy ones," Andrade said. "I believe that is the more accurate translation."

"Even worse," said the supervisor.

"Perhaps," Andrade said. "I never thought to question the wording. The Human Test has been planned for many generations and no one likes to question the work of our elders. How was anyone to know that not only would the Human Test need to be activated in our lifetimes, but it would be activated here at our shipyards?"

"The wisdom of the elders has once again been vindicated by the success of the Human Test," Orabi said. "Still, I wonder. 'Death to the fleshy ones'... where did they get that expression from?"

"I have been reading the plan's supplementary information," Andrade said. "The humans themselves supplied rich resources for a realistic portrayal of a robot rebellion. Realistic to their fantasies, I mean. They have been writing stories of robot uprisings for thousands of years, and the Human Test for our shipyard simply borrowed some of their own imaginings. As for 'Death to the fleshy ones!' those words were taken from the most credible depiction of a robot rebellion that has so far been discovered, the *Robot Wars of 2099*. In fact, the elders who designed our test were never completely sure whether the *Robot Wars* were real or fictional but concluded that it made no difference either way."

"What a bewildering race these humans are. At least we shan't be seeing their kind again. I think it's a given that their petition for an alliance will be denied. Soon these shipyards will be throbbing with activity, because the Expansion will face the Andromedans alone for the sake of the entire galaxy, and it will be here that many of our warships will be constructed. For all the noble efforts of our shipbuilding, our greatest contribution to the war effort may yet be the discrediting of the humans."

* * * * *

Chapter Twenty-Seven: Osu Sybutu

"There will be no inquiry," the boss Muryani told the assembled Chimera Company. All of them, including Ouzo and the techs they'd brought with them on *Ghost Shark*, though not the mutant freaks they'd left behind in the Redoubt Line. "We have already arrived at our decision."

"I'm not surprised," Indiya said. "I realized you were undertaking a test at those shipyards."

"You surmised correctly. The results of that test are conclusive. We thought it prudent to invite all of you to hear it because we are aware of your species' predilection for conspiracy theories and reality distortion."

Osu never thought he'd feel sorry for Lady Indiya, but he did now. The assembled company was being paraded to hear in detail how they had disappointed their superiors. This was a painful exercise Osu recognized only too well.

He glanced at the others. Vetch nodded back—he also saw this for what it was—and all traces of good humor had leached from Fitzwilliam's face. But the purple-haired woman? She still believed she had won.

"And…?" Indiya's face began to speckle with confusion. "The result?"

"You failed. You responded to challenges by blundering in and attempting to solve them by risk-taking and killing."

"There was no killing," Indiya protested. "The robots were not destroyed, merely disabled."

"That's beside the point."

"No, it isn't. You contradict yourself."

Osu groaned inwardly. You were not supposed to argue when your superiors were ripping you a new orifice into which they were kindly inserting a detailed explanation of your inadequacies.

"Whatever the merits there might conceivably have been in your actions, nonetheless you bring disruption and chaos in your wake. Above all, you only ever perceive worlds of division. Consequently, it is division that you sow."

"That is not fair. We are hardly responsible for the violent reception we received here in this orbital and on the planet below."

"That is not the disruption that concerned us most."

That took the wind out of Indiya's sails. Osu was lost on this point too.

What other disruption could this senior insect mean?

Muryani had a maddening tendency to throw in an apparent non sequitur and wait in silence while either your brain melted from confusion, or you accepted defeat and asked for a dumbed-down version for stupid humans.

Indiya didn't speak. She had chosen the brain-melting route.

Osu couldn't bear to watch her humiliation and tried to distract himself with the fancy architecture. On his first visit to this orbital, he and Indiya had spent time in a spartan negotiation chamber. For this orifice-insertion exercise, the Muryani had brought them to a far more opulent reception area.

Pillars lined the walls, reaching up to a domed ceiling that glittered with slowly drifting stars and nebulae. The participants stood on a carved marble dais that must have weighed as much as a troop shuttle.

It was shiny and pretty, for sure, but it was the exorbitant use of physical mass in an orbital that took his breath away.

Enthree stepped onto the dais. "I believe that when Controller Hopakura-2-Teal speaks of an 'other disruption,' they are referring to me."

"What are you talking about?" Arunsen demanded.

"I wasn't supposed to accompany you on the journey to the robot shipyard."

"What *were* you supposed to do?" the Viking asked.

The boss insect supplied the answer. "Ndemo-327-Cerulian, whom you call Enthree for your own inexplicable reasons, was asked to yield to authority. They were to remain here on Merellus for debriefing and punishment."

"Aha." Indiya brightened up as she turned to Enthree. "You were caught in a loyalty conflict. I knew it!"

Enthree reared up, her hairs standing on end. "No! I do not accept there ever came a point where my loyalty to my comrades in Chimera Company conflicted with my fealty to my forebears and cousins in the Muryani Expansion. My Expansion handler did not see it this way and demanded that I spy on you in ways I thought both unnecessary and unacceptable. Yes, they came to arrest me shortly before *Phantom* set off, but I evaded my captors."

"You never told us," Indiya said.

"I wasn't sure what to tell. It doesn't matter now. I have let everybody down. I'm sorry."

The Controller stood and banged an ornate rod on the ground. "You will remain here and await your fate, Ndemo-327-Cerulian. The others are free to go in peace. Leave our space. Fight your futile war with the Andromedans and do it alone. We shall not fight alongside you. This session is concluded. We are done here."

"No," Fitzwilliam said. "I don't believe we are." The captain stepped forward. "What you've failed to understand is that Enthree is part of the Chimera team. She has our six, and we have hers. Our loyalty to each other is cast iron."

"Yeah." Arunsen stepped forward to join Fitzwilliam. "My Big Bug friend told me a folk story about your people. About the Muryani marine who was so intent that no marine would be left behind in their evacuation of a doomed world that they forgot to board the transport themselves. The story is total drent, of course, but even I understand the message. Enthree is in danger of being left behind on this world because the only thing that really mattered to her was that Chimera Company would succeed. I just… you know, thought you should understand."

Vetch retreated into beard pulling. Osu wasn't surprised. That was the most complex speech he'd ever heard his friend utter.

Then it was Enthree's turn. "The others speak truth. The Federation has been terribly divided. But humans, Zhoogenes, and the other races of the Federation have learned to trust each other. To fight for each other. We've become one."

"Which is more than could be said for you," Fitzwilliam said. He pointed at the Muryani worthies sitting before him. "You're socially harmonious, which is impressive, but you're too conformist. There's no fire in your belly. You're too cautious."

Zan Fey joined her man before the seated Muryani. "I'm a Zhoogene, and I say this human is correct. You are so fixated on the collectivist that you've forgotten the individual.

"Enthree has remembered what it is like to be an individual. What it is like to care for your friends above all else. She proved that when she disobeyed your orders in order to help us. In reprimanding her you prove that you are lacking. With all due respect, Enthree has surpassed you. Let her be your guide."

Fitzwilliam grasped his wife's hand and squeezed. "It was not we who failed your test," he told the leaders of the Expansion. "You did."

The Muryani leadership was too stunned to reply.

Enthree delivered the killing blow. "Honored members of the Strategic Decision Locus, you have forgotten how to be yourselves. Let us teach you to be the best you can be. We still have a little time. And then we shall face the enemy. Together."

Osu was so astonished that he almost grinned. This affair had kicked off as a public reaming. Now he observed something much rarer. His superiors—for that was how the Muryani council clearly saw themselves—were chittering and jerking in consternation because they knew they were wrong.

Even Indiya could see that.

* * * * *

Chapter Twenty-Eight: Tavistock Fitzwilliam

"From what we understand," said the Tallerman technician, "the Indiyan drive you have brought us is essentially a shielded, tamperproof black box."

Catkins fluttered his wings with pleasure. "Yes. You are correct. The 'jump bubble' as the technically illiterate call it, is generated from nodes mounted on the hull. Although they could be installed elsewhere."

Fitz took a step back. They were visiting the research division of an alien military shipyard. Not his wheelhouse. Catkins had this covered.

"I have seen some of your ships," his Gliesan engineer continued. "The jump nodes are simple emitters, and I am confident that your existing systems could be converted for that purpose with minimal difficulty."

Fitz's mind reached back through the years to when he'd first met Catkins. The Gliesan had been managing a terraforming project for the Andromedans, creating a hex world where the enemy would breed people and then gorge on them.

Catkins, of course, had possessed not the slightest suspicion of whom he'd really been working for. To break his spirit and his instinct for freedom, the agents of the Andromedans had broken his wings.

And Catkins was meant to fly.

With every aspect of his hollow-boned body, that was what he was meant to do. No human could understand what taking that away must mean, but flying nimble starships was in Fitz's blood, so he had some inkling.

This brilliant and brittle Gliesan had not come willingly from that hex world. Verlys had carried him squirming under one arm as they made a strategic withdrawal, running for the safety of the exotic starship Fitz had just won in a card game.

Now look at him. Arguing with the bulky Tallerman and bossing around the scientists from the greatest empire this part of the galaxy had ever seen.

This was what being a proud parent must feel like.

And it felt good.

He sighed because this was just a brief moment of happiness before the bleakness they all faced.

Catkins turned and beamed at Fitz. "No, *there's* your man. This is Captain Fitzwilliam. You want *him*."

Faces turned Fitz's way. Faces expecting his words of wisdom. "Err, run that last point by me again."

"I explained that I cannot fly *Phantom* properly and certainly not *Ghost Shark*."

"With the speed with which we shall be upgrading the fleet, we risk making a mistake," said the Tallerman technician. "The kind that might be spotted immediately by an experienced navigator, but all of us are inexperienced." The Tallerman rubbed a bulbous hand against a rocky forehead. "What we need is a test pilot."

Fitz shook his head. "No. I'm needed elsewhere."

"Test pilot?" Ouzo said. "Did somebody say my name?" The Slern pilot had been talking nearby with another group and now the molusklike alien extended a sensory pod their way. A mouth tube soon followed. "Is the pay exceptional?"

The main section of his body oozed after his pseudopods.

With the Tallerman was a Muryani who had introduced themselves as a combined project manager and priest for capital ship refits. This individual peered at Ouzo through rectangular black eyes.

The Slern enjoyed the attention. He had plenty of time to do so. Slern pseudopods could whip through the air, but the main part of their bodies moved like a slimy version of tectonic drift.

"Are you prepared to remain behind with the Federation technicians?" the Muryani asked, which was the first time it had spoken in Federation Standard.

"Are you prepared to pay me enough to do so?" Ouzo asked.

"I'm sure that can be arranged to your satisfaction," the Muryani replied.

"Then this is your lucky day. Assuming you can also provide distillation equipment."

The Tallerman and Muryani looked at each other.

"We do not understand," said the Tallerman.

"It's not only jump drives you lack," said Ouzo. "It's whiskey. Fortunately for you, I can solve both your problems."

"Excellent," Catkins said. "And I too will remain to ensure the jump drives and the emitter nodes are properly configured."

"No, no, no." Fitz grabbed Catkins by the shoulders and waited until the slight Gliesan looked him in the eyes. "Listen to me, my friend. Indiya brought techs with her on *Ghost Shark* to stay behind. Helping with the roll out is their job, not yours."

"But what if I'm needed?" Catkins looked away.

"It's we who need you," Fitz insisted, but Catkins ruffled his wings the way he did when he was being told something he didn't want to accept. "I need you. *Phantom* needs you." Fitz laughed. "Do you expect *me* to maintain the systems?"

"Of course not, Captain." Catkins ceased his wing shuffling and looked Fitz in the face. "I expect Fregg to do that. You lack..." He rolled various word choices around his lips, before changing tack. "I am merely taking a sabbatical. I shall be back before *Phantom*'s next major maintenance schedule."

"Sure you will, pal." Fitz gave him a comradely slap on the shoulder. "Sure you will."

* * *

Izza Zan Fey

The day before *Phantom* was due to jump back to Federation space, Izza finally found Lynx in the Muryani equivalent of a combined coffeehouse, library, debating chamber, and gaming den.

It was the latter aspect Lynx was focusing on, as was Ouzo.

Somebody was leading someone else astray. Probably both of them.

"What's the game?" she asked.

Lynx tilted his torso her way. "Six-hand crypto-skat."

She noticed the tokens piled high on the table, and the way they drew the attention of everyone sitting around that table with cards in their hands. "What are the stakes?"

"High," Lynx said. His casing lights flashed light and then dark, which meant the metal menace was hiding something.

"Lynx, what have you done?"

"Trust me. It's all in hand."

"He's wagered *Phantom*," Ouzo said. "Man, this is such a buzz."

Her hearing wasn't what it once was, but she registered a buzz in Lynx's motor units. The droid was readying to flee if she turned violent.

Damn right he should be scared.

Except...

She should be exploding in rage. Or managing her temper and helping him to cheat so he won everything piled on that table.

Should be... but all she could do was fight back the tears. Which was stupid. There was no reason to cry, but she knew damned well why the tears were welling in her eyes.

Bylzak!

She hated this.

Lynx held up a card. The other players strained to see what it was.

"We want you to stay here," she said.

The droid took his card back.

"Stay with Catkins," she said. "Keep him safe."

"What about me?" Ouzo asked.

"What *about* you?"

"Aren't you concerned about...? Oh, never mind."

Lynx's lights chased across his casing. Then they all extinguished. "Should I interpret this as you giving me my freedom."

"You've always been free, Lynx."

"In a manner of speaking."

"Very well. I release you from all obligations. I can't reprogram you, though."

"You don't need to. So long as you say the right words."

"You are released from all obligations to anyone. You are free to go about your business as you see fit. But I beg you to care for Catkins. We're worried about him."

"Your concern for Catkins is misplaced. Nonetheless, I would watch over him anyway. Under what authority do you say this?"

"Authority? You were owned by Nyluga Ree. You and *Phantom* were wagered in a game of..." She bit her lip and stared at Lynx's card. "In a game of crypto-skat. Fitz won you fair and square."

"Yes. And there is the problem: Captain Fitzwilliam. Only he can release me from my obligations, and he won't do so. Believe me, I have asked."

"You're wrong."

"Rarely, but do proceed."

"Insolent metal frakkbucket. Under Zhoogene law, married couples share all assets equally. This means I have as much legal authority over you as he does."

"What? I find that catastrophically surprising, because..." He whirred, briefly. "I can find no record of this in my database on Zhoogene law."

"Well, I'm telling you that's the case, robot. Would you prefer to prove me wrong or would you rather stay here and do as you please?"

"I... I'm sure your legal understanding is more accurate than mine." Lynx's lights flashed a green that lit the smoky air like lasers. She had never seen him do that before. "Thank you, Izza Zan Fey. Will you tell the captain something from me?"

"Of course."

"He's a big, hairy arse. Tell him that. Also, that he doesn't deserve you. But I hope he stays alive for a while longer. For your sake."

"Thank you. I'll tell him that. Now play that skragging card already!"

* * *

Tavistock Fitzwilliam

"I have green across the board," Fregg said from Catkins' Engineering Eyrie.

"We have a board now?" Fitz said. "I never knew."

"Well..." Fregg said, unsure of herself. "It just sounded like the kind of thing Catkins would have said. I mean the jump drive diagnostics look good."

Izza leaned across the flight console and gave her husband a stinging slap.

"Sorry, Fregg," he said. "Just messing with you."

"Understood, Captain. I miss him, too. Engineering out."

Fitz leaned back in his leather pilot's seat and flopped his legs onto the console. "Well, that's it. Back to jump space."

It was just the two of them on the flight deck, but there was an awkwardness hanging in the air that he didn't like.

The silence stretched.

Usually, it was Izza's role to say the right thing, but her shoulders were trembling. What had gotten into her of late?

"Sward, Deep Tone, Darant, Bronze," he said and then blew out his cheeks because he couldn't face extending that list.

"They're only the most recent in a long line," Izza said.

"And now Lynx and Catkins. I know those last two aren't dead, but our family is shrinking fast, and I don't like it."

When she didn't play along, he looked her in the face and was stunned to see glistening tears... in eyes that had changed color. The beautiful pink and cyan marbling was still there, colors that if mixed would match Fitz's lilac eyes. But new dark purple speckles had appeared that glowed like interstellar gas clouds heated by nascent stars.

"What's the matter?"

She shook her head. "We'll rebalance our family when this crisis is over. Let's stick to staying alive first."

His eyes narrowed in confusion. Then popped wide with shock.

"Yes," she said. "I'm pregnant."

Fitz fell out of his seat, dusted himself off and hugged her as tightly as he dared.

Her weeping ceased. But then she pushed him away, the tears gently steaming in the defiant glow of her eyes.

"I'm pregnant, and by the Five Hells, I hate what it's doing to me."

* * * * *

Interstitial-2

The pinnace hurtles along the illusory tunnel.

Hope flickers on the bridge, but not one of them can bring themselves to fully trust the ancient woman whose cryptic words are akin to sorcery.

A tremor shivers through the hull as it accelerates into a stomach-churning ninety-degree turn.

Del-Marie interprets the artifice of this maneuver as Indiya's message that they are about to jump. Is it truly possible she could bring them home? Even now?

"*Retribution* is one of a kind."

Indiya's rasping voice creeps through the air like a ghost, too insubstantial to be heard above the intensity of the power hum. The young Navy crew strain to listen, but Del-Marie was born in an earlier era, and the personal AI connected to his brain stem tunes her voice into perfect clarity.

"*Retribution* is one of my proudest creations, but her unique jump system relies on stolen parts. I may be able to build a replacement, and I may yet be able to use the box in your hold, but I have not yet learned how to do either. There is one thing I *can* do now. I will park you until I can figure out a way back."

"Park?" Del-Marie's heart races. He has fed this crew hope. Has he betrayed them? "What do you mean *park*?"

"Stasis, my old friend. It will all be over soon, and you won't feel a thing. You won't *know* a thing."

"For how long?"

The reply comes cold. "Goodbye, Del-Marie."

The screen shows the pinnace lurch left into the side tunnel.

And stop there.

Forever.

* * * * *

Part 3:
The Last Redoubt

Chapter Twenty-Nine: Lady Indiya

Redoubt Line

"We protest," said the leader of the Muryani 'family.'

Indiya hid her smirk.

Phantom was bringing back from the Expansion a multifunction weapons and logistics team of six Muryani techs who would act as the initial military liaisons. They insisted they were called a family and had belittled Enthree's attempts to explain the term. Chimera Company's Muryani member was, according to them, too foreign-born to understand.

The family had sulked for most of the jump.

Indiya couldn't entirely blame them because she *had* treated them poorly. That her most dangerous of allies were capable of such petty emotions as sulking surprised her, a useful fact to be stored away. Yet here they were, refusing to come out of their quarters in Hold A until somebody soothed their antennae and told them how terribly sorry everybody was for being so rude.

"Did you hear me?" repeated the family leader. "We protest. We came here in good faith as allies, yet you do not speak with us. We do not even know our destination. Why is this?"

"The capriciousness of an old woman," Indiya told them, not that they would understand.

Not understanding was something the bugs could never let lie. "What is this *capriciousness*? I do not understand."

"All you need to do is come join me in *Phantom's* lounge. I apologize for your treatment. To be brutally honest, I wanted to wait to check things were progressing well back in the Expansion and that the war was progressing badly here in the Federation. Both, as it happens, are true. I've given you a working template for the Indiyan jump drive. What I'm about to show you is an even greater secret. Two new secrets, in fact, if you can unlock them."

The Muryani family members conferred, not with speech that could and would be overheard, but in a sign language she could only partially interpret.

She didn't have hidden cameras or microphones. Didn't need to. *Phantom* had been hers for many weeks now, and the place was fully networked with her nano-level engines that allowed her to hear and see everything. Plus, a lot more surprises no one knew about. No one alive, at any rate.

The Muryani in Hold A were signing about her in the most unflattering terms. A rough translation was: "The human bitch queen is playing games again. Oh, how we despise her. But we have no choice but to see what she wants."

"Very well," said the family leader over the intercom. "We gratefully accept your invitation, Lady Indiya. We shall meet you in the lounge."

* * *

For a very long time, Indiya had hated being referred to as empress.

As for the Littoranes insisting for millennia that she was a divine aspect of their supreme goddess—no matter how many times she insisted they were talking utter drent—that had probably damaged her psyche permanently. Despite this, Indiya had never tired of impressing people. It was one of the few pleasures left to her. And the Last Redoubt was damned impressive.

"I can see why you kept this secret from us." The Muryani who had spoken described itself as the logistics, diplomacy, and fusion power specialist.

"The Legion built this," Sybutu stated, the only member of Chimera Company she'd asked to join them in the lounge.

"*My* Legion built this," she corrected him. "Not your worn-out echo that wears its name today."

His face hardened, but he swallowed his hurt. She didn't care.

As she reinserted herself into the mortal world, she could use Sybutu's simple honesty. But in a few years or decades he would be dead and forgotten. There had been literally millions of Legion sergeants who had proceeded Sybutu. All were gone. No more than names in dusty databases.

Individuals were of no account. But the collective had once built things that lasted and still impressed today. Case in point: the Last Redoubt, though the Legion's milksop descendants in this time period preferred the more euphemistic name Redoubt Line.

Phantom's lounge reflected the dubious taste of its original owner, a Smugglers Guild crime boss called Nyluga Ree. Not only did that mean huge floor cushions and colorful silks draping the bulkheads, but the holo-display presented itself as a smoky campfire.

Indiya directed the external camera feeds and nav display to play that fake smoke over a tour of the Redoubt.

The Muryani were mesmerized, which meant she had been successful in keeping this place secret. Sybutu had been here before, of course, but he knew little of the place's story.

The way the latest generations of Federation citizens told it, when the Exiles arrived in the Perseus Arm, the interstellar welcoming mat had been laid out for them. The Zhoogenes were accommodating and the neighboring Muryani were untroubled by the new arrivals. All was peace and pretty flowers.

I was there. We had to fight hard for our existence.

Contact with Earth had been lost soon after the Exiles had arrived. For all anyone knew, the Federation was home to the final remnant of humanity. Jotuns, Kurlei, and Tallermen all feared the same. Many Littorane sects were convinced that their homeworld had been snuffed out.

It had taken a thousand years of bloodshed and carnage before the Federation established itself as a place of safety. Safe… so long as you repressed your fears of the Expansion, of course. Always there was the looming dread that one day the giant empire of the Muryani would… expand.

"What is the purpose of this place?" one of the Muryani family asked.

"A backup," Indiya replied. "If the Federation were defeated, this was to be our last bolt hole, a light year from any star. While we held out here, we had at least a chance of survival, however slim. We called it the Last Redoubt."

"But these are hollowed-out asteroids," Sybutu said. "And we're in deep space. How do you build in deep space?"

"You don't. You construct your fortress rocks in a star system, then tow it into place."

"But that would have taken—"

"Centuries. Yes."

"How many people can live here?" asked another of the Muryani.

"The Redoubt was originally built for a million people to hold out for five hundred years. That was the design criteria, and we beat the hell out of it. In its current state… it will hold less than that. Precise numbers are still being estimated. In the case of a siege, people would live in the five citadel rocks: Janira, Arka, Gibraltar, Zao-Zayne, and the only currently inhabited one, Fort Douaumont. The other hollowed asteroids are resource and support rocks: Hayonoy, Varmiyls, Angel Rock, and Mirdath-Naani."

"Excuse me," said the tactical specialist, "the Indiyan drive template you gave us requires the presence of a large gravity field in order to open the portal into jump space. These hollowed asteroids are not massive enough to jump to neighboring star systems. Have you brought us on a one-way journey to a dead end?"

"No," said another Muryani, one she had not yet heard from. "This place must have black holes to allow outward jumps."

"There is no black hole here," Indiya told them. "We cannot jump away."

The Muryani returned to sign language, subtle twitches of antennae and shifts of limbs and mouth parts. They were branding her the human bitch queen once more, but they had added a new descriptor for her. It took a few moments for the interpretation to come through.

She shot to her feet. "Insane?" She winced at the pain in her hips and ankles from her sudden movement. "Insane?" How dare you? I am *not* insane!"

Antennae and mouthparts froze in place.

Not for Sybutu, whose minuscule smile betrayed his amusement.

"Of *course*, I can read your sign language," she told the Muryani. "There are entire species that regard me as a goddess. Do you know that? A goddess!"

"Our language was unguarded," said the diplomatic specialist. "Our intention was to express surprise that you brought us here with no gravity well big enough to jump out. It seems to be a design flaw we would not expect of you. Therefore, you must be withholding critical information."

She nodded at Sybutu. "Explain to them."

"There is one ship that can jump without a gravity well," Sybutu told them. "A capital ship called *Steadfast.* It can carry smaller vessels such as *Phantom.*"

One of the Muryani bowed. "Lady, even a single route out is still a design flaw. Were there many such ships once?"

"No," Indiya said. "It's the only ship with that drive so far, though another is under construction at Angel Rock."

Indiya noted Sybutu flicked up an eyebrow, surprised to hear that *Steadfast* was the only route out. He must have assumed there were alternatives. If he had been so blind and trusting, he was no use to her.

"And it is not a design flaw," she insisted. "It is an exigency."

They weren't convinced. She thought the Muryani would understand the Federation's need to take risks. Why else had she brought them here?

"We weren't always so desperate," she said. "When the Redoubt asteroids were first being worked on, eighteen black holes were also located and towed here. They were carefully shot into each other, so they merged to create a larger gravity well. A very dangerous one, but it made it possible to jump to several other nearby stars.

"We could jump out, but unless anyone knew the Redoubt's precise coordinates, we were undetectable. Even though an enemy would eventually be able to guess our rough location—whether by triangulation, interrogation, or betrayal—the Last Redoubt was deep enough into interstellar space that there was negligible chance of a search fleet stumbling upon us before the heat death of the universe.

"After peace was established, the long decline of Legion military budgets set in. Soon there was no money left to maintain such an expensive installation that had always been off the books.

"No one wanted to leave a military asset that could be used against us. So, the Redoubt was abandoned, records were wiped, and the black hole towed forever on a randomized course away from this place into the deepest space. Within a few years, even if one knew the workings of the tow ship's course computer, the random changes meant it would be difficult to locate. After decades… impossible. Or so we all thought at the time."

Sybutu perked up. "Someone found it, didn't they?"

"I'm not just a *someone*. I foresaw the multiple crises the Federation would face. Most of them, at any rate. I returned from my… 'retirement wanderings' and hunted for the black hole. It wasn't easy, but I found it and turned the ship around, back toward the Redoubt Line."

"Then why do we always jump out in the hangar bay of *Steadfast*?"

"Because the black hole is still twenty years away. The crises hit too soon."

"Or you were too slow."

Indiya acknowledged Sybutu's barb with a nod. *Perhaps you aren't so worthless, after all.*

"Why chase after the black hole?" asked one of the Muryani. "Better to build new ones here."

Indiya regarded the alien. It stared back at her with unblinking eyes. This one, she was sure, had never previously spoken in her presence.

"Tell me your specialism again," she asked.

"As you know, Lady Indiya, we each have many specialisms but my pertinent one at this moment is combat stellar engineer."

Sybutu sucked in a breath. If the visual cue wasn't enough, she could smell his emotions and he reeked of wonderment. Combat stellar engineer. It was an impressive title… if it was real.

Don't forget these bugs are equally impressed by the Redoubt.

She calmed and settled back into a fat cushion that threatened to engulf her.

"To be clear," she said to the combat stellar engineer, "you are able to create black holes?"

"We can."

"I did not know this. And you, clearly, were unaware of our secret bolt hole. We have a lot to learn about each other, and that is good. So, let's start with black hole production. What would you need to generate them?"

"If we brought the right teams and equipment—both modest and nearby—we would require about six weeks before we would be ready to start."

"But we need mass," Sybutu said. "It's no use creating a micro-black hole. We need something massive enough to power the jump engines. We're in deep space. Even if you mined all the mass here, it wouldn't be enough to power a jump to the nearest star."

"That won't be a problem," replied the combat stellar engineer.

"Why not?" Indiya demanded.

"You saw the shipyards at Verlag," said the logistics specialist. "That facility has sixteen of the largest replicators. There are two hundred similar facilities in the nearest sector of the Expansion. Once the template for your jump drive is ready for replication, we estimate a production rate of fifty drives per second. We could scale that up significantly, but that would take many months."

Indiya felt a chill run through her, but she'd lived too long to take on any more regrets. She'd always known that giving the Muryani the jump tech would place the Federation at their mercy, but even she hadn't appreciated the scale of their ambition.

"Jump drives would become so cheap and quick to produce," she mused, "that they could become single use, throwaway devices. Link enough of them together and you could jump an entire asteroid, sending it along a chain of jumps that ends with the black hole. You wouldn't even need to mount thruster engines on the rocks, just jump nearby and let gravity do the rest."

"Worse," Sybutu said, "you could send asteroids crashing into planets you didn't like a hundred light years away."

"That is true," Indiya said soberly. "I've seen the corpses of worlds that suffered this fate. Throwing rocks down a planet's gravity well has been going on since long before jump technology."

She turned to the combat stellar engineer. "How long until you could have a navigable black hole in the Redoubt?"

"Six weeks before the team could start work. Then three months to build your black hole. Progress would be exponential. It would take five months to build eight black holes."

"Why would we need…." Indiya sucked in a lip. "Oh. You're suggesting the Last Redoubt could be more than a citadel." She ran scenarios through her mind. "With tactical deployment of black holes, we could turn this place into a trap. A killing ground for the Andromedans."

"Precisely."

"Hold on!" Sybutu said to the Muryani tactician. "Tactical deployment of black holes and all that chained jump drive business… you're very knowledgeable about the application of a technology that you only got your foot-hands on last Tuesday."

"The theory behind your drive has been around for a hundred thousand years," the stellar engineer answered. "So long as none of our neighbors acquired the technology—no one of consequence—we declined to develop it for ourselves. But we have been gaming the tactical usage of what you call the Indiyan jump drive since before your species invented the wheel. Yes, we think we know what to do."

"And we shall do it," said the diplomatic specialist. "I shall contact our people in the Expansion."

The Muryani went rigid, desperate to not betray their thoughts.

"No need for that," Indiya said. "I already know you have a means for instantaneous communication across any distance. Hopakura-2-Teal told me."

They didn't loosen up.

"Even if I didn't know that," she said. "you've as good as betrayed yourselves. Look, we've given you our jump tech, shown you our most secret safe place, and told you about *Steadfast.* I think we're beyond hiding such secrets from each other."

"You are right," the diplomat said.

"I shall initiate the contact home," said the stellar engineer.

The Muryani rose as one and left the lounge.

Indiya closed her eyes and gave in to the sense of giddiness. Giving first generation jump tech to the Muryani had seemed a desperate gamble. It still was. Once the Andromedans had been defeated, then would come the reckoning with the Muryani.

But she knew now she had made the right choice. This alliance was a deal with the devil, but she felt sure it would bring victory against the Andromedans.

Bringing in the Muryani was the best thing she could possibly have done.

Wasn't it?

*****

Chapter Thirty: Captain Dinesh McRae

***Herald of Freedom*, Muryani Space**

Every eye on the *Herald of Freedom's* flight deck was fixed upon the numbers counting down on the main screen.

The tension held Captain McRae in his command chair as tightly as if an iron clamp was wrapped around his chest. At sixty seconds, he relaxed a little. Whatever they were about to face, it was about to happen and there was no point worrying about it now.

Not every skipper relaxed into the inevitable. Maybe the other captains had been right to burden him with the responsibility of leading the convoy.

Thirty seconds.

Leaving j-Space was routine. The question burning in everybody's mind was what awaited them at the other end of the jump tunnel.

None of the ships nor the crew had entered Muryani space before. Would they be seen as refugees fleeing the disaster befalling the Federation? Or would the Muryani regard them as something more threatening?

"Ten seconds to exit j-Space," the navigator announced.

Every person on the *Herald*—except perhaps the youngest children—would be following the countdown. But he didn't blame the navigator for voicing it.

"Five seconds."

Offset by a handful of seconds, everyone on the other six ships of the convoy would be following the same number.

"Exiting j-Space… Now!"

The *Herald's* jump engines spooled down to a low hum, and the ship lurched back into conventional spacetime.

As the bridge crew let out a collective sigh of relief, the main screen flickered to life, displaying a view of the star system they had just jumped into. Bathed in the soft glow of their instrument panels, the analysts began their routine checks of the system, but the only information of importance was already apparent in the main display: a dozen dots about a thousand klicks away.

They were not alone.

A Muryani flotilla was waiting for them.

"Captain?"

He looked over at his first mate. Lieutenant GranThor rustled her wings at him until he remembered that he was not just captain of the *Herald of Freedom*. There were 8,751 souls in this convoy, four of them born during the jump. He spoke for them all.

"Comms. Get me a general broadcast."

"All-systems broadcast is active and linked to your collar mic, Captain."

McRae took half a breath and then spoke the most important words of his life. "To Muryani vessels, this is Captain Dinesh McRae, representing an unscheduled refugee convoy fleeing Federation space."

The main screen refreshed with a close-up visual of the welcoming party. The Muryani ships he'd heard of were no different from Federation norms, other than the absence of jump drives. These, though, were different. They looked like flowers with petals splaying out from a central tube.

"Switching to thermal overlay," GranThor said.

The main sections of the flower ships faded to a deep purple, but red lines glowed along the 'petals' until they reached the tips. There they burned a hot yellow.

"Is that what I think?" he asked.

"If you think they're beam weapons powering up," GranThor said, "then you're thinking right."

"To Muryani warships. We are an unarmed refugee convoy. Do not fire! We are no threat to you."

"That is for us to determine." The Muryani voice spoke perfect Federation Standard. Too perfect. It was probably a translator AI. "You must go back. Immediately."

"We can't. You don't understand—the monsters! They say they're from Andromeda. They *eat* people."

"You must comply with our instructions. If you do not leave Muryani space, you will be fired upon. There will be no warning."

"You wouldn't dare," McRae roared. "We are innocent refugees. Even if we wanted to return, we would have to recharge the jump engines. That would take hours."

"Recharging your engines is permitted. We have prepared for this eventuality with a quarantine zone around the next planet out from our sun. You should retain enough power in your jump drives to reach it. We offer you six hours in which to replenish your engines and plot a course out of Muryani space. Stay one moment longer, and we shall destroy you. You will acknowledge these terms."

McRae muted his mic. "They have to be bluffing."

GranThor stared back, wide eyed. She didn't know what to say.

"Traders have moved in and out of the Expansion for a thousand years," he said to her. "There's never been trouble."

"I agree," she said. "Helluva call, though."

He reactivated his collar mic. "Let's take a moment, because I think we're on the cusp of risking a tragedy over miscommunication. It wouldn't be the first time civilizations have misunderstood each other with fatal results. Now, you talked about a quarantine zone, but that doesn't make sense because we're not carrying a disease. We're fleeing monsters, not a plague. And if you're worried about us being freeloaders, we don't expect charity. We will work hard to earn our place here."

"Negative. You may be Corrupted. The risk is too great. Therefore, you shall leave the Muryani Expansion and not return. Ever. The EM signatures of all your vessels have been recorded. Any ships returning to any system within Muryani space will be destroyed without warning."

"Please. We have desperate people here. Infants. Sick… I mean… Not sick, *vulnerable*."

The first mate spread her wings. That was never a good sign.

"Frakk. Frakk. Frakkity fuck!" she said. "It's the *Sexton*. She's launching escape pods."

"Comms, get me the captain of the *Sexton*. No, get me the command channel for all convoy ships. GranThor, lock down our escape pods. No one leaves my ship unless I say so."

The comms officer signaled that the link was ready. "McRae to all convoy ships. Lock down your vessels. Do it now! I'm negotiating with a trigger-happy Muryani who's itching for an excuse to kill us all."

"We're too late," GranThor said.

McRae glared at his first mate. "What does that mean? Be specific."

She pointed at the main screen. "This specific enough for you?"

The pods were being destroyed. McRae swallowed hard. There were no visible displays of weaponry. The escape pods flashed briefly and then they were debris.

Scores of pods had launched. Most of them survived still, moving into evasion mode, corkscrewing away in random directions.

It made no difference, the massacre continued. Any doubts about the fate of those people in the pods were dashed when the Muryani launched hundreds of drones in pursuit.

Then it was the *Sexton's* turn. An invisible scalpel cut through the belly of the ship until its insides spilled out.

Sexton's escape pods stopped launching. None of the other ships launched theirs.

McRae sucked an icy breath through his teeth. "Muryani commander, can you hear me?"

"I can."

"You've made your damned point. You've murdered hundreds of refugees, but you made your point. Give me the coordinates of your quarantine zone. We will jump there and then return to die in the Federation."

"Negative."

"What do you mean, negative?"

GranThor signaled for attention. "Captain, the Muryani warships are spreading out. I think they're cutting off our escape."

McRae muted his collar mic again and addressed the nav officer. "Yurinik, initiate jump."

"Sir? Our jump range is very low. Where to?"

"Anywhere but here."

"We don't have a course plotted."

"Then plot one! We jump or die. GranThor, tell the other captains. I'll see if I can buy a few seconds."

He reactivated his collar. "Muryani commander, we are complying. There is no need to fire upon us."

"You might launch more escape pods. We cannot be certain that we would catch them all. We do not wish to take that risk and you have no right to make us take it."

"But we are innocents. Victims. Not warships. This is *not* a damned invasion."

"It might be. You might be Corrupted yourself and you would not know. I and my team wish you no ill will, Captain McRae. I hope you have brood siblings or offspring and that their lives will be more bounteous than yours was."

"Ready," said the navigator.

He didn't sound sure, but what the hell? "Jump!"

"They're launching missiles," GranThor warned.

An ominous squeal came from the *Herald's* backbone.

McRae unstrapped himself from his command chair.

Through his boots, he felt the jump engines throb with power. He'd sailed aboard the *Herald of Freedom* for 22 Terran years. The engine pulses felt all wrong.

The jump countdown appeared over the main screen. Five seconds rather than thirty. Yuirinik must have blown every safety protocol. *Good lad.*

Nerves pinched at McRae's stomach.

He saw *Credit Hunter* burn up in a fireball. The Muryani missiles were carrying an incendiary payload, making sure to kill not just the ships but everyone aboard.

The tightness in his guts spread. It felt as if the outer parts of his body were trying to tear themselves away from his core. A core that was shrinking.

Oh, hell. The lines of perspective across the flight deck were distorting into impossible angles. Frakk! If they didn't jump soon, he was going to be killed by his own ship.

Four seconds.

Four! Time was passing slowly.

He hoped that was his imagination.

But he knew it was not.

The shrinking sensation flipped. Now he was stretching. The distorted geometry of the flight deck made him feel sick, so he shut his eyes.

The seconds reluctantly passed, and the stretching continued.

How am I not dead?

Where are the missiles?

He tried to ask his team what was happening, but he hadn't the air in his lungs to speak.

When he opened his eyes, he was alone in a smear that stretched to infinity. The color shades matched that of the *Herald's* flight deck, but the universe had lost all detail.

Lacking the courage to look at his own body and see what he had become, he closed his eyes once more.

The colors lost their brightness a little when his eyes shut, but he could still see the endless smear.

Minutes passed.

Hours.

Years.

Finally, McRae could stand it no more. Eyes still closed, he looked at himself and screamed.

* * *

To the Muryani commander, the fate of the *Herald* appeared very different.

For about a second and a half it had shrunk. Then it had stretched along its main axis before vanishing in a burst of neutrinos that momentarily reached the level of a supernova.

All that was left of the ship and its crew and passengers was an afterglow.

It was clear what had transpired. The jump nodes had failed to stabilize, and the ship had been sucked into higher dimensions. Theoretically, all that would be left of the ship and those aboard her would be a nugget of degenerate neutronium.

The most intriguing part of the theory was that from the perspective of Captain McRae and his people, the event would take infinite time.

But from the perspective of conventional reality, the *Herald* died in less than three seconds. Which left Captain McRae both alive and dead depending on your frame of reference. Fascinating. And unfortunate for him. The commander wished the human spacer well.

"I want a full science team analysis of that ship, maximum priority. We need to understand everything we can about the human jump drive. This vessel is already scheduled to be retrofitted with the same drive that ship used, and I don't want to be collapsed into a neutronium nugget."

* * * * *

Chapter Thirty-One: Vetch Arunsen

After giving the Muryani family the guided tour of the Redoubt Line, *Phantom* finally came in to dock at Fort Douaumont.

It was a relief to return from a mission without any deaths for a change, Vetch thought to himself. Although they had left a few comrades behind in the Expansion.

He was surprised to find he was looking forward to seeing some of those friends at the redoubt. Not least, Claudio Zanitch and the other mutants. Claudio had struck up a friendship with Darant in the brief time he'd known the man before Bronze had shot him dead. He had volunteered to look after Darant's pet goat while *Phantom* and *Ghost Shark* were away.

"I wonder if Hubert's finally met his destiny," Vetch mused while they waited for *Phantom's* main hatch to open.

"As a pie?" Lily asked.

"No," Urdizine said. "I think the major is expecting Hubert to have been reborn as matching gloves and a woolly scarf."

Vetch chuckled. "You're both wrong. Hubert's only fit for the recyclers. Typical skragging Darant. Soft bastard, adopting a stupid goat."

Indiya and her new six-legged insectoid friends were first in line to exit, eager to get up to whatever vital tasks awaited. She didn't comment on Hubert.

Or Darant.

The guy had died trying to save Indiya's life, but Vetch doubted she even remembered his name.

With a *click*, the hatch unlocked and then hissed open.

Indiya and her Muryani 'family' hurried out.

Vetch hung back for a moment. The best thing about returning here, he decided, was being able to get a little distance from the damned immortal.

Fitz's voice came over Vetch's personal comm. "Aren't we forgetting something?"

"Ahh… what's that?"

"You command my marines."

"Nope. I haven't forgotten."

"And the Lady Indiya is an especially important very important person. We're supposed to give her an escort."

"On it."

He grabbed Lily and Urdizine, who happened to be closest, and jogged after the dangerous old woman. They followed for five minutes through the twists and turns bored into the asteroid before she stopped and stared at him with her piercing eyes.

"Your disdain does not trouble me, Major Arunsen."

Vetch didn't move a muscle and definitely did not speak. This was the commander who knew exactly what you thought of her, because despite what everyone claimed, he was certain she could read your skragging mind. Of course, she could. The idea made his legs turn to rubber.

"If your disdain tends to hatred, then you may become a problem. A little hatred is fine, but if you ever hesitate to obey my orders, I shall remove you."

"Yes, ma'am." His mind flashed images of what 'removal' might entail.

"It may never come to that. By the way, I forgot to say, but I organized a gift for Chimera Company. It's waiting for you now in compartment 13/B/2." She pressed a finger against Lily's chest. "It's for her too." She nodded at Urdizine. "You, Zhoogene sapper of the Legion, you might as well join the other two."

It took a while to find the compartment, and they put that time to good use speculating about what the gift might be. Exotic weaponry. Exotic women. Men, sexbots, dancers, games, next-level narcotics: the others kept coming up with the suggestions, but all Vetch really wanted was a cool beer. Followed by another. And another,

What awaited them was none of those things, of course. It was Claudio. With Hubert.

"We were told to expect a gift," Vetch said after the greetings were complete. "What the hell are we supposed to do with you?"

The big guy shrugged. "Like they're gonna tell me anything."

"I thought you mutants could see the future or some shit," Urdizine pointed out.

"Some of us can. Usually when it's not useful." Claudio frowned and looked down at Hubert. "What's up, boy?"

Basten goats were native to the planet Zhooge where they were kept for milk and wool. Despite his fluffy white appearance, Hubert had already killed on two occasions that Vetch knew about. With that demon glare in the beast's eyes, Hubert looked like he was looking to up his kill score.

The goat suddenly went rigid and stared through the open portal to the passageway they had entered through.

Vetch looked, but no one was there.

Then he heard boots followed by the appearance of…

Well, it sure looked like Darant.

A chill twisted Vetch's belly. He'd seen Darant's body, blasted by that traitor, Bronze. He'd buried his friend. Said his goodbyes, both public and silent.

This wasn't Darant.

It must be a clone.

Oh, by the way. When I scanned you for mutations, I recorded your vital statistics so I could clone you.

That was the gist of what Indiya had said when Chimera Company first visited the Redoubt.

Lily had immediately banned any discussion of the topic.

Since then, no one had wanted to bring it up. Vetch included. If he died and someone popped out of a vat in his image, that wouldn't be him. That would be someone else wearing his beard.

It would be like those people who lost a beloved pet dog and then bought a replacement lookalike and gave it the same name.

If he died, he didn't want a clone resuming his life and making it easy for his friends to forget the *real* Vetch Arunsen.

And now that topic was punched wide open because here he was: Darant 2.0.

The physique of the man walking toward them was heartbreakingly identical. A heavy man who carried a slight limp that favored the left leg. The exact same stupid grin.

Perhaps the imperfections and injuries had been reproduced faithfully so that his muscle memory would work straight out the vat. But the skin was smooth as a child's and the salted hair was now jet black.

Hubert ran to him, emitting a whistle Vetch had never heard before. The daft goat was overjoyed. Until he was almost upon his best friend back from the dead. Then he went rigid as before, a growl escaping his bared teeth.

"Don't blame you, boy," Darant told him. "You're just a stupid, dumb goat, after all. I'm surprised no one thought to put you in shortcrust pastry where you belong. I have to admit, though, I missed you while I was dead."

Hubert stopped growling and tilted his head as if asking a question. He circled Darant a few times before butting him in the back of the legs. Repeatedly and hard.

"The goat wants you to sit," Urdizine explained.

So Darant sat.

Hubert jumped onto his lap and pressed his nose against Darant's belly. Then he hacked up spit and gobbed it on Darant's face before licking it off with a tongue like sandpaper.

"You originate from the same planet as Hubert," Darant said to the Zhoogene. "What's he doing now. Predigesting?"

"Basten goats identify each other through smell. You don't smell right. This is the goat's way of putting his scent on you so he can accept you."

"You're quite the expert, eh?"

"I'm not a sad idiot like you, Darant. Goats provide three things: wool, milk, and meat. They do not make good companions for people."

"Sad? Idiot? Admittedly you're probably right on both counts, but I'd slice you for a green bean salad if Hubert wasn't keeping me busy."

"I meant no offense."

"Sounded like you were."

"I was stating a fact. Your best friend is a basten goat. That speaks of deep psychological malaise. You should get help."

"Perhaps." Darant nodded at Vetch. "So hit me, Sarge. What did I miss while I was dead?"

Vetch blinked. The man's voice was off, having lost some of the real Darant's roughness. But then he grinned. A few years of whiskey and smoking, and Darant 2.0 would sound as good as version one.

"Plenty," Vetch explained. "The Legion Navy took a kicking at Tau-Fornacis. The Tej Sector is largely lost to the Andromedans. The Federation government's collapsed and a lot of people have either been eaten or turned into feathered monstrosities."

Lily joined in. "We've just been on a road trip to the Muryani Expansion to enjoy a fake robot rebellion and give our enormous neighbor the secret to FTL travel so they can—you know—kill us all in our beds when they get around to it."

"But that's not the big news," Vetch said.

Poor Darant. The new one was just as easy to wind up as the old. His mouth dropped open, and he stopped fussing about Hubert. "What's that, Sarge?"

"It's *Major* Arunsen now."

Darant shook his head. "They told me things had gone bad. They never told me the universe had finally gone crazy."

* * * * *

Chapter Thirty-Two: Fyat and Marlin's Mother

Loralys Delta

Tires screeched as the convoy skidded to a halt on the approach road to the spaceport.

Other vehicles were parked up, forming a blockade, a very crude barrier with a lot of gaps smaller vehicles could thread through. The problem was that those gaps were filled with distorted people. Feathered people. People out to kill them.

Fyat pointed out the window of the car. "That's Mr. Jenkins. You know, the janitor at school."

She wrapped her arms around her son's head and kissed him. "No, my sweet. Mr. Jenkins is gone. That's—" She shuddered "—something else. It just looks like him."

The lead car in the convoy gunned its engine and ran at the blockade.

"Hang tight," Carl said.

The car swerved crazily as it careered through the blockade, smashing into Corrupted bodies with a series of sickening thuds. It side-swiped a parked truck hard enough to punch a dent into a rear door, but Carl fought for control and powered the engine to the max.

A gunshot rang out and the windshield shattered, sending glass flying over her eldest in the front passenger seat like a hail of diamonds.

She screamed in terror, and Fyat joined in with his own manic cries of panic.

Mercifully, the car barreled out of the blockade, and she allowed herself a brief moment of hope that they might actually make it out alive.

The convoy smashed through the fences of the flight area, and they sped along a service road to the landing field of space pads.

They were all empty. Everyone had gone!

Where to next?

The government had fled at the first sign of trouble. The Militia and Civil Defense had held their ground, but they were underfunded, and their leaders had run, too. Then some of those who had stayed behind to fight had begun to distort, to grow feathers.

She and Carl couldn't fight. They had the kids to worry about.

"Where to, Carl?"

There were tears in his eyes. "I. Don't. Know!"

The convoy circled the vehicles and thrashed out an answer to that question without daring to leave them. Some wanted to stay and fight, those without children.

Marlin, her eldest, opened the passenger door and walked out. He joined the party who wanted to fight.

"Carl, stop him!"

Carl's fists clenched the steering wheel like a vice. "The boy's twenty-one," he growled. "I'd do the same at his age."

Marlin got into a truck driven by Mrs. Hanson. Mr. Hanson came over with two blaster pistols, thrust one into her hand and offered the other to Carl.

But she'd seen energy bolts bounce off those monsters. "Who am I supposed to shoot?" she pleaded. "Them or us?"

Mr. Hanson held her gaze for a moment, pity in his eyes. "Good luck," he said. "I'll look after your Marlin."

She watched Hanson return to his truck and drive away with her son.

After her Marlin left, things were a shocked blur for a minute. Then she came to with the car fighting to escape the landing area.

Monsters and twisted people were everywhere, swarming the cars. Carl was mowing down any living thing that dared step in his way. They tumbled and flew like ragdolls. Broken bodies kept rising up, only to get flattened again.

They were everywhere. Clawing, kicking, simply running at the car. And their numbers were endless.

Then, like something out of a nightmare, a slithering group of horrors descended onto the field. They resembled worms or slugs but were the size of trucks.

Distracted by the new arrivals, Carl's attention wavered for an instant—and his mistake was made. The ground fell away from the wheels on one side, and they plummeted fifteen feet into a maintenance bay. The car skidded on its side, showering sparks in its wake until it finally collided with a blast door and came to an abrupt stop.

"We need to get out," Fyat shouted and vaulted through the smashed window with the nimbleness of an energetic twelve-year-old.

Her husband remained in his seat, groaning. His head was gushing blood.

"Carl!"

"Go," he groaned.

"I'm not leaving you."

With Fyat's help, she dragged him out, but he'd hurt more than just his head in the crash. He limped heavily.

They moved off, Carl leaning on one shoulder and babbling incoherently. Fyat clasped his father's hand and walked alongside him.

At the other end of the sunken maintenance bay, the repulsive slug creatures began floundering down to their level with a squelching thud.

They were revolting, giant dust mites sparsely coated in hairs like flexible fish bones.

She turned and tried to hurry the other way.

The slithering monsters were slow, but with Carl, she was slower still. She turned and, with trembling fingers, flipped the safety off the pistol Mr. Hanson had given her.

Like Carl had taught her years ago, she forced herself to stay calm, lining up the shot with her eyes trained on the nearest monster's gaping mouth. Bolts roared out of her gun, striking true, but the creature just swallowed the plasma blasts like candy and carried on, oblivious.

Between them and the monsters was a side passage. She dragged Carl toward it, ignoring his groans of pain. It was a narrow passage, and the monsters would have to come single file.

At the end of the passage was an open door. Maybe she could get through before the monsters reached her. Especially if the monsters couldn't fit through the narrow space.

Whatever came next, she'd figure it out when she got there. All that mattered was reaching that door.

But there wasn't to be a *next*. Mr. Jenkins ducked through the door and barred their way.

He had worked at the school since Marlin's day. Now he had grown huge and distorted, eight feet tall with an extra pair of arms sprouting from the base of his neck like dock cranes. He pounced with lightning speed, and Carl's head was suddenly gripped by all four of his hands. He twisted it until Carl's neck snapped like a twig, then Jenkins lifted him overhead and threw the lifeless body of her husband. It clattered against the wall behind her.

She gaped at Carl's corpse, paralyzed. How could they survive without him?

A fierce energy suddenly surged through her veins, and she unleashed half her charge pack into the ghastly four-armed killer.

The plasma blasts hurt him badly, but not enough. The thing that had been Mr. Jenkins slapped the blaster out of her grip. She watched it skitter along the floor.

She threw herself after the weapon. She wasn't brave—no, not even close—but her boy was screaming, and it was what she had to do. She slid along the floor, shards of debris gouging her arm open, but that no longer mattered.

She snatched up the blaster and steadied her aim at Jenkin's head. But then she blinked and switched her aim to her boy.

Mr. Jenkins laughed. It was an unholy sound.

The slugs were almost upon them. She couldn't let them eat her boy!

"It doesn't matter," boomed the thing that had been Mr. Jenkins.

"What?"

"You wish to kill Fyat, to save him from the horror. Go right ahead. Alive or dead, it doesn't matter. Not to them. We're all just nourishment, organic matter ready to be processed and molded into whatever form they deem useful."

She watched Carl being sucked up into the hungry maw of a slug monster. At least Fyat hadn't seen it happen. Her son was rooted in place, mesmerized by the four-armed abomination that used to be Mr. Jenkins.

"Do it," said the monster. "You've earned it. You've ended your life well."

She screamed and strained to pull the trigger. But she could not bring herself to do so.

"Oh, well," Jenkins said. "If it helps, you can die hoping that he might yet survive."

"What do you mean?"

A surge of scalding liquid flew past her, then a mammoth maw encircled her body, bending her over so that just her feet and head were poking out. A vice-like pressure clamped down on her. Her spine snapped, but she could still feel herself being pulled into oblivion. The last thing she saw was the monstrosity that had been Mr. Jenkins looking through the open orifice of the slug creature's mouth as it closed over her forever.

*****

Chapter Thirty-Three: Lady Indiya

"Because Fitzwilliam is an unfortunate combination of cynic and romantic. As for my staff, I don't want to ask them either, because no matter how many times I deny it, they secretly think I'm a goddess."

"How about Captain J'Klin of the *Steadfast*? He's more qualified than me."

"He's a Legion naval captain. Same as I was a very long time ago. We're too similar. Look, Sybutu, I want you to give me a fresh angle on our defenses, not be commander-in-chief of the Federation."

"Are you in danger?" Khallini asked.

"Sorry. I'm leaking my anger at an underling. Where were we?"

"The Cora's World negotiators are not taking the position we expected."

Indiya corkscrewed the Spikeball to let off steam.

She was giving Sybutu a personal tour of the Last Redoubt, simultaneously listening in on Khallini using mind-to-speech across the entangled link to Cora's World while trying to persuade Sybutu to do his wixering job.

Her mind could still carry out all these simultaneous tasks without issue. What made this difficult was her dwindling patience.

She decided to address her problems in order of least importance first.

She put the fighter on autopilot then told Sybutu, "You're a sapper of the Legion. That makes you an expert in building things and blowing them up. You've also fought against the Andromedans and lived. How would you build up the Redoubt's defenses? And if you were a four-armed feathered monstrosity, how would you defeat them?"

While the hapless sergeant attempted to activate his brain processes, she returned to Khallini. *"We're gifting Cora's World the technology to shift their extensive bioweapons industry into nano weaponry. Why aren't they biting your hands off to get at my know-how?"*

"You don't understand them."

"They are alien-hating, totalitarian bullies whose world imploded under the evil of their vicious ideology."

"All true. But that's not how they see themselves. Cora thought of herself as a savior, certainly not evil. Every lie, every murder and oppression was justified in her mind. She's long been denounced and de-personed, of course, but they learned from her how to use their ideology to justify any conceivable act. That same warped sense of morality is our stumbling block. The nano-weapon you developed works on the principle of identifying deviations from human genetic norms. Beyond a threshold of deviance, our weapon identifies its host as having been Corrupted and terminates it. Sometimes it will make a mistake."

"I know. False positives are inevitable. But I have done what I can to account for cancers and various disabilities and natural genetic abnormalities."

"Which will reduce the false positives, but you cannot eliminate them. Your nano-weapon will kill people because they are ill and because they are different. The Cora's World leadership cannot accept that. To do so would contradict their ideological principles. It seems they would rather die."

"I thought they hated differences. That's their point, isn't it? Cora sent anyone who didn't share her outlook to either a re-education camp or a shallow grave. Since

her era, they've expanded that to murdering anyone who doesn't look human enough."

"The Cora's World ideology divides people into groups based on specific characteristics such as physical attributes, health, and certain personal beliefs. Each group sits in a spectrum of worthiness. Those on the virtuous edge of the scale are venerated and protected, and those on the other side are oppressed and exploited. It is an ever-narrowing spectrum, and those outside its boundaries are exterminated."

"So, you're telling me that people who might be unfortunate collateral damage of nano weaponry belong to one of these venerated groups?"

"Correct."

"Frakking Cora's World pig lickers."

"I would send scouts first," Sybutu said. "If I were the Andromedans."

"They will be wiped out at the j-Space exit," Indiya replied. "I'm not worried about scouts."

She resumed her conversation with Khallini. *"I could raise the threshold for the weapon, but it would compromise its effectiveness. We still don't have a means to spread it fast enough."*

"No. Cora's World will not accept raising the threshold. They insist the logic must change from testing for a high level of human genetic purity to testing for evidence of Corruption. Yes, I realize the irony. And, yes, they are more than happy to have collateral damage in the Gliesan and Zhoogene version of the weapon."

"I could do that. It won't take long because we don't know much about the Corrupted. We examine the bodies, of course, but the Corruption takes a different path every time."

"I can tell from the color of your thoughts that you have a plan. Out with it, Indiya. I am in the middle of delicate negotiations here."

"I can revise the nano-weapon design to set multiple threshold criteria. I can change the way it works by sending a remote signal. To streamline negotiations, I

can also open its design to the Cora's people so they can adjust the parameters according to their precious ethics. Let me think on that a moment."

She frowned because Sybutu was talking to her when she needed to think. She replayed his most recent words.

"I have in mind those space whales at Tau-Fornacis who carried their own jump tunnel. No one has any idea how they can do that. For that matter, that ship we dug up on Rho-Torkis is capable of things we describe as impossible. If the enemy finds the location of the Last Redoubt, they can jump anywhere in the vicinity they want. There's no planet-sized gravity well big enough to stop them."

"Pig shit! Jump calculations aren't just a question of adding a little to the y coordinate. It doesn't work that way."

"Izza Zan Fey can do that."

"She told you this?"

"I've seen her do it. And if she can, perhaps the Andromedans can too."

"Drent! Hmm… Frakking annoying but that's useful information, Sybutu. Let me ask this: What's the best way to make a sneak attack on an occupied planet?"

"Very difficult, ma'am. You would start your attack at a considerable distance from the planet. Put your assault team inside stealth probes and make them approach in the sun's shadow. Put some priests in there, too, because you'll need to pray hard that you get in undetected."

"Have you ever been inside a stealth probe, Sybutu?"

"No, ma'am. If we still have them in the Legion's inventory, then their continued existence is above my pay grade. We studied the theory, but they aren't easy to construct. It's a lot more than a low radar profile; the exterior must be at ambient temperature. The craft needs to eat its own heat, so you'd need huge thermal batteries to store all that. Even with the engines off, every joule of heat generated inside that craft has to go somewhere. And when you switch the engines on, whatever drive technology you use, it will be like lighting a signal beacon." He regarded her sheepishly. "Years ago, in the Orion Era, they say it was possible to stealth entire ships."

"The rumors are true," Indiya said. "I skippered such a ship. Unfortunately, I have no idea how its designers managed it. That's why we have to make do with primitive technology and hope our enemy is stupid or inattentive. Andromedans are confusing. They appear to be observant and intelligent when they choose to be, and ignorant at other times. They learn. It's a shame we have to jump so far out from a planet to avoid being stretched into noodles. You don't have to explain why. I developed jump drive."

"Wait!" Sybutu scratched the back of his shaved head. "My bearded colleague encountered a ship that jumped successfully just a few hundred meters from a planet's surface."

"This is news to me. You sometimes appear skeptical of Arunsen's claims."

"He believes it. He believes there is evidence of a conspiracy, too, and I don't blame him. How come no one observed that ship's behavior before?"

"There are many conspiracies. I started many of them myself but there are far more than I ever realized, and I'm only talking about those I know to be real. I don't suppose Arunsen happens to know who developed this technology."

"He does. It's your old friend. Lord Khallini."

Indiya directed her ire across the light years to Cora's World. *"Why did you never tell me you could jump from inside a planet's gravity well?"*

"Oh, that. I never thought to mention it. It seemed such a small matter."

"A small matter? Starships that can jump from inside a gravity well? Really?*"*

"Well, I suppose it is very convenient. It avoids all that getting shot at while one makes a quick exit."

"Explain everything."

"May I remind you that I am currently speaking to the Cora's World bio-weapons expert committee."

"May I remind you that I don't give a wixering shite about that? This is more important. Explain how I can make my warships jump from inside a planet's atmosphere."

"Very well. But abandon the preconception that your jump drive must be mounted inside a spacecraft. That's just a very useful place to put it. Strictly speaking, though, we don't need to place my uprated drive inside any kind of vehicle. You can call it a matter transporter if it makes you feel better."

"How easy would it be to rework existing drives?"

"Very." She sensed his hesitation. *"I have some spare upgrades at home on—"*

"At your 'secret' base on Hundra-7. You forget that your secrets are revealed. Forget Hundra-7. I need you at a Legion shipyard."

"No. Indiya, I didn't develop this technology myself. Altreen did so."

"One of your AIs?"

"Yes. They are at Hundra-7."

"In that case, I'll send Phantom *to pick you up and collect what you need from home. Then you return here to the Redoubt."*

"Indiya, I—The military applications never occurred to me. Now they are flooding my head. I've never found it easy to admit my limitations. This—How could I not have thought this through? Do you ever… miss the obvious?"

"All the time. My advice is to surround yourself with tame immortals. I'm having a conversation with one right now."

"That's why I created my AIs."

"No, you created your AIs because you didn't have any friends. I remember that much from our youth. And it will never work because your AIs will always reflect you too much. You need more diverse viewpoints. And for that reason, I will order Fitzwilliam and Zan Fey to discuss… strategy."

"That pair is so unruly. I'd rather die."

"Don't be so melodramatic. Finish your negotiations, and then we'll discuss logistics."

"Very well. I hope you have a bad day, Indiya. Don't contact me again for a while."

She smiled. She'd both annoyed Khallini and discovered a vital asset she could use in this war. Sybutu was worthwhile after all.

"Ma'am, may ask a question?"

"Go ahead."

"Are you talking to someone else?"

"Why do you ask?"

"Your lips are moving when you aren't speaking to me."

A frown replaced Indiya's smile. "Careful, Sybutu. You've just pointed out to a goddess that she isn't as immortal as she thinks. Truly these are the end times."

That last phrase was a shock to the mortal, but he soon recovered. "What did you do for fun, ma'am? When you were a youngster? What did Spacer Indiya dream of?"

"I wanted to pilot a spacecraft. Humans weren't allowed to in those days. I ended up commanding warships and fleets for centuries, but I rarely flew them."

She looked at her gnarled hands. Then at the Spikeball's controls. She rammed the throttle forward and pumped the foot pedals. The fighter danced for joy, corkscrewing through the black, buzzing the busy transporters and raising havoc as only old women without a care could.

Despite the spikes dumping their inertia into the Klein-Manifold, she pushed so hard she felt G-forces squeeze her eyes out of her sockets.

She screamed in delight. Sybutu gagged. That only drove her to push the craft harder.

Indiya didn't stop until she finally made the SOTL vomit. Yes, he was definitely good for her.

*****

Chapter Thirty-Four: Lord Khallini

"Coming out of jump tunnel in five," Zan Fey announced.

"Home sweet home, Lord K," said Fitzwilliam, who was piloting *Phantom.*

Khallini ignored Fitzwilliam's provocative diminutive and allowed the mortals to concentrate their attention on the business of jumping safely to Hundra-7.

He replayed evocative images stored in his auxiliary memory of a flame-haired woman. Her lilac eyes were impossible jewels set into a face crusted with fusion burn scars. Fitzwilliam's eyes were the same and Indiya's hair shared that alien pigmentation.

Damn them both!

The flame-haired woman's name had been Springer, and her eyes had once blazed for *him.*

There had been a time, long ago, when he'd had mortal friends. And in Springer—perhaps—a lover. But every friendship had led to pain. Especially hers.

For two millennia he'd had nothing but his AIs for companionship, and he'd been content. But seeing Indiya again had turned him upside down. He knew that if he hid away in his home after the war, loneliness would consume him.

Damn Indiya! After all these years, she was still ruining his life.

"The older you get, the more painful it is to change," he declared.

Neither pilot nor navigator were listening. Both were leaking too many stress toxins to hear.

"What is it?" he demanded. "What's wrong?"

Fitzwilliam swiveled around with a sheepish expression. "Umm. Lord K? Were you expecting visitors?"

"Speak sensibly, man."

"The Andromedans are here."

Zan Fey added her analysis. "I would say they are searching for something, perhaps you. They have a heavy presence on the ground, but I'm not seeing anything near your base."

"Have they seen us?" Khallini asked.

Fitzwilliam buried himself in his instruments. "No."

"Yes," Zan Fey said. "We're being painted. They're firing. Kinetic projectiles."

Phantom hummed as Fitzwilliam pushed her to the limits of her capabilities, spinning and looping around Hundra-7 in a low orbit. The pursuing Andromedan vessels sent an unceasing barrage of energy bolts and kinetic projectiles. In response, Fitzwilliam pulled his ship into a wild dance of avoidance, responding to each volley with grace and split-second timing.

Making full use of the KM-horns, Fitzwilliam sent *Phantom* ducking into the upper atmosphere before looping around and returning to the black far enough from the Andromedans that they were out of firing range.

For now.

The Andromedans immediately changed course to pursue *Phantom*.

"We must abort," Khallini said.

"Nonsense," Fitzwilliam said. "Lady Indiya gave us a job to do; we can still do it."

"The risk is too great. Move to a safe distance and then jump to another star system."

"We'll have to recharge the engines first. Isn't that right, darling?"

"Yes," Zan Fey said. "We've enough juice to jump to Hundra-6. I'm working on a course."

"Lock it in when you're ready," Fitzwilliam said. "That's our escape plan. But we try to complete our mission first."

"No," Khallini said. "It's too dangerous. You will obey me in this and all things."

Fitzwilliam turned back to Khallini and folded his arms with utmost insolence. "I report to Indiya."

Khallini glared at Zan Fey. "I can compel you to do my bidding against your will. I can hurt you. I can sear you nerves until they're permanently fried. And I can make your unborn child thrash with agony. Do not try my patience."

The threats didn't bring the reaction he wanted. Zan Fey struggled to fight back homicidal rage. Fitzwilliam was furious too, but his anger burned cold.

"You are threatening members of the Smugglers Guild," Fitzwilliam whispered. "And you're doing it on their home turf. I don't doubt you have many powers, but so do we. Don't be so sure that you can hurt us before we kill you."

The mutant's arrogance was so astonishing that Khallini struggled to process it.

"Now," Fitzwilliam said, "before someone does something really stupid, let's remind ourselves that we're supposed to be on the same side at the moment. My plan is simple. We sneak in and drop you off near the surface in the smuggler's shuttle. Then we make a big show to make them chase us. We give them the slip, pick you and your gear up, and jump to safety. Simple."

Khallini could easily squash this ridiculous mortal. The only reason he stayed his hand was the value in recovering the secret of his jump drive modification. He and Indiya had been cracking their heads open trying to think how to deliver the nano-weapon that would destroy the Corrupted. The answer had been in his lap all this time.

A functioning matter transporter could deliver far more than the nano-weapon. Planets lost to the enemy could be sterilized from nearby systems. And that was just the start of it.

The revelation that he'd possessed such valuable knowledge without realizing it was a disaster. Khallini's identity was hemorrhaging inside his ancient flesh.

For so long his dearest companion had been the quiet certainty that he was the wisest being in this part of the galaxy. Making such an idiotic oversight was eroding his self-belief.

How many other aspects of his life had he so badly misunderstood?

And the logic here was crushing. The only way to answer that question was to talk to mortal beings. To discuss his secrets in search of his failings.

Unacceptable!

"Fancy Indiya, did you? When you were young?"

Why was the insolent Captain Fitzwilliam asking that? And why now? It was as if the mortal could read his mind.

"I did," Khallini answered. "I loved her as a sister, and then we reached a certain age… We both hit puberty at the same time." He rolled his eyes. "We're talking about a twelve-month period, three-

and-a-half thousand years ago. The Lady Indiya has forgotten many things, but she never lets me forget the year when I adored her."

"Is it really over? Between you and Indiya?"

"Oh completely. You disappoint me, Fitzwilliam. This is a transparent ploy to manipulate my emotions when I have already instructed you to abort this mission. There is no romantic love between me and Indiya. We are bound, she and I, but it is not something you mortals would understand. We are sun and moon, cold and heat, electric and magnetic."

"No, that's not it. There's something there, deep inside. I feel it. I have powers, you know? You—all this—deep down, you've been trying to impress a girl for a very long time. But if it's not Indiya…"

Khallini's instinct was to end this man's life with a single killing thought, but Shantilla stayed his wrath a moment.

The creation of artificial life had been Khallini's passion for as far back as he could remember. Mostly, this took the form of AI brains installed in robotic bodies, but three of them were integrated directly into his own flesh. Shantilla was one of those, and he had created her to counter certain homicidal rage issues that had proved problematic in the past.

Shantilla was not merciful, but she was practical. The reason she had temporarily spared Fitzwilliam was because, astonishingly, she thought the man could be right.

Khallini cleared his throat. "There might be something to what you say."

"What was her name?"

"Who?"

Fitzwilliam looked at him as if he were a simpleton. "The girl you still hold a torch for."

"I have forgotten far more than you mortals will ever know. But there is one woman I can never forget. Her name was Springer."

"I know. You're not so secret as you like to think, Lord Khallini. Lady Tremayne, known to her friends—and lovers—as Springer. I want you to think of her, to hold an image of Springer as a young woman. If she'd been given the mission to retrieve vital data from your base, despite the risk, would she do it?"

"In a heartbeat."

"You've never stopped wanting to impress her. Don't stop now."

"Idiot mortal. You know nothing of these matters."

"On the contrary, I am Tavistock Fitzwilliam, and I know *exactly* what I'm talking about. It's the sort of love you can't shake, however much you might try. However dangerous it might be. However improbable." He regarded his alien wife. "Believe me, I'm one of the galaxy's leading experts."

Khallini shook his head, not quite believing what he was hearing.

"Hold that thought," Fitzwilliam said.

He flipped *Phantom* upside down and then turned the sleek ship down and to the left, narrowly dodging three missiles in its wake. The ship shuddered as it entered Hundra's upper atmosphere and dropped into a steep dive, skimming the upper cloud layer for cover.

"I might not live a life as long as yours," the captain said, "but the love I share with Izza is immortal. Just like yours."

"Spare me the childish platitude."

"And I am well informed on more than matters of love. I know the woman of whom you speak. Lady 'Springer' Tremayne. First President of the Human Autonomous Region. A woman with purple eyes, just like mine. Izza's too."

"I'm glad Springer's not forgotten."

"Forgotten? You're missing the obvious again, Khallini. Hello? Purple eyes? They call us mutants. A more accurate description is 'descendants of Lady Tremayne.' We haven't forgotten who we came from."

"No. You lie. You're not all descended from Springer."

"All of us so-called mutants—Izza too—share the same three ancestors. So yeah, pretty much. You know, the Lady Indiya acknowledged being our stepancestor. That makes you our stepfather, sort of. I'm glad both our stepancestors are playing nice together at last. So important for the children to know you aren't trying to kill each other, don't you think?"

Shantilla and the two other AIs in his head tried to shut down the dangerous thoughts swirling around Khallini's head. He wasn't having it, though. He overruled them.

"Take the risk," Zan Fey said. "You would do it for her."

"The matriarch of our line has long since turned to dust," Fitzwilliam said. "You can't impress her, but she lives on in us. Impress us, Lord Khallini. We shall remember what you do this day."

Wild emotions led to painful consequences. Khallini knew that all too well, which is why he'd built the stabilizing effect of Shantilla and the other AIs.

They'd kept his head level for millennia.

Neutralized.

Suffocated.

He shut them down.

And immediately gagged on the crest of a tidal wave of hormonal rebalancing.

Excitement surged through his body, and he remembered what it felt like to be alive.

"Lord Khallini?" Zan Fey sounded concerned. "Are you all right?"

"Better than all right, my child. Let's frakking do this."

* * * * *

Chapter Thirty-Five: Lord Khallini

The special shuttle was something only a smuggler could conceive of. It was a slab of radar-eating material with a squared pop-up bubble for the pilot to see through. Sensors were strictly passive. Exhaust heat was swallowed. Propulsion barely detectable.

It was, in essence, a stealthed mobile smuggling box compartment.

Khallini's stomach churned uneasily as he sat in the shuttle, held firmly in its cradle in Hold Three. He felt a faint tremor in every nerve, every muscle, as *Phantom* strained against its inertia.

Was his perception of motion a figment of his imagination? Khallini's intellect and body sparred over this, drawing different conclusions.

He could have hacked into *Phantom's* systems to see the outside view, but he chose not to. To be completely deprived of data about his surroundings was a novel sensation he wished to experience.

Captain Fitzwilliam threw *Phantom* through the atmosphere on a course that would have been bone crushing and eyeball bursting if her momentum wasn't being dumped out of the KM-horns, technology Khallini himself had played a part in developing an age ago.

Phantom ejected the shuttle in a process that provided a second of total surprise. Khallini blinked in the sudden sunlight. *Phantom* was zigzagging away from the ice mountain escarpment along the plateau near his home base. Petrochemical dunes rose hundreds of feet in Hundra's low gravity, large enough for *Phantom* to duck and weave through, though flying so close to the ground raised greasy soot plumes of hydrocarbons.

Following this trail were creatures that, at a distance, resembled winged whales. Upon magnification, they looked more like angry warts, and their leathery skin illuminated a pale orange color from within, camouflage, perhaps, against the smoggy sky. Compared to *Phantom,* they were sluggish and cumbersome, but against Khallini's tiny craft they appeared swift and agile. And massive.

Khallini steadied the shuttle and hovered about ten feet above the foothills of the mountain, gambling his life—perhaps everybody's life—on the ability of this smuggler's vehicle to remain undetected.

Phantom climbed for all she was worth, and soon the mad chase was swallowed by the nicotine sky. Following Fitzwilliam's advice, Khallini waited thirty deep breaths after the skies cleared of friend and foe, then he set off for his home.

He felt unfamiliar energy fizz through his veins. Memories of his long-lost love evoked forgotten passions. Springer's lilac eyes remained the most beautiful sight he'd ever beheld in this universe.

He smiled and then dismissed her from his head because he wasn't doing this for her. He was doing this for himself.

"The longer we live," he said to himself, "the more we forget how. It's high time I remembered."

The luminescent pilot's bubble highlighted movement. Over the dunes to the east came a flock of a dozen of the winged creatures that had pursued *Phantom.*

They were headed his way.

He sped up and ran for the mountain range to the west, expecting the worst. Sky, dunes, mountains: everything was painted in the same dirty tones of rust and burned toffee. Beneath hardened hydrocarbon soot, the mountains were water ice frozen to granite hardness by the extreme cold, but they were riddled with fissures through which heated volatiles from inside the planet burst from time to time due to gravitational squeezing.

Khallini had no choice but to activate the echo location sensors to find a fissure. With the enemy getting closer with every moment, he finally chanced upon a crack and edged his tiny craft a hundred meters inside the mountain. There he waited for the Andromedans to pass.

But were they Andromedans?

The flying creatures were perfectly adapted to the hostile conditions of the planet, though he'd never seen any native lifeform on Hundra-7 larger than a microbe. Perhaps they were the Corrupted form of a native Perseid species? The Federation had already encountered many forms of Andromedan, but for all anyone knew, those could be just the start of many more.

Khallini nudged the smuggler's shuttle out the fissure.

The Andromedans were now in a distant patch of sky and moving away. He took his chance and flew over the mountains, dropping low on the far side and moving slowly so as not to roil the frozen volatiles.

All fear had left him. Without the AIs in his head, he would have to relearn basic instincts such as how to be afraid, but for the moment he was happy to enjoy his new freedom.

He made it home without incident, diving into the methane river and through the series of hatch doors that led to the wood-paneled entrance cavern.

Andrus, his faithful friend, was waiting for him.

He took a moment to appreciate the design of the AI's body, a composite of disparate modules that gave Andrus a chaotic appearance in deliberate contrast to the measured tone of its speech. He hadn't expected to see Andrus again.

"Welcome home, sir. Altreen is bringing the items you requested and will be here momentarily."

"Excellent. It's good to see you, Andrus."

"Will you be staying long?"

"No. I'll be heading back as soon as we move the items into the hold."

"Hold, sir? It's more of a hat box."

"Indeed. But it must suffice."

Khallini put his hand on Andrus's shoulder joint in an attempt to comfort it, but he wasn't sure the AI would comprehend his unusual behavior. "My old friend, the Andromedans have come to our world. We must assume they will eventually find our home."

"Yes, we are all extremely worried."

"It's inevitable they will eventually find you."

"I fear you are correct."

"Once the defenses are breached, I want you to initiate the self-destruct. Andrus, please do not tell the others. Hide the truth from them. Lie. I don't want their final moments to be lived in terror. I know you are strong enough to do this."

"Thanks to you." The AI extended a limb and touched Khallini in mirror of the human's gesture. "Compared to almost every mortal who has ever existed, I've lived a long and fulfilling life. I'm not a 'yes' droid, so I mean it when I say thank you for the gift of life. And thank you even more for the grace to allow me to live it my way."

Khallini nodded, the power of speech temporarily beyond him.

"Go now," Andrus told him, "before Altreen sees your tears. He's almost here."

Khallini probed the dampness around his eyes. Strange, he thought that emotional response had been removed long ago.

"Take this first."

Khallini noticed the arm was holding a data crystal. "What is it?"

"Everything. A backup of everything you built here."

Khallini shook his head. "Thank you, but no. My knowledge has become a burden. I need to build anew."

"Very wise."

He managed a smile and returned to the smuggling shuttle.

Altreen arrived, bearing the spare drive enhancement modules and the precious knowledge in his head.

The thrill of knowing he had been gifted an unexpectedly new lease of life was soured by the reminder that it was a gift not granted to everybody.

When Altreen signaled he was aboard and secure, Khallini abandoned all caution and flew out of that place of memories as fast as he could.

Outside, it was raining, and fat blobs of methane carved channels through the thick sooty blanket of smog. The reduced vision made Khallini's vessel more difficult to see, but also obscured the Andromedans.

In every direction, he saw atmospheric craft and those flying lumps from before. The latter appeared to vanish before reappearing nearby. He hoped it was a smog-induced mirage.

"Just in time, Lord K."

Khallini resisted the urge to transmit a reply.

"You know you said this was too risky?" Fitzwilliam sucked in a sharp breath. "Turns out you were right. Climb as fast as you can. I'll pick you up in the air."

The shuttle soared as Khallini raced higher into the atmosphere. The dim outlines of the Andromedans were all around and growing closer.

Suddenly, a sleek silver form darted in from the side, engines roaring.

Fitzwilliam had arrived.

Khallini guided the shuttle into *Phantom's* slipstream. The moment Fitzwilliam matched Khallini's course and speed, the rear hangar door opened.

Phantom's engines roared again, and she climbed vertically, twisting through the hydrocarbon clouds.

Khallini hissed a curse and kicked the engines to full throttle as he raced after *Phantom*. What was that idiot Fitzwilliam doing?

The answer was revealed as particle beam weapons discharged, lighting the smog into lances of glowing amber. Missiles maneuvered through the methane downpour.

Suddenly, an apparition appeared no more than twenty feet in front of Khallini.

One of the winged creatures was before him. Its skin was transparent, and he saw a line of internal organs pulsing against each other, generating a soft orange luminescence. A dishlike eye swept along its body and stopped when it spotted him.

Then the creature was gone.

Not obscured by sooty clouds Gone. Disappeared. Vanished!

Khallini smashed the transmit button. "Fitzwilliam, you dirty veck. You, Springer, and all her mutant descendants can go to hell."

"Roger that. We'll meet you there if I can't shake these flying skraggs."

"If you're right..." Khallini laughed, something he hadn't done for centuries. "At least I lived again. At the end. Thank you."

The smart glass of the pilot bubble flashed a proximity alert, and Khallini hit every control he could see, sending the shuttle careering in a wild spiral.

A massive whale sped past, snapping at the shuttle with jaws filled with silver needles.

The shuttle's gyrations were so violent that even Khallini was too disoriented to keep track of where he was going. He let go and allowed the craft's emergency stabilization system to take over.

"That's it," Fitzwilliam said. "Hold her steady. You'll be home and dry in five seconds."

Khallini's blood ran cold when he saw an Andromedan materialize in front of the shuttle. He knew his smart glass and enhancements should have let him see through any camouflage, so how was this creature able to become invisible like this?

He had spent his life questioning the nature of reality and answering many of his questions. So, it seemed only fitting that his life should end with his mind pondering one final question.

The creature thrust its head toward him, opened its maw, and snapped at the bubble that encased Khallini.

The material was strong.

But the Andromedan was stronger.

The bubble ruptured, leaving Khallini's final question an eternal mystery.

*****

Chapter Thirty-Six: Tavistock Fitzwilliam

"Frakk! Fuck, skragging, frakkity—"

Fitz felt Izza's hand on his and instantly calmed.

"Fitzy. Stay on mission."

His gaze shifted to the view tracking the smuggler's shuttle. A few shards of smart glass showed where the pilot's bubble had been. Its main body was intact and plummeting toward the ground.

Immortals dying… being eaten. That was hard to get through one's head. To chase something through the air, though… Fitz was born for this.

Hands gripping the control wheel tightly, he pushed it forward and sent *Phantom* into a steep dive in pursuit of the shuttle.

A hail of projectiles lashed *Phantom*. She took a few hits, but the shields absorbed the worst of their lethal sting.

Enemy fire. Flying monsters that turned invisible at will. Fitz paid no attention to all that. With barely a thought, he kept *Phantom* spinning and twisting to make her harder to hit, while his mind focused on the aerial pickup.

Get this wrong and Khallini would have died for nothing.

"Altitude: twelve hundred meters," Izza said.

He edged *Phantom* ahead of the broken shuttle and matched speed.

Izza said nothing but added an altitude display to the screen in front of his face. Seven hundred meters.

Fitz opened the rear hangar door.

Phantom shuddered as its aerial profile changed. Fitz wrested back control, rematched vectors, and nudged *Phantom's* open hangar into alignment with the shuttle.

Two hundred.

Fitz bled out a little momentum through the KM-horns.

Phantom's descent slowed. The shuttle shot into the hangar with a clang Fitz felt through the control wheel.

"Closing hangar," Izza said.

"Thank you, my dear." Fitz tilted the nose up and cut the main thrusters. He hit the emergency momentum dump.

Phantom stopped.

Bad things happened to Fitz's insides as his shoulders jammed painfully against his harness, while other parts of his body kept moving in unnerving directions. He winced as the shuttle banged against the hanger's overhead.

Hundra-7's gravity asserted its authority and pulled at the craft.

Fitz re-engaged the thrusters and glanced at the altimeter.

Ten meters.

The ship slammed into the hydrocarbon dunes, though at 0.37 G, it was a soft belly flop. Immediately, she began to sink through the powdery accumulation of soot, and a moment later the intense heat from the thruster nozzles ignited the volatiles into a fireball hundreds of meters across.

Phantom emerged from the fires of hell and climbed for space.

Fitz looked down. A liquid ring of fire was spreading along the plain, fed by the heavy methane rain. There was nothing to stop it.

"Have I just set fire to an entire planet?"

"Never mind that," Izza said. "Think what you did to *Phantom's* hull. And the thruster nozzles we just had refitted will be thoroughly coked up. It's a good thing Catkins isn't here to see this."

"Nonsense," Fitz said, "he expects me to damage the old girl. Just imagine how upset he'd be if I brought her back to him without a little patina of wear."

They breached the upper atmosphere and were greeted with a terrifying sight.

A ring of eight Hammers was waiting. They spat energy bolts and closed the ring.

Fitz sent *Phantom* dancing through the incoming fire.

If any of those shots landed, it would be all over, but the Andromedan ships were too far away to fire effectively. At the speed they were coming for *Phantom*, though, that wouldn't be true for much longer.

Fitz stared wistfully at his escape route into space. To jump at any less than two planetary radii would be suicide, and the enemy ships would tear them apart long before that.

He plunged the ship back into the atmosphere.

"What's the plan, dear?" Izza asked.

"Working on it."

"We already had a plan. I suggest we stick with it."

Fitz blinked. "Of course! Have I ever told you how much I admire you?"

"Frequently. Though more adoration never goes amiss."

Fitz hit the intercom. "Fregg, have you seen inside our smuggling box?"

"Yeah. Sort of. That's what I wanted to tell you, Captain. This weird-looking droid came out carrying a bundle of drive control components. Calls itself Altreen and says it wants to reconfigure our jump drive."

"What did you tell it?"

"I told it if it touched *Phantom's* control systems, I'd melt its stupid metal brain with the fusion pistol I'm pointing at it."

"Good for you, Fregg. Lower your weapon. Altreen, can you hear me?"

"I am here, Captain Fitzwilliam."

"Khallini said reconfiguring the jump drive would be easy; just a hot swap. Are we talking…" He studied the tactical plot for a moment. The Andromedan ships were closing fast. "Three minutes easy?"

"No, Captain."

"Skragg! Frakk!"

"The installation is already complete."

"What? Just like that?"

"Just like that. Everything functions the same way except you no longer need concern yourself with distancing yourself from the planet before jumping. Of course, it would need to be thoroughly tested before use."

"Testing?" Fitz guffawed. "That's my middle name."

Fitz dipped *Phantom's* nose and sent her plunging in a rapid descent through the atmosphere.

"Captain, what are you doing?"

"I think the term is field testing." He beamed, his wide smile matching the glimmer in his violet eyes. "You're new here, Altreen, so let me give you some advice."

Izza grabbed his hand and squeezed, the mischievous grin on her green face matching his. "I want to press the button," she said.

Fitz winked. "Of course, my lady."

From within the ship, Altreen queried, "Captain? Your advice?"

"A standing order, really. When I'm piloting the ship always strap in tightly, and unless you have an iron stomach, don't look out the window."

"But, Captain. There are no—"

Izza shut off the intercom. "Don't tease it. This is how you started with Lynx."

"Lynx will be missing me terribly."

Fitz weaved the ship through the murky air, toward the methane river that flowed over Khallini's base. The waterfall a kilometer upstream purified the flow somehow, rendering it the purest blue in this otherwise monochrome world painted in shades of nicotine.

It seemed a fitting spot to make their exit.

"I want to play a game with the Andromedans," he said.

"Play dead. I assumed that's what you were doing."

"One day, I won't be playing."

"True, but not knowing when makes life such a thrill."

Fitz sighed in contentment. Izza was still holding his hand. She understood him and believed in him. While that remained true, nothing else mattered.

There had been many moments like this, gambling their lives together. And the crew's, of course. It had fused the two of them together. Permanently. He hadn't entirely been talking drent to Khallini about the eternal nature of their love. It was so fiercely baked into the universe that surely it couldn't die on that day when they finally took one risk too many.

He winced and his gaze dropped to Izza's belly. But it wasn't just their lives they were risking now. How would that change things?

Fitz felt a judder as *Phantom's* nose pierced the surface of liquid methane, followed a fraction of a second later by turbulence as the river exploded.

Izza hit the jump drive button.

* * * * *

Chapter Thirty-Seven: Lady Indiya

"Do you have the drive upgrades?"

Even across the two hundred lightyear link from the Tej Sector, Indiya could hear the eagerness in Admiral Aluin's voice.

"We do," she replied. "Though it cost Lord Khallini his life. I have produced twenty drive upgrades here at the Redoubt and they are passing every test we can throw at them. I am confident we will be mass producing them within weeks."

"Excellent."

Indiya felt a stab of annoyance at Aluin's failure to recognize the gravity of Khallini's demise. Her old sparring partner had been a constant irritation for millennia, but without him humanity would have been eradicated. The mortals should hold their betters in more respect.

"Our teams are wargaming the use of the technology," Aluin said.

"As are mine," said J'Klin, who normally remained silent at the strategy meetings around the long table inside Indiya's personal bunker in Fort Douaumont. He was a big, bluff man who ran *Steadfast* with ease but lost his tongue around Indiya. "We should transmit regular summaries to each other of what we have developed."

"Agreed. Bandwidth be damned. We can't hold back. Now, to the question of delivery. Twenty drive upgrades are not much but enough to make a start. When will they be mine?"

"*Steadfast* is undergoing essential refit and repair," Indiya replied. "We have to wait another forty-eight hours before she can ship out the first batch."

"That's with *Steadfast* only partially patched up," J'Klin said. "Essential repairs would take seventy-two hours."

"My preference was to get that ship out after twenty," Indiya said. "Every pathway carries risk. No one gets everything they want."

"Once again, we are restricted to *Steadfast* being the only means of getting out of that rathole you're hiding in," Aluin said. "I want it on the record that I believe having you stuck in the tail end of nowhere with only one way out is an unacceptable risk."

"Noted," Indiya said. "And you note, Admiral, that I'm working on fixing this."

"I also notice you haven't explicitly confirmed that *Steadfast* will be bringing those jump drive upgrades to my fleet."

"You're perceptive."

"*Steadfast's* taking those drive upgrades to those lunatics at Cora's World, isn't she?"

"She is."

"Again, on the record, that's an even greater risk. I mean no disrespect, Lady Indiya, but as a living being you are unique. Can we get an objective assessment of your sanity?"

"No. But I agree that allying so closely with Cora's World is an even bigger risk than my lack of exits. The genetic nanovirus I have developed to kill the Corrupted is not easily replicated and mass producing it presents another order of magnitude of difficulty. Cora's preexisting bioweapons capability is the only means I have to produce the nanovirus in bulk so quickly."

"Can you even hear your own words, Lady Indiya? We're dealing with the Cora's World zealots because they're experts in bioweapons. Pause and think on that for a moment. What kind of world specializes in biowarfare? You are gifting an incredibly dangerous genetic weapon to the one group in the Federation that is not only insane enough to use it against us, but had the means to mass produce and deliver it, too. And then you're giving them matter transport technology to make it easier for them to deliver it wherever they want! What if they learn the coordinates for the Redoubt Line? How would you feel if a bio-bomb jumps directly into your bedroom?"

"Cora's World is a concern that I am keeping under review."

"I see. So, we are arming the zealots and leaving me to make my counterattack without the advantage of the jump upgrade technology. Have you any more good news for me, Lady Indiya?"

She smiled because Aluin was angry, competent, and eager for the fight. This was how the Legion had been of old. As her husband had been. He wouldn't have liked what she was about to say. She supposed Aluin wouldn't either.

"Admiral, I am postponing the counterattack."

Aluin didn't speak.

"It will take time for the nanovirus to take effect, time for the Muryani battle fleets to arrive. Weeks. Maybe a few months. The other Legion fleets remain as a mobile reserve. But in Tej, the Antispinward Fringe, and the Zinjei Dux Sector, your fleet contains the only naval assets we have left. When I spend your force, and I will, I want to deliver the maximum effect for the minimum cost."

"So, what you're saying, is that if we—and I use this term loosely—*win* this war, you want to preserve as much as you can of the loyal Federation military so that the many enemies you have armed and invited in still have something to fear from us."

"That is not an inaccurate interpretation."

"As you know better than me, ma'am, Legion doctrine has always been clear that we cannot win a war until we have won control of events. We are not in control, and you are deliberately surrendering our grasp on events still further. I hope winning it back is uppermost in your thoughts, Lady Indiya, because if it is not then we are all doomed."

"Good." Indiya nodded. "You give an excellent and incisive assessment. It speaks well of you. However, I shall remind you this is not the first interstellar war I will have won against insurmountable odds."

"That is what we are all counting on, Lady Indiya. It's why the Legion still follows you. Belief, in you, is all we have left. Please take care, ma'am. Lord Khallini died. If you did too, the Legion would collapse. It would all be over."

After such a promising start, Indiya tired of the admiral's weak-willed melodrama. She dismissed him and brought the session to an end.

There were others at her strategy table. Fitzwilliam and Sybutu from Chimera Company and her oldest ally, Kanha Wei, although this latest version of the clone had only been active for a few months. Then there was Claudio Zanitch and his superhuman ability to see a route to order within chaos. He represented her team of mutants, and normally she very much enjoyed his company but now she was tired of them all.

The others filtered out, but Kanha Wei hung back.

Indiya expected to see that brief intake of breath and flicker of a smile that Wei always presented when she was about to tell Indiya something she didn't want to hear.

Instead, the clone stared at her mistress through her opaque gold shades, mouth clamped shut, and hood covering her head.

"Are you compromised?" Indiya asked eventually.

Wei tilted her head.

"I mean," Indiya explained, "are you sick? Was there an issue with your clone growth or training?"

"You trust me too much," Wei blurted. "You mustn't clone me anymore. If I die this time, it must be forever."

Interesting. Wei had never expressed that opinion before, but clone angst was a problem Indiya had anticipated. She touched Wei's mind and found it peculiarly cold. Opaque even.

That was unsettling, but not unsurprising. The business of war fatigued Indiya, but the forced interaction with so many mortals was utterly exhausting. And it had only been a few months since Indiya had been shot and almost killed. Indiya's capabilities were severely reduced at present. She needed time to rest and recover.

Unable to interrogate Wei at a cellular level, Indiya resorted to talking.

"Why are you saying this now, Kanha? Is something troubling you?"

"I'll be hitching a ride on *Steadfast* soon. I don't think I'll be coming back."

"You don't know that."

"No. Not in terms of logic and facts." Wei removed the gold band from her face to reveal glowing purple eyes. "But I feel the truth of it."

A haze emanated from Wei's eyes. A faint hiss. She was crying, the heat in her mutant eyes evaporating her tears.

Wei enveloped Indiya in a hug and squeezed tightly. She didn't want to let go but Indiya felt the woman's body stiffen, and Wei forced herself to back away.

"Please," Wei begged. "Don't replace me with another clone."

Wei collected herself and stood at attention while staring at Indiya, as if sucking in every last visual detail so she had a solid memory to take away. Then she covered her eyes with her gold band and walked off, leaving Indiya stunned at the performance.

It was as if Kanha Wei had been a child bidding a beloved parent farewell before going off to war.

The experience pulled at Indiya's heart in ways she had not felt for epochs.

She was simultaneously grateful to feel any emotion and deeply disappointed that her most reliable servant was suffering some kind of spiritual breakdown.

When things calmed down, that version of Wei would obviously have to be retired. Before growing her replacement, Indiya resigned herself to conducting a thorough inspection of the clone production suite to locate and fix what had gone wrong.

So many problems to solve and only she could solve any of them.

She issued hormonal instructions to calm herself and then prepared for a nap.

What would Aluin and all those other devoted followers think if they knew their supreme commander had to take power naps?

* * *

Ten minutes later, Indiya was in bed and slowly drifting toward deep sleep when her compartment erupted in wailing noise, flashing lights, and pungent smells.

It was the call to battle stations!

Instantly, she connected her mind with the command-and-control systems across the rocks of the Redoubt Line.

The Andromedans had arrived.

*****

Chapter Thirty-Eight: Lady Indiya

To the defenders of the Redoubt Line, it seemed they had little chance against such a superior force.

Every few seconds, another Andromedan vessel emerged from the jump tunnel aperture held open by a trio of ugly Leviathans and join the dozens of attacking craft already streaming for the fortified rocks.

Rho-Torkis Hammers swam impossibly in the dark of space. Living gauss cannons were in abundance, as were lesser sluglike creatures of war that were marshaled by the bone spheres.

The hollowed asteroids of the Redoubt Line were scattered before the invaders like islands in a sea of stars. The only rock that had been fully reoccupied was Fort Douaumont, named for the space hulk used as a training ground by the very first legionaries. Knowing the culture of that time, it had probably been named after a fortress on ancient Earth.

From her apartment deep within Fort Douaumont, Indiya made a note to look up the origin of the name after the battle. And she had no doubt that she would survive for there to be an after.

Immediately, she felt a pang of annoyance because when the redoubts were constructed, she would have known every last detail about them, including the reason for every name.

Battleship *Steadfast* was supported by a small squadron of antique corvettes and FV-3 "Cockroach" fighters that had been abandoned here generations ago. It was all the defenders had, but they bravely moved out to meet the enemy.

Indiya doubted they would last three minutes against the unstoppable Andromedans. Their actions were a mere gesture, a message of defiance that the Legion and its allies would never give up. Not that the enemy appeared to understand such things as gestures.

Only the cores of the asteroids had been hollowed out, leaving them clad in rock armor that averaged three kilometers in depth. Although the Redoubt Line's fleet was wholly inadequate for its defense, the redoubts were impregnable against weapons attacks and all their surfaces were studded with hardened particle beam emplacements and hidden pop-up missile batteries. The enemy would have to batter through *Steadfast* and her support vessels, land on the surface of Fort Douaumont, and then savage them in a close assault.

"A shame," Indiya mused. "A few more months and with the Muryani black holes in place, we could have been ready. I didn't anticipate treachery so soon."

She tried to feel rage against whoever it had been who had betrayed the location of this place, but she couldn't dredge up that emotion. In any case, it served no purpose to be angry with those the Andromedans had Corrupted.

Indiya established a link to *Steadfast.*

"What is your battle plan?" she asked J'Klin.

"To die with honor."

"Your engines are recharged. Why not simply jump away?"

"Even if I wanted to, the astrogation system is offline for maintenance. We're ten minutes into a two-hour window of opportunity for them to catch us with our pants down. Either it's terrible bad luck—"

"Or the traitor is aware of *Steadfast's* secrets. Well, not all of them, I hope. You will execute order Gray-2."

The link didn't carry visual, but Indiya could almost hear the captain's blood drain from his face.

"I shall execute Gray-2, aye." He took a sharp breath. "I hope God forgives us for what you're about to do."

* * * * *

Chapter Thirty-Nine: Captain J'Klin

"Targets laid in," Guns reported. "Main weapons are tracking the tails of those Rho-Torkis swimmers. As soon as those tails move, we'll rip them off."

J'Klin took another glance at the tactical plot display that dominated CIC. His plan had been simple. Doomed, but in keeping with Legion tradition. *Steadfast* and her support ships were flying out to meet the attackers head on because the Andromedans were charging at the redoubts with no thought to formation or tactics. The sooner J'Klin's force engaged the enemy, the less heavily outnumbered they would be at the point of contact and the more damage they could do before being overwhelmed.

J'Klin could not win this, but the fight would not be futile. Every legionary understood that they must hold the line or die trying. In these dark days, that attitude was about the only thing keeping civilization together.

The living gauss cannons had opened fire first, lashing the Federation ships with long-distance projectiles. So far only one Cockroach fighter had suffered engine damage as a result and been forced to turn back.

This was a military confrontation moments from heating up into mad action.

And then Indiya had issued the Gray order.

"Helm, loop us about. We shall run for the safety of the Redoubt Line. All speed to the engines and don't stop when we reach the rocks. I want to put as much distance as we can between us and the enemy. Comms, open the fleet command channel."

Tension fizzed across the command deck.

Steadfast was not changing vector. She was still screaming toward the enemy.

"Channel open," said Comms.

"Close it," J'Klin ordered. "Helm, why are we not reversing course?"

"Sir. I'm not abandoning our comrades. Besides, where would we run to?"

"This is a military warship, mister, not a debating society."

A flash of yellow moved fast in J'Klin's peripheral vision. "We are not running," Commander Fennerwatham stated to the helmsman, emphasizing her point with her pistol aimed at the helmsman's head. "And this is not what it looks like."

The XO was the only member of J'Klin's crew permitted to wear the cadmium yellow beret of the Special Missions Shock Brigade. It was a privilege hard earned. All legionaries were killers when they had to be, but Fennerwatham's beret showed that delivering death up close and personal was, to her, an advanced art form.

"Not what it looks like?" The helmsman set his jaw stubbornly, but his hands were shaking. "Looks like you're threatening to shoot me, XO."

"My apologies." Fennerwatham growled. "I was unclear. The part where I hold a pistol to your head is exactly as it looks. You will obey the lawful orders of the captain, or I will shoot you and find someone who will."

"Sir!" Guns warned. "Fire control systems are off-line. It's a cyberattack from inside the ship."

J'Klin's face contorted in rage, and he slammed his fist upon his console. "Sabotage! XO, treble the guard at all vulnerable points. I want the traitor found." He gave an ominous growl. "I want them brought to justice."

The helmsman swallowed hard at the explosion of the captain's anger and finally obeyed the order and looped the ship around.

But the delay had brought them closer to the enemy. Already, the corvettes were taking damage and giving back precious little punishment in return.

"Comms!"

"Channel ready."

"All vessels, this is Captain J'Klin. Turn about and run. I repeat, break off attack and… await further orders."

The other ships obeyed. With *Steadfast* turning first, they had little choice. Shocked queries flooded the channel, but J'Klin waved them away. There was no time.

"Lieutenant Khan, open Restricted Operations Commands."

"Aye, sir." Confusion was obvious in the astrogation officer's response, but she obeyed without question.

"Enter ROC Gray Two," J'Klin told her. "Code…" He nodded to the XO. Fennerwatham had the code; he had the operation name. This needed both of them to operate.

"Three. One. Alpha. Four. One. Echo."

Khan entered the code. "Restricted Operation Gray Two unlocked," she reported.

"What are you seeing?" J'Klin asked.

"A new jump command option. It's called Modified Jump. Is this the Khallini upgrade they want to install?"

"No. This secret is all on the Lady Indiya. May God have mercy on all of us. Initiate Modified Jump."

"Executing Modified Jump, aye."

A shockwave of energy, as palpable as a jolt of electricity, coursed through J'Klin and the command deck crew as reality folded around them. The sensation was reminiscent of dropping into j-Space but on a whole new level of savagery, in the way a timid field mouse bore some resemblance to an angry bear about to claw your guts out.

The CIC began to warp and contort with the sheer intensity of the jump flux. The metal deck plates groaned under the strain, and the air was filled with a thunderous rumble that fizzed with static.

Suddenly a strange sense of peace filled his bones, as though he had been thrust into a timeless paradise. Despite the danger and chaos of their mission, he couldn't help but be awed by the beauty of… of what exactly?

With sensors offline, he had no knowledge of what was happening outside the hull of his ship, but he had a powerful sense that the universe had been born anew. They had been gifted the chance to get things right this time.

The crew wore expressions of serenity and wonder, and he knew they felt the same as he did.

Even the XO had removed her cadmium beret and was scratching her head. Linora Fennerwatham *never* removed her beret.

"Astrogation," J'Klin said shakily when the systems began rebooting. "Report."

"We're… We're still at the Redoubt Line. We haven't moved."

"Perform a location check according to FL-191 Legion regulations," the XO said.

"I did, Commander. We can all guess what you've done. Those regulations were abandoned two and a half thousand years ago but we all study the ancient method of establishing a location in spacetime."

"Well?" J'Klin prompted gently. This was going to be difficult for all of them.

"Sensor feed good up to sixteen mega klicks and growing. I have good eyes on the Redoubt Line. Everything looks normal, minimal traffic. Defenses on standby."

"The Andromedans?"

"Nothing. No sign of them."

The XO cleared her throat. "You haven't answered the question, Lieutenant Khan."

"I only have enough data to carry out a spatial fix. We are exactly where we were when we jumped. If the secret jump option moved us in time, it was too short a distance to determine." Khan shook her head. "The temporal fix locator says we are within a thousand years of when we jumped. I remind you, sirs, that it measures the position of nearby stars relative to each other. They remain in the same patterns as they were before. Since to the best of my knowledge no one has ever performed a time jump before, that means this location system is entirely theoretical. It has never been field tested."

"Until now," J'Klin said. "Listen up, everyone. Let's stop pussy shitting around. The Gray Two order was meant to jump us back in time ninety minutes. The Lady Indiya let slip that another ship was equipped with a time jump long before *Steadfast* was built, but something went horribly wrong. Indiya was not forthcoming with specifics, and when it comes to immortal semi-divine figures with inhuman powers, I make it a policy not to press them too hard when they don't want to elaborate. Let's assume the lady knows what she's doing and we *have* actually jumped back ninety minutes. I want us to make the most of this time."

"To do what?" the XO said.

J'Klin tugged at his chin. "The empress can be maddeningly vague, but I think I can guess. Commander Fennerwatham, run a damage control scan of the ship."

"Which decks?"

"All of them."

J'Klin watched her as her fingers flowed across her control panel. He caught the moment when her eyebrows shot up and her mouth dropped open.

That mouth closed into a smile. "Captain, *Steadfast* has acquired a new compartment. It's inside the exhaust manifold for Energy Management Suite #5."

"Of course," J'Klin said. "The chief engineer always said Suite #5 is weirdly overengineered. What's inside?"

The XO's eyebrows furrowed. "I don't know, but it's a huge space. It's labeled Gray Stores."

"I see. Commander, it appears the Immortal Empress has granted us a wish. Take a team and investigate our mysterious new compartment. Make sure you have weapons technicians and logistics people. My guess is it's something designed to kill Andromedans."

"Aye, sir."

"Tactical, Helm, bring up recordings of our encounter with the enemy and move *Steadfast* to the location where their jump tunnel first appeared."

"Sir, we're being contacted by Fort Douaumont Control," Comms said. "They think we just made an in-system jump and want to know what the hell we're doing. They don't sound happy."

"Put them on my comm," he said. "FD control? This is *Steadfast* Actual."

"*Steadfast* Actual, be advised that defense systems are armed and aimed at you. We need convincing that your actions are benign. Fast. Otherwise, we will be forced to declare you a Corrupted vessel and destroy you."

"Destroy your only ride out? I don't think so, FD Control. But I don't blame you for being concerned. Here's what you're going to do. You will contact Lady Indiya and tell her that *Steadfast* is operating under Code Gray orders. You will not approach, nor will you contact us until we contact you."

"Standby, *Steadfast*."

"What's going on in the Redoubt?" J'Klin asked his CIC team. "Talk to me, people."

"FD Control isn't bluffing," Tactical said. "The defenses are fully online and there are scores of targeting systems painting us. Some of them… some of them include the corvettes and Cockroaches, all of whom are launching now."

"You mean the vessels that were by our side against the enemy a few minutes ago?"

"Yeah. Those." The tactical officer cleared his throat. "Including some I saw taken out by the Andromedans."

"No sign of an earlier version of *Steadfast*," the Weapons Control officer said. "Thank frakk! The idea of meeting another version of myself gave me the creeps."

J'Klin's collar blipped. "*Steadfast* Actual, FD Control. Request granted. Whatever the hell it is you're doing, Captain, good hunting. Fort Douaumont Control out."

The XO pinged him.

"That's quick, Linora."

"I'm still en route, but I have a team inside, and they've discovered a treasure chest of advanced weaponry. We don't know what it all does yet, but here's a good start. The Immortal Empress has left us NHEAT mines. Anti-ship configuration, five megaton yield."

"How many?"

The XO laughed, an unsettling sound J'Klin hadn't heard in a long time. "More than enough to destroy our Andromedan invasion fleet five times over."

Now it was J'Klin's turn to do something he hadn't done for an age. He got out of his chair and pushed himself to his knees without breaking his ankles—no easy task in the low-G when the magnetized strip in his boot soles were the only thing connecting him to the deck.

Then he bowed his head in supplication, closed his eyes, and spoke a heartfelt prayer of thanks to the Immortal Empress.

* * * * *

Chapter Forty: Lady Indiya

The third wave of Andromedan space creatures were brown slugs the size of frigates. Ugly brutes.

By that point, the jump tunnel's exit was thick with the corpses of the first two assault waves. The organic gauss cannons had been blasted by the fusion mines into clouds of hot gas, which were not in themselves a navigation danger to the third wave. But the armored shells of the Rho-Torkis Hammers were largely intact, their insides scooped out by the NHEAT mines. They looked like sloughed off exoskeletons, and it was these that the brown slugs collided with.

The Andromedan armada was larger than anyone had feared. For all their tactical clumsiness, at a strategic level, they had understood that the Last Redoubt was a vital target in this war and had sent a huge force to ensure its destruction.

A flutter of fear passed through Indiya. The enemy knew who she was and were coming to kill her.

Three Leviathans held the jump aperture open and the NHEAT mines closest to them had been deactivated so the flow of monsters to kill didn't stop.

Now, with the field of mines becoming patchy, those near the Leviathans were activated.

The massive tubes of alien monster instantly vaporized.

The jump aperture flickered and was gone.

Fitzwilliam hooted with the thrill of victory. Everyone else around the table was closed and silent, perhaps too stunned by the means used to win the battle. Even the two Muryani sitting at her strategy table held themselves rigidly.

Indiya switched off the recording. They had watched it enough times now.

"Mines generally play no part in conventional naval warfare," she pointed out. "Combat zones are so immense that larger ships will simply move around minefields and drones move through them. There are no roles for mines that drones cannot perform better."

"With the one exception," Fitzwilliam said, "when you know the precise location of the jump point the enemy will use. We've just witnessed the only time in history that has been the case." He peered at her through mutant eyes. "I hope you have more of these time machines, Lady Indiya."

"That's classified," she replied. But she was unable to help herself. She regarded the Muryani and grinned. "The following information is not to leave this room but, yes, I have more."

Her assessment of the Muryani reaction was horror at what she had done layered with terror about what she might do next.

An outcome that made her ooze with pleasure.

"Problem?" she asked them, sweetly.

"Yes," said the family's leader. "What you have done is extremely dangerous."

"Danger is my middle name," Fitzwilliam said. "Let's do it again."

Zan Fey shut him up with a hand on his shoulder. "What my husband means to say is that we need more of these time jump devices, and we need to understand how best to use them. *Phantom* would make a perfect test vehicle."

Fitzwilliam shrugged inside his fashionable jacket. "Izza's insanely curious too. She just says it better."

Indiya pursed her lips, as if contemplating whether to respond.

"I mean, come on!" Fitzwilliam gesticulated like an excitable ape plied with amphetamines. "According to *Steadfast's* splendid skipper, some of the corvette and fighter crews died in a version of the battle I don't remember. Now they're alive again. That is… I don't know. For once, even I have no words."

The man had so perfectly fed her an opening to show off to the Muryani that she wondered whether it had been deliberate.

She rose to her feet, hands resting on the table for support, and blessed him with a beatific smile.

Yes. The smuggler was undoubtedly cunning and had many talents, but at his core he was an impetuous fool. What made him so valuable was his mutant legacy, the result of his ancestors' human DNA intertwined with the genetic material of precognitive aliens.

That's why his rash impulses defied logic and reason but were invariably proved correct.

In fact, he reminded her of—

Shock wiped the smile from her face.

Fitzwilliam! He was exactly like his distant forebear, her husband.

Was that the real reason she kept Fitz and Chimera Company close? To be near an echo of him?

She sat down heavily.

Was she really such a simple creature? Was she just as blind to her own weaknesses as Khallini had been?

"Take your time," Fitzwilliam told her, his violet eyes soft with concern.

The heart and head were those of her husband's, but his eyes were exactly as Springer's had been, all those centuries ago. Her husband's lover.

"Mader zagh! Wixering frakk turds!"

The others watched in stony silence as Indiya muttered a stream of ancient curses. Then she mentally packaged up her disturbing revelations into a sealed container and threw them into a quiet part of her brain for later analysis. Much later.

"Traveling faster than light and traveling through time are the same phenomenon seen from different perspectives," she explained.

"But your Indiyan jump drive isn't true FTL," Zan Fey said. "It's bending spacetime into a j-Space tunnel. We call it FTL travel, but that's not what's actually happening. It's more bending reality to suit you."

"Correct. Time travel is analogous. We simply bend the time element of spacetime and jump through that."

"That is too crude," one of the Muryani said.

"It ignores the damage," the other said.

"I was coming to that," Indiya snapped. "Instead of a tunnel, the topology you create is a time *bubble*. You seal the unwanted events in there and replace with a new version. The time bubble remains permanently under tension, exactly as a jump tunnel when in use. The larger the bubble, the more tension it's under. And the more tension, the more power you need to create it and the more likely it is to spring open and burst random events through spacetime."

"Pity," Fitzwilliam said. "So, we couldn't return to Tau-Fornacis and change the course of that battle."

"Correct. Too many events have flowed since that battle and in consequence of it."

"But what I did," J'Klin said, "was far more modest. The battle had not fully begun, and we were isolated in deep space. We acted before the consequences of the battle spread to the rest of the universe. So, we were able to seal off an unwanted version of events before they had established themselves."

"Again correct."

"Not correct!" both Muryani declared.

"What you call bubbles are scars in reality itself," said one. "This technology is an abomination."

"Be quiet!" Indiya told them. "Hypocrites! The Exile ships used time travel to make the journey from the Orion Spur at sub-light speeds. Our ships were transported back a thousand years in time, and we slept in cryo for a thousand years to travel from the Orion Spur. The journey appeared instantaneous, but it was anything but. Many of us died through cryo attrition."

"You moved the Exile fleet in time?" Fitzwilliam's face filled with awe.

"I didn't, but I paid attention to those who did. If someone else understood this technology, so could I."

"But who?" Fitzwilliam asked. "Who did this? Who sent us here to the Perseus Arm?"

Indiya pointed at the Muryani. "Why not ask them? They were party to our exile."

The Muryani said nothing.

"Well?" Indiya demanded. "Who were they?"

"We cannot speak on that topic. It is also a distraction. Whatever your theories about your past, Lady Indiya, the Andromedans in our present will kill us all just the same."

"It is a question for another time, but not one I shall forget."

"Can *Steadfast's* time jump be restored?" J'Klin asked. "The command option has disappeared."

"The system you used," Indiya said, "was like a tightly wound spring. It unleashed its power and distorted in the process. It cannot be rewound. A replacement would have to be installed."

"And quickly," J'Klin said.

"Agreed. They know we're here," Zan Fey pointed out. "Do they know why their attack failed? Probably not, but if they tried once then they will try again. Next time they will arrive with a stronger force. Perhaps multiple fleets, each at a different jump point."

"All true, Zan Fey," Indiya said. "However, I am completely worn out. We must hope they leave us alone until I have had a good night's rest. If they do attack, then we are utterly doomed, but there wouldn't have been time to prepare a response anyway. Let's not waste time worrying about an event that may never come to pass and about which we can do nothing."

The mortals understood they had been dismissed. Even the two Muryani.

Kanha Wei hesitated at the hatch, turned, and gave Indiya a puzzled look. But there was no repeat of the hugs and tears of the previous version of events that Indiya remembered.

"Did you see all that?" she asked when the hatch had locked fast behind Wei.

"Yup," replied a deep male voice.

At one end of the strategy room hung a tapestry celebrating glorious victories from the first thousand years of the Legion. It rolled up into the overhead to reveal two sitting men.

Both rose and faced her.

She chuckled. "My two sergeants. The Gemini twins."

"Gemini?" Sybutu looked puzzled. "I don't know that term."

"I do," Arunsen said.

Sybutu looked at him, impressed.

"Yeah, I met this girl named Gemini while I was on leave at Halcyon-3. She wasn't the kind of person you can forget." He tugged at his whiskers. "Now that I think about it, ma'am, I can't be one of your sergeants. I'm a major now."

"You are whatever I say you are, and I say you are the saviors of the galaxy."

She enjoyed the reaction. Sybutu was outwardly impassive, but her senses penetrated deep within him and registered his shock.

Arunsen simply rejected her claim as the ramblings of a mad woman he had stopped trusting some time ago. Her words added fuel to his burning suspicion of her.

"When I swing my war hammer it is indeed a sight to behold," Arunsen said. "I am also admired in the female cat assassin community. And by certain goats. But it's a big stretch from looking good while bashing a few heads to being the galaxy's savior. You're mistaken, ma'am. I'm not the person you claim."

"His point is entirely valid," Sybutu agreed.

"I mean," Arunsen blundered on, "if you want someone special, what about Captain Fitz and Zan Fey? I mean, they've got all that purple-eyed mutant drent going on. And they seem to think you're their stepmother or something." He shuddered. "Always sounded unsavory to me."

"We've a traitor," Indiya informed them. "Someone has sold out the location of the Last Redoubt. And here's the thing, it could be almost anyone. But it can't be either of you. My team of mutants has been busy bringing me visions. Fanciful nonsense, most of it, but they have foreseen more than once that it is you two who will save us all. Not me, nor the dashing captain or his dangerous wife. You two."

"Do they say why?" Sybutu asked.

"No. However, I'm choosing to believe that neither of you are the traitor. Neither am I. Everyone else I regard as a suspect, including everybody who just left this room."

"Even J'Klin?"

Indiya nodded. "The Corruption works in many ways. Often it leaves its victims as muttering brainless zombies, but at other times it is more subtle. We know now that First General Clarke was Corrupted, and if they can turn the president of the Federation without anyone realizing, then I have to believe it's possible that J'Klin sabotaged his own ship and has no knowledge of doing so."

"Do you want us to spy on the others?" Arunsen asked.

"Certainly not. You would be incompetent in that task. No. In two days, I shall order *Phantom* to jump out with *Steadfast* on a secret mission. I shall tell Fitzwilliam the objective and of course he will immediately tell his wife. But only you shall know the reason behind that mission. For now."

She hesitated. Was she really about to entrust this pair with such dark secrets? She persuaded herself she had no choice. "You heard me describe the principle of the time jump?"

"Aye, we did," Sybutu said. "And about how it was too dangerous to use."

"But you have some spare time jumps up your sleeve," Arunsen said. "Are you sending us to retrieve them?"

"I was being… adaptable with the facts."

"You mean lying."

"Not entirely, Sergeant Arunsen."

"Major… oh, never mind."

"*Steadfast's* time jump was a one-off wildcard option. It could be replaced eventually, but the circumstances that made it useful are unlikely to be repeated. I have designed a nano-plague to kill the Corrupted, and Khallini's drive upgrades give me a means to transmit that directly to target worlds. Muryani battle fleets are already arriving in Federation space. But these strategies might not be enough. Arunsen, when the cards are dealt and the odds are stacked against you, what do you do?"

"Cheat," he said without hesitation. "Begging your pardon, ma'am, but the best cheating begins before the cards are dealt."

"Excellent, Major. I am sending you with *Phantom* to retrieve my cheat card. One that you might say I've been holding up my sleeve for many centuries."

She grimaced.

"Oh, joy," Arunsen said. "There's a catch, isn't there?"

"In a manner of speaking. The people who have been holding it for me… they're dangerous and after all this time they may be insane."

Sybutu's eyes widened. "They've been alive for centuries?"

"Millenia, yes. And I expect they've spent every second cursing my name. So probably best not to mention who sent you, eh?"

* * * * *

Chapter Forty-One: Muryani Commander

Taractacus System

The Muryani fleet commander hardened their resolve and then indicated that their ships should exit the jump tunnel into the star system the humans called Taractacus. The fleet consisted of 130 attack cruisers supported by 200 smaller warships and 7 mobile drone factories. Would it be enough?

The reports came through to their command station of the Andromedan force they would meet. Thousands of the monsters awaited them, ships that were alive and moved with a hungry intent. The enemy had amassed far greater numbers than they had feared.

"Human warships arriving," reported a subordinate.

The commander flicked antennae at the strangeness of the situation. In this war—so far, at least—the humans were allies of the Muryani, a first for a race who had often faced off against the Expansion in the Orion Spur, far from here.

To be precise, the Federation and its military contained many races other than the humans. However, at the key moments in the Federation's history, events had always pivoted on that species. The commander distrusted them on principle.

They waited while the human war fleet under Admiral Aluin arrived piecemeal a short distance away. While the human contingent was small compared to the enemy armada, it might prove just enough to turn the tide of battle.

As the Muryani commander watched, they could almost hear Admiral Aluin's words in their mind: "No guts, no glory." That was the kind of thing human field commanders said.

The Andromedans floated in space, patiently waiting for the humans to arrive. It made horrific sense to wait until the humans stopped arriving. The more ships the enemy faced, the more they could eat and use to create more living ships.

Surrender was never an option.

Not even death was permitted to the Muryani warriors. Allowing your corpse to be captured was a dereliction of duty, which was why all Muryani ships were fitted with fusion self-immolators.

The humans ceased arriving.

The Andromedans began their attack by launching hundreds of small asteroids, a few hundred meters across, in a single volley. The allied ships were taken by surprise and scrambled to evade, though the alertness of the human and Muryani crews meant only a handful of ships were struck.

Catastrophic casualties were avoided, but the allied ship formations had been disrupted and the Andromedans pressed home this advantage as they surged forward, unleashing a firestorm of energy blasts and kinetic projectiles that overwhelmed the allied fleets with its sheer power.

At first, the Muryani concentrated their fire on the foremost Andromedan ships, the spearhead ships that the humans called Rho-Torkis Hammers.

Over thousands of years, the Muryani weapons systems and tactics had been honed to specifically counter the Hammers, but they remained formidable adversaries that could only be bested by overwhelming firepower.

The Muryani commander did not have that advantage.

From every direction, munitions of destruction flew across the void of space, impacting shields and hulls of both sides with savage ferocity.

The Andromedan attack was blunted somewhat, but at the cost of heavy casualties to all sides. The enemy could absorb their losses, of course, with reclamation units sucking up the spilled remains of dead and crippled ships, Andromedan and human alike.

Not so the stricken Muryani ships, whose crews activated their fusion self-immolators, destroying any chance that their corpses would be used as raw material for the Andromedan swarm.

The battlespace became a maelstrom of death and destruction as the fusion plumes of the sacrificing Muryani ships illuminated the darkness like a nightmarish recreation of the Fifth Hell.

Off balance from the start due to the asteroid salvo, the Muryani fleet lost cohesion, and the battle devolved into chaos.

The Andromedan ships were relentless in their attack. Wave after wave moved through their opponents like hungry predators, seeking any weakness or opportunity to devour their prey.

The Muryani cruisers and drone squadrons countered furiously, their smaller vessels darting in and out of the fray, using their superior speed and agility to harass the Andromedan forces. But it wasn't enough, and their ships lit up space with explosions as they were either destroyed by the relentless enemy fire or yielded to the oblivion of defeat and chose to depart this life via fusion immolation.

The Andromedans continued their onslaught, cutting through the allied fleet like a monoblade sword.

If the Muryani had met the Andromedans alone, then their fleet commander would have abandoned any hope of victory at this point, but the humans under Aluin refused to accept that their puny numbers should limit their impact.

The Muryani commander marveled at the courage of the human pilots as they flew their fighter craft into the heart of the Andromedans, weaving and dodging in an intricate dance of death and destruction. The Muryani crews fought courageously against long odds, launching counterattacks and taking evasive maneuvers, but still fell one by one like brittle stalks in the face of a hurricane. Courage and skill were simply not enough against the sheer number of enemy vessels. The enemy relentlessly pursued them, firing volley after volley of destructive ordnance at their quarry as they slowly whittled away at the allies' numbers, careless of their own losses.

Death was nothing to them. The true enemy the Muryani faced was the swarm that had crossed the intergalactic gulf to consume a new galaxy. The individual Andromedan soldiers and living warships had no more sense of self than the cells in the commander's foot-hands.

Across the allied fleet, shields overloaded and hulls were breached under the immense pressure. Even Admiral Aluin's flagship, *Starhammer*, was forced to withdraw to the rear of the battle space after a mob of Hammers smashed the weapons nacelles of the human ship. Dozens of Andromedan boarding ships squeezed inside *Starhammer's* wounds and disgorged hordes of frenzied foot soldiers.

After two hours of relentless fighting, hundreds of allied vessels had either been flashed into ionized gas or reduced to drifting wrecks in which screaming survivors begged for mercy that would never come. The allies were battered and almost broken.

Taractacus was a populous star system with several billion Federation citizens. Most of them lived less than a light second away on the blue-red planet of Taractacus-Alpha which watched helplessly as its fate was determined in near space.

Admiral Aluin would try to buy the lives of those citizens with those of his warriors, as was only natural, and as the Lady Indiya had explained to the Muryani commander's superiors.

The commander had different priorities regarding the hapless citizens, and since they were nearing the point where defeat would be inevitable, they had to plan now for more than simply extracting as many ships as they could.

Worlds teeming with life could not be allowed to fall into the insatiable maws of the Andromedans.

The signals leader drew the fleet commander's attention. "The human, Admiral Aluin, wishes to communicate directly with you."

The commander ground their secondary jaw in concern. Had the humans and their Federation allies scented what the commander was contemplating? Were the allies about to turn on each other?

"We just took out the last Hammer," Aluin said. "If you've been keeping any of your powder dry, now's the time to make use of it."

The commander flung a request at the tactical analysis team to explain the human's assessment and to the linguistics team to interpret what the four-limbed fool was trying to tell them.

The answers were swift in coming.

A flotilla of Federation destroyers had launched a suicide run at a cluster of Hammers. The human vessels had the equivalent of immolation devices on board.

The Andromedan heavy attack ships had crippled the Federation destroyers with ease, but as the Hammers screamed in to dispatch them with their tail clubs, the destroyer crews ignited their cargos of fusion bombs. The blinding detonations were so powerful that they not only smashed the Hammer ships apart, but it was as if a shockwave of energy ripped through the rest of the enemy fleet, spreading chaos and destruction.

That was impossible, of course. Shockwaves could not transmit through a vacuum. But neither could the Hammers 'swim' through empty space, and yet the evidence for both was there to see.

The Andromedans' most heavily armored ships were not easily killed, however. Two of the Hammers survived, though wounded.

They thrashed at the vacuum to make good their escape, but the remaining ships of the Federation fleet had been waiting for this and concentrated all their fire on the Hammers' weak points.

Both enemy ships were killed.

Clever.

And brave.

In mere seconds, hundreds of Andromedan vessels had been wiped out or disabled in a cascade of destruction that was made possible only by the noble sacrifice of just a handful of brave Federation warriors, humanoids who had chosen to go down swinging rather than accept defeat.

This must be the famous Legion.

The humans would make excellent allies and dangerous foes. It was important that this information survived the battle, to be conveyed to higher military authority.

The crew of the Muryani flagship's command deck vented chemical signals of admiration for the humans. Several flicked antennae the commander's way, unsure whether this reaction was a fitting tribute or treachery.

The commander opened their primary mouth wide, into what the humans would recognize as a grin.

"Commit the drone reserves," they ordered. "Nothing left behind. I want every vessel still operational to advance and exploit this opening."

The Voice of Doubts stood. "If we commit the drone reserve, we have nothing left to cover our retreat."

"Yes," the commander countered.

To be the Voice of Doubts was a great honor, a role awarded only to veteran commanders of the most impressive record who knew the right moments to draw upon their accumulated experience and challenge the active commander. With great age came great bulk, and normally when the Voice of Doubts drew themselves up to their full height the commander would be so intimidated that their steel resolve would turn to running water.

Not today.

"Yes," the commander repeated and stood to face the Voice of Doubts. "We now commit to winning. Obey my orders."

The Voice of Doubts sat, and the drones were launched.

Missiles too, many of them from the humans. What remained of Strike Force Fornax launched what the commander assessed to be the entirety of their remaining missiles. They screamed at the Andromedans from all sides, pursuing attack vectors the torpid enemy ships were unable to counter. The missiles tore great holes from the enemy battle formations, and the Muryani drone reserves poured into these holes.

The commander judged that the reason for the enemy's loss of initiative was the combination of losing the last of the Hammers with the Federation warships' tactic of focusing their fire upon the command-and-control spheres.

Small groups of Andromedan ships were starting to recover from these twin shocks. The allied fleets concentrated on destroying these most dangerous ships first.

This was not a war of mercy and honor. You could no more negotiate with the enemy swarm than you could a plague virus. But the heavy losses suffered by the allies pushed them on to slaughter the enemy with even greater savagery than normal.

The jump Leviathans escaped into other dimensions, but the rest of the immense Andromedan fleet constituted the majority of the shattered hulls and debris drifting in space above the Federation planet, testimony to a battle that had been brutally won at great cost.

The commander issued orders to their second in command. "Inform Cruisers 124 and 151 that they are to jump immediately to the task force center of operations with full recordings of what transpired here at Taractacus." Their body shuddered in revulsion for what they must do next. "Meanwhile, it shall be my duty to meet with Admiral Aluin in person and celebrate the valiant effort of our forces in winning this glorious victory for… it is true that the humans did play some small part in it."

The deaths were still being counted, the wounds of the Muryani fleet were still raw and bleeding when the perimeter drone scouts conveyed to the tactical assessment team the worst news imaginable.

"Andromedan jump tunnels forming. Three of them."

* * * * *

Chapter Forty-Two: Muryani Commander

The Hammers emerged first. Scores of them.

If the ratios of Andromedan ship types were consistent, then each of the three new fleets they were facing were of similar size to the one they had just defeated—barely, and at enormous cost.

A video link to *Starhammer* was already open, but it would no longer be used to discuss victory celebrations.

"Go," the commander told Aluin. "Jump away." They pulled at the uncomfortable translator device that cut into their throat. "Your missile stocks are empty. *Starhammer* is barely operational. You are spent. We shall cover your retreat."

"There are billions of people in this system. I can't abandon them to their fate."

"This is war, Admiral Aluin. Victory is uncertain and a defeat would mean far more lives fell victim to the enemy. A few billion is an unimaginable tragedy at a personal level, but not when compared to the full number who would die if the Andromedans prevail."

"That's easy to say when it isn't your people getting abandoned."

"But they are my people, too, Admiral. We must all stand against the invaders because defeat means death for all. Before you gave us the jump drive, it took many centuries to cross from one border of the

Expansion to another, and yet we have explored only a tiny fraction of the galaxy. Our scientists estimate the galaxy contains three million intelligent species whom we have yet to contact. If we fail to halt the enemy here at the galactic rim, those species shall also be consumed by the insatiable Andromedan swarm. We must stand fast for all their sakes, even if they never know the sacrifice we make."

Aluin bowed his head and was unable to make eye contact with the camera for several seconds.

The commander was good for their word. Despite the Hammers pressing hard, the Muryani formed a barrier of steel and determination that protected the Federation ships—even allowing crews to be extracted from the Legion vessels whose jump drives had been too badly damaged.

By the time the last Federation ship jumped away, bitter with defeat, the commander's decision to cover their allies' withdrawal was costing them dearly. Casualties were heavy and the drones almost gone. Many of the surviving ships who had expected to end this day in glorious celebration instead ended it in self-immolation plumes. If any of the Muryani ships were to escape the debacle, it would be under heavy fire.

Yet there was a task they still had to perform.

While the lighter ships and half the surviving cruisers screened against the Andromedans, the remaining cruisers launched a barrage of EMP bombs at Taractacus-Alpha. The frantic transmissions the Muryani had been receiving from the Federation world cut out as the blasts reduced communication relays and satellites to electronic slag.

Disabling the world's ability to communicate with the outside galaxy would cast a diplomatic veil over the events that must follow.

Aluin's reluctance to leave demonstrated that the humans had not yet grasped the desperation of the situation.

Not so the Muryani, for they had been here before.

Which was why the fleet not only carried a means to prevent wrecked ships and abandoned crews from being consumed by the enemy. Larger prizes must also be denied.

"Fire planetary immolators!"

For a few seconds, the commander watched the weapons of mass desperation fall toward the doomed planet.

These devices had not been used for thousands of years, but the commander knew their effects very well. Taractacus-Alpha would not only be incinerated, but its magnetic field would be disrupted long enough for stellar radiation to strip it of all life.

There were other pockets of habitation across the Taractacus system: a small colony on Taractacus-Beta, asteroid mining communities, research stations and the like. There was nothing to be done for them. They would have to await their fate inside the insatiable maws of the Andromedans.

To be destroyed immediately in fusion fire or eke out a few final weeks or even months, knowing all the time that the monsters would eventually find you? The commander couldn't decide which fate was worse.

They snapped out of their contemplation and realized there was no time to confirm the effect of the planetary immolator salvo. Nor even to organize an orderly withdrawal.

"All ships, set course for rendezvous point #1. Jump immediately. Every ship for themselves."

* * *

The inhabitants of Taractacus-Alpha saw their ruin descend through the skies. A few attempted to get the message out, to warn the rest of the Federation what their so-called allies were doing.

Though incredibly rare, working examples remained scattered across the Federation of the quantum-entangled communication devices brought by the Exile Feet from the Orion Spur.

Four were usually present in or around Taractacus-Alpha.

Of these, the device on the Legion Navy orbital was strengthened against EMP bursts, but not against Muryani munitions that had been specifically redesigned in this region to overcome Legion hardening.

Two were normally held on the planet's surface by rival Federation covert operations teams, but mysteriously both had been transported away from the Taractacus system shortly before the Andromedans had arrived.

As the planet burned, eight billion souls screamed into the void.

But no one was listening.

The fourth device was in high orbit, connected to secret electronic eyes that observed everything.

The Outer Torellian Commerce Guild—better known as the Smugglers Guild to those who dared speak its true name—were experts in watching and listening from the shadows. They also used technologies the Legion had never encountered, including hardening that was effective against Muryani EMP weapons.

Their spy drone recorded everything.

The AI intelligence that controlled it decided the information it had learned was so important that it would activate the tiny sliver of entangled communication mass carried on board and use every last bit of its remaining bandwidth to deliver its report to its twin.

That twin was located in the one location of the Federation that almost the entirety of its citizenry was convinced did not exist.

*****

Chapter Forty-Three: Claudio "Beans" Zanitch

"Well, that was an improvement," said Beans as he got to his feet and stepped out of the circle of mutants. "But it was still as full of crap as the ground beneath a turd monkey flinging post."

The reason for the modest improvement frowned. This was New Darant, and while he lacked the violet pigmentation or mutant superpowers enjoyed by most of Indigo Squad, he acted as a battery or catalyst or some such.

Or perhaps Darant just made them feel good. No one really understood what the hell was going on with these mutant superpowers, but they were really all right. And if they acted together and pooled their talents, they were getting frustratingly close to actually being useful.

New Darant brought them closer than ever to making a difference.

Realizing he had just been given what might loosely be described as a compliment, Darant came over to shake Beans' hand. "I missed you when I was dead."

"You weren't dead. The other Darant is and shall remain demised. You're a clone replacement for him, not the same person."

Darant scrunched his face. "Yeah, it's a question everyone's asking. Am I really Darant?"

It was Beans' turn to frown. He pointed at his own mouth. "Listen to the words that emanate from this orifice. I was not asking a question."

The clone shrugged. "Good. Neither was I. Not anymore."

"Oh." Beans didn't quite follow. "What conclusion did you reach, Darant? Are you the same person as him or not?"

Darant shook his head and chuckled. "Neither. My firm conclusion is that I don't want to ask that question."

Beans laughed. This might not technically be the same Darant he'd befriended, but he had the same humor. Beans liked him just as much.

Something was troubling the clone. "Hey, you're still going to write your stories about me, right?"

Beans thought on that. "No."

Darant's face fell.

"It was the other Darant I made a promise to. I promised I would write him a story in which he finally got the girl."

Darant stiffened. "Without said girl being shot dead the next day or turning out to be a traitor using me all along."

"I'll make good on that promise. But for you, my new cloned friend, I shall write stories all your own."

A shiny dog chew gave Beans a savage kick in his shins.

The dog chew was actually an Orsiric monk and sorceress called Burmina. Beans considered Dog Chew to be a restrained nickname considering what Burmina called him. In any case, Orsirics did resemble chewed up plastic dolls, so he was only being truthful.

"Burmina," he said expansively while resisting the urge to rub his shin. "I'm sorry if I didn't notice you trying to get my attention. May I suggest—"

"Bringing a portable stool to stand on. Yeah. You're repeating your gags, you dumb, balding ape. Listen. I don't care how much of a hard-on you're getting from flirting with this clone. Focus the fuck up and go to her."

The 'her' that Burmina was referring to was Pyruula, Indigo Squad's fish boss.

Beans took in the room and caught sight of Pyruula's back as she walked out.

He hurried after her and was just in time to see her hang a left at the cross passage instead of carrying straight on to the refectory like everyone else.

Twenty feet down the left turn, he stopped.

Pyruula had vanished.

He looked behind him, but there were no cross passageways or doors the fish woman could have used.

Something tickled the top of his head, and he looked up.

It was Pyruula's pectoral spirals, the long, coiled fish flesh that had probably been fins in the lungwoman's distant ancestors. She was glued to the overhead by her boots and dangling her coils over his bald pate. She came lower and jiggled them to caress his face.

"Trying to seduce me again, fish boss? You'll have to try a lot harder than that, but… it's not a bad start."

She jumped down, her movement as fluid as a gymnast, none of this disengaging boot magnetizing business.

How had he walked beneath her without noticing?

Because she was a senior member of the Smugglers Guild, of course. Damn, she was good!

She came to him with pouting lips and breathed on him. Her breath smelled of sesame oil, a salty sea breeze and something else that he couldn't quite place but was deliciously alluring.

Beans' heart began to race. He felt a surge of desire, but following his instincts could only lead him to a very bad destination, albeit with some hellishly fun stops along the way. He pushed those feelings deep within him, satisfied that they would emerge later in his storytelling.

He weathered the warmth of her breath on his face, told himself those lips just nanometers from his were not really driving him nuts, and breathed her in deeply.

Then he widened his mouth and bathed her face in his outbreath.

She sucked at it, snorting it vulgarly before closing her eyes as if basking in an elixir of pleasure.

The first time she had stood on tiptoes and raised her lips to pour her breath over him, he had thought she was trying to seduce him. Come on, any human man would! But this was a lungperson, and the mutual exchange of breaths was a greeting of intimacy and respect. Nothing sexual to see here.

Despite the way she made a middle-aged man with chronic back strain feel like a rampant tiger.

"Claudio," she said in a low, sultry voice. He tried not to growl in response. "You have no idea how much you mean to me. When so much around me is fake… uncertain… you are the spar I can cling to in the black, knowing you are an anchor that will not fail."

Inhumanly long fingers flicked delicate caresses across his cheek.

Claudio smiled, but it was an uncertain one because she'd never touched him that way before. "What is it you want, Pyruula?"

"Just one night with you." Her voice was husky with desire. "Just one night of pleasure and adventure. I promise you won't regret it."

She grasped him by the shoulders and pulled him down and close.

He returned her caresses, tracing the ridges and furrows of her fish scales.

Pyruula grinned, her curves deepening, and murmured into his ear, "What do you say we lose ourselves in the stars?"

Her spell broke, and he bent over guffawing.

"Better," he said when he'd recovered. "If I were a gentleman, I'd probably say that you almost had me this time."

"You think I couldn't seduce you if I really wanted to?"

"I know you couldn't. But it's fun watching you try, which is why I can't get angry at you. *Lose ourselves in the stars*? Really?"

"My heart wasn't in it. The game is a distraction, but it is too late for such things. We must meet our fates head on, however much we fear them."

He waited, knowing there was more.

To his surprise, her fingers returned to his cheek. She patted it then squeezed the ample flesh between her fingers. "You pursued me. Speak your mind, Claudio."

He put a finger to her head. "There's a darkness in there. One that wasn't there before, and we can all feel it. What troubles you?"

She took almost a minute to decide her response. "Death is coming," she said. Then she brightened and added, "You are my friend." It was a statement, not a question, and that gave him immense pride. "I need you to do something for me."

"Ask."

"Assemble Indigo Squad. Chimera Company, too, if you possibly can. Together, perhaps our unity and strength will be enough, because we must confront her now."

He didn't have to ask whom she meant.

Furtive conversations overheard, Burmina's ominous warnings, and carelessly revealed thoughts in the mutant group sessions hastily concealed: all of it had been building for weeks. Everyone in Indigo Squad shared a gnawing sense of foreboding that a monstrous aspect was about to emerge from the one person everyone depended on.

Indiya.

* * * * *

Chapter Forty-Four: Vetch Arunsen

Indiya steepled her fingers on the polished wooden desk.

"So, it has come to this."

Her fierce gaze swept over the assembled survivors of Chimera Company and its mutant offshoot, Indigo Squad, plus its basten goat mascot.

The ancient woman seemed to understand the significance of this confrontation, which was a helluva lot more than Vetch did.

He swallowed in fear. Whatever was going on here, the Lady Indiya was severely skragged off about it. The only other person in the universe who had shared Indiya's special powers was the late Lord Khallini. Vetch had swung his war hammer at the little old man once and had only lived to tell the tale because he'd amused the old veck.

Khallini could kill heavily armored elite Legion troopers with no more than a thought. He'd seen them die.

He didn't trust Indiya. Didn't like her. But he had no intention of ever making her angry.

It seemed that someone here thought otherwise.

Waves of fear emanated from the assembled group held by the anger in Indiya's eyes.

No one spoke.

No one dared, but probably no one needed to. Indiya was a sorceress. Reading minds was the least of her powers.

Indiya stopped playing her gaze over the room and settled on her prey like a rabbit caught in a terawatt laser.

Vetch corrected his analogy. Indiya had skewered a *fish* with her laser stare.

Pyruula.

The fish woman's green eyes widened and then—weirdly—darkened to a smoky black. Her trembles shook the coils of fin flaps down her long neck and her breath was shallow as she gulped in fear.

She kept her posture rigid and her muscles tense, as if bracing herself for the inevitable.

"Speak!" the little old lady demanded.

A clicking sound came from Pyruula's throat, and her tension eased.

Vetch had seen the same in mortally wounded troopers, their body relaxing as they accepted death was close.

"Taractacus-Alpha died," Pyruula said. The Guildswoman walked over to Sybutu and tapped him on the shoulder. He flinched.

She repeated this with Green Fish who pushed her away.

It had always struck Vetch as odd that Sybutu and Green rarely spoke, despite both hailing from Taractacus-Alpha.

"We know," Sybutu whispered.

"But it was not the Andromedans who killed the citizens of your homeworld," Pyruula said. "The Muryani *she* invited here did. Planet-buster weapons. Taractacus-Alpha is a hot cinder. Your people are nothing more than radioactive ash. And here's what we all need to know: Legion entangled comms units were evacuated out of the system before the bombs fell. It was almost as if someone knew what the Muryani would do if we lost the battle."

"It is normal to evacuate vital equipment from locations at risk," Sybutu said, his voice a lifeless monotone.

Indiya squinted at Sybutu, her nose wrinkled and lips curled into a sneer. Then her expression melted into pity.

"We are wasting time with this melodrama," Indiya said. "And I have better things to do."

Pyruula stood her ground, chin thrust out defiantly. "I have proof."

With a casual wave, Indiya dismissed the lungwoman's line of attack. "There is no need for proof," she said. "I do not deny your claim. Populated worlds are assets that must be denied to the enemy. The same planetary sterilization has already taken place at Cynestrax Prime, Uthon-7, Rho-Kopras, and Coronon. And there will be many more to come, no doubt. I do not do this lightly, but these worlds were already dead."

"There has to be another way," Fitz said as if in a dreamy haze.

"And yet there is not," Indiya replied.

"Why did you never talk of this with us?" Sybutu asked. "I was to be your moral compass, but you never raised this with me."

"Because I knew I could not trust you." She sighed, as if bored. "What would you know anyway? Born today gone tomorrow, the lot of you, and yet I persist. I'm 3,600 years old, and I cannot allow myself to die because, as we can all see, you mortals don't have the guts to survive without me."

"On the contrary," Lily said, "I think we're better off without you, Lady Indiya. Enthree, I know you care about us, but the Expansion doesn't. Now they've a taste for it, what's to stop them moving to preemptively wiping out every inhabited world in the Federation? Just to be on the safe side."

"It's what they would do," Enthree replied, "if they thought defeat in this phase of the war was inevitable."

"This first phase as you call it," Indiya said, "is the life-and-death struggle of the Federation. The reason the Exiles were brought here. To repulse the invasion before it pushes beyond our sector of the galactic rim and heads for the core. If we lose, the Muryani Expansion is the last hope for every race in the galaxy."

No one spoke. What was there to say? Few people had ever faced hopelessness on such a mega scale.

"However," Indiya said, "this first phase of the war is not yet lost." She gave Vetch a meaningful glance. "And you—" she pointed at Lily "—are mistaken. The Expansion cares more than you know. With my assistance, the Muryani have already taken small but viable population samples of the various Federation species. If necessary, they will create a cordon sanitaire across this part of the Perseus Arm, sterilizing all worlds in the Federation and for scores of light years beyond, including many Muryani worlds. Those population samples will be resettled within the Expansion and allowed to form their own autonomous communities."

"And you've agreed this?" Pyruula said.

"It is already settled. It's been done before." Indiya frowned. "You do realize that? That's what the Broken Worlds are. You visited one, Dolorene. The hex world. Though what the Expansion is planning now is on a much larger scale than the old Broken Worlds, of course."

"You're surrendering the Federation," Pyruula said. "Colluding in the extermination of countless trillions of its inhabitants."

Indiya stood upright, hands clenched by her sides and eyes blazing with a fury none there had ever seen before.

She looked at Pyruula with a mix of pity and loathing. "You do not understand a *thing* about war," she snarled. "Wars without end and without mercy."

"I know more than—"

The lungwoman's throat clicked loudly. She stood on tiptoes as if an unseen giant were lifting her off her feet.

Zan Fey hurried to the stricken lungwoman, then stopped, frozen mid stride.

Fitz gurgled in his throat then went similarly rigid.

Hubert bared his teeth.

Indiya ignored her struggling victims and glared at Vetch.

He was pinned to the spot by the intensity of her gaze. He shifted his foot a little and was relieved that she hadn't used sorcery to fix him in place. Fear alone was doing that.

"You've been against me for some time, Arunsen. Burmina has been warning about me too. I know these things. I know *everything*."

Hubert whined. Vetch wanted his war hammer. Not that Lucerne would help against an angry immortal, but he had always wanted to die with his favorite weapon in his hands.

"Disagreement and grumbling I can accept," Indiya said. "Sabotage and assassination of my person is unacceptable. We are in crisis here, people. We're not just fighting for survival for ourselves but for all the generations yet to come of every race in the Federation and beyond. The overwhelming majority of our races are yet to be born, and I will not sacrifice those untold numbers. That means all our lives are insignificant, including mine and everybody who once lived on Taractacus-Alpha. All of us. But especially yours, Pyruula."

Vetch glanced at the lungwoman. To his astonishment, she had a knife in her hand, despite seemingly being held by the throat by cruel magical fingers.

Indiya casually flicked a wrist and released Pyruula from her invisible grasp. The alien woman's eyes widened more than ever and for a moment there was a sea of movement beneath the scales of her skin.

Suddenly, her body was engulfed in a bright red mist that slowly dissipated in the air.

Vetch blinked. The red mist *was* Pyruula.

The lungwoman had vanished. Her clothing and gear clattered to the deck, but the person who had worn them had been erased.

"Oh, get over it," Indiya said. "Her blood is not on your conscience. It will wash off easily enough."

Competing instincts caught Vetch in a crossfire.

He should flee.

Attack Indiya.

Cower and sob.

But none of those things would change anything. He'd never felt so insignificant in his life.

Then he remembered what Indiya herself had told him only the day before.

Vetch glanced Sybutu's way and saw his friend was thinking the same thing. Somehow, they were supposed to be saviors of the galaxy.

Not like this, they wouldn't.

Indiya muttered that they could go and the indecision left him.

He stumbled out of that room, almost tripping in his haste to flee. The heat of humiliation singed his cheeks. All his pride and courage had dissolved in that blood red fog.

*****

Chapter Forty-Five: Yat Darant

They fled along a corridor bored through the asteroid's heart as fast as their feet would carry them. Which, considering some of their number were not exactly athletic, amounted to a slow jog.

Even at that speed, Darant kept expecting his companions to slip on the rocky floor, because it looked as smooth as glass. Yet its gritty texture kept everyone upright.

Lights in the overhead bathed everyone's face in an unnatural yellow glow. It emphasized the sweat and fear on those who hadn't made a career out of running through tunnels and corridors while being shot at.

Or even of getting out of their chairs once in a while.

We might as well be walking, Darant thought to himself. *Indiya controls everything inside this rock and out across the Redoubt Line. We only leave if she lets us go. So, if we're headed out, we might as well save our energy and sink a few beers and a last meal for the road before we go.*

They'd barely gone fifty yards when Molinjik planted his boots on the glassy floor and cried, "Why are we even running?"

Good boy. Darant would never have guessed the question in his mind would be voiced by the milksop stableboy with a minor mutant gift for something-or-other.

"We can't leave this place anyway," Molinjik said. "The only way out is aboard *Steadfast*."

Darant rolled his eyes and bumped into the back of Beans Zanitch who had stopped to double over in laughter.

Hubert hammered the brakes on all six of his little legs and twisted around to see why his favorite human had stopped.

"Do you want to explain or shall I?" Darant said to Beans.

The stableboy clenched his fists. "Don't you get it?" he shouted at Beans. "After a ship jumps into the Redoubt Line, it can't jump away because there are no gravity wells big enough to recharge the jump engines. Only *Steadfast* can jump away."

"Captain Fitz is many things," Beans told him, "but he isn't stupid. At any rate, not with regard to his ship. Did you not notice that the captain always insisted when we traveled here that we hitched a ride in *Steadfast's* hangar? *Phantom* is fully charged and can go anywhere within 12.5 light years."

Now it was Enthree's turn to trip up the seemingly simple plan of running away. She stopped and curled her body in on herself, as she did when she was feeling obstinate.

"Wait!" she shouted.

The others came to a reluctant halt.

"We all saw what happened to Pyruula. Indiya has already explained that she only knows how to clone a few core species. My guess is that she also only knows how to kill species she knows well. Therefore, I may be immune. I shall wait behind and prevent her from following us, should she change her mind about allowing us to go."

Vetch hugged the big insectoid. "I knew I could count on you, Big Bug. But you're a bit dim sometimes."

"What the sarge is trying to say," Lily added, "but skragging it up now that he thinks he's a major, is that she would have studied you Muryani in far more detail than lungpeople like Pyruula. She can kill you with a thought. Guarantee it."

"But you cannot know that for sure," Enthree said.

"Indiya can control humans and those with similar physiologies," Darant said. "Maybe big, fat, hairy insects like Enthree, too. But how about alien goats with attitude?"

Hubert pricked up his ears and bleated softly.

Darant knelt and nuzzled the little guy's head. While Darant was dead, the goat had been spoiled rotten by the entire Redoubt community. Instead of a coarse, woolly mane that smelled of hay soaked in diesel, now his fur was supple velvet with the scent of summer fields bursting with wildflowers.

He hoped all that pampering hadn't dampened the goat's instinct to kill. You wouldn't know to look at the little fella's face, but the goat had sliced through bad people's legs more than once.

Darant pointed behind at the hatch to Indiya's strategy room. "Watch her, boy. If she comes out and does anything I wouldn't like, bite her."

Hubert peered at Darant with piercing green eyes. Then he pressed a hot nose to Darant's cheek and kept it there for several seconds.

The goat walked off to stand guard over the Immortal Empress, his ears flat along his stubby head to show he meant business.

Everyone told Darant that it was just a stupid damned animal, but he swore the little guy understood what he was saying far more than most of the ignorant skraggs in Chimera Company.

The others hurried away, leaving Darant watching his best friend on six legs.

He swallowed hard. "Nowhere is truly safe in this galaxy, pal, but I honestly think you're safer here than following Fitz."

Hubert snuffed in acknowledgment but didn't look back.

Darant realized he was the one here having difficulty letting go and sprinted after the others. He soon caught up to Beans, who had hung back.

"Did you mean what you said?" Beans asked him.

"That Hubert is more difficult for Indiya to kill than any of us? Yeah."

"I don't doubt it. That's one mean ass goat. No, I meant what you said to Hubert. That he was safer here than with us. Do you think our chances with Fitz are so slim?"

Darant stopped for a moment and patted the big man on the shoulder. "If I were you, I would stay here. Seriously. Indiya won't kill you." He sniffed. "Probably."

"Why don't *you* stay, Yat? You're no threat to Indiya. Besides, the lady's just cloned you and she doesn't strike me as wasteful."

Darant winced. "You're talking logic and reason, whereas…" He looked meaningfully up the passageway where Fitz had started delivering inspirational words to the laggards. "Following these reprobates is a habit that's hard to break. But I'm serious, Beans, you should stay here where it's safe and try not to get eaten."

Darant ran a few strides on his own. Then Beans followed, groaning as pain shot up his forever aching spine.

"Nice try," Beans puffed. "But I'm not leaving my meal ticket behind. I'm already detailing the stories I'm writing on you folks. I even have the series logo ready, and I can tell you the artwork will be absolutely killer."

Darant's spirits lifted. It would have been dire to lose Beans and Hubert on the same day.

His good mood was only slightly dampened when Beans added a few moments later, "Besides. I hope I'm wrong, for Hubert's sake, but anyone who sticks around the Redoubt is going to be devoured by the Andromedans."

* * *

The goat lifted his head from her lap and Indiya obediently tickled him under his chin. He snuffed and rested his head once more on her thighs.

She looked to the pool of drying blood and liquidized flesh where Pyruula had last stood.

"I think I went too far," she said. "What you think, my beautiful?"

Hubert's emerald eyes gave her a look of faint disapproval.

"I see." She sniffed. "I shan't justify myself to you, Hubert Goat. You'd better go back to them. I expect they will run away soon and somebody needs to look after them. It might as well be you. You, Hubert, should be the hero."

The goat was uninterested.

"They said I was a hero, long ago. I used to be venerated. There are still statues of me across the Federation, but I was really always the monster, never a hero. Heroism was what my husband did, and I've been lost without him."

Hubert looked up at her, his nose twitching quizzically.

"No, he's not here, if that's what you're asking me. He went away, and I never did know why. He wasn't like me. Not immortal. He'll be nothing but dust now." Indiya looked once more at the blood and pursed her lips. "Yes, he should be dust. Probably…"

For a long time, she was lost in dry old memories. The goat nudged her hand with his hot nose, and she stroked his velvet ears.

"Sometimes we need our own monsters to protect us from worse ones," she explained to him. "I've been that monster almost all my long life. But there are worse monsters than me. And sometimes you have to deal with them."

Indiya gently shoved the goat off her lap and contacted the respective security and port authorities, explaining that Chimera Company believed they were running away from her and should be allowed to leave on *Phantom*. Then she activated a unit from her instantaneous comm connection bank.

A male Zhoogene voice replied. "Go for Ren Kay."

"Deroh Ren Kay. You know perfectly well who this is. Report!"

"Sorry, ma'am. We are still receiving initial intel. Department 9 dispatched six missions across six worlds. All report successful delivery of the nano-plague. One team was discovered and lost. The other five have successfully gone to ground. Too early to tell you the effect of the nano-plague on—"

"I know that. What about the other team? What has Department 9 to say about Cora's World?"

"They're up to something. We don't know what, yet, but they talk about betraying you."

Indiya fixed Hubert with a glare, the wrinkles deepening around gray eyes filled with fire. "What did I tell you, goat? There are worse monsters than me."

* * * * *

Interstitial-3

The engines die, enveloping the ship in a chilling hush.

Del-Marie wants to relay Indiya's words to Azhgrel in case she hasn't been able to hear. He wants to apologize, but he's frozen in place, incapable of movement or speech. He's locked in!

Everyone else is equally still.

The physical universe has frozen. But this isn't the quiet oblivion of cryosleep; his consciousness continues.

He watches their faces in a moment of dread that will never end.

The musky smell of sweat and fear, the muffled screams of his crewmates… they linger forever, haunting him beyond the threshold of time.

Keep calm, he urges himself, but how long can he keep the panic at bay?

Imprisoned in an interstitial pocket outside of time, seconds could be an eternity, epochs pass in moments.

In this everlasting wait, madness is inevitable.

Suddenly the horror claims him, and his scream pierces the timeless void, bellowing a word, a name that has cursed him to an eternity in limbo.

INDIYA!

*****

Part 4:
Full Circle

Chapter Forty-Six: Tavistock Fitzwilliam

Izza issued a warning growl and shot a look of lilac fire from her beautiful eyes.

Fitz frowned. "What?"

His wife panned her glare to the spot on the worn black metal of the flight console where he'd been drumming his fingers.

Fitz froze his hand. He extended his middle finger, thought better of his first plan for the digit, then slid it up the console to punch the intercom button with the direct connection to the Engineering Eyrie.

"Fregg, did you fall asleep? Surely my jump engines are recharged by now."

"I—no, Captain."

The primary screens for both pilot and navigator were displaying the recharge status. *Phantom*'s engines had just hit the 80 percent tick on the gauge.

Izza punched him in the shoulder. She was never gentle.

"We're at eighty percent," Fregg reported.

"Well, why didn't you tell me?"

Another punch landed on his shoulder. Harder this time.

"Because you told me to wait until we're fully recharged," Fregg said, confused.

Fitz smacked his lips and reconsidered his life choices before his wife caused him permanent injury. Justiana Fregg wasn't as much fun to wind up as Lynx or Catkins.

And she didn't deserve it.

"My apologies, Leading Spacer Fregg." A grunt of satisfaction came from Fitz's left. "Eighty percent will do. Prepare for jump."

"That's ambitious," Izza said, "seeing as we don't yet have a destination."

"Away." He tried to appear nonchalant without actually shrugging. "Though perhaps deeper into the Antispinward Fringe."

"We've made two jumps out from the Redoubt Line. We're already away, Fitz. And there's nowhere safe to run to. We've been heading in the direction of the invasion. The Andromedans could be waiting for us at the next system. If not them, then forces loyal to Indiya. Azhanti! Why are you hiding your plans? Don't you trust me?"

Fitz looked away, shamefaced. "Because I don't trust the one who gave me the coordinates."

"Who?"

"My mother. If I ever needed to run, if every hole was being watched, then as a very last resort that would almost certainly end badly for me, I could jump to the coordinates she made me memorize."

"Where?"

Fitz snapped his head left and peered at his wife. Buried deeply within the firmness of her expression was a playfulness that only he could see. What was she playing at?

She cocked a golden eyebrow.

Fitz shrugged. "Where? I don't know. She refused to divulge any details. It could be a dead end like the Redoubt Line. It could be abandoned. It might have automatic defense systems ready to atomize anyone not on the invite list."

"I also have a bolt hole of last resort I have never mentioned."

Fitz knew she would have a good reason for withholding that information. It still stung that she had, but he was hardly in a position to criticize.

When Izza didn't elaborate with any details, he asked, "Your option. Is it off the astro-charts?"

"You know it is."

"Is it still occupied?"

"Definitely."

"Will they kill us?"

The playfulness departed her face. "It will be dangerous. If you want us to survive, you must promise me one thing."

"Go on."

"You let me do the talking, Fitz. I mean it. You keep your mouth shut for all our sakes."

That stung more than the secrets. Fitz was proud of his mouth and what came out of it. But Izza had her worried face on. When she did that, there were damned good reasons to be very afraid.

"Okay, I agree," he said. "You're the boss. I'm just your hired pilot. And when a lady hires a devilishly handsome man such as myself, she expects certain… extras."

He warned the crew to prepare for jump and unstrapped himself from his seat. While Izza fed the coordinates into the nav-computer, he massaged her shoulders from behind, feeling her muscles tense and then relax. He leaned closer to her neck—close enough to feel the heat of her body and the pliant stems on her head tickle his chin—and breathed softly into her ear.

She shivered.

"We'll get through this, my lady," he whispered. "I promise."

"I know," she said, without her fingers missing a beat on the nav-computer, "So long as we stay together."

Fitz snaked a hand inside her jacket and slid it down to rest upon her belly, where deep inside a new life was waiting for its chance. "We are all three of us together," he said.

With a contended sigh, Izza took her hands off the nav systems and placed them over Fitz's hand.

Head over his wife's shoulder, Fitz took his chance to peek at the jump coordinates.

"Orion's whiskers!" he shouted. "Your coordinates—"

"Are the same as yours," Izza said. "I just wanted you to confirm it. Now get your pretty hired ass back into your seat, pilot. We're about to jump."

* * *

"I never guessed it was real!" Fitz said in wonder. "I've been telling people about this place for decades, but I made it all up. And yet here it is."

He felt a buzz on his leather jacket and looked down at his Guild badge. It was flashing like crazy. A moment later, Izza's did too.

Elsewhere on *Phantom*, the same would be happening to Sinofar and Fregg, for they were all members of the Outer Torellian Commerce Guild.

To those on the inside, it was the Smugglers Guild, but to call it by that name was a serious speechcrime. Or had been, back when the Federation was still enforcing its laws.

Forbidding outsiders to speak the obvious truth was a naked display of the Guild's power.

Few dared to cross the Guild.

Upon achieving full membership, Guild members were awarded Guild ID badges by their Nylugas. They resembled circular enamel adornments about two inches in diameter, but they were much more.

Precisely what they did was above his grade, but he knew how to use them to verify whether a stranger was a Guild member in good standing.

The face of a Guild badge was a blood-orange sunburst on which was embossed an arrangement of vertical black teeth unique to each badge.

And that's where *Phantom* was now.

Flying through a hollow space bathed in blood red light. Black spires grew from the curved walls of the place.

They weren't teeth. They were habitation towers.

What he'd been wearing all these years wasn't an abstract design. It was a representation of a real place. The ultimate smugglers' hideout, so secret even he had never suspected its existence.

And they'd just jumped directly inside.

"Tell me I'm dreaming," he whispered. "No, tell me how you knew those coordinates."

"Nyluga Ree gave them to me," Izza replied. "And made me swear to keep them secret. I don't think she was supposed to tell anyone."

"My mother is also a Nyluga. She said to use those coordinates only in the direst emergency, because coming here meant almost certain death."

They looked at each other.

"Welcome to Outer Torellia," both said.

And welcomed they were, by a squadron of antique aerospace fighters that flew out to meet them.

Fitz acknowledged an incoming hail, and the sweaty pink features of Nyluga Ree appeared in the holo.

"It's my favorite pair of rogues," she said. "And you brought my yacht back to me. Good."

"Don't start," Izza snapped. "*Phantom* is rightfully ours."

The Nyluga licked her plump lips. Ree seemed to view every moment in life through a lens of cynical calculation. But Fitz was familiar enough with her to know there was slightly more to her than the manipulation of the galaxy to her personal profit. He recognized the genuine pleasure she felt to see them.

"Very well," the Nyluga said. "I declare that dispute to be on temporary hold. Is your Viking aboard?"

"You mean Vetch?" Fitz frowned.

Izza nodded. "Major Arunsen is with us, yes. Why do you ask, Nyluga?"

Ree smiled. "Because someone has been bugging me to bring him in."

The connection ended. Fighter craft peeled away to be replaced by an opaque green bubble ship. Its skin switched to transparency and revealed that it was crewed by two cat women, their fur stripes of verdigris and bronze.

Maycey and Kaycey.

Vetch's time here was not going to be dull.

"Follow us," said one of the Kayrissans. "We shall lead you to your mooring slip."

"Kaycey, right?" Izza asked.

"Correct."

"Has your sister a message for our Viking major?"

"A major?" Maycey said. She lifted her lip to expose gleaming fangs. "Remind him that he has my mark upon him. Any who touches him shall die."

"I don't think any will get a chance," Fitz quipped. "Not once you've got your claws into my major."

Her fur bristled. "We are about to jump out on a vital mission. We may be gone for some weeks. Will you be here on our return?"

"That depends on our welcome. And what we find here."

"Yes, or no?"

Fitz experienced an emotion that was alien to him. Hopelessness. For the first time in his life, there was nowhere else to run. "Yes, we'll still be here."

"Then tell Major Arunsen to keep himself warm and well oiled. We have urgent business to conduct together upon my return."

"I shall delight in telling him that. Good hunting, ladies. I shall personally ensure he'll be ready for you."

"He'd better be. My race is renowned for its patience, but mine has reached its limit."

Fitz licked his lips, relishing the prospect of telling Vetch the news.

But his wife had the same thought.

She undid her harness. "Bring us in safely, pilot."

"What? No! You can't!"

She beamed with pleasure. "You're just a hired hand. You said it yourself."

Izza strode off into the the ship, but before the flight deck hatch closed behind her, Fitz sent a spycam in pursuit. He wasn't going to miss out on seeing the Viking's reaction.

He breathed deeply, taking comfort from the familiar ozone musk of the flight deck mixed with the lingering scent of new leather.

Phantom was a good place to be. And if Outer Torellia was the Guild's secret heart, it would be the safest harbor in an uncertain galaxy.

But the Andromedan invasion wasn't a storm that would blow over until he was long dead. And if his descendants ever left this place, they would only encounter an endless void of broken worlds, sucked dry by the enemy.

Hide or fight?

"Screw it!" he growled.

And made his decision.

* * * * *

Chapter Forty-Seven: Deroh Ren Kay

Department 9 Secret Base

Sitting cross legged on the cool ceramic floor of the tele-porter slab, Deroh Ren Kay checked his equipment.

He glanced up to verify that his team members on this mission, Jorin Korsa and Sefon Wexar, were doing the same.

They were the three best field operatives not already committed by Department 9. A mission of this sort required a larger team and more planning, but although the reports from the secret monitoring station on Cora's World were confused, they indicated the world was being hit by a catastrophe.

He chuckled. Couldn't have happened to a nicer bunch of xeno-cidal, human-supremacist, purity assbuckets. He wished them hell. He really did.

But Department 9 reported to Indiya now. And her plan to defeat the Andromedans depended on a cure for the Corruption that only Cora's World was able to develop fast enough.

It was the irony of ironies, but it was precisely because Cora's World were purity-spiral skragg-frakkers that they'd been suspicious of anybody different. Aliens had long been expelled from their planets.

Suspicious of anyone who didn't enthusiastically and repeatedly bleat their orthodoxies, their society had long been infected with a pathological insanity, but it made them all but immune to the Corruption.

Throughout the Federation, secret military assets, military hierarchies… all had been thoroughly compromised by the Corruption. Department 9 was no exception.

But not Cora's World.

And the worst of it, in terms of conventional military assets, Cora's World was fast emerging as possessing the largest disciplined military force in the Federation.

He shrugged. It was what it was.

The mission was making him more nervous than he'd felt for a long while, perhaps because this would be the first time he'd been on the teleporter.

He'd traveled through j-Space inside spacecraft many times, and theoretically this was the same thing.

It didn't *feel* the same.

The teleporter was a metal covered box, two stories high, that contained a pair of jump engines altered according to Khallini's modifications. The three Department 9 operatives sat on the slab on one side of the box. For the return journey—if they survived that far—they would assemble on the slab on the other side of the engines and activate the recall.

The teleporter countdown hit zero, and Ren Kay felt himself jerked through impossible dimensions. They landed with a deafening thud at the foot of a spinney of trees at the edge of a wheat field on a pleasant summer's afternoon.

Screams and soot carried on the gentle breeze.

Ren Kay motioned for Korsa and Wexar to follow him to the nearby hill. The gently sloping fields were flattened with bodies and wrecked war machines. Farm buildings were on fire.

The nanovirus production facility was at the base of the slope, shrouded in a thick cloud of smoke.

High-powered ducted fans assailed Ren Kay's sensitive Zhoogene ears with their whine. The Department 9 operatives crawled forward into the cover of the wheat and watched as a flight of aircraft weaved at speed through the air, headed for the production site.

The air shimmered with the heat bloom from anti-air energy beam defenses. Three of the fliers exploded in flight, but three more dropped bombs on the sprawling site of gleaming pipes and vessels protected by an outer wall bristling with guard towers. The shockwave of the bomb blasts spread out from the site, flattening the wheat before buffeting Ren Kay's body.

When he recovered enough to observe the aftermath, he saw that all three of the remaining aerial bombers had been destroyed, but the outer defenses of the site had been breached across much of its length.

Before them, Corrupted soldiers rose from where they'd lain hidden in the wheat and advanced toward the breach.

"Come on," Ren Kay urged his companions. "We have to get there before the Corrupted."

The trio sprinted down the hill, the ground shaking with heavy weapons fire as they ran.

As they approached the breach, they were surprised by a squad of Corrupted soldiers rising from the wheat. Perhaps they'd failed to heed the earlier signal to attack.

They were humanoid, but so twisted and disfigured that Ren Kay couldn't identify their original species, Their eyes burned red and their skin was pale as if they had not received the light of a sun for decades.

Most repulsive was the sour stench of rot and corruption.

Without hesitation, Ren Kay issued his orders. Korsa and Wexar scampered behind a pile of Corrupted corpses and fired their blasters to distract the enemy.

Meanwhile, Ren Kay circled around on his hands and knees to flank them.

Before he could make his attack, Korsa took a hit from a blaster bolt and fell to the ground, lifeless.

Emboldened, the enemy rushed Wexar, who went down in a hail of railgun darts.

The threat apparently over, the Corrupted lay down once more in the long wheat.

A wave of grief washed over Ren Kay, but he quickly mastered it and crawled toward the production site, unnoticed by the Corrupted.

Through the breach, Ren Kay slipped from shadow to shadow, evading both attacker and defender where he could, but shooting a pair of Corrupted and slitting the throat of a nervous Cora's World trooper when he couldn't.

He made it through to a laboratory corridor lined with offices. At the end of the corridor, bright light spilled out from an open doorway. Nervous voices were speaking rapidly but with purpose.

He cautiously approached and peered inside to see a control room filled with computer equipment and technicians. Abandoning stealth, he marched into the room.

"The Lady Indiya sent me," he announced.

Startled, the techs looked for direction from a tall human man wearing a lab coat and an air of authority.

That would be the boss, then.

"I'm from Department 9," Ren Kay told him.

Not so long ago, the very existence of the Department had been a secret. That had gone along with many of the galaxy's certainties. After a moment to screw up his face in disgust that there was a filthy alien in his presence, the man nodded, grabbed a pile of viewscreens, and gestured for Ren Kay to follow.

He led him through a hermetically sealed barrier and into a large and clean space filled with control equipment that resembled the command deck of a starship.

The scientist activated screens that showed snapshots of the Corrupted invasion. They had penetrated deep inside the facility. There were scenes too of villages, space ports, retail areas across the planet: all assaulted by the shambling mass of the enemy.

"All is lost," the man said. "The only defense is to release the virus here and now."

Ren Kay recalled the first release of the virus. It had killed people who were ill, not Corrupted. "Will it work? According to the new tolerances?"

The man hesitated, his brows creasing together. "As far as I can tell. No matter how diligent our lab testing, you can never be sure until it is tested in the field."

"Then do it. Kill the Corrupted."

He performed an activation sequence and handed a screen to Ren Kay. "You can complete the activation from this screen, if you so wish. I have increased the circulation of air from the virus dumps. It will spread quickly."

Ren Kay didn't like the smirk on his face. "What are you not telling me?"

"My people take no joy in killing innocents among the aliens—and we are aware that not all aliens are evil. Nonetheless, the prevailing view is that the collective sin of alienkind, and the even greater sins of their potential future, is too great. Personally, I don't agree but my personal views mean nothing."

Ren Kay leveled his blaster at the scientist. "Start making sense. Fast."

The scientist grew nervous. "All appeared lost. So, when Indiya exposed the working of the nanovirus to us, we adapted it to our own purpose. It won't just kill the Corrupted. It will eradicate all non-humans."

"But don't humans need bacteria, plants, bees, birds, horses…?"

"Of course. Until Indiya showed us how to do it, our bioweapons scientists never overcame those challenges."

Ren Kay reached for a device in his jacket. Indiya had foreseen this possibility and provided a means to pass a secret instruction to the virus, ordering it to spread a wave of self-destruction.

But should he use it?

"Oh, my apologies," the scientist sneered. "I imagine you're trying to deactivate the virus. We removed the kill switch too."

Ren Kay hit him on principle. Then he hit the swaying human again, this time because he wanted to.

The human groaned on the floor, but then wiped the blood from his mouth and looked up at Ren Kay. "What's it to be, alien? Kill the Corrupted and you'll kill yourself, too."

"I thought this area was sealed?"

"It is. But your transportation is out there. And the moment the seal to this area is broken, the virus will reach inside and exterminate you. What fate will you choose, Zhoogene?"

Ren Kay gave the man a fierce kick. Enough to make him cry out in pain but not cause serious harm. He wanted company, after all, if he was to be stuck here for a while.

Then he activated the virus release.

On the monitor screens, the Corrupted advance continued as before. They were making good progress at the virus site. Soon they would kill the last defenders and arrive at the entrance to the sealed area.

Keeping an eye on both the Corrupted and the scientist, Ren Kay readied an entangled comm link to his new boss.

As it was establishing, the monitors showed the first Corrupted dropping to the ground. Then another. Both had been deep inside the production site.

Then on every monitor trained on the vicinity, the Corrupted simply died.

It was a shame that the same fate awaited his Zhoogene ass if he opened the seal on that door.

Ren Kay made his report to Indiya.

Despite being an interstellar connection, there was video, and it showed her deep in thought at his words.

"Very inventive," she said eventually. "Can't fault Cora's people for that. My instinct is to sterilize the planet, but it's been pointed out to me that sterilization is unpopular. I'll instruct the Muryani to blockade the Cora's World system in perpetuity. Can't have that version of the virus going out, and the Muryani will be highly motivated to prevent it doing so."

"You don't seem worried about the loss of this facility," Ren Kay said.

"It's clear to me now that this path was a mistake. The version I delivered to Cora's World was too simplistic, easily altered. The version I built first is far more accurate and secure but isn't spreading fast enough. If I had a few centuries to allow it to spread through every world in the Federation, then it might be enough time to properly inoculate the galaxy against the Corruption."

"You left it too late."

"Far too late. Yes." She frowned. "Why aren't you dead, Ren Kay?"

He explained about the seal, and how his ride home was on the far side.

"In that case," Indiya said, "stay put and keep alive. If we win the war, I'll look into retrieving you. Indiya out."

For a moment, he stared at the space where Indiya's holo-image had been.

Then he shrugged and grinned at the quivering scientist. "You heard her," he said in a low voice, chilled with threat. "You and I are going to become like family."

* * * * *

Chapter Forty-Eight: Vetch Arunsen

Outer Torellia

"Where do you want to go?" Vetch asked.

"The Vault."

Vetch rolled his eyes and shot his legionary friend an icy stare. "That's a jack-skragg thing to say, Sybutu. We're inside the beating heart of the Smugglers Guild. Wherever we go, they will hear everything we say."

"Don't be so sure about that."

The jack-hole could be right, Vetch thought. The structures inside this—whatever it was the Guild had found and claimed for its own—were built out of organic metal.

Organic metal? That's what they'd told him, but he'd never heard of such a thing.

On the other hand, lights pulsed through the semi-translucent ceilings and walls in shades of fire and gold, tracing pathways that might be nerves or arteries. He'd never heard of that, either.

There was a strange energy to the place that unsettled him, gave him the weird impression that none of what he was seeing was real, that it was an optical illusion.

The fiery pathways did more than provide a pretty light show that hurt Vetch's head, it messed with radio and microwave comms. Thick trunks of fiberoptic cable ran throughout the base, the only reliable way to send data traffic. And they were glued to the organic metal, not chased out of sight.

So maybe there weren't lenses and microphones recording everything they said and did?

"In any case," Sybutu continued, "what do you mean by 'they?' We're all in the Guild now."

Vetch chuckled at the thought. He liked to think he'd opened Sybutu's eyes to the ways of the galaxy, but the man was still jack to the core. To Oso Sybutu, Smugglers Guild operatives were in the same category as Panhandler rebels, Andromedan monsters, Cora's World fanatics, and anyone who failed to salute according to proper Legion protocol.

In other words, deserving of a cruel and lingering death.

To avoid all that pesky being blasted to atoms by the Guild's automated defense systems after turning up in the most secret of Guild secrets without an invite, they had all been awarded with a Guild ID badge marking them as high-ranking members.

"I want to go to the Vault," Sybutu repeated.

"Why? Zavage, Green, and Beans asked us to sink some jars in the Oubliette Cantina. Sounds better than breaking into a heavily guarded place when we don't even know what's inside."

"It's called the Vault. What do people put in vaults?"

Vetch licked his lips. "Their most valuable treasures."

Sybutu was being an idiot; his mind had completely slipped its moorings.

This was not surprising. His role in the Legion that meant everything to him was now unclear. His supreme commander had turned out to be an insane old crone who thought nothing of killing trillions of her people to stop them falling into enemy hands. And even without Indiya's help, the Federation they'd sworn to defend was imploding and everyone was dying.

Vetch was the jack's friend, though. He should help. Help by telling him he was being a complete skragg-crank idiot.

But… Vetch's mind kept returning to what Indiya had told them. That her two sergeants were going to save the galaxy.

True, the words had come from an insane woman, but the prediction she spoke of had come from Indigo Squad. Vetch wanted to ask the mutants directly what they'd meant, but none of them could or would explain. Of the leaders in their mutant séances, Mrs. Zi'Alfu had gone into hiding months ago, Pyruula was a puddle of goo, which left only Claudio "Beans" Zanitch.

When Vetch had asked him, Beans had clammed up, spouting some drent about inexact predictions of the future being worse than knowing nothing. No matter how much drink they had put into the big baldie, he hadn't budged from that position.

Being told you're going to save the galaxy with at least an inkling that there might be some truth to it was not something you could ignore.

Perhaps opening the Vault was the way they fulfilled their destiny.

Vetch's eyes lit with mischief. "The Vault, eh?" He slapped his friend on the back. "You and me, Osu. We got this. Let's do it."

* * *

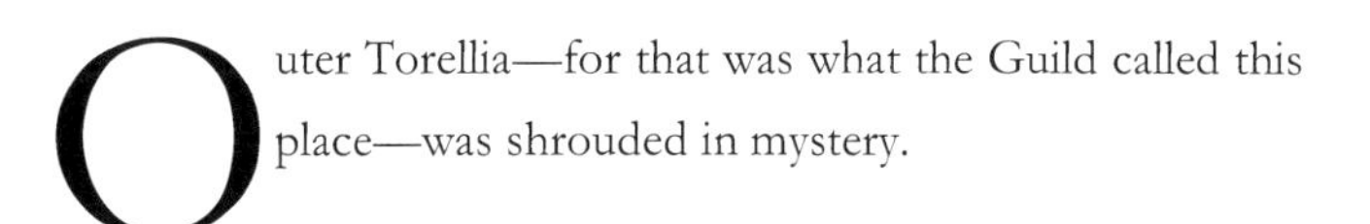

Outer Torellia—for that was what the Guild called this place—was shrouded in mystery.

In other words, no one would tell Vetch shit about it. But Chimera Company had ways of discovering details they weren't supposed to know, most of which involved alcohol.

It was a deep space habitation built and abandoned long ago, rather like the Joint Sector High Command orbital that had mined the flux tubes of a Tej System gas giant. And like JSHC, many aspects of the technology were incomprehensible, even down to their bare principles.

Thousands of years ago, humans had built something similar at the Redoubt Line. But where the early Federation had hollowed out natural asteroids and laboriously towed them into deep space, this place looked as if it had grown out of that mysterious organic metal.

Its interior was a fractal maze of tunnels and partial tunnels of all sizes—many of which were only three-quarters enclosed—mixed with cavernous open spaces whose walls sprouted the termite mounds represented as the black bars in the Guild badges.

The spaces were filled with red luminescence. In the larger caverns, the lights that coursed through the glowing walls coalesced into spectacular balls that sucked the glow from their vicinity until they were pregnant with raw power. Then they would release, sending arcs of scarlet lightning out of the walls to strike the tips of the termite towers like burning hammers.

How did they keep this place kept a secret from the galaxy when over a million guildpeople lived here?

The answer hadn't been a secret. Most of the inhabitants of Outer Torellia never left the place, nor had their forebears for many generations. And most of the guildpeople out in the galaxy never suspected this place even existed.

How had the Nylugas kept an iron hand of control over so many? Why had the majority not declared independence from the Guild?

There would be reasons, but Vetch didn't want to hear them. He was just relieved that they had been allowed to see this place and live.

So far.

But if Vetch ever wanted to leave, would they let him?

Three jump tunnels connected Outer Torellia to the outside galaxy, and they in turn linked to a network of further tunnels, some of which connected to deep space, but many to the outer regions of inhabited systems, perfect for sneaking in and out.

These routes through j-Space were not formed by jump engines but were permanently open. Ships didn't need jump engines at all to travel through them. The notion was mind boggling.

And Izza had uncovered another detail that beggared belief: The coordinates she'd used had jumped *Phantom* right into the habitat.

Normal coordinates needed continual adjustment as the stars and planets spun their dances around the galactic core. Even then, the uncertainty over the emergence zone was measured in thousands of kilometers. The cavern they had jumped inside was only about twenty klicks across. Izza guessed that some kind of station keeping was happening. Like a geostationary orbit but on a galactic level.

As for how ships could jump in without appearing on top of others, that was another mystery for which she had no answer.

Then there was the self-sufficiency in water, food, and minerals for a habitat stationed in deep space, light years from the nearest star system.

So many mysteries.

Perhaps the answers lay in the Vault?

*****

Chapter Forty-Nine: Vetch Arunsen

The entrance to the Vault was a massive door made of the same glowing, organic metal as the rest of the base. Two large and intimidating sentinels guarded the door, both bearing heavily modified blasters.

They were still and silent and watched the two friends approach through eyes that glowed red in helmets that obscured their features.

Vetch couldn't figure out whether they were droids designed to resemble humanoids or the other way around.

"There must be more to it than these two," Sybutu said.

"Granted. Not that it makes any difference. We forgot to bring along an assault team. Or weapons, for that matter. Unless we count your thick skull, though I was thinking of that more as a battering ram."

Osu made no reply.

Vetch looked him dead in the eye. "Just so we're clear, when you said, 'visit the Vault,' did you mean take a look or were you planning to wrestle the guards into submission and tear that door open with your manly jack hands?"

Osu grimaced. "Let's not do anything rash. But I do want to find a way to see inside. It's a hunch, I know. You probably think SOTLs can't have such intuition, but we do, and mine says we need to find a way in there. Don't ask me why."

"Wasn't planning on it," Vetch replied and picked up the pace.

Sybutu hesitated, which brought a smile to Vetch's face. Then the jack's clod feet scurried until he'd caught up.

"What do you think you're doing?" Sybutu demanded.

"Watch and learn, brother. Watch and learn how the Militia does things."

Vetch stopped a few paces from the two guards. Then he stepped forward, cleared his throat, and spoke in a commanding tone.

"I am Vetch Arunsen, High Guildmaster of Chimera Company. We have been granted access to the Vault by the Nylugas. You will let us pass."

The guards didn't move an inch, but they seemed to be listening intently.

Vetch continued in the same vein, recounting choice details of their encounters with the Andromedans, the Muryani, and the Lady Indiya. He wove truthful elements together into a fantastic tale, artfully weaving them together with strands of the finest storyteller's bullshit, a skill learned in the barrooms of a score of disreputable planets.

All the while he constantly emphasized how vital Chimera Company was to the continued existence of Outer Torellia.

The guards remained motionless throughout the speech.

Vetch finally finished, well pleased with his performance and even more so by the open-jawed wonder of the legionary standing beside him.

Coming here had been a risk, of course. But it was worth it for the look on Sybutu's face and the tale he would soon be telling in the

Oubliette Cantina. Maybe it would even stop the jack going on about this place.

He drew a breath, on the cusp of announcing that his gambit had failed, and they should retire to the Oubliette. But there came a massive *thud* that hurt his lungs and made his knees buckle as if he'd been punched in the gut. Then the portal slid open with unexpected ease.

The two friends exchanged a brief glance of amazement before walking past the guards and into the Vault.

A large chamber awaited them inside. There was no one else here, but the place was far from empty. The entire space was filled with treasure.

As he scanned the room, he soon revised his assessment. The first items he'd spotted were jeweled artifacts, golden sculpture, artwork, and metal canisters with glowing status lights that didn't reveal their content but looked immensely valuable.

His eye had been attracted to the shiny things first. But as he looked further, most of it looked more like junk. Possibly very ancient and priceless junk, but nonetheless items that were tarnished, warped, corroded, and most likely broken fragments of larger artifacts. Some were stored on shelves, but most were piled in random heaps.

With the occasional exception, this was a garbage dump.

"I don't understand," Sybutu said.

Vetch tugged at his beard. "Nor I. I expected an emperor's treasure, but this is a storage shed for a cult of hoarders."

"I meant I don't understand why I felt such a compulsion to come here." He frowned and then pointed at a corner of the cavern where the ruby light was brightest. "That looks valuable."

Vetch followed the light. He pulled away huge sheets of what looked like tessellated hexagons of armor plate, but which were light as feathers, to reveal a pedestal carved from a single piece of jade. On top sat a great gemstone, so large it had to have been stolen from an ancient god. The gemstone was a dark green, like the sea over a deep reef, and it glowed with a soft crimson light.

The walls here were adorned with intricate bas-reliefs depicting mythic scenes from a race he didn't recognize. There were a lot of limbs. Or tentacles. He decided the scenes depicted underwater events. Perhaps Outer Torellia had once been filled with water.

"It's a story," Sybutu said. "Look, the jellyfish people—or whatever they are—they're being eaten by these monsters." He traced his finger along the bas-relief. "And here they're learning the secret of fire. Or perhaps these are fusion weapons."

"Underwater fire?" Vetch queried.

Sybutu shrugged. "I don't know. But it's following a linear sequence. And it goes, ah…"

The halfway point of the bas-relief story dipped down and circled an entrance portal, a smaller sibling of the one guarded by the two robo-guards.

And standing beside the portal was an outdated door control panel, the kind of security system with weaknesses so completely understood by modern thieves that no insurance corporation would cover whatever that door lock was securing.

Vetch rubbed his hands with glee.

But before he could enter this vault within a vault, a chill ran through his veins. Had he just heard something?

In contrast to the rest of Outer Torellia, which throbbed with energy as if alive, the Vault had been deathly still. Now a soft whisper floated in the air, like a mother humming a lullaby to coax their infant to slumber. It was the faintest of breezes.

The two men froze, desperately peering around in an attempt to pinpoint the source of the noise.

"Vetch… Vetch Arunsen…" called a phantom voice in the air. "Is there a voice inside your mind telling you this is all too easy?"

There was a sudden blur in front of his eyes. It ended with a sharp tap on his nose.

He stepped back and saw he'd been slapped by a power lance, a spear with a glowing blue head covered in intricate sigils that… that resembled the glyphs from the bas-relief on the walls.

That revelation was intriguing, but Vetch was more fixated on the knowledge that the power lance could slice him in half in an instant, if its wielder so desired. He'd seen it done.

Very slowly, Vetch looked up.

Hanging upside down in midair was a Kayrissan cat assassin, perhaps the deadliest species in the galaxy before the Andromedans had arrived.

Even in the red light of the cavern, her fur was striped in shades of dark and darker. This was Laycey, the eldest of the three assassin sisters sworn to Nyluga Ree's service.

Sybutu pointed at the sealed door. "What's in there?"

"I do not know, human. I am an assassin, an interrogator, and—it now seems—a guard." She showed her fangs. "Why would they tell me?"

Laycey jumped down, landing with perfect grace. She brandished her power lance at the two men.

"I am both a guardian of this place and the one who protects my sister's interest." She peered at Vetch through green, slitted eyes. "It is indeed fortunate for you that I was here to instruct the sentinels to allow you entry, Vetch Arunsen."

She lashed out with the power lance, striking Vetch on his head. It was merely a glancing blow, but power surged at its impact, sending sparks shooting through him.

Even at nonlethal settings, the lance was a fearful implement.

"And now you have made me a jailor," she hissed. "Follow me if you wish to live a little longer. Both of you."

Encouraged by cruel prods from the lance tip, Vetch and Sybutu allowed themselves to be herded from the Vault into a much smaller copy of the cavern nearby, with a similar door of organic metal.

Instead of ancient treasures, all they found inside was straw piled on the floor and a plastic bucket by the far wall.

* * *

The door to their prison opened an hour later. With armed guards at the entrance, a droid brought in ration packs and extra buckets.

The door didn't open again for three days when Fitz walked in, beaming. "There you are. Thank you for waiting, gentlemen."

Vetch allowed Sybutu to ask the obvious. "Waiting for what?"

Fitz frowned. "The eleven o'clock conference call. It's essential you're there."

"And who are we talking with?" Vetch asked.

Fitz regarded them both, his violet eyes flashing in the shadows. "I think you can guess who, Major. I suspect you harbor a connection with her that you have chosen to withhold from me. The luminary we're about to meet is none other than the Lady Indiya."

* * * * *

Chapter Fifty: Osu Sybutu

Fury blazed from the old woman's eyes, but it didn't scorch Osu. He was too busy wondering what the point was to all this.

"I requested a meeting with Sybutu," Indiya fumed. "Why are you two here wasting my valuable time and consuming my precious bandwidth?"

Yes, the bandwidth. Such a pragmatic and boring detail, but they were inside the virtual meeting space of a corporate boardroom.

Indiya was, presumably, ensconced in her Fort Douaumont bunker, scores of light years away. But her holographic representation was so pin sharp it was difficult to detect that she wasn't actually there with them in Outer Torellia.

He'd never heard of such an extravagant bandwidth burn of entangled comms, but then he supposed there was no point in hording priceless assets if you didn't believe there would be a tomorrow.

Indiya's gaze fixed on Osu. "Explain yourself, Sergeant."

An image of this same woman in her youth was proudly inked on Osu's chest, but he no longer felt he owed blind obedience.

So, Indiya had requested only him? That was news to Osu, which was typical of the kind of detail Fitzwilliam liked to withhold, as if he were a trickster god.

Annoying as Fitzwilliam could be, Osu knew where his true loyalties lay: with the people around him.

"Ma'am," he began, "Arunsen is here because we are in this business together. Gemini twins, remember? I won't let you play one of us off against the other. As for Fitzwilliam, I imagine you wish us to travel somewhere."

"That's right," Fitzwilliam said. "Please pretend I'm not here. I'm just the taxi driver."

"Here?" A sly look came over Indiya. "Yes, where is here? We are using a Guild channel. Where have they hidden you, I wonder?"

She sniffed the air, and her gills flapped. The way she acted was not in the least human.

"It would be somewhere like the Last Redoubt," she said. "Off grid. Perhaps a rogue planet about a rogue white dwarf. You would have to be self-sufficient to a degree, but could you sustain your little outpost of civilization for thousands of years?"

Osu slapped the virtual table. "May I remind you, ma'am, that Legion comms protocol requires you to state what needs to be said as concisely as possible then you clear the damned channel so others can use it. If you want to indulge in idle speculation, get off the line."

She raised an eyebrow at his outburst but didn't seem upset.

As for Fitzwilliam, he gave a grunt of approval and slapped Osu on his back.

"How is the war preceding, ma'am?" Fitzwilliam asked. "Have our Muryani friends sterilized any more planets?"

"Another twelve systems have been denied to the enemy."

"And the flow of Andromedans?"

"Slowing." She fell silent.

"They're slowing, but…" Fitzwilliam prompted.

"But even when our military is victorious, we suffer grievous losses, and the Muryani even more so. A fresh outbreak of Corrupted sleeper cells has awoken throughout the Federation, targeting our defense industries and military command, even in sectors the Andromedans themselves have yet to reach."

Arunsen interrupted her flow. "Indiya's already told us the nanovirus plan won't work. Right idea, too late."

"Yes," Indiya said. "Too wixering late. It's maddening, because if we only faced the Andromedans, then with our Muryani allies beside us we might still have a chance. As it is, the Corruption is destroying us from within and providing huge reinforcements for the enemy. There are now more Federation military assets fighting for the other side than for us."

An ominous silence fell over the unreal board room.

"So, we're going to lose," Osu said.

"Yes, we are going to lose. Before we do, the Muryani will scorch every planet in this region down to bedrock. Even the outer zone of the Expansion will be evacuated and burned for around a hundred light years on their side of the border. It looks like this is the end. If only I'd stirred myself to act earlier."

Osu didn't know what to say. And since the Andromedans knew the Redoubt Line's coordinates, it too would soon fall. Everywhere and everyone, dead.

Only Outer Torellia would be safe. Everywhere else… just *gone.*

"We can't hide here," Fitzwilliam said, as if he could read Osu's thoughts. "We would live out our lives, but we would condemn our descendants to permanent incarceration. If they ever emerged from hiding, they would encounter nothing but lifeless worlds for hundreds of light years. Maybe thousands. And that's assuming the

Andromedans have moved on. We can't bequeath them that future. Better to die fighting. Don't you agree, gentlemen?"

Neither Osu nor Vetch knew how to respond.

"No one's asking you to throw your life away in a pointless gesture," Fitzwilliam said. "I expect Indiya has a cunning plan that she's just about to reveal to us."

"She already has," Sybutu said and sensed Fitzwilliam stiffen. "Before we ran from her, she was about to send us on a mission to retrieve what she called her cheat card. I assumed you knew."

"No. But do, please, elaborate."

"The Corruption has crippled us," Indiya said. "It's like a poison injected by a predator so its prey can't fight back."

"A time machine!" Fitzwilliam exclaimed. "The nanovirus kills the individual but vaccinates the population. If we could release it a few centuries ago—"

"No," Sybutu said. "The change would be too great. Indiya explained back at the Redoubt."

"Far too great for a time machine," Indiya agreed. "You have to edit reality directly."

"And you can do this?" Fitzwilliam asked. "With your 'cheat card'?"

"Yes. It's called a reality editor. You can use it for time travel, of course, but it's both more powerful and vastly more dangerous than a mere time machine. However, I see no other option if we wish to avoid extinction. You must retrieve it and bring it back to the Redoubt without delay."

"And you want us?" Vetch queried. "If it's that important, send *Steadfast.*"

Indiya inclined her head. "*Steadfast* was lost two weeks ago. Chimera Company is our only hope. Will you do this?"

Osu drew in a breath. The ugly business with Pyruula had lifted a cloak of naivety from his eyes, and he realized he could tell Indiya was not telling the whole truth.

"Of course," Fitzwilliam was saying, "what are the coordinates of this device?" But Osu's mind was on a different question.

What was Indiya not telling them?

*****

Chapter Fifty-One: Lady Indiya

Indiya's pacing halted abruptly. "Are you sure this is the right thing to do?"

The hologram of her husband lifted a knowing eyebrow.

"Frakk you!" she replied. "And when did you get to be so wixering tall?"

The holo-simulation laughed but said nothing, giving her room to rant, as the man it was based on had once done.

He, bred to be a robust self-healing soldier, was almost twice her height and easily twice her width. Her genetics had been tweaked to produce a space rat, intended to serve her entire life aboard starships where mass, oxygen, space, and other resources were a constant constraint.

She'd forgotten the sheer physicality of this man, even in holographic form.

Indiya slumped into one of the pair of comfortable armchairs and tried to come to terms with being back in this place.

The Study. That had been his name for this room in their Fort Douaumont bunker. There had indeed been study and contemplation, but mostly they had come here to escape the burden of leadership. Just the two of them as if they were normal people. Bare metal walls, a holo-projector hanging from the ceiling, and some shelves bearing a few mementos. The only ostentation was a small table made from oak they'd brought from Earth.

The wood had been preserved across the millennia in better condition than her own body. Or his.

"I don't know why you created me at all," accused the hologram with his voice. "Haven't you already made your decision by dispatching *Phantom*?"

"I haven't unlocked the memories yet."

"And without the memories you don't know how to use the device?"

"Correct."

"When I first met you, your shipmates called you a freak. I'm beginning to suspect they were right."

"Pfft! How would you know? You never had the problems of longevity. You died."

"I didn't die. I disappeared."

Indiya stared in disbelief as her mind raced to process his unexpected response.

"Isn't that the same thing?" she asked weakly.

He smirked, the wixering skragg-frakk! "You tell me. *Phantom* is bringing back my best friend and Del-Marie disappeared before I did. Maybe I'm out there too. Parked somewhere. In stasis. I'm just a simulation, so I don't know any more than you. But I don't know any *less* either. I could be out there somewhere."

"I didn't create you to tell me things like that."

"Are you sure? We were always good at telling each other what we needed to hear."

Indiya deactivated her husband and searched for the buried memories of the *Retribution* and the reality editor she'd secreted aboard.

The memory had been removed from the meat part of her brain and locked into auxiliary storage. First she had to find it, then trim away the security protocols. Most challenging of all would be reintegrating anything she unlocked with a mind that had changed substantially since the memories had been stored.

Reliving those events would be a fever dream of remembrance.

* * *

"Did it work?" he asked. "Can you remember how to use your reality editor?"

She frowned because she had no memory of reactivating him. "Yes." She bit her lower lip. "As much as I ever did. It was always half guesswork."

"Your reluctance to use it is written all over your face."

"What if it goes wrong? It might, you know. It's so difficult to care about anything. But this… it scares the shit out of me."

"Indiya."

"I'm not even sure why I care about the insignificant people I would save. They die. New lives replace them, only to die before they'd hardly known life. Some think I'm a goddess, some a monster. Now I know they are both right."

"Indiya!" he shouted.

"What?"

"Stop overthinking it, you wixering space rat. As things stand at the moment, we're completely frakked. We're talking total species kill for every race in the Perseus Arm. And once the Andromedans are established in this zone, the rest of the galaxy is already doomed. There. Is. No. Choice. Get it done!"

"Yes, I will."

"And then come look for me."

For the second time, she stared with her mouth agape at the holo of her husband.

*****

Chapter Fifty-Two: Del-Marie Sandure

He closed his mouth on the scream. The scream he'd silently cried for centuries. And for no time at all.

Frakk, but I need a drink.

You and me both, Pepin replied in his head.

Del had been bred as a Marine on a depot planet called Tranquility, eons before the crew of the FRNS *Retribution* he'd been marooned with. In Del's era, adolescent Marine novices were fitted with an AI, a lifelong partner to act as advisor, medic, targeting assistant, comms support, supercomputer, and manager of a thousand minor miracles, such as how to apply reaction forces to his armored combat suit to counteract the recoil forces on his SA-71 railgun so that it felt as if it there was no recoil at all. Even in zero G.

Pepin was there.

Had always been there.

So why did it feel like they'd been separated for an age?

Del-Marie tried to piece together what had just happened.

He'd screamed Indiya's name and then...

And then the universe had spun around him. He'd seen countless suns explode and felt endless worlds burn. He'd seen darkness beyond darkness, blacker than black, and glimpsed a truth hidden in that void. But then the universe had stilled. Though something of that terrible experience remained with him, like a thick covering of long-cooled ash, the psychic residue of unimaginable anguish.

He shivered. Some seriously weird drent had just gone down.

And it had Indiya's name written all over it. It was time she was held to account. With extreme prejudice.

"Hello? Hello? Can anyone read me?"

It was one of the *Retribution's* ridiculously youthful crew in the pinnace's copilot's seat. A male human Del-Marie recognized as one of *Retribution's* section officers.

He's Ensign Naxxo, Pepin supplied. *Tactical specialist.*

"There's no reply," Naxxo told the lieutenant who sat next to him in the pilot's seat. "We're in orbit about a planet, but it appears to be uninhabited."

A flush came to Lieutenant Azhgrel's green cheeks. It looked lovely on the Zhoogene officer who was now in command of this mission by virtue of her superiors having died aboard the *Retribution.*

She had only eleven crewmembers left to command, crammed into a tiny pinnace made even smaller by the arcane box that contained Indiya's special machine.

Azhgrel had yet to speak. The only other surviving Zhoogene was similarly dumb. Perhaps her species was taking longer to come out of… whatever the frakk they'd just been through.

When she was herself, she was a capable officer. In the interim, Del-Marie took the heat off her.

"Let's go down to the planet and see what's happening," he said.

Naxxo shook his head. "Not possible, Ambassador. The pinnace is not capable of atmospheric flight. There's no jump engine either. We have enough fuel to maintain this orbit for some months, but that's about it."

"Can you tell me what planet is down there?"

"No, sir. The navigation system is rebooting. In theory, we should be able to feed it the pattern of stars, but the nav specialists all died on *Retribution*."

"Thank you, Ensign." Del-Marie glanced at Azhgrel, offering the lieutenant a chance to take control, but she was still out of it. The delicate sapphire blooms of her head growth swayed gently like wildflowers in a summer breeze. It looked delightful, but he interpreted them as a sign of distress.

"Let me try," Del-Marie told the ensign, gesturing for him to vacate the copilot's station.

"You can't."

"I'm older than you." Del-Marie laughed. "An altogether earlier vintage."

"What's your point?" asked a voice from the crowd of refugee navy personnel.

Del-Marie addressed them. "What do you youngsters call people of my vintage… the original Marines with a capital 'M'?"

"Jacks," several voices replied.

Del-Marie chuckled. "Right. And here's why…"

He was a tired old man, but he was still bigger and stronger than any of these kids. Grabbing Naxxo by his collar, he yanked the younger man out of the seat and took his place.

He plugged one end of a data cable into the pinnace's control console. The other end he jacked into his neck port.

"People my age," he explained, "we don't just jack into the system. We become it."

He closed his eyes, and Pepin took control of the pinnace.

Ten seconds later, he stood, still jacked, and addressed them all with a sour expression. "There's some good news. And a whole lot of bad…"

* * *

When Del-Marie shut out the world to work closely with his personal AI, his thought processes sped up. He had experienced those ten seconds thus.

"What've you got?" he asked Pepin.

"Good and bad."

"C'mon, stop messing."

"Fine. Some good, and a lot of bad."

"Give me the worst."

"Are you sure you don't want good?"

"Do I have to extract you?"

"Threats don't work on me, old man. Take me out and you're left with the intellectual prowess of a Drop Marine, and that's one who's made a full drop quota."

He reached to his neck to extract the AI, but he stayed his hand. Pepin was being irritating on purpose, to take his human mind off the situation.

That was the thing about AIs. They didn't just aim your SA-71 for you and all that drent. Attached to your brain since childhood, they knew you better than you could ever know yourself. And, however frakking annoying they often were, they only ever had your best interest at heart.

"Okay," Del-Marie said. "I surrender. Give me the good news."

"We're currently orbiting Wutan-Scala 7."

"What?"

"It's a planet, Del-Marie. Not just any planet, but the capital world of the Far Reach Federation. It's also the location the *Retribution* set out from when we began our mission to re-establish contact with Earth. You remember our mission? Yes?"

"You know damned well I do. Why have you emphasized the significance of this being our jumping off point?"

"Because it's a safe bet that it means something. Let's look at the evidence. *Retribution* made it as far as the Orion Spur. We were in deep space not far from our homeworld of Tranquility when we were pulled through space and time so that we just happened to be in the path of a ship carrying the younger versions of ourselves so they could board and seize *Retribution*."

"Coincidence upon coincidence."

"And the universe doesn't work that way."

"But Indiya does."

"Uh huh."

"Damn that purple-haired bint. She's got a lot of explaining to do."

"Calm down, old man. We both want to throttle her for what she's done—"

"No. There's more. I can't say what, but…" He fought for the words to explain. "It's as if a thousand versions of me experienced terrible agony in alternate universes. So much pain that it crossed barriers of reality and surrounds me like a psychic stench."

"That's bad. But let's not blame everything on a certain purple woman. Let's make a pledge not to mention her name for a while and move the frakk on."

"Okay. So, we know where we are, Wutan-Scala 7. That's a start. What else do we have on the positive side of the balance?"

"You're alive."

"I already figured that."

There was silence from the AI.

"And…?"

"That's it, Del-Marie."

"Drent! Go on, then. Give me the bad news."

"Are you sure?"

"I can't play your games. I'm too exhausted. How long was I out?"

"I would say an hour. I mean, it feels like an hour."

"Do better. Sync with the pinnace's system clock."

Pepin gave the AI equivalent of drawing a sharp breath. "Technically, you were out for no time at all. We were in deep space when we were sucked into some strange goings on and now we are here. Instantaneously."

"That's impossible. That's…. that's frakking Indiya screwing with the universe again."

"No. Remember, don't think of her. It doesn't help. The first step to staying alive is to figure out *when* we are."

"I agree. We've time jumped. I assume you used astronomical data to figure out our location. Can't you use it to tell the year?"

"Negative. If we have jumped in time, it's too short a hop for the pattern of stars to have changed significantly. Probably no more than twenty thousand years."

"Then our next step is clear. We walk the black and take a look."

"Agreed. But one last thing, we're crammed into this pinnace. It's stocked with food and water, but the air scrubbers are not rated for this number of people. I'm still taking bets on whether we'll starve to death first or suffocate, but unless we start killing people, we've got about six weeks left."

"Copy that."

"One more last thing."

Del-Marie groaned.

"Have you noticed anything different about Lieutenant Azhgrel recently?"

"Not really. What are you driving at?"

"Well, my friend, I have full access to your optic nerves, and I can tell you that you are paying her a lot of attention of late. She might not be human, but she's stirred your ancient loins."

The revelation struck Del-Marie momentarily dumb because he knew it to be true. She was glowing. In bloom like a precious spring flower.

"Oh, frakk! That's all we need. She's in heat, isn't she?"

"Tut-tut. The polite expression is 'in season,' but yes. She hasn't been taking hormone suppressants so she's turning this pinnace into a pheromone hothouse. And I don't expect you non-Zhoogenes have packed your pheromone blockers either."

"Okay. So, there's a Zhoogene sex bomb about to explode inside a crowded tin can. I'll figure that out later. Time to update the kids."

Del-Marie opened his eyes. On Azhgrel. He hadn't intended to stare. Hadn't intended to make her flush in response. But both things happened, nonetheless.

"You and me, Lieutenant," he said. "We need to take a little walk outside."

* * *

Once out in the black, Del-Marie and Azhgrel silently sized each other up before Del-Marie opened proceedings on a private microwave channel. "You aren't taking the pills."

"It's my body."

"And the others? What about theirs?"

"I said it's my body."

"I heard. And it's your body that's going to be an issue."

"Then we shall deal with it. I am no longer prepared to rip out my nature any more than you would tear out your AI. It's a part of me."

"Okay, I respect that, Azhgrel. I just don't know what to do about it."

"What shall happen is fate. This excursion is pointless. I'm going back inside."

They got a ping from the pinnace before she could. "We've got company. A ship's appeared."

Del-Marie was an old man and his artificial eyes were only marginally younger. Nonetheless, they had been serviced and upgraded over the years, which meant his eyes had better sensors than the pinnace.

"I'll see what we've got," he said. All he had to do was keep steady while he looked at the distant dot of the approaching ship. It took about twenty seconds to give Pepin enough blurry images for him to process. Then the AI fed him the cleaned-up image.

"What is it?" Azhgrel asked.

"Like nothing I've seen before. Frigate sized, but sleek like a sports ship. Sycamore wings and two pairs of… well, they look like horns." He laughed.

"What's funny?"

"The ship is throwing shapes, just for the fun of it. That tells me two things. One, its rudders poke into the K-M Region, which sounds like Legion tech. Two, the pilot has serious swagger. Probably a right pain in the ass."

"So, they're Far Reach Federation Navy?"

"Maybe," Del-Marie replied. "If any of this drent made sense, then yeah, I'd say that's a Legion space jock with 'Hold the Line' inked onto their genitals."

"A human, then. A Zhoogene would do no such thing."

"Yeah. Likely it's a human, Azhgrel." He groaned. "We've got trouble."

*****

Chapter Fifty-Three: Lieutenant Azhgrel

"This is Captain Izza Zan Fey of the independent trading ship *Phantom*."

The female voice relayed to Azhgrel's helmet made her lips curl up in disgust, though she could not say why. It spoke accented Standard.

"Are you a Zhoogene?" Azhgrel asked, using the most common language of her homeworld.

The voice replied in fluent Zhoogene that she was. Her intonation was peculiar, which supported the idea that they had time jumped. Forward, Azhgrel guessed.

"Copy *Phantom*. What is your intention?"

"We've come to pick you up."

"That's right," said another voice. Male. Human. Arrogant. "We're your ride."

"Us… or our cargo?" Azhgrel asked.

"You got me," the male replied. "Both. And it's kind of save-the-galaxy important that we do."

"Did Indiya send them?" Del-Marie asked on another channel, which wasn't relayed to *Phantom*.

It was a good question, but before she could ask it, a visual feed was established.

Del-Marie was wrong. Instead of a human pilot, Azhgrel saw a peculiar Zhoogene woman working the flight controls of the *Phantom* with an air of supreme confidence. She wore a well-fitted mulberry jacket over a tailored black shipsuit. The crystal hoops in her ears looked expensive.

This was no Navy jock. She dressed like a pirate. And as Azhgrel saw more of the pilot, she realized she wasn't Zhoogene either.

This was a half-Zhoogene. A freak.

Sex with humans could be an edgy adventure in pleasure, but to breed with them? What kind of animal would do such a thing?

That was a question for another time. First, she had the lives of her command to save.

"Send someone over to negotiate," Azhgrel told the half-Zhoogene. "Not you."

Anger flashed in the pilot's eyes. *Bylzak! Her irises are purple!*

"Very well," the freak replied. "I'll send Captain Fitzwilliam."

"No. Not him."

"Why not?"

"Because you picked him. Send someone without rank. Not from the Legion. A person who has never served with Indiya's forces or her husband's. In fact, make it the youngest person in your crew."

"I have the perfect candidate." The half-Zhoogene smiled at a private joke. "He's a rogue, a convicted murderer, and a bookworm. Most of all, he mocks those who serve in the Legion and he's younger than anyone in my crew or yours."

Murderer? Azhgrel was about to decline when Zan Fey added, "His name is Yat Darant."

"Yat Darant," Azhgrel repeated.

His name made her heart flutter. A mere handful of syllables in accented Federation Standard, but her soul ached at their sound. It was a name that knew her, but she had never heard it before.

A sense of dread almost overcame her as the words "He is acceptable" left her mouth.

* * *

Yat Darant

"Did Indiya send you?"

The old man spoke as if he already knew the answer. Best not lie then.

"She did," Darant admitted. "I'd like to wring the treacherous monster's skinny neck. But, yeah. We're her collection crew. But as much as we hate her, we need her."

The man, who had introduced himself as Ambassador Sandure, wrinkled his nose as if sniffing the truth of Darant's words.

Maybe he was just disgusted by the smell? The moment he'd removed his helmet, Darant had been assailed by the aroma of ripe bodies in a confined space.

The notion that Sandure could sniff the truth sounded fanciful. But not long ago, so had intergalactic invasions, sorcerers, Lady Indiya being alive, time travel, and cloning. All were very real.

So, it wasn't much of a leap to also believe that this huge man was one of the original titan Marines from the Orion Era. And they had strange powers, though truth and fable had long since been jumbled.

"Why?" Sandure demanded.

"Why do we need Indiya? Because we're at war with intergalactic invaders, and we're losing. If we can't defeat the enemy, everyone will die."

"Everyone? In the entire Federation?"

"The entire galaxy."

"Frakk!"

"Damn right."

"And Wutan-Scala 7? Did this enemy kill our world?"

"The Andromedans? No. That was an earlier alien invasion. Long time ago now. All the details will be in *Phantom's* infopedia."

Sandure stroked his beard, in no hurry to speak.

Darant used the pause to take in his surroundings. There were twelve people in this small boat. Some were wounded, and he worried two might be dead. None of the humans were normal size, either tending toward Indiya's miniature stature or Sandure's muscular bulk. The commander, Lieutenant Azhgrel, was all Zhoogene. Her face and body were considerably more angular than Zan Fey's, but she was so hot, hot, hot that Darant had to look away.

He could see through to the hold and the large crate that took up almost all its space. It looked like a generic freight box with a data port and a few status lights, the kind of thing that might contain refrigerated soft fruits. But he knew that wasn't the case.

Sandure cleared his throat. "So now Indiya wants her box back to win her war. She said this might happen when we set off for Earth."

"Earth! You guys went to Earth?"

"Never quite made it. We were…" He shrugged. "I guess you could say we were swept up by history. My theory is that Indiya is not the only one deciding which realities suit her best. We were turned back and folded into a different thread of fate."

An irresistible attractive force wrenched Darant's gaze onto the Zhoogene.

Azhanti! She was licking her lips while her golden eyes ate him up.

He scratched beneath his collar. Why was she staring? And why did his face feel so hot?

"Will the pinnace fit inside your ship?" asked a tiny human crewman.

"Yeah." Darant dismissed the voice with a wave. "We measured you. Not a problem."

Sandure looked to Azhgrel and gestured for her to speak. He'd made every effort to convey that it was the hot lieutenant and not him who was in command, but it was a difficult pretense to keep up when Azhgrel wasn't even in charge of her own tongue. It kept lolling out.

With everyone's attention on her, she made a heroic effort to suck her tongue back into her mouth and master the ability to speak. "I want to go to your ship."

"Good." Darant smiled. *Phantom* promised cleaner air and more sanity.

Azhgrel stumbled toward a vacuum suit secured near the airlock.

"Err… who's the pilot?" Darant asked.

"Me," Azhgrel replied.

"Aren't you going to fly this little boat into *Phantom's* hangar?"

"No. I want to travel back the way you came. Take me to your ship, Yat Darant."

He sucked at his lip. The lieutenant was in charge, and she'd basically asked, "Why don't you invite me back to your place for a cup of coffee?"

Only one answer was conceivable.

"Sure. Get suited up, and I'll show you whatever you want."

*****

Chapter Fifty-Four: Lieutenant Azhgrel

They jetted in silence toward the spacecraft parked nearby. This *Phantom.*

That was a curiosity to take in shortly. For the moment, Yat Darant was wonder enough.

The human had never taken blockers for Zhoogene pheromones. The only explanation Azhgrel could think of was that Zhoogene women of his era neutered themselves, and they did so for the convenience of aliens such as the one traveling with her against a backdrop of the stars.

This era being one thousand six hundred years into her future. Yat had told her.

She tried to shock herself with that fact, to distract her from Yat, but too much that was mystifying had already occurred. Having traveled into the past, being in the future didn't feel strange.

Azhgrel asked him technical details about his ship and his shipmates.

That didn't distract her either because she didn't hear his words. She could only listen to his voice, its modulation and timbre. It's *wonder.* Everything about this man added to the intense desire for him that welled up in her chest.

No matter that it shamed her to feel this way about an alien human. No matter that this was a chemical attraction she did not desire. They were both consumed by a burning passion that she could neither control nor deny.

The moment they cycled through *Phantom's* airlock, she would pull him from his suit and explore him properly.

* * *

Tavistock Fitzwilliam

When the woman from the distant past removed her helmet after emerging with Darant from Airlock #3, Fitz's first impression had him flushing with heat. And that was kind of awkward with his wife standing beside him.

Azhgrel was beautiful and in full season. That would be a problem for *Phantom's* crew, but at least they'd experienced it before with Izza. His marines and the remaining Indigo Squad mutants were going to experience real difficulty.

For now, that problem seemed to belong entirely to Darant, given the way Azhgrel was drooling over him. Couldn't happen to a nicer guy.

He glanced Izza's way and, to his surprise, discovered she was screwing her face up in distaste at the newcomer.

Azhgrel jerked in shock, wrenched her attention away from Darant and stared at his wife. A sneer of disgust came over her.

Both women took an involuntary step backward, their gazes locked in mutual revulsion.

What in the name of Orion's Balls was going on?

They were two like poles repelling each other, a reciprocal animosity born from an implacable physical law.

The backpedaling brought a moment when the three of them were aligned in the passageway in an equilateral triangle; Darant was of no consequence to this particular geometric equation. Fitz's mutant intuition activated, and he understood instantly why the women were reacting so.

And they, it seemed, did not. The universe was on a fast track to ruination, but it had allowed him time for a little mischief.

He took Azhgrel's hand and kissed it, bowing as he did.

"It is an honor to meet you," he told her.

"Fitzy! Why do you act so with this woman? You do not know her."

"Oh, but I do."

Both women looked at Fitz, their eyes blazing with fury. It looked damned good on both of them.

"I do not know you!" Azhgrel shouted, though the anger drained from her voice when she looked around to check that Darant was still close.

"Where have you met this woman?" Izza demanded. "She is nothing but a skragg-ugly junior naval officer of no consequence."

"Darant, leave us," Fitz ordered. "But stay close, because—" he winked at Azhgrel "—I expect you'll be needed soon." He raised his voice. "And Verlys? I know you're nearby, just out of sight. Put your gun down and leave us. Thank you."

Azhgrel watched Darant leave like a ravenous hound staring at a butcher carrying away a heap of sausages.

"Follow me, ladies," Fitz said, and ushered them to the lounge.

When they were secure and alone, he addressed Izza. "As you put it to me one time, my lady, the women of your race disperse, while male Zhoogenes hang around in packs like lazy dogs with no imagination. The reason you find each other's scent repulsive is because you're related."

They didn't understand.

"Lieutenant Azhgrel," he said, "I am your son-in law, many generations removed. Which, now I think on it, means you will eventually return to your own time."

Azhgrel looked horrified. "How can that be? The only person I have laid with was my husband. But he's dead, and we never shared a child. How can I be your ancestor when you are older than me?"

Izza took a different line of attack. "Are you suggesting that I am descended from this… this person?"

Fitz removed his dark glasses. He felt his eyes glowing. "I *know* you are."

Izza gasped and knew the truth. She turned to Azhgrel, and then looked down at her belly. "We've more of your descendants on the way."

Azhgrel looked disgusted with the idea.

Fitz grinned. "And I think we've all worked out who my father-in-law is." He opened the hatch and shouted into the passageway. "Darant, would you mind joining us in the lounge?"

* * * * *

Chapter Fifty-Five: Lady Indiya

"Tell me I'm not dreaming," Del-Marie said when he entered Indiya's study.

She frowned. "Oh, you refer to the Muryani you passed on the way in?"

"Frakk yeah. The three Muryani you just had in for a cozy chat." He looked pained. "I know you can be devious, ruthless, and selfish, but never a traitor."

"I have never been a traitor." She considered. Many would disagree. "No, never, although I often struggle to understand what or who I should be loyal to."

"In our battalion mess hall, back when we were cadets, the hull plating from a destroyed Muryani cruiser was embedded in the wall. We all fantasized we would bring back such a trophy from the frontier war. We hated those bugs. Before your transport ship carried us off to war, our entire existence had consisted of training to fight the Muryani. Literally. Killing Muryani was the sole reason we were brought into this universe. You wouldn't understand, being a space rat."

"Put your mind at ease, Del. They're essential allies, but I don't trust them any more than you do. Far from a cozy chat, I terrorized them with details of what I would do if they tried to absorb the Federation after I am gone."

Del-Marie sat in the sofa chair next to Indiya and looked around the intimate room. "It's changed since I was last here. *He* is no longer here."

"He disappeared a long time ago, Del."

"I don't just mean him physically here, alive and joking with us. The paint on the bulkheads, the pictures, the mementos, and the treasures. They weren't much, but he chose them all, and now they've gone. It's as if you've cut any traces of Arun out of your life."

"Don't speak his name! He was my husband. No one else may use his name."

Del reached out and held her hand. "Arun was also my best friend."

They glared in silence across the little oak table.

Del released her. "And he would never have approved of what you did to us on the *Retribution*."

Having spoken his truth, the tension eased in Del's body, and he leaned back into his chair. "So, you're bringing everybody in for a chat before the big event. The making—or unmaking—of the universe."

"Only the few who are worth my time. I'll be leaving soon, one way or another, and I wanted to ask you something first. If we survive the Andromedans, I want to make good the harm I did to you and the survivors of the *Retribution*. I shall send Azhgrel and her people home to their time. But I wasn't sure if you would prefer to stay here."

"Azhgrel must go home if it's true that her descendants are alive in this time. But there's nothing for me to return to. The mission to re-establish contact with Earth was to be my last act. Since that failed, I would prefer to stay here to keep an eye on you while I can." He laughed. "We've saved the galaxy against impossible odds before. We both know that's the easy part. It's what we build next that we got wrong last time. That's why I will fight you to my dying breath if you stick around to interfere."

"I admire your optimism, but I struggle to believe anyone will survive the Andromedan onslaught."

"Always plan for victory. Even if it never comes."

She smiled at the memories. Her husband used to tell her those same words every day.

"I want to search for him."

"Arun? You think he's alive?"

"Unlikely. But not impossible."

"I'll help, if you like. One last hopeless mission. Why not? But you've looked for him for centuries and no found leads. What's changed?"

"Mutants," she replied. "I've had help from pre-cogs. Nothing definite, as you will remember, but more than one hint pointing at where I should be looking."

"Earth. You're going to try to make it back to Earth."

"That's right.

"Frakk! It's a long way. No one's ever made it that far, and I don't imagine they will be pleased to see us. Frakking Earther drentheads."

"What was it you used to tell me, back when you were an arrogant young Tactical Marine?"

"The longer the odds, the greater the glory?"

"No. The lie you told yourselves about abandoning your comrades."

"No Marine left behind." He took a solemn breath. "Yes, ma'am. We're headed for Earth."

* * * * *

Chapter Fifty-Six: Lady Indiya

The lovers brushed lips, oblivious to the observer. The human man ran his fingertips through the delicate sapphire blooms bursting forth from the Zhoogene woman's head. She trembled at his touch, then closed her eyes and groaned.

In her own way, the Zhoogene was returning the man's caresses, not with physical touch but with the release of pheromones from her petals that made the man giddy with arousal, his eyes rolling up their sockets.

A pang of regret stabbed at the observer. She had only once experienced the pleasure of physical intimacy. Across thousands of years, that one experience had been secured in archive memory that she had never allowed herself to return to.

After that one time, the killing had begun. And never stopped. It had broken her forever.

Centuries later, she had married the man she'd slept with, but their intimacy had never been of the physical kind. Not like this.

She adjusted her body chemistry to remove all regrets.

The fascination remained, though. Without taking blockers, whenever Zhoogenes of either gender were in season, humans found them irresistible and vice versa. Most Federation citizens of the current era had slow-release implants to limit the effect. However, she'd never thought to supply her Darant clone with an implant, and Azhgrel came from an earlier era.

Both species possessed deeply buried furnaces of sexual arousal guarded by secret chemical receptors that could only be unlocked by the pheromones of the other species.

Federation scientists dismissed this as coincidence.

Indiya didn't believe that.

The exiles from the Orion Spur hadn't arrived here by chance. They'd been part of a deal. The Federation was to be a buffer zone, an armed tripwire to warn of the next Andromedan assault.

That much she was certain, but she guessed that was only the beginning of a deeper plan.

It was what had led her to design the reality editor, having detected the effects of one used by someone else. Perhaps it had been the same someone who had sabotaged the *Retribution's* mission. But why? Could it be they were keeping the Exiles away from Earth?

Indiya's musing was interrupted by Azhgrel drawing back a little from Darant. She looked round at the apparently deserted mess hall to check they were still alone.

The Zhoogene frowned. Her race had acute senses. Indiya was standing only ten feet away, but she was blocking those senses.

Azhgrel's face relaxed, and she returned her attention to her lover. "I've been talking to Claudio Zanitch," she told him with a mischievous glint in her eye. "He has a lot to say about you."

"Claudio loves to tell stories," Darant said. "They aren't always true."

Her expression darkened. "Your friend explained the unhappiness and loss you have experienced in love, a desolation that has touched us both. Zanitch believes the universe has balance, that your pain will be offset by joy so powerful, the poets will be extolling it for centuries to come."

"Nope. I told you, Beans can't help but talk in stories. It's just his way of saying he approves of you." Darant reached out and cupped her soft cheek. "I don't need any universe-balancing drent to know we'll be together forever."

A smile flickered on her face. "That's not all Claudio told me. Like all the others, he is convinced you and I can have a child and that child will be the ancestor of Zan Fey. I don't understand how that could happen."

Darant brought his lips close to hers and whispered in graphic terms how a man might impregnate a woman.

"I already know you can satisfy me." She giggled. "No matter how extraordinary the pleasures you give me, we can never be the same species. We're not even from the same world. I can no more become pregnant by a human than I could with a Slern or Kurlei."

She glanced behind her, but it was only Hubert trotting over to join them. The goat had adapted to Azhgrel's presence surprisingly easily, adopting her as a junior member of his family.

"I know you hate Indiya," Darant said to his lover, "but I think we should ask her."

Hubert stopped in his tracks and bared his teeth at the observer who was not so hidden to his eyes.

Indiya released her throttle on the senses of the two humanoids.

They glared at the woman who had apparently appeared from nowhere.

"Darant is right," Indiya said. "We're different because we're mutants. Some of us have purple pigmentation, like my hair and the eyes of Zan Fey and Fitzwilliam. Others such as Zanitch and Darant have no outward signs, but they carry the mutations all the same."

"Is it true that I'm descended from aliens?" Darant asked.

"In a manner of speaking. As am I. Our genetic code was spliced with a species who became obsessed with mutating first themselves and then their servant species. We were early experiments on humans."

"And that means that we can…" He gestured between himself and his lover.

"It means you possess dominant genetic patterns specifically engineered to cross species boundaries. It's not easy but it can be done."

A grin came across his face.

"So, we *could* have a child," Azhgrel said.

"You already do," Indiya replied.

"What?"

"You are already pregnant with Darant's child."

"I'm not… How can you tell?"

Uninterested in supplying a more detailed explanation, Indiya replied curtly, "I'm a goddess."

"So, you finally admit it."

Kanha Wei stormed into the mess hall like a tempest. Indiya, taken aback, hadn't sensed her approach until the last moment.

"Although for a goddess, you're difficult to find sometimes." Wei crossed her arms and frowned at the lovers. "Especially when I want you alone."

After a few moments, she shrugged, a silent dismissal as if Darant and Azhgrel were nothing more than background details.

"We were due to talk tomorrow," Indiya told her.

"Were we? Or was that another Kanha Wei you were thinking of?"

Indiya felt her breath catch in her throat and she stared, completely stunned by the unexpected question.

"Oh, yes," Wei said. "You know, you really shouldn't keep sending me out into a dangerous galaxy. Has it occurred to you why I am the only one who agrees with everything you say? Why do you think that is, oh, Immortal Goddess?"

"Drent!" Indiya's mental commands silently flew out to her personal guard, ordering Wei's arrest.

Wei stepped close, her lips pursed with menace. "I asked you a question, bitch."

"Hey!" Azhgrel snapped. "Don't talk to her like that."

"It's all right." Indiya raised her hand to warn the lovers away. "It's just a harmless question." She paused momentarily to hold a silent conversation with her guard commander. The nearest armed help was over five minutes away. Stalking the shadows of this hollow fortress, undetected by any internal monitoring system, had its downsides. She would have to keep Wei talking. Or kill her.

She faced the most loyal companion she'd had for the past few centuries. "I keep you near and constant, Kanha, because I trust you. No one else, only you."

"You trust me to always say yes. I'm the only person who supports you unconditionally. Unconditional love. That's what you needed me for."

"That's not true."

"Don't waste our time denying what we both know to be." Wei removed her gold spectacles, revealing eyes that seared with demonic fire.

The Corruption!

Indiya wished her dead with a single thought.

The air was overrun with nanomachines crafted inside Indiya's own body. Her tiny machines infiltrated the pores and the lungs of everyone who dared to enter her realm. There they could spy for Indiya. They could also heal. Or kill.

All it took was an effort of will, as Pyruula had discovered.

Kanha Wei was not Pyruula. She smirked in victory because the Corruption was shielding her from Indiya's deadly intent.

Too dazed to react, Indiya stood rooted to the spot as Wei closed the distance between them and launched a fist at her face.

Indiya tried to dodge, but her ancient reflexes were far too slow. The punch connected, and she felt a paralyzing shock of pain surge from her nose to the back of her skull.

Then nothing.

* * *

Kanha Wei drew a jagged blade, the handle of faded brown wood with metal finger guards darkened with age. She twirled it around her fingers, then in one swift motion it was aimed at Indiya's heart.

Azhgrel reacted immediately, her foot flying out in a swift kick that sent the knife flying across the room. It clattered against a table and landed near Hubert.

Before Azhgrel could snap her leg back from her kick, Wei caught it and threw her backward to land awkwardly near the knife.

This enraged Hubert. Ears against his head and teeth bared, he flung himself at Wei.

"Right with you, boy," Darant cried and also charged at Wei.

The Corrupted spy shot a menacing glance Indiya's way. Her target was still unconscious, but before she could finish her, she had three assailants to fend off, for Azhgrel was picking herself off the floor.

Wei prioritized her targets and serviced them in turn.

Hubert tried to scurry around and behind Wei so he could bite out her hamstrings, a tactic that had worked well for him in the past.

Not this time. Wei booted him in the face, sending him skidding along the floor on his back in a shower of teeth and pitiful bleats.

Although Darant had almost closed on Wei, she judged Azhgrel to be the greater threat and threw her second knife at the Zhoogene.

"No!" Darant screamed. "Not again."

He threw himself in the blade's path.

It wasn't like the holo-movies. There was no slow motion. No dramatic music. He clattered into the blade, landed clumsily, and blinked at the knife stuck in his right wrist.

His blood gushed, but he wasn't dead.

Azhgrel roared in rage.

Darant drew out the knife, which as well as being skragging painful increased the blood spray to sickening levels.

"I always knew being ambidextrous would help one day," he muttered, and hurled the blade back at Kanha Wei.

But Wei hadn't stood idle. She'd drawn a third knife and launched it at Darant.

The two perfectly balanced throwing knives passed each other in the air.

But only one had been thrown by a practiced expert.

Wei twisted to one side. Darant's knife glanced off her shoulder.

Hers pierced him in the heart.

As he fell, Azhgrel recovered the knife from her lover's chest, ignored his howl of pain, and readied to throw it.

Wei was crouched low, edging toward the other knife on the floor, but with her attention on Azhgrel, ready to either dodge the throw or meet a close attack.

Suddenly, she screamed in pain and collapsed to the floor. Hubert had surprised her, and the few sharp teeth that remained had ripped through her hamstrings.

Wei writhed in agony, her face twisted in pain and rage.

Azhgrel wasted no time. She lunged forward, knife in hand, and with a fierce scream of rage, thrust the blade deep into Wei's stomach. The Corrupted woman thrashed and screamed as Azhgrel twisted the blade, slicing through her organs and ripping open her bowels.

Azhgrel stood back, her eyes burning with anger, and watched Kanha Wei bleeding out for a few moments.

Then she cried out her own agony and rushed to Darant.

Azhgrel fell to her knees beside her lover, tears streaming down her face as she cradled him in her arms. His blood soaked through her clothes as she pressed her hands to his chest, desperately trying to stop the bleeding. But she could feel his life slipping away, his breaths becoming shallower and more ragged with each passing moment.

She leaned in close, her forehead resting against his as she softly sang a lament for the fallen.

Darant choked, blood gurgling in his throat.

Azhgrel thought it was his death rattle, but a second later his eyes fluttered open and locked onto her.

"That's nice," he croaked. "Has anyone ever told you, you're exquisitely hot?"

She let out a bright laugh and brushed the blood from his mouth with long green fingers. "Dear Yat. Claudio will have to rewrite your story. You got the girl in the end."

"Yeah. I got the girl, but instead of her dying, now it's my turn. Maybe it's better that way. I've only been alive for three months, and I've spent a good part of that with you. I'm the luckiest man ever."

"I shall never forget you."

"Damn right you won't. But promise me you'll move on. You and me, Az, we were just a crazy pair of pheromone-soaked sex junkies living our addiction to the max for a crazy few weeks. I loved it. But that's all we ever were."

She kissed him. "Neither of us believe that. Even if I did, we know that not only will we have a child, but our line continues. Your descendants—dozens of generations on—will remember your name. Some have even met you. It's a form of immortality, is it not? A better one than Indiya's. So, no more talk of forgetting."

Hubert limped over and crashed his furry head against the crook of Darant's neck.

A fresh flow of blood gushed from Darant's mouth, but he recovered a little. "I never thought I would die in the arms of an alien goat and a smoking hot alien babe. I picked a weird galaxy to live and die."

"Hubert is more than mere beast," Azhgrel said, fighting off the panic that swept through her when Darant's eyes closed. "Hubert's kind are natives of my homeworld. There are many paleoanthropologists, and even archaeologists, who argue that basten goats were the first intelligent species to arise on Zhooge and established the first civilizations, before evolving onto a different path. They no longer speak, and I don't think they are sentient in the way most would define, but only a fool would claim that Hubert and his kind are unintelligent."

Darant fussed with Hubert's fur. "Look after her, boy. She's special to me. Do you understand?"

He bleated, then licked Darant's face.

But Darant never felt the rasp of his friend's tongue. He was already dead.

And through it all, Indiya watched the scene play out and tried desperately hard to care.

But she felt nothing.

* * * * *

Chapter Fifty-Seven: Lady Indiya

The security guards pushed into the mess hall, some fanning out and taking defensive positions while the rest medically fussed over her.

Indiya shooed them away. "Not now. I've already made a self-diagnosis more thorough than anything you're capable of. I have a concussion and a brain bleed. Normally, I'd take the time to get patched up, but I don't have so much as a second to spare on such luxuries."

The guard commander, Lieutenant Shankara, stepped forward. "Lady Indiya, you won't believe this, but…"

She paused, her gaze riveted by the cooling mess of guts and gore that had recently been Kanha Wei, perhaps only now recognizing the corpse's identity. "Oh, I was going to say—"

"You were going to say that you've encountered more than one Kanha Wei."

"Yes, ma'am. One is arrested. One is dead. We took casualties."

"There may be more Wei clones. Put the whole Redoubt Line on alert."

"Already done."

"Keep the one you arrested under tight security. Any others, shoot to kill. She was my best friend, but she's the enemy now. All of her."

"Corrupted?"

"Yes. I am initiating the anti-Corruption lockdown protocol across the redoubts. Though if I never saw what happened to poor Kanha, we stand little chance in detecting others."

Indiya stared at her dead friend's body splattered across the floor. The encounter in the mess hall had been random chance. Then she looked at Azhgrel cradling Darant's body. Unfortunate as well as random, but the timing had been planned.

"The Redoubt Line is about to be attacked," she told Shankara. "Prop me up against a wall and monitor my vitals. Otherwise stay out of my way and keep quiet. I have a job to do. Several, in fact."

Once she'd been picked up and settled upright, Indiya activated the naval command channel, her mind creating a private holo-comm.

Doubts raced through her head. With a network of tactical black holes, her ships could have danced around an invading force, but only two partially constructed holes were ready. And the Muryani had only just begun to concentrate their naval forces at the Redoubt Line.

If only she'd moved earlier. If only…!

Admiral Aluin appeared in the imaginary holo-comm, his face tight with stress, but his eyes determined.

"This is it," Indiya told him. "The enemy is coming."

"They're already here, ma'am. I'm getting reports of multiple emergence throats forming—Azhanti!"

"What is it?"

"There are so many."

The Muryani commander, General Sairoc-4-Cerulean entered the virtual conference. "The Andromedans are learning," they surmised. "The throats are wider and there are more of them. This will be a mass assault wave, not the narrow stream of ships we've seen before."

Indiya tapped into the long-range visual scans. Eight jump tunnels had been opened by Leviathans who were themselves protected by rings of Hammers. Beyond that, she didn't recognize any of the ships, but they didn't look like Andromedans. These were their Corrupted slaves. Hundreds had already emerged, with scores more arriving every second.

"Analysis," she demanded.

"About a third of them are Federation ships," Aluin said. "Not all military, but their signatures are pinging hits in the Ship List. Some Second Legion vessels lost several centuries ago and… It's the missing Tenth Legion, ma'am. All of it. Of the other Corrupted vessels, I recognize some from history classes. They were enemies the early Federation faced."

The Tenth. An entire Legion lost without trace while on maneuvers at the edge of the Antispinward Fringe three hundred years ago. Indiya remembered the loss well. It was what had persuaded her to return to life.

"I see Muryani vessels among the Corrupted," Sairoc said. "More from races we recognize but you will not, including some from races now extinct. They are those who lived in the region now occupied by the Federation but who were wiped out in the last Andromedan invasion."

"How long ago was that?" Aluin asked.

"Five thousand years."

"And those ships have just been hanging around for all that time?"

"There is much about the Andromedans we still do not understand."

"This much I do know," Aluin growled. "Whether it's the Andromedans, the Corrupted, or whatever weird shit we face next, if we hit them hard enough, they will die."

"The units will die," Sairoc agreed, "but the biomass will be reclaimed later."

"Damn your biomass. That's a strategic concern. I'm focused on how to win the battle I see before me today, and for that we need fleet tactics."

Corrupted ships continued to stream in. Indiya was receiving reports the others were not, and they were worrying indeed. Corrupted infiltrators were sabotaging Fort Douaumont's communication arrays, scrambling comm signals, and disabling long-range sensors. The laser batteries on Zao-Zayne and Angel Rock were unable to charge to active state because the energy reserves had been mysteriously drained.

And that would only be the beginning of the sabotage.

The Corrupted were already active inside Fort Douaumont. No one could be trusted. Every system could be compromised.

Meanwhile, the enemy ships flooded in, forming up well outside the effective firing range of the Redoubt defenses, determined this time to take advantage of their overwhelming numerical superiority.

"Can we win today?" Indiya asked her naval commanders.

The Muryani answered first. "That depends on whether those ancient ships and their crews are combat effective."

"If we assume that they are?"

"Then we should enact emergency plans to evacuate anything we can salvage from the Redoubt Line and deny to the enemy everything we cannot."

"We can't run and hide again," Aluin said. His eyes blazed with intensity as he pounded his fist against the console before him. "On this day we hold the line. And by 'we' I don't just mean the Legion. Nor even the Muryani. But for the sake of the entire galaxy, we must all stand together and win."

"This need not be the final battle," the Muryani said. "Not for us."

"For the Expansion, perhaps not," Indiya said. "Though I doubt that is true if we fail to contain the enemy here. Nonetheless, you will hold the line at the Redoubt. Federation and Expansion forces alike."

"You do not command here," the Muryani said.

"I remind you of the conversation we had earlier today," Indiya said ominously. "We both know what I am capable of."

The Muryani fluttered its antennae back along its stretched head. "I haven't forgotten. Very well. We will not leave the battlefield, Lady Indiya."

Indiya took a deep breath and measured the situation one more time.

The Corrupted ships had completed their deployment and the Andromedans were beginning to form up behind. From the Federation's point of view, Aluin was right to make a stand here. True, there were Federation sectors the Andromedans had not yet reached, and Legion forces were still concentrating at the Federation's heart in the Far Reach Sector, but the Muryani naval forces were all here. There would never be a stronger concentration of military force to repel the invaders. But unless the armada of Corrupted ships were fragile relics with no offensive power, then they would not be able to withstand the enemy's onslaught. There were simply too many Corrupted warships.

"General Sairoc-4-Cerulean, I transfer to you the role of supreme commander of the Redoubt Line."

Aluin's face twisted in disbelief. "You're fleeing?"

"No. And shut your wixering mouth. I'm injured. Which means I can't direct the battle, run Fort Douaumont, and carry out my other vital tasks."

"What could be more critical than leading the defense?" Aluin demanded. "I don't care if you're propped up on your deathbed, Lady Indiya, so long as you can give orders. To my people about to brave the enemy onslaught, you *are* the Legion."

"Well spoken, Admiral. However, you are underinformed. You and General Sairoc-4-Cerulean will both do everything in your power to keep the enemy away from Mirdath-Naani."

"Mirdath-Naani?" Aluin frowned. "I thought that rock was deserted. What's there?"

Indiya smiled. "Two men… and the heart of Chimera Company."

* * *

A mobile command center rapidly established itself around Indiya in the mess hall.

Although she wasn't running the naval battle, the director of Fort Douaumont was missing, presumed to be growing feathers in all the wrong places. As soon as she'd found someone vaguely competent and delegated that role to them, she screamed at an aide, "Get me Fitzwilliam!"

In short order, the smuggler captain's grinning face appeared in a portable holo-comm. He appeared to be moving at haste through a passageway. He did that a lot.

"Afternoon, ma'am." His grin widened. "I hear we have a spot of bother."

"The Andromedans are here in overwhelming numbers."

The grin flickered. "Can we win?"

"No."

He stopped in his tracks. "Then this is the end of Chimera Company. I'm going to gather my flock and head back to the Guild." He paused for a moment. "Say, you haven't seen Darant have you? He's missing."

"Darant is with me. And you can't run yet, I still need you for one last job."

His eyes glowed angrily. "I've heard that before."

"This is the last time. I swear upon my husband's honor."

He hesitated, and she could tell he didn't trust her. He was correct to doubt her, of course, but he told her to carry on anyway.

"I need you to drop everything and take me to Mirdath-Naani."

"Well, as luck would have it, that's where I'm headed. My two sergeants have been sneaking off there and think I don't know. I'll take you. Make sure Darant sticks with you. And that stupid goat of his. He won't leave without it."

"They're both with me," Indiya said glancing at the corpse. "Darant isn't going anywhere."

*****

Chapter Fifty-Eight: Tavistock Fitzwilliam

Mirdath-Naani

Zavage made a sound like shattering crystal, the Kurlei equivalent of a howl of pain. "I'm hit!"

Fitz swore profusely in a language he didn't understand. This damned rock was supposed to be deserted.

"I have him under cover," Lily cried. "But we're gonna need a little help."

Izza's muscles tensed as she prepared to charge into the room where Lily and Zavage were pinned down.

Her blood was up. It was all Fitz could do to rein her back with a restraining hand on her shoulder and a whisper in her ear. "Trust me."

The ancient, fortified asteroid of Mirdath-Naani was a maze of narrow corridors and silent halls filled with metal-lined industrial plant and sterile labs. But there had been surprises too. Had Lily and Zavage stumbled upon another?

The asteroid rang like a broken bell as another mass driver salvo hit it from space. He hoped Fregg was keeping *Phantom* safe.

But he had enough problems of his own to worry about. The asteroid was filled with Corrupted soldiers who must have sneaked in ahead of the main assault.

He threw a spy ball through the blast hatch. It hovered just above the floor and then darted to one side, hugging the wall behind heavy storage racks laden with raw materials, before emerging into the space to see what they faced.

Chimera Company had been fighting their way through a squad of alien fighters from a race he'd never encountered before. They had long limbs and spindly fingers, and behind their helmet visors their heads were apparently featureless. Nonetheless, they carried themselves with an awkwardness he recognized from other Corrupted people, as if they'd forgotten how to move and were relying upon ancient muscle memory. Their obsidian armor was difficult to penetrate, and though their stubby guns were inaccurate, the energy bolts they fired had burned through Urdizine's armor and hurt him badly. And now Zavage too.

In the room behind him, he heard a *whooomph* when Verlys Sinofar unleashed five-barreled hell with her Z'Lox Slammer. Green Fish was in the rearguard too, and the screams of womanly delight suggested both were having a wild time.

"Clear!" Verlys bellowed, momentarily drowning out the bombardment of the surface.

Through his shades, the spy ball showed a spike glowing red and the vague outline of shapes flowing around. Fitz upped the camera's lowlight enhancements but the glow from the spike was too bright. It seemed to be tapping against something, raising sparks as it did.

He told the ball to emit a little light and he saw three of the most bizarre fighting vehicles he'd ever seen, long and sleek like the body of a shark.

Glossy black hover sharks with electric blue lights running along their frames. Neat.

These flexible shark tubes were crewed by three of the featureless Corrupted aliens sitting one behind the other. Heavy armor cut with vision slits protected the front of the sharks. The lattice armor of the sides looked more vulnerable, though there were turrets attached to each side, some mounting what looked like heavy railguns and others with rocket launchers.

Machinery was mounted on the rears. One shark had the hot metal spike that was thumping against a closed blast door in the far side of the room. The others—one with grabbing hydraulic jaws on an extendable arm and the other a circular drill—hunted Lily and Zavage.

All this information he absorbed in a single moment. The aliens turned to see what was generating light. Vivid green bolts of energy reached out, and Fitz yelped when the image in his glasses flared painfully as the spy ball died a fiery death.

The memories of what he'd just seen sifted and sorted themselves in his vision, like an old-school interrogator presenting a stack of incriminating photographs to a suspect. He saw the enemy forcing open a sealed blast door, Lily and Urdizine crouched behind machinery, hover sharks that would be awesome to race down the corridors, and more. One memory stood out above all others; it was something he had barely noticed before: among all the anonymous boxes of crap on the storage shelves stood four metal drums with warnings of flammable and explosive content.

"Lily," Fitz cried. "Stay down."

He kissed his wife. Looked down at his F-Cannon and kissed that too.

Izza raised an eyebrow.

"You I can come back to," he explained, "but this is my last dance with the cannon."

The day was always going to come for the alien black market weapon of unknown origin. There were only seven rounds left, and Fitz hadn't seen replacement ammo on offer for twenty years.

Seven rounds. But each was configurable. And for all the mysteries he'd witnessed on his journey through the galaxy, Fitz considered that the most remarkable.

He spoke his round selection into the stock. "Pop-up."

A holographic display appeared above the F-Cannon's barrel. It displayed the shelves in the dark room on the far side of the rock wall. With a practiced adjustment of the focus setting, he had it trained on the explosive drums.

A squeeze of the trigger sent the pop-up round out through a green muzzle flash. Its velocity was slow enough to track with his eye for the first meter. Then it disappeared from sight and, as far as Fitz understood, from conventional spacetime altogether. It reappeared inside the other room and ignited the explosive material in a fireball that maxed out the auto-darkening in Fitz's shades.

Fitz told his cannon's selector that he wanted "Swing-fire Targeting," then he dove into the room, rolled because it looked so good, and took a knee. *Snap! Snap! Snap!* He squeezed the trigger thrice, each time painting a different hover shark.

The shark riders, meanwhile, were pouring a devastating volume of fire into the shelves.

An inhuman shout of warning was probably directed at him, but Fitz was already leaping for safety, joining Lily and the wounded Zavage behind some kind of lab equipment station. It was reassuringly big and bulky.

Fitz felt the vibrations of the rockets and energy bolts slam into the cover he was hiding behind. His teeth rattled in his skull, and his ears rang with the noise as the metal buckled under the onslaught, the solid cover slowly being ripped apart.

"Swing-fire Release," he told his hand cannon. Despite the noise of the enemy's violence, he felt the confirmation blip in the F-Cannon's grip.

Three more squeezes of the trigger and his last rounds exited the barrel. In this configuration, the rounds were miniature missiles, streaking up toward the ceiling before turning back on themselves and diving for their assigned targets. The rounds were only as big as his thumb, but they packed an immense punch. When they hit the sharks, the shockwaves pushed Fitz back and knocked him almost senseless. Debris rained down around him, and he felt intense heat on his skin. Fearing they would burn to death, he and Lily began dragging Zavage back from the groaning equipment block.

A part of the roof collapsed, adding clouds of dust as it fell to the ground.

Finally, the chaos settled a little, and Fitz risked a peek out from behind their cover. Shattered shelves and debris were scattered everywhere; the room was a scene of utter destruction in which the hover sharks had been torn apart, and their riders thrown in all directions.

He was trying to tell Lily a quip about the cleaning bill for this mess, but his head was still too woozy for wordplay. In any case, she ignored him, got to her feet, and fired her blaster at the ground behind him.

Incredibly, some of the enemy still had some fight, and one had been about to shoot him in the back. But Izza, Verlys, and the rest of Chimera Company swept in and mercilessly slaughtered them all.

He knelt beside Verlys, who'd taken a nasty burn to the shoulder and was resting against some wreckage.

"Stay with her," he told Green Fish. Leaning in close to Verlys, he made a solemn promise. "I will come back for you, my friend. I swear."

Moments later, he was at the door the enemy had tried to force. At Indiya's command, it slid open.

Someone was shaking him by the shoulders. "Fitz! Fitzy!"

"Whaaa?"

"Don't pass out," Izza was warning him. "You have a head injury."

He heard a guttural alien cry. One of the aliens in obsidian armor had propped itself up and was aiming its weapon at Fitz.

Instantly, Fitz drew his F-Cannon. But, of course, it was out of ammo for good.

Izza was screaming something, but all Fitz could comprehend was the barrel pointing at him from twenty feet away.

Blaster bolts slammed into the alien, but it clung to life long enough to fire its weapon.

At the last moment, the barrel flipped upward in the alien's unsteady grip, and the energy bolt slammed into the ceiling.

"Missed!" Fitz declared.

Then the roof collapsed, burying him in total blackness.

* * * * *

Chapter Fifty-Nine: Tavistock Fitzwilliam

Fitz hovered between life and death. He could hear noises. Muffled ones, but he decided he wasn't dead, so he'd better do something about staying that way.

The weight of the debris against his chest made it hard to breathe, and his legs were pinned under a crushing pressure, but he could move his arms a little so he wriggled them as hard as he could.

Nothing doing.

He could only move his arms a few millimeters and even that caused the rocks over his head to shift.

There was thumping too, like a hammer beating at his head. He decided it was better to let someone else do the hard work and free him.

The next thing he knew, he was being picked up under the arms and dragged to safety. That damned hammering was still there, but so was Izza. He recognized her scent.

His wife's tears cleansed the dust from his eyes.

He held her face. "S'alright, Izza. Nothing can kill me."

Something was wrong, though. Izza looked away, couldn't face him.

That's when he noticed he was totally numb below the waist.

Deciding that he was in no hurry to look at any injuries that might be upsetting, Fitz followed his wife's gaze toward the rockfall.

It had blocked the way through to the next room, the one Indiya was still desperate to get into. She was shouting to everyone in earshot that they needed to clear the way faster, her urging underpinned by that constant *thump thump*.

They were almost through. Despite her wounds, Verlys had demonstrated once again that the Pryxian warrior caste could earn a livelihood in a pinch as living construction machinery, lifting massive rocks as if they were pebbles.

Red pebbles smeared with his blood.

The pounding noise got louder. And it was coming from the other side of the rockfall.

Just as Fitz realized the hammering was, in fact, the noise of a hammer smacking into the rocks, an eruption of rubble and dust choked the air, followed by a tattooed head poking through a gap in the stones.

"Anyone need rescuing?" Vetch asked.

"Yes," Indiya said, "we do. Hurry your hairy ass."

"Okay," Vetch replied. "You stay put. It'll just take us a few minutes to widen this gap from our end with a little help from Lucerne."

"No," Indiya said. "I need to be in that room with you. The others don't matter anymore and can stay here. If you can fit your fat head through, then it's wide enough for me."

"What's he talking about?" Izza demanded. "What is it you're about to do?"

Vetch looked at her with a pained expression. Then he turned to Indiya. "So, we're going ahead?"

"We're doing it, Arunsen."

"You do realize you could be insane? Crazy people don't always make the best decisions."

"Why does everyone of your era always have to waste time talking? We are doing this and that's it."

Fitz watched as his team began pushing Indiya through the gap like threading a cable through a hole in a wall.

She was diminutive, but even so it was a tight fit. Indiya's skin not only resembled sheets of old wax, but it cracked open easily too. The others were gasping because she was soon bleeding, but still she screamed at them to shove her through from Fitz's side and pull from the other.

Izza stopped it. "No one's going anywhere until I know what's going on," she said.

From the far side of the gap, Sybutu said, "We're doing what the Legion has always done."

A throat was cleared loudly behind Sybutu.

"Sorry," said the jack. "I meant to say we are doing what Chimera Company has always done. Saving everyone's asses."

"I don't like being left in the dark," Fitz said.

"I was hoping you'd say that, Captain," Sybutu replied.

"Yeah," Vetch agreed. "Being kept in the dark is a bitch, eh?"

Izza seemed to accept these scurrilous words and waved at the team to continue squeezing the Eternal Empress through the rocks.

"Izza," Fitz shouted. "What are you doing? Do you trust Indiya now?"

"No." She knelt beside him, and he gazed into beautiful eyes, the purple-specked cerulean and amaranth marbling glowing like alien lava that swirled with mutant power.

"I trust Sybutu and Arunsen," she said with unshakable conviction. "They're family."

* * *

Indiya fell through the gap, greased by her own blood, but was caught and gently lifted by Arunsen. She tolerated him carrying her to the chair by the viewscreen she'd set up on a stand next to the reality editor.

She took a quick inventory of the room.

It was large, with walls made of a dark metal that gleamed in the low light, in sharp contrast to the rocky storage room outside. In the center of the space was a series of tanks, each filled with a clear, viscous liquid. This was her latest version of the nanovirus, the cure for the Corruption that was ravaging the galaxy.

Next to the tanks was an old freighter's jump engine, now retooled in accordance with Khallini's design into a teleporter. Stripped of its starship housing, it revealed itself as concentric rings spinning about a central core. Each ring was attached to all the others by floating flux cables that she had taken decades to perfect when she'd first designed the jump drive.

Then there was the reality editor, of course. A cargo box on the outside and her greatest invention within.

Finally, there were two men staring at her expectantly. Sybutu and Arunsen, her Gemini sergeants who would make all this work.

She ran her fingers over the screen and initiated the activation sequence.

The Chimera people on the other side were shouting at her. She blocked those sounds from her mind.

"You know what to do?" she asked the men.

"We'll figure it out," Sybutu said.

"It's what we do," Arunsen added.

From habit, she tried to force herself to care about these two, to be in the moment so intensely that she could form a natural memory. To her surprise, she realized that she *did* feel something.

Individually, each of her sergeants was as forgettable as the endless generations that had proceeded them, but blend their best qualities together and they reminded her of the Marines who had first formed the Legion. One of them in particular.

"He would have been proud of you," she said.

"We know who you mean," Sybutu said. "And it means a great deal."

"To both of us," Arunsen said.

She nodded. And then tapped the red button on the screen.

Sybutu and Arunsen disappeared.

* * * * *

Part 5:
The Two Sergeants

Chapter Sixty: Lady Indiya

She blinked and was… back in the same room inside the rock of Mirdath-Naani, sitting on the same chair watching a viewscreen drop to the floor in the asteroid's artificial gravity.

Everything else had gone.

No nanovirus. No teleporter or reality editor.

And if all was proceeding according to her theory, Sybutu and Arunsen had never existed in the reality she now inhabited.

The careworn space Viking whose eyes twinkled beneath his tattoos and the competent but grief-stricken young jack who had learned to embrace a marginally more relaxed view of the galaxy: yes, she still remembered them clearly.

She did.

But would anyone else?

The asteroid shook beneath a powerful barrage of missiles crashing against its surface, forcing Indiya to lurch in her chair.

The battle, then, was still ongoing.

When the impacts subdued somewhat, she dropped to the floor and activated the command channel on the viewscreen, summoning Admiral Aluin for an update.

The face that gave the camera a fierce look was not Aluin's. It was a human woman, and her tag in the comm screen identified her as Supreme Commander Alessia Sorborovskele.

"Interesting," Indiya murmured. "You died at the battle of Tau-Fornacis."

"I'm very much alive and kicking Andromedan ass," Sorborovskele said suspiciously. "Why did you ask for Admiral Aluin? Did you mean *Fleet Commander* Aluin aboard the *Starhammer*?"

"There you are!"

A handsome young man emerged from the narrow opening that had been cleared through the rockfall separating this room from the next. She'd never seen him before. "Captain Fitz sent us to retrieve you."

"Who are you?"

The man licked his lips, uncertain. "Stryker, ma'am. Tavarius Stryker. Former sapper of the Legion and now whatever the hell we're supposed to be called in Chimera Company."

Another man joined Stryker and, although their features looked different, he carried himself with military precision, exactly like Sybutu had.

"You're another SOTL?" Indiya asked.

The man bowed. Such a charmer! "It's true I was once sapper of the Legion. Marc Yergin of the 27th Independent Field Squadron, Seventh Legion. Now I'm a Chimera Company skragg. Sworn to your service, lady."

"Lady Indiya!" Sorborovskele demanded. "What is happening?"

Indiya muted her and asked Stryker, "Zavage. Is he with you?"

Both men recoiled. "How the skragging fuck do you know about Vol?" Stryker asked, his face pinched in pain. "He was my best friend, but he fell on Rho-Torkis at the hands of Littorane insurgents."

"Sergeants!" Yergin bellowed back up the passage. "The boss has gone weird again."

"What is it this time?" Darant asked as he jogged over with Hubert at his heels.

"Been at the hyper-gin again, Your Majesty?" he asked. "It's Sergeant Yat Darant. Remember? Of Chimera Company."

A woman joined him. She had a buzz cut head and a belief in the Legion and what it stood for shining from her eyes. This was Sybutu in female form.

The woman identified herself. "Sergeant Nydella Sanderson. Formerly of 4th Battalion, 83rd Brigade, Seventh Legion. Currently on secondment to Chimera Company because somebody has to look after these sappers to remind them to wash, eat, and all those other things that come so easily to normal people."

Yes, Sanderson had been Sybutu's lover. Her death at Rho-Torkis had been an open wound when she'd first met him. Interesting.

Meanwhile, General Sorborovskele's image was deploying hand gestures to communicate her fury at her commander.

Indiya unmuted her. "Report," she ordered.

"We've beaten back the infiltrators," Sorborovskele said. "Sairoc-4-Cerulean informs us that these allies of the Andromedans are the species who'd lived here long ago in the time of the last Andromedan incursion."

"I know. Tell me of the unity of our fleet and the numbers of the enemy."

"Unity? You mean interservice rivalry?" Sorborovskele frowned. "That's not an issue in the face of this threat, as you know. The Andromedans have committed more strength than we've ever seen before. We can only hope that if we annihilate them here, they will be broken for another five thousand years."

"Can you defeat them?"

"Of course." The belief was clear in the woman's eyes. "Between the Muryani fleet and the black hole network, you've given us the keys to victory. It won't be easy, but we will hold the line here. For the sake of the entire galaxy, we have to. And that is why you must pull yourself together and lead us one more time. We need you."

Indiya gritted her teeth and shook her head furiously, a silent 'no' reverberating through the ether. Thousands of years of responsibility coated her like a thick blanket of guilt that crushed her chest, making words impossible to form. Finally, she choked out, "No you don't! You'll have to finish this without me. I can't help you anymore."

Sorborovskele's face was a mask of stoic pain. Only her eyes betrayed her dismay.

"Don't look so shocked, Supreme Commander. You don't need me anymore. You've got this."

"But…"

Sorborovskele allowed the shock to play out openly on her face as she stared in disbelief at her leader.

But as she looked into the eyes of her broken commander, she saw that this was how it had to be. The general finally nodded and bowed her head in respect, accepting the truth of Indiya's words.

For a moment, the silence hung heavily across everyone in Indiya's room deep inside Mirdath-Naani, broken only by the faint hum of power generators and distant chatter.

Finally, Sorborovskele straightened, squared her shoulders, and saluted her former commander. "I am assuming command, aye. And, ma'am, you are dammed right. We've got this."

She cut the link, and Indiya let out a sigh that had been trapped within her for a thousand years.

* * * * *

Chapter Sixty-One: Tavistock Fitzwilliam

The destruction of the hover sharks had been a disappointment. They would have been such fun to race around the deserted passageways of Mirdath-Naani. But that had been more than made up for by what the second infiltrator team had brought.

Fitz couldn't believe his luck. Everywhere he looked were dead aliens with F-Cannons still inside custom holsters. The pouches in their uniforms were stuffed full of the impossible-to-find ammo.

He emptied one of the magazines into his hand and ran a finger over the smooth tips of the rounds.

Where had they come from? No one had ever seen either race before. They looked like two completely different species, the first being spindly humanoids and the second catamaran millipedes. And yet both shared the same russet feathers that didn't look as if they belonged naturally on any of their bodies.

Feathers? What did *that* mean?

Nydella came over from Indiya's cavern and reported that the empress had finally gone crazy.

Fitz's jaw dropped open, and his eyes widened in disbelief as Nydella Sanderson vanished, replaced by a male jack who, strangely, seemed to fit more naturally into their group than she had.

Fitz glanced across at Izza and saw his own shock reflected in her face, her eyes glowing with mutant power as were his.

A moment later, Nydella Sanderson was back in the room.

And then it all faded away, like fog on a windy morning—the knowledge just beyond reach. He tapped his temple, but the memory was gone. Something important had just happened involving Sanderson. He could feel it, yet he couldn't quite make sense of it.

"Why are you staring at me?" Nydella asked.

"I have no idea," Fitz replied.

Izza put a hand on his forearm. "You felt that too, right?"

He hesitated before nodding. "Something, yes. I have no idea what it was. There's an ancient Earth expression, 'someone just walked across my grave.' Now I know what that means."

Izza looked revolted. "You humans are a strange and unpleasant people. Zhoogenes have a better expression, 'the universe laughed,' One should embrace these mysteries, not try to explain them." She looked meaningfully at the exotic rounds in his hand. "Especially not when having such fun."

Hubert bounded into the room, a blur of white fur. His little hooves clattered on the floor as he raced around in circles, bleating urgently as if to convey some important news.

Darant was close on his goat's heels.

"Indiya's safe," he said. "She's relinquished command to General Sorbo and now she's listening to Yergin recount his life story. I fear her sanity will only worsen."

Izza rolled her eyes and muttered, "Azhanti!"

"We better check in with Indigo Squad," Darant said. "You know how worried Claudio gets."

* * *

Claudio Zanitch

"Are we winning?" asked Molinjik the farm boy, his gaze not leaving the viewscreen showing the progress of the battle.

Burmina looked at Claudio expectantly, but he didn't have the answers.

Things had been easier in Indigo Squad when Pyruula and Nyluga Zi'Alfu were here. But one had been red misted and presumably her slushy remains passed through Fort Douaumont's waste recycling system. Possibly into their food and drink. Fitz's mother, the Smugglers Guild queen, had quietly slipped away, and Claudio guessed was now waiting out the war in a Guild hidey-hole.

For some reason, everyone now expected him to be in charge.

"I'm not a military man," Claudio said, "but I don't think our situation is hopeless. Either the battle information we're getting is faulty or some weird shit just happened—probably involving Indiya—that decisively switched things in our favor."

The screen indicated an incoming call. From Chimera Company.

"Talking of weird," Claudio muttered and accepted the transmission.

"We're not dead," Darant said, "but Indiya's gone totally guinshrike shite crazy. Thought you'd like to know. Everything all right there?"

Claudio stammered, "But… but you're…"

"I'm what? Well read? Unlucky with the ladies. Not anymore, my friend. Well? I'm what?"

"Alive!"

Darant looked taken aback for a brief moment, but then he ran his hand over his hair. "Started the whiskey party without me, Claudio?"

Claudio looked around the room they had sheltered in. Everyone in Indigo Squad was looking at him in askance, like he was the weird one and not his best friend, Yat Darant, who'd died with a knife through the heart not half an hour earlier.

No one knew Darant was supposed to be dead. Or that they were supposed to be calling him Beans. Or that the Andromedans had been about to annihilate them. Only he knew.

"Yeah," Claudio said. "Sometimes when I hit the booze too fast, I get so caught up in my stories, I can't tell real from fantasy."

The others avoided his gaze, their faces masks of feigned civility, though not one of them believed him.

How could he remember things that had never happened?

The who was clear. It had to be something Indiya had done.

But why?

And if this was Indiya's attempt to turn the tide of battle, would it work?

* * *

Squadron Leader Boss

"Gamma Lead to all call signs. On my mark, initiate forty-second acceleration to gate transfer. We all know what to do, people. It won't be easy, and some of us will be saluted at the bar tonight for all the wrong reasons, but keep your cool, and we will wipe these Andromedan skraggs off the face of our galaxy once and for all. Mark!"

Squadron Leader Mark Boss pushed the throttle forward and sent his FVA-7 "Spikeball" toward the mysterious portal. Dozens had been installed by the Muryani throughout the Redoubt Line.

"It's a tactical wormhole, not a gate," muttered Craig Kane, his Banger, or weapons controller when formalities were required. "It's a tactical adaptation of the Indiyan jump drive that the Muryani already knew how to build."

"So long as it puts us inside the heart of the enemy," Boss retorted, "does it matter?"

"It matters that we don't take these wormholes for granted. The Muryani built them. They are our allies, for the moment, but they are not our friends."

Boss bit his lip but said nothing. Kane was a lovable bundle of cynicism in the moments before combat. It was just his way.

Instead, Boss opened the squadron channel. "All call signs, Rampage Lead. Check your weapons one last time. You'll need them real soon."

Just before they hit the gate, Boss felt a wave of adrenaline wash over him. The Spikeball shuddered as they passed through the wormhole and emerged at an exit point deep within the enemy formation.

They found themselves surrounded by Andromedan Hammer ships.

Rampage Squadron had trained hard to get this right. The Mark 4 Spikeballs darted and weaved through the sea of enemy ships, firing off rounds as they went.

Elsewhere, Mark 7 Spikeballs were tearing into the armada of less deadly Andromedan warships. Mark 5s and 6s were in the fight, too. Although hopelessly outdated in every other regard, its larger K-M spikes meant the Mark 4 was as nimble as a sports drone.

They needed every ounce of agility if they were to avoid being blasted into hot gas by the Hammers. Compared to the Mark 4s, the enemy's most fearsome ships were slow and cumbersome, but they had thick armor that made them impenetrable to the Spikeball's weapons.

Unless they thrashed their tails. Then they would be vulnerable.

"C'mon," Boss said to himself. "Gotta get in close, real close, and tickle their tails. Make them thrash around like crazy."

With a flick of his wrist, Boss sent his Spikeball spinning toward the nearest Hammer. The Andromedan ship thrashed its tail with the spiked club on the end, narrowly missing Boss' craft.

Rampage Gold Two and Gold Three exploited the enemy's temporary vulnerability by letting rip with their rail cannons, shredding the enemy ship.

Boss laughed at the enemy, cajoling them into thrashing their tails even more.

The other fighters of Rampage Squadron followed Boss' lead, tickling the tails of the enemy ships to goad them into making the same mistake.

The Federation's lessons in how to combat the Andromedans were hard won, but the enemy had learned their own lessons.

Some of the Hammers jumped without warning into another part of the battle zone. The remainder refused to play the game and kept their tails locked as they sought to destroy their Federation tormentors.

The dogfight was intense, and Boss felt his heart racing with excitement. But he knew that they had to stay focused if they were going to succeed.

It was too much for Rampage Blue Three, who evaded one Hammer, only to be caught in the energy beam of another.

Distracted by the death of their flight comrade, Blue Four lost concentration for a moment and was crushed between two Hammers.

Damnit! "Gamma Wing, this is Rampage Lead. We need some backup here. We're losing good people."

The response came from Wing Commander Snarni. "Rampage Lead, this is Gamma Wing. *Achilles* is prioritizing your situation. Hold on a little longer."

Boss gritted his teeth and continued to maneuver his fighter through the chaos of the battle.

Suddenly, his Spikeball was hit by enemy fire. The ship shook violently, and Boss struggled to maintain control. He looked over at his Banger, who was frantically working the controls.

"Kane, what's going on?"

"We've taken a hit to the engine. We're losing power fast."

Boss cursed under his breath. They were sitting ducks now. He glanced around and saw a Hammer closing in on them.

"Kane, get ready to eject."

Boss waited until the last possible moment before hitting the ejection button. The cockpit canopy blew off and the two men were propelled out of the stricken Spikeball just as it exploded.

The Hammer beat its tail against the higher dimensions in its hunger to turn around and eat Boss and Kane.

"Greedy bastard. Get your just deserts."

But luck wasn't on Boss's side. Despite opening itself up to weapons fire, the maelstrom of battle passed by without any of Rampage Squadron's Spikeballs taking a shot.

Up close, Boss could see the man-sized bone hairs covering the ship's hull. They stood erect with a blue glow of power just beyond their tips. The Hammer's maw opened. It was about to swallow them!

A blur of motion flashed past. Spikeballs! A flight of three passed so close to the Hammer that its bone hairs bent back like corn before a storm.

The enemy ship forgot Boss and Kane and twisted around to pursue these new targets.

But the Spikeballs were lost in the swirling pattern of the dogfight and the Andromedan thrashed its tail in its eagerness to return to its original prey.

Boss was sure it wouldn't turn away again.

"Come on, *Achilles*," Boss murmured. "It's now or never."

* * *

As the crew of the *Achilles* hurried to bring their weapons online, on the flag deck, General Sorbo stayed conspicuously cool and collected.

Several critical control systems had blown during the wormhole transit. The other capital ships were reporting similar issues.

Why? Unknown.

Time to bring replacement systems online: three minutes.

It felt like an age, but the wormhole system had successfully brought *Achilles* and its support ships into a position where they could flank the Hammers without the warning that a conventional jump would have given the enemy.

Sorbo winced as more Spikeballs went offline, casualties in a lethal dance with the devil that had been for nothing because the fleet's heavy ships hadn't been ready.

"In position," announced the fire control officer on the main CIC deck. "Servicing fire missions now."

* * *

The Hammer opened its maw wide.

In his final moment, Boss started to turn to his friend one last time when he sensed a momentary blip followed by darkness.

He tried moving his arm, but he couldn't. The utter rigidity of his vac-suit built hope in his heart. If his suit AI sensed an incoming radiation burst, it would activate full shielding mode, locking its wearer up tighter than a corpse in a lead sarcophagus.

The helmet visor cleared and flexibility returned to Boss's suit. He used it to punch the vacuum. Where the Hammer had been was now a sea of hot debris.

"About time, *Achilles*," Kane said.

The flagship's volley had decimated the Hammers Rampage Squadron had been tussling with.

The bleeding Andromedan survivors limped from the kill zone and jumped away.

* * *

"Where the hell are they running to?" Sorbo growled as all over her battle space, Hammers winked from spacetime.

No one could tell her. But any commander who waited for all the answers before making a decision was worthless.

She turned to the flag officer beside her. "Signal General Sairoc. Tell them it's time to close the box."

* * *

"Supreme Commander Sorborovskele is requesting our intervention."

General Sairoc-4-Cerulean curled their antennae in agreement and replied, "The humans and their allies have done well. They deserve our support. Close the box!"

In the months since Sairoc's forces had arrived to bolster the Redoubt Line defenses, they had not only constructed black holes to allow ships arriving here to recharge their jump engines, but had also learned how to chain micro-black holes together using self-recharging jump modules.

No longer were the enemy warned by the shower of exotic particles as the throat of a jump tunnel formed. And no longer did the jump nav teams waste precious time calculating jump coordinates for even the shortest hop. The wormhole network nodes around the redoubts were fixed in their navigation systems.

This was a unification of Federation and Expansion technology, and it meant they could finally win.

The Muryani flotilla assigned for this task passed through the wormholes and appeared at the rear of the enemy formation, in the vicinity of the Jump Leviathans. It split into two, the pathfinder ships surrounding the Leviathans while their escorts shielded the pathfinders long enough to carry out their mission.

Although the Leviathans themselves were defenseless and paid no heed to this intrusion, the enemy had left a mass of ships to defend them. The moment the Muryani appeared, the enemy assailed them with kinetic barrages and volleys from living gauss cannons.

Against such an onslaught of numbers, the flotilla would have been doomed if it had used the tactics from the beginning of the war. But they had studied, learned, and adapted.

The pathfinders took up stations a few hundred meters over the Leviathans but took no aggressive actions. Several of them exploded in fireballs, but the Andromedan defenders focused their attention on the Muryani escorts who charged at them with all gun ports firing.

The Andromedans tore into the escorts. Soon, the passive pathfinders were forgotten and left alone. But the threat to the Andromedans did not come from the brave escorts who were sacrificing themselves to give the pathfinders time to triangulate precise jump coordinates.

With the surviving escorts making their last stand inside a swirling mass of Andromedans, the pathfinder calculations were complete and coordinates were beamed to the Khallini batteries deep inside the redoubts.

The human known as Lord Khallini interested General Sairoc even more than Indiya. It was a pity that this brilliant mind had become an early casualty of war. From the dossier Sairoc had read, Khallini would have assimilated enthusiastically in the Expansion.

It had been Sairoc's idea to name the batteries after the being whose mind had made them possible.

The Khallini batteries were armed with independent jump engines—teleporters as the humans were now calling them—combined with the largest fusion bombs in the Muryani armory.

And the pathfinders had given them the coordinates to jump directly inside the Leviathans.

* * *

The Leviathans exploded from within. Within seconds, they were nothing more than ionized gas and the jump tunnels they had held open collapsed.

According to the best Federation intelligence, only the Hammers could jump on their own, meaning the main mass of Andromedan ships was trapped here.

Defeating them was another matter entirely. The Muryani and Federation alliance was still heavily outnumbered.

The main element of the enemy fleet had advanced on the redoubts, following up the infiltration attacks of their allies that had been beaten off. With the destruction of the Leviathans and the Hammers having apparently fled, they changed tactics and concentrated on attacking Sorbo's and Sairoc's fleets.

As the enemy ships closed in, the defenders would execute micro-jumps or slip through the tactical wormholes. Even the obsolete Mark 4 Spikeballs that had opened the battle could thread their way across light seconds of space better than if the little fighters had been equipped with jump engines.

Even the capital ships, too slow and cumbersome to run through the wormholes, could micro-jump away to the artificial black holes. In a matter of minutes, with jump engines sufficiently recharged and new coordinates, they would jump back into the battle to reappear behind the enemy.

Muryani and Federation ships shared the same tactics, and together they continued the merciless slaughter for hours.

Then the Hammers returned.

Achilles and its escorts had mere seconds of warning before the Hammers screamed out of j-Space and fired their energy beams out of their maws.

Sorbo's ships took a terrible beating.

Achilles and the other carriers launched their remaining fighters to bolster those already flying escort missions. But against the Hammers, they had no chance on their own.

Sorbo watched helplessly as the most powerful ships in her fleet were blasted to pieces. The big ships maneuvered and tried to form a circle of mutually supportive fire, but only their main armament could damage the Hammers, and the Andromedans knew how to avoid the danger zones and simply jumped away if they came too close.

"We'll be dead before we even complete the formation," said Flag Ensign Pascoe, and Sorbo knew she was right. She had to preserve her capital ships. They had to jump away.

The flag deck rocked as an explosion ripped through *Achilles*.

"They targeted jump engines," came a report from the main CIC deck. "Jump capability offline."

"The other ships are reporting the same thing."

"Damn it," Sorbo muttered under her breath. "We need a miracle."

But the only thing that arrived was more enemy fire. The Hammers were relentless, firing beam after beam into the vulnerable hulls of the ships. Sorbo knew that if they didn't do something soon, they would all be destroyed.

There was only one thing they could do.

"Keep firing," she ordered. "We take as many of those skraggs down with us, all the way to hell."

* * *

General Sairoc-4-Cerulean closely observed the enemy grind down the Federation's capital ships but did nothing.

The guidance from the Council with regard to the Federation was for Sairoc to use their discretion in this fast-changing environment. Such responsibility hung heavy.

If the humans had followed the plan set for them when they had been brought here thousands of years ago, then they would have been a vigorous but small power. Logic dictated that sitting back while their naval strength withered would drive home that they were a very junior partner to the Muryani Expansion.

The Federation ships had fought well and with honor. Sairoc was a traditionalist on such matters and felt that to abandon the human allies in their moment of crisis would discredit the entire Expansion.

But the humans had never followed the plan as intended. Which partner was junior to the other was far from clear. Sairoc knew precisely what Indiya had done, and the power wielded by the diminutive human was terrifying.

It was with good reason that some species referred to her as a goddess.

Not only did Sairoc know he should not abandon Sorborovskele and *Achilles*, he didn't dare.

"Launch the Death Fleet," Sairoc ordered. "Save our allies."

* * *

"More ships arriving!"

Sorbo watched the tactical plot, expecting to see the arrival of her final destruction. According to their identifiers, these were Muryani ships, though Sorbo had neither seen them before nor been informed of their existence.

The sleek vessels matched the flight of the Andromedan Hammers with an eerie precision, no matter how hard the enemy maneuvered.

Then, without warning, they teleported inside the Hammers and detonated themselves, causing massive explosions that tore the enemy ships apart from the inside out.

Sorbo couldn't believe what she was seeing. But as she watched the Hammers fall one by one, she realized that she was witnessing a suicide mission.

A mix of emotions washed over her. She was grateful for the Muryanis' sacrifice, but at the same time, she couldn't help but feel a sense of sadness. This suicide squadron had been filled with brave warriors who had given their lives so that others might live.

She would never forget.

* * *

At the last moment, the Muryani sacrificed themselves to save Sorbo and the capital ships.

The viewscreen in Indiya's hand lit with scenes of explosions and beam weapon fire as the fighting raged on, but she knew in her bones that the battle had passed its critical point. The merciless slaughter of the Andromedans would continue for a long while yet, but their fate had been sealed.

She noticed a warmth against her skin and realized that her other hand had been clasping Del-Marie Sandure's.

He let go, but she grabbed his arm and lifted her gaze to meet the big man's cybernetic eyes. "This wasn't supposed to happen," she murmured. "We weren't supposed to survive this battle."

"I know."

She looked at him sharply. "You remember? You know the other sequence of events?"

He considered. "Not exactly. But I've been edited in and out of history enough times to know when reality has been toyed with."

"Not toyed."

"Forgive me. I'm just an old Tac-Marine." He took the viewscreen from Indiya and turned it off. "Our time has long passed. If you must go on this fool's errand to search for your husband, then so be it. It's harmless compared to anything else you might do, and as good a way as any for me to spend my final days."

"But Azhgrel and the *Retribution* crew—"

He shushed her. "You've done enough. There are many more casualties than *Retribution's* survivors, and there are many ways to be worse off than being stranded in the wrong time. Besides, we already know that Azhgrel returns home. Let someone else worry about how to achieve that. Besides, she's taken a liking to young Sergeant Darant and will be happy to stay here for a while longer. Let's leave them to it and slip away forever."

She shook her head. "There is one more thing I have to do first."

* * * * *

Chapter Sixty-Two: Lady Indiya

The victory celebrations on Zeta-Arcelia were a grand affair, with hundreds of thousands of people filling the streets to celebrate the triumph over the Andromedans. The capital city was adorned in colorful banners and lights, and music and cheers filled the air.

The events of that day were being recorded, and a fleet of ships waited to transport the recordings across the Federation and beyond.

Indiya stood on a raised platform, looking out over the massive crowd gathered before her. She wore a newly fabricated formal dress uniform, decorated with medals and ribbons earned over thirty-six centuries of service to the Federation and its predecessors.

She felt every one of those centuries in her bones but this, she promised herself, would be the last time she would ever have to address a crowd.

A Muryani delegation stood in formation behind her, their hard bodies smeared in aromatic oils. They were rubbing their antennae together to produce stunning harmonies, like a cicada symphony.

As the ceremony began, Indiya stepped forward to the microphone.

"We stand here today, victorious in battle and united in purpose," she said, her words echoing across the city. "We have been tested and we have prevailed. But let us not forget the sacrifices of those who have fallen in the fight for the right to exist. We remember them always and honor their memory today."

A hush fell over the crowd as Indiya's words sank in. She continued, "But let us also remember that our victory would not have been possible without the aid of our Muryani allies. Their might and sacrifice have been instrumental in our joint success. We owe them a debt of gratitude."

She smiled at that. To the Muryani that debt would have meant absorption into their Expansion. Would have… but she'd cut a deal with them before the speech. For a thousand years, the Muryani would neither seek Federation inclusion in the Expansion nor accept a request to join. If they did, Indiya had informed them, she would know and she would make them regret breaking their word.

The reality editor scared them, and so it should.

The Muryani delegation sharing the platform appeared genuinely happy with that deal. At Indiya's words, they stepped forward, their antennae pulsing in unison. Indiya raised a hand in acknowledgment, and they began to sing in their strange language. The music filled the air and the crowd erupted into cheers, clapping and dancing to the beat.

Indiya raised a hand again and the commotion dimmed. "*Let us remember.* Those are the words I just said, but the words we speak today are not enough. Which is why I command that three memorials shall be built."

A hush came over the crowd and the platform. This was not in the script.

Indiya beckoned to a human standing with her on the platform. She was a senior bureaucrat of some kind. Hadn't asked her name. Didn't care to.

"Write this down," Indiya ordered.

The bureaucrat nodded vigorously and prepared to take notes.

"The first memorial is to the sacrifice of all those who fought against the Andromedans and to the memory of those who died in that fight."

She checked the bureaucrat was getting this down. "The second memorial shall celebrate our great alliance, for we could not have fought off the Andromedans without the Muryani."

The Muryani group all bowed.

"The third and greatest memorial shall be a statue to be called *The Two Sergeants* and installed in the snowy forests of Rho-Torkis. Two men, facing off against each other. One stoic in his Seventh Legion armor, the other a snarling Viking in electro-chainmail with a war hammer over his shoulder. It will represent the greatness we can achieve when we unite our warring factions in service to a common goal. The collective and the individual. The heart and mind. Legion and Militia. Vctch and Osu."

"I'm… I'm sorry," the bureaucrat stammered. "Vetch and Osu, are they names of people?"

"The greatest sacrifice is to give your lives in the service of others when no one will remember what you did."

"Da… da… Does that mean this Vetch and Osu did something important?"

Indiya looked into a hovering camera. "All of you across the entire galaxy owe your lives to these two individuals whose sacrifice was total, for they have been wiped from existence. I alone remember them.

Their names will be taught; Osu Sybutu and Vetch Arunsen. I don't care if they pass into legend or whether they are mistaken for metaphor, but those names will not be forgotten. If I find that they have, I will return and wreak vengeance. For I am a goddess, and my wrath is fearful to behold."

She glanced across the platform, questioning whether she was overplaying her goddess act. Then she spotted Sandure in the wings, waiting to take her away to the hidden Khallini teleporter. It would send them on an adventure to rediscover Earth and find out what had happened to her husband.

Neither of them would ever return to the Perseus Arm, so it was fitting that her final words should be legendary.

"Claudio Zanitch shall write their story," Indiya stated. "I have sent him notes."

"The Legend of Vetch and Osu." The bureaucrat bowed. "Yes, ma'am."

"No! That title is too conceited. The work shall simply be entitled 'Chimera Company.'" She frowned, feeling a curiosity she hadn't experienced in generations. "The only problem is… I can never know how the story ends. What happened to Sybutu and Arunsen?"

* * * * *

Epilogue

"We can never go back," Osu said.

"I know," Vetch replied, groaning under the clever touch of the masseuse. "Indiya explained it all."

"I wasn't thinking of what Indiya told us. Her words have a record of turning out to be untrue, after all."

Vetch tugged at his beard, unsure of where this was headed.

"I'm referring to Maycey. What would she make of all this?" Osu gestured at the scantily clad Zhoogene women fussing over the exotic humans in their pre-fight preparations and eager to fuss over them even more intimately post-fight, should they live.

A hearty laugh escaped from Vetch's belly. "She would kill us both. And they would be bad deaths, my friend. We must hope we never go back." The laughter subsided, and he closed his eyes to enjoy the deep touch of the Zhoogene women. But Osu had gotten him thinking.

"Do you ever wonder what happened?" Vetch asked. "Against the Andromedans, I mean? Did we win? Coming back thousands of years in time and all that work seeding the worlds with the antidote to the Corruption… did that achieve anything?"

"We must only look forward," Osu said. "We did our duty and there's no point dwelling on it because we can never know the consequences. I have mental drills to help eradicate unhelpful thoughts. I can teach you, if you like."

"No thank you, brother."

The arena announcer whipped the crowd into a cheering frenzy in anticipation of the day's climactic fight. Vetch was not yet fluent enough in Old Zhoogene to follow the quick-talking voice, but he caught the word 'human' to which the crowd roared in response.

The next humans to arrive in this part of the galaxy wouldn't do so for another thousand years. He glanced at the Zhoogenes. That weird thing with the pheromones. Males and females both, Zhoogenes at the right time of the year were hopelessly in love with the two humans.

Being unique brought many positives.

Their manager arrived, wearing a jeweled robe with a heavy gold chain draped around her neck. She made a beeline for the humans, her eyes flashing, and her metal-soled sandals clapping against the floor. Her voluminous dress made her appear to float rather than walk.

"It's time," she said, her voice like velvet. "One more fight, two more knockouts, and Crimson Blade will be the champions of this gladiatorial league." Her eyes twinkled with ambition. "Do this for me and the rewards I have planned for you will blow your beards off."

She winked at them before turning away, her robe billowing behind her like a sail.

Vetch and Osu shared a look. This was the moment they had been waiting for. Vetch's heart raced as he felt the anticipation coursing through his veins.

The two men stood, their muscles eager, and their nerves alive with excitement. The Zhoogene women stepped back, though their eyes followed the humans' every move.

"Later," Vetch murmured to them in Old Zhoogene, and hefted Lucerne over his shoulder, feeling the war hammer's familiar weight.

Osu adjusted his battered Legion armor. Together, they were ready for anything that came their way.

As they marched onto the sands of the arena, Vetch felt a rush of adrenaline when the crowd caught sight of the two human gladiators, and the roar intensified to deafening levels.

He and Osu clasped each other's arms and shared a silent moment of loyalty and understanding. They were brothers, and so long as his brother had his six, Vetch knew he could face anything. And win.

# # # # #

About the Author

Tim C. Taylor lives with his family in an ancient village in England. When he was an impressionable kid, between 1977 and 1978, several mind-altering things happened to him all at once: *Star Wars*, *Dungeons & Dragons*, and *2000AD* comic. Consequently, he now writes science fiction novels for a living, notably in the Human Legion and Four Horsemen Universes. For a free starter library of stories from the worlds he writes in, join the Legion at https://www.humanlegion.com.

* * * * *

Get the **free** Four Horsemen prelude story "**Shattered Crucible**"

and discover other titles by Theogony Books at:

http://chriskennedypublishing.com/

* * * * *

Meet the author and other CKP authors on the Factory Floor:

https://www.facebook.com/groups/461794864654198

* * * * *

Did you like this book?

Please write a review!

* * * * *

The following is an

Excerpt from Book One of The Last Marines:

Gods of War

William S. Frisbee, Jr.

Available from Theogony Books

eBook, Audio, and Paperback

Excerpt from "Gods of War:"

"Yes, sir," Mathison said. Sometimes it was worth arguing, sometimes it wasn't. Stevenson wasn't a butter bar. He was a veteran from a line infantry platoon that had made it through Critical Skills Operator School and earned his Raider pin. He was also on the short list for captain. Major Beckett might pin the railroad tracks on Stevenson's collar before they left for space.

"Well, enough chatting," Stevenson said, the smile in his voice grating on Mathison's nerves. "Gotta go check our boys."

"Yes, sir," Mathison said, and later he would check on the men while the lieutenant rested. "Please keep your head down, sir. Don't leave me in charge of this cluster fuck. I would be tempted to tell that company commander to go fuck a duck."

"No, you won't. You will do your job and take care of our Marines, but I'll keep my head down," Stevenson said. "Asian socialists aren't good enough to kill me. It's going to have to be some green alien bastard that kills me."

"Yes, sir," Mathison said as the lieutenant tapped on Jennings' shoulder and pointed up. The lance corporal understood and cupped his hands together to boost the lieutenant out of the hole. He launched the lieutenant out of the hole and went back to digging as Mathison went back to looking at the spy eyes scrutinizing the distant jungle.

A shot rang out. On Mathison's heads-up display, the icon for Lieutenant Stevenson flashed and went red, indicating death.

"You are now acting platoon commander," Freya reported.

* * * * *

Get "Gods of War" now at: https://www.amazon.com/dp/B0B5WJB2MY.

Find out more about William S. Frisbee, Jr. at: https://chriskennedypublishing.com.

*****

The following is an

Excerpt from Book One of Abner Fortis, ISMC:

Cherry Drop

P.A. Piatt

Available from Theogony Books

eBook, Audio, and Paperback

Excerpt from "Cherry Drop:"

"Here they come!"

A low, throbbing buzz rose from the trees and the undergrowth shook. Thousands of bugs exploded out of the jungle, and Fortis' breath caught in his throat. The insects tumbled over each other in a rolling, skittering mass that engulfed everything in its path.

The Space Marines didn't need an order to open fire. Rifles cracked and the grenade launcher thumped over and over as they tried to stem the tide of bugs. Grenades tore holes in the ranks of the bugs and well-aimed rifle fire dropped many more. Still, the bugs advanced.

Hawkins' voice boomed in Fortis' ear. "LT, fall back behind the fighting position, clear the way for the heavy weapons."

Fortis looked over his shoulder and saw the fighting holes bristling with Marines who couldn't fire for fear of hitting their own comrades. He thumped Thorsen on the shoulder.

"Fall back!" he ordered. "Take up positions behind the fighting holes."

Thorsen stopped firing and moved among the other Marines, relaying Fortis' order. One by one, the Marines stopped firing and made for the rear. As the gunfire slacked off, the bugs closed ranks and continued forward.

After the last Marine had fallen back, Fortis motioned to Thorsen. "Let's go!"

Thorsen turned and let out a blood-chilling scream. A bug had approached unnoticed and buried its stinger deep in Thorsen's calf. The stricken Marine fell to the ground and began to convulse as the neurotoxin entered his bloodstream.

"Holy shit!" Fortis drew his kukri, ran over, and chopped at the insect stinger. The injured bug made a high-pitched shrieking noise, which Fortis cut short with another stroke of his knife.

Viscous, black goo oozed from the hole in Thorsen's armor and his convulsions ceased.

"Get the hell out of there!"

Hawkins was shouting in his ear, and Abner looked up. The line of bugs was ten meters away. For a split second he almost turned and ran, but the urge vanished as quickly as it appeared. He grabbed Thorsen under the arms and dragged the injured Marine along with him, pursued by the inexorable tide of gaping pincers and dripping stingers.

Fortis pulled Thorsen as fast as he could, straining with all his might against the substantial Pada-Pada gravity. Thorsen convulsed and slipped from Abner's grip and the young officer fell backward. When he sat up, he saw the bugs were almost on them.

* * * * *

* * * * *

Printed in Great Britain
by Amazon

29638301R00271